NOWHERE TO RUN

Books by Robert Daley

NOVELS
The Whole Truth
Only a Game
A Priest and a Girl
Strong Wine Red as Blood
To Kill a Cop
The Fast One
Year of the Dragon
The Dangerous Edge
Hands of a Stranger
Man with a Gun
A Faint Cold Fear
Tainted Evidence
Wall of Brass
Nowhere to Run

NONFICTION
The World Beneath the City
Cars at Speed
The Bizarre World of European Sport
The Cruel Sport
The Swords of Spain
A Star in the Family
Target Blue
Treasure
Prince of the City
An American Saga
Portraits of France

ROBERT DALEY
NOWHERE TO RUN

WARNER BOOKS

A Time Warner Company

This book is a work of fiction.
Names, characters, places and incidents are either the product of the author's imagination
or are used fictitiously, and any resemblance to actual persons, living or dead, events,
or locales is entirely coincidental.

Warner Books, Inc., 1271 Avenue of the Americas, New York, NY 10020

 A Time Warner Company

Printed in the United States of America
First Printing: October 1996
10 9 8 7 6 5 4 3 2 1

Library of Congress Cataloging-in-Publication Data
Daley, Robert.
      Nowhere to run / Robert Daley.
           p.   cm.
      ISBN 0-446-52063-2
      1. Man-woman relationships—France—Fiction.   2. Americans—
Travel—France—Fiction.   3. Police—New York (N.Y.)—Fiction.
I. Title.
PS3554.A43N68   1996
813'.54—dc20   96-3146
                                                                         CIP

Book design by Giorgetta Bell McRee

≡ BOOK I ≡

≡ CHAPTER 1 ≡

He stood at the edge of his wife's cocktail party, a big man, six-two, about two hundred pounds. He had a crooked grin and a nose that teenage fistfights had somewhat disarranged. Unlike the other guests, who were more formally dressed, he wore jeans and a blue sweater over an open-necked multicolored shirt.

The apartment was sixteen floors above the street and overlooked Central Park, a posh address, the poshest, and there were times, tonight for instance, when he was not comfortable there. In his hand he held a glass of designer water of the type favored by his wife's crowd, and he watched them buzzing around her, or around each other. Flora and her partners owned a decorating shop on Madison Avenue across the park, and these were people she did business with: antique dealers, gallery owners, other decorators.

A man he did not know came up to him and said: "You're Mr. Simpson, right, Flora's husband? The cop?"

Dilger tended to look at people as if he would later have to identify them in court. He said: "Simpson is Flora's name. My name is Dilger."

"Right. Sorry."

The man was tall, thin, with a gray goatee, no mustache.

"I'm from Chicago," he said.

Most of the women present, including Flora's two partners, sported butch haircuts. Most of the men were the kind who stood with one hand fluttering, or else turned inside out on one hip.

"So what breed of dogs sniffs out the bombs?" the man from Chicago said. "I'm real interested in dogs."

Because just then Bulfinch came into the room, Detective Dilger failed to respond. Instead his eyes narrowed, and he watched him.

"I was loaned this German shepherd by the Seeing Eye people," the man from Chicago said. "Part of a program they have. I raised him from a pup."

A maid took Bulfinch's coat. He swiped a glass of champagne off a passing tray and moved toward Flora.

"Well, about six months ago I had to give the dog back to be trained for his life's work."

Bulfinch embraced Flora, kissing her on both cheeks.

"I was devastated having to do it. Devastated."

Herbert Bulfinch: to Detective Dilger he looked like a middle-aged fag art dealer, which he was, and not a bit like a crook, which he also was.

"Tomorrow Gus—his name is Gus—graduates from Seeing Eye School. So that's how I happened to be here in New York. Flew in from Chicago to attend Gus's graduation."

This statement caught Dilger's attention. "You flew in from Chicago for a dog's graduation?"

"Seeing me at his graduation will mean a lot to Gus."

Dilger had a rather wide, fleshy mouth, and when something amused him, as now, his grin showed all his teeth. "Graduations call for gifts," he said. "So what did you get for the dog?"

"Gift?"

"You can't stiff a dog at his graduation."

Bulfinch wore leather trousers and a leather vest over a white shirt with big blousy sleeves. Flora had him by the arm and was introducing him to someone.

"What about it?" said the man from Chicago. "What breed sniffs out the bombs?"

"Excuse me," Dilger said to him, and he began to make a passage through people toward Flora. One or two voices called out to him in passing, and he smiled or waved, but did not stop.

When he reached his wife's side, he nodded at Bulfinch and said: "Evening, Herb."

The dealer mumbled something.

Dilger's big grin had come on and was focused on his wife. He was about to walk out on her party, and the grin was a kind of peace offering. "Gotta go now, Babe," he said.

"Just wait a minute," she said, "just wait a minute."

Nodding again at Bulfinch, Detective Dilger started back the way he had come. His wife's face had got very dark very fast. He had seen this and was aware of her trailing him through the crowd because he could hear voices calling out to her along the way.

When they reached the vestibule Flora fairly hissed at him: "You're the cohost. I need you here."

"Gotta go to work, Babe."

"You promised you'd stay." Her voice must have come out louder than she intended, for she smiled broadly all around at anyone who might be watching.

"I said I'd stay as long as I could, and I did." Flora was Dilger's age exactly, thirty-three. He counted this the best age for a woman. Her body was still long and smooth, her blond hair thick, her face still unlined.

He put his glass down on a sideboard. "There's this job I have to do," he said, reaching into the hall closet for his leather jacket. It was winter outside. The day had been cold and the night would be colder still.

"You've always got a job to do."

"I told you I wouldn't be able to stay long." The art dealer having been localized, it was safe for the detective to proceed to the next step. He was anxious to get to it.

"Every time I depend on you, you're not there."

"Now, Babe . . ." Dilger's teeth showed again, and he bent to kiss his wife, but she averted her face. "Well," he said, "maybe if I hurry I can get back before the party ends."

He had no intention of returning to her party, and his wife knew this.

The door having closed behind her husband, Flora turned and found herself facing the dog lover from Chicago, at whom she threw a tight little smile.

"I just had a long talk with your husband," the man said.

Flora made her smile broader. "Can I get you more champagne?"

"Abrupt kind of fellow, isn't he?"

"He can seem somewhat abrupt," conceded Flora.

"In fact, he can even seem downright—"

"Let me get you more champagne," said Flora, and she plunged back into the crowded room.

It took her a few minutes to separate out a man named Gartner, the lawyer who handled her contracts. Still smiling and nodding across at guests who caught her eye, she said to him: "How do you get a divorce in this state?"

"Well, well," he answered, "finally coming to your senses."

She gave him a look.

He laughed and sipped from his drink.

"What's the answer?" she said.

Immediately, the lawyer put on his sober, professional face. "Then it's not a rhetorical question?"

She gave a slight inclination of her head.

"You mean to divorce your husband?"

Flora saw across the room that more guests had arrived.

"Here's my card," said Gartner, still treating the matter lightly. "I handle divorces too." Then he added: "But let me give you a word of advice as well. Don't play with fire."

"What's that supposed to mean?"

"You may get burned."

Again wearing her bright hostess smile, Flora made her way toward the foyer and her newly arrived guests.

During the next two hours she smiled so hard and so often that by the time she went to bed her cheeks hurt.

Removing the police plaque from the windshield, Detective Dilger shoved it under the seat, then made a U-turn into the heavy northbound traffic. This caused much screeching of brakes and some fist waving, which he ignored.

There was frost on the roofs of the parked cars and steam coming up through the holes in the manhole covers. The wheel was cold in his hands. He sped four blocks up Central Park West to 81st Street, where he turned down into the transverse and crossed the park under the bridges.

Coming out at 79th Street, he waited behind cars for the light to change, then drove down Fifth Avenue as far as 68th, where he turned left into the side street, passing the elegant town houses on both sides with cars parked solid along the curbs. Turning left again at the corner of Madison, he moved slowly uptown, passing in front of his wife's shop, which was shuttered and dark. A few doors farther on was Bulfinch's gallery, and he slowed almost to a stop as he came abreast of it.

To either side of the front door were display windows with the security grills pulled down. Behind the grills stood illuminated paintings, a single big one in each window. One was a very dark portrait, the other an equally dark landscape. Bulfinch was considered the city's foremost expert on old masters, so this was what Detective Dilger, who knew little about art, supposed the two paintings to be. The interior of the gallery was dark, empty obviously, which caused him to nod to himself and then, once he was well past, to speed up as far as the next corner, where he turned into the side street. At Lexington he started downtown. The 19th Precinct station house was on 67th Street, and he pulled to a stop in front.

Nodding to the uniformed cop on security duty he went in past him. At this hour all the radio cars were out on patrol.

There was a policewoman at the switchboard, a sergeant behind the desk, and the captain's office door was closed. The 19th was one of the city's oldest houses, built in 1887, a tall narrow building with board floors and a wooden staircase just beyond the entrance. Dilger went to the staircase and up four flights and into the locker room.

There were many lockers, 250 or more in rows, and Dilger's was in the second row on the left. The room was empty. After working the combination he pulled open the steel door. Inside in a plastic bag hung the uniform he was obliged to own but no longer wore. He thought of it—when he thought of it at all—as the suit he would get laid out in, if he got killed, and if the department classified it as an honorable death. He had no intention of getting killed, honorably or otherwise. On the hook opposite hung the gunbelt that went with it, its holster containing his service revolver with its four-inch barrel. He had owned this gun since the police academy but carried only a so-called off-duty gun now. It was smaller, two-inch barrel, only five shots, but more than enough. Nothing was going to happen to him, not tonight, not any night. Shootouts happened mostly on TV. A detective his age had to be unlucky, stupid, or crazy to find himself in a shootout, and Dilger was none of these things, he believed.

On the floor of his locker was the satchel he had come for, and he withdrew it, banging the locker door shut behind it and spinning the dial.

He went down the stairs two at a time but on the second floor ran into Lieutenant Connor, commander of the 19th detective squad, Dilger's superior, who had just come out of the men's room apparently, for he stood in the hallway still zipping up his fly.

"The Park Avenue burglar just struck again," said Connor.

There had been a series of burglaries of luxury East Side apartments.

"I'm shorthanded," added Connor.

"Take a look at the chart," said Detective Dilger. "You'll find I'm not on it."

Connor was new. It was said he was soon to make captain. He had come in screaming about lax bookkeeping and promising to shake up the squad.

"So sign in and help out on this job and I'll give you comp time at a later date."

"Not possible," said Dilger.

"Maybe I can arrange overtime."

The department had been cracking down on overtime money. Coming from a man bucking for promotion, this was a major concession.

"I'd like to help out," said Dilger. "But—"

"Then help out."

"Can't."

"Are you a detective or what?"

"I'm a detective who happens to be off duty," Dilger said, and he gave his huge warm grin.

"An attitude like yours, you could be back swinging a stick."

Detective Dilger had no desire to be flopped back to uniform. He also had no intention of groveling. The inflexible grin was as far as it went.

"What's in the bag?" Connor asked finally.

"Just some personal stuff," said Dilger, already moving. As he started down the stairs he called back over his shoulder: "I really am sorry I can't help out, Lieutenant."

The last part of this scene was witnessed by Detective O'Malley, who also had just come out of the men's room and who followed Dilger down the stairs and out onto the stoop, where both men breathed in the cold night air.

"Watch out for that guy," said O'Malley. "You get on his shitlist, you got problems."

"Nah," said Dilger, "nothing to worry about."

A car went by in the street and both men watched it.

O'Malley was older, a heavyset man, stolid, and although Dilger most often worked alone, he had worked with O'Malley more than with any other of the precinct's detectives. They had

9

spent hours together, eaten hundreds of meals together, and in the manner of police partners knew more about each other than men were supposed to know.

"So what are you working on?" said O'Malley.

"Who knows?" said Dilger. "Most likely nothing."

"You got something." It was a statement, not a question.

"I don't know. Probably not." Dilger gave him the grin. "If it's anything, I'll tell you tomorrow."

"Jack, the talking head," commented O'Malley. "You talk a lot but you don't say anything."

Dilger gave him a wave over his shoulder and got into his car.

He drove out onto Madison again, heading uptown toward Bulfinch's gallery. When he passed it he noted that the window lighting, and the dark emptiness inside, were unchanged, and he turned at the next corner and parked at a fire hydrant in the middle of the block. The street was dimly lit, the lamplight filtering down through the branches of leafless trees. There being no pedestrians in view, Dilger opened his satchel, pulled out a telephone company uniform and hard hat, and began to struggle out of what he was wearing and into the uniform. Obviously he could not have changed in the station house. Just as obviously he could not go home to change. He put on horn-rimmed glasses and clapped the hard hat onto his head. Most witnesses to crimes described hats, glasses, mustaches, and beards, if any. Dilger knew this. They never saw the face at all.

In the rearview mirror he scrutinized himself and then both sidewalks. Still no pedestrians.

He went around to the trunk. His civilian clothes in the satchel went into the trunk, and he lifted out a telephone company toolbox.

The trunk lid slammed, and he took a final look around.

Still no one.

Detective Dilger, transformed into a telephone repairman, sauntered down the sidewalk.

Bulfinch's gallery fronted onto Madison, but the entrance to the rest of the building, twenty or thirty floors of luxury apartments, faced East 74th Street. An awning with tassels hanging from it ran out to the curb. It was spotless. With the birds we got in this town, thought Dilger, they must wash it once a week. Its brass supporting poles shone, as did the enormous brass carriage lanterns to either side of the door.

A uniformed doorman, epaulets on his shoulders, gold braid on his hat, waited in the doorway.

Detective Dilger, who had not seen this particular doorman before, flashed what could pass as telephone company credentials. "You got trouble on the top floors," he said.

Most New York doormen hardly spoke English. This one said: "I call super," and moved toward his switchboard.

But Dilger stopped him by saying: "I hear you do a real good job here." He spoke slowly, not wanting the man to miss the compliment.

"Who tell jzou dat?"

"That old lady you're always so nice to."

The doorman grinned with pleasure.

"Any of our guys been around here today?" Dilger asked carefully. If his handiwork downstairs had been discovered—and sooner or later it would be—he could be walking into a stakeout. The FBI could be waiting for him, or detectives from Internal Affairs, even detectives from some other squad.

"I see no one," said the doorman.

"Maybe someone came by and asked for the super?"

"No, I see no one."

"I'll go talk to the super," lied Dilger. "Let him know I'm working in the building."

"He in his apartment. I show jzou where he live."

"You better stay at your post," said Dilger. "I know where to go."

The door to the basement was beside the elevator. Opening

it carefully, Dilger listened, but heard nothing. As soundlessly as possible he descended the stairs.

In the corridor below he again paused to listen. In front of him was the laundry room, and he opened its door and looked in. One of the machines was tumbling; otherwise the room was empty, and he let the door fall closed. The super's apartment was in the back, his windows giving onto the rear courtyard. Walking instead toward the front, Dilger pushed open the door to the storeroom. It was in this room that the binding post was located, with his gear attached to it, and where, logically, anyone waiting for him would hide, and he listened for the sound of someone breathing. The sound of a stakeout breathing.

Finally he reached in, flicked the lights on, and peered all around. No one.

The binding post was across the room. He studied it from a distance, as if by approaching no closer he remained uncompromised.

His wire looked the way it always had. It led out of the top of the box. It was gray, same as real telephone wire, but it was in plain view, and it wasn't supposed to be there. A real telephone guy would come in here to repair something, or because someone upstairs ordered an extra line, and he would spot it immediately. Plenty of extra lines going in these days, for faxes usually. Suppose Mrs. Richbitch upstairs thinks her maid should have her own fax, or her kids need a fax so they can fax their homework to school. The telephone guy comes down here to make the installation, sees the illegal wire, and five minutes later this place is crawling with federal agents. They trace the wire up to that ceiling beam there, and then along the underside of the beam to the point where those old doors are stacked against the wall. The wire drops down behind the doors, and that's where they find Dilger's tape recorder. Then what? They set up a round-the-clock stakeout. They arrest whoever comes back to service the wire.

Though the wiretap had been in place two weeks, none of

this had happened yet, apparently. There were fifty or more apartments above Dilger's head and three businesses out front. Had no one ordered new service or developed line trouble in that time? How far could he push his luck?

Wearing his phony uniform Dilger had come back to change tapes every two days, sometimes a familiar doorman to get by, sometimes a new one like tonight. So far he had avoided the superintendent altogether. The danger had increased exponentially. He knew this. Was what he was doing worth going to jail for? The hairs on the back of his hands seemed to stand up straighter each time, and they stayed upright longer. These were physical reactions he could not control. An intellectual decision to ignore danger was all very well, but the body did not always agree.

He had been in the storeroom more than five minutes by now, looking around, listening, snuffing the air the way an animal might, his shoulders tense, the hairs on his hands signaling as always the immense risk. These were sensations most men avoided. A few, and Detective Dilger was one, enjoyed them. In fact there were times when he loved them. Tonight seemed to be one of those times, perhaps because it was so different from his wife's stupid cocktail party.

The doorman, meanwhile, had rung the superintendent's apartment, informing him in Spanish that a telephone repairman was in the building.

Moving to the stacked doors, Detective Dilger dragged his tape recorder out from behind them. It was a voice-activated Panitel 121, and he noted that a considerable portion of tape had been used. Walking back to the binding post, he pulled open its small steel door. The setup looked just as he had left it. Bulfinch had two lines, the bottom terminal pairs on the right-hand side, and Dilger's wire was attached to both of them.

He heard the footsteps then, and just had time to reach into his toolbox for a screwdriver, and to rip out several wires, any wires, before the storeroom door was pushed inward and the super entered.

A Hispanic, Dilger judged. Dark-skinned. Dark trousers, a white shirt buttoned tight across his throat, a red rep tie. Probably had started as a doorman himself but had improved his lot, and wearing a tie at this time of night was the way he proved it to himself, not to mention his staff.

"Evening," said Dilger. "You got some telephone problems on the top floor."

The super said: "Jzou got a work order?"

"In my pocket," said Dilger, who was still fanning out wires. "Show it to you in a minute. Better get this mess straightened out first, though, don't you think?"

He had about seven wires fanned out, seven phones out of action upstairs. The super stood near the door looking suspicious, and Dilger reached into his toolbox and withdrew the hand phone, thrusting its clips inside the box, attaching one to a bolt, the other to some insulation, and then dialing a number at random. "Number two one two," he said into the dead phone. "That you, Charlie? It's Pete. Yeah. Well, let me try it. Call you right back."

To the super he said: "Be with you in a jiffy," and he moved the fanned-out wires this way and that, whistling cheerfully as well.

But the super remained in the doorway. Dilger's tape recorder was in plain view on the floor beside the doors where he had left it. The way to keep the super from glancing over there was to keep the man's focus on him and on the binding post.

For five minutes, perhaps more, he whistled, hummed, asked inane questions, and the movement of tools, wires, and hands inside the binding box never stopped. Finally, because the super did not move, he pretended to reattach the hand phone and to redial the same number as before. A second "conversation" ensued, replete with invented phone numbers and pseudo jargon which Dilger supposed would be incomprehensible to anyone, much less a man whose first language was probably Spanish.

After disconnecting the hand phone a second time, Dilger pushed his glasses more firmly onto his face, then stared in puzzlement at all the wires. "This is more complicated than we thought," he said to the super. "Why don't you go back to your dinner. I'll knock on your door on the way out, and we'll have a chat."

He began slowly, meticulously, one by one, to replace the wires.

Still the super waited in the doorway.

"I'll be about twenty minutes, I'm afraid," Dilger said.

There was another long pause during which the super remained fixed in the doorway.

"I wait for jzou in my apartment," he said.

"Right," said Dilger, apparently concentrating on the binding post.

He did not look up until the heavy door slammed shut. When it did he gulped air, could not catch his breath, and was conscious of how much he had sweated.

And yet the quickened heartbeat and the frissons moving up and down his spine were delightful. Although his immediate instinct was to run over and hide the tape recorder, he didn't do it.

Calmly, almost casually, he finished reattaching the torn-out wires.

But the adrenaline high was followed by a depression just as deep, as he was forced to admit to himself that the wiretap ended tonight. He and it were burned. Another visit to this basement was out of the question.

When all the wires were back in place he went across and picked up his tape recorder. Once again he noted how much tape had been run off, and this almost made him change his mind about aborting the tap.

He put the tape recorder into his toolbox, then began to roll up his wire.

Stepping out into the corridor, he carefully closed the heavy storeroom door, and on tiptoe moved to the stairs and climbed them. At the top was another door. This too he closed without sound, and he strode out across the vestibule and out the door to the sidewalk. Here he encountered the doorman for the second time.

"Jzou see the super?"

"Yes I did," said Detective Dilger. "I've got another emergency just came in, so I have to hurry. Tell him everything is shipshape now, and I'll see him next time."

Though feeling the doorman's eyes on him all the way to his car, he did not hurry. The car was too far up the street for the man to see what it was or get a plate number.

Dilger drove back across the park to the West Side and into the schoolyard on 77th Street, which was deserted at this hour. There he got out and changed back into jeans, sweater and overcoat, this time standing up under a naked basketball rim to do it, no wriggling. He could see his breath as he changed. His telephone company outfit, fake glasses and the hard hat went into his satchel.

He was eager now to listen to his tape, but not here. This schoolyard was well enough lit for his car to be visible from the street. If the cops who patrolled this sector were on the ball it would attract their attention. Any minute a radio car might drive in and park beside him. The cop serving as recorder would get out and ask who he was and why he was parked in the schoolyard, while the other cop called his plate number in to Central, just in case. Of course he could flash his shield and they would back off, but there would be a record of the incident, and this he did not want.

Flora's cocktail party would not be over yet, so he could not go home either.

He drove out of the schoolyard and up Amsterdam several

blocks until he found and pulled into a metered parking spot that was empty. After flicking off his headlights he lifted the recorder onto his lap and rewound the tape, then began at last to listen to whatever he had taken all tonight's risks for, and all the other risks over the last two weeks as well.

≡ CHAPTER 2 ≡

Jack Dilger's mother was a college girl from the New York suburbs. His father, who was from Oklahoma, played third base for the Yankees. They brought Jack home from the hospital to an apartment they rented on the West Side near where he and Flora lived today. His earliest memories were of that apartment and of the streets outside. His parents had liked the bright lights, apparently. They were always out nights after games whenever the Yankees were at home. They were killed in a car crash in Florida during spring training. Both were twenty-eight years old. Their son, Jackie, was six.

His maternal grandparents took the boy in. They had disapproved of their daughter's marriage from the start, and more so now. As they saw it she had thrown her life away for a few short years with an uneducated lout whose only skill was swinging a bat. Now in their sixties, they resented their grandson's intrusion into their retirement years. They resented the boy himself, and so sent him at the age of ten to a military prep school in Pennsylvania. Summers they sent him to camp in New Hampshire.

His school was run by the Irish Christian Brothers, who taught him Catholicism, discipline, and sports, more or less in that order. There was compulsory attendance at Mass at six-thirty each morning, and military drills later in the day. The good brothers believed that only corporal punishment could curb obstreperous boys. Regulations were strict, and punishment for infringements were meted out at the front of the classroom while the other boys watched. There was one brother who favored a length of rubber hose across the buttocks. The pain was considerable, the ignominy too. Most preferred eighteen-inch rulers across outstretched palms. This made for considerable pain also, which young Jack Dilger took pains to conceal, never bursting into tears, as other boys often did. Instead, he would give his already big grin and pretend the brothers couldn't hurt him. This earned the motherless boy the admiration of his classmates, which he liked, as it was virtually the only admiration he ever got. In classrooms he was attentive if the course interested him, and smart enough when he chose to be, but he found most courses boring.

Each day after school came games and sports which were played all over the small campus. Individual brothers served as moderators, and most often they took part, tying their cassocks up to their waists and running back and forth as fast as any kid. Jackie played all sports but was never the athlete his father had been. His favorite sport was football. He played linebacker on the school team and enjoyed hitting into kids from other schools. He got in a number of fights with other kids, and although he lost some of them, he never showed that the punches hurt him, was never reduced to tears, never quit no matter how hurt he might be.

This was Jackie's life for seven years, an all-male world with no house mothers, no nurses, not even nuns, no girls or women anywhere who might have softened its impact.

Summer camp was an all-male world also, but there was a girls' camp about a mile away through the woods, and beginning at a certain age he and other boys would slither through the woods like Indians intent on giving the girls a good fright. By his mid-teens, still slithering, his object had changed. Instead of scaring girls he preferred spying on them, and he and other boys learned which trees one could climb that would give a view into their lighted windows. In this way he got occasional intimate glimpses that fired his imagination, an initiation of a kind into sex.

When he graduated he was nearly eighteen. He was supposed to spend several weeks at home before starting his job as a camp counselor, and he was to go on to college in the fall—his grandparents were certainly willing to finance college. But they were not a bit glad to have him at home. He was aware of this; he was interrupting their routine. He wandered around. He knew no one in his grandparents' town, was bored by the idea of another summer in the north woods, and he was not really interested in more education. He was lonely. Perhaps he already missed the discipline of prep school. One day he cleaned out his savings account, rammed his few hundred dollars into his pocket, left a note behind, took the train to New York which he had now decided was his true hometown, and signed a four-year enlistment in the United States Navy. His first night in boot camp all his money was stolen while he slept. It was an important lesson: if you did not protect what was yours you would lose it.

He went to sea on a cruiser named the USS *Salem*, which, as it happened, had been assigned to the Mediterranean as flagship of the Sixth Fleet. The flagship took part in exercises at sea of course. It also put into ports from Gibraltar to Turkey, the whole fleet did, showing the flag. Jackie went ashore in Spain, Sicily, Greece—everywhere the ship docked—and although he gawked at his share of tourist attractions, most of his time was spent cruising the streets for girls. He soon came to see himself as an outcast. So-called nice girls would have nothing to do with sailors in uniform, especially sailors traveling in bands. Officers could keep civilian clothes in their cabins and rarely left the ship in uniform. Sailors, however, were not permitted even to own any, partly because there was no room in their crowded quarters belowdecks, partly on the theory that in foreign ports it was easier to keep track of young men in sailor suits than of young men who looked like everyone else.

In Athens Jackie bought jeans, a flowered sports shirt, and espadrilles, and had them gift wrapped. The package was small and innocent-looking, and after that he smuggled his package on and off the ship in each liberty port in turn. This lasted until the cold weather came. Instead of wandering aimlessly about, one sailor among many, he would change clothes in the toilet of the first bar he came to, check his uniform and the gift wrapping with a sympathetic barman—a barmaid was surer if there was one—and then move alone through the streets in search of young people's hangouts. These were dark cellars usually, full of noise, smoke, and girls eager to try out the rudimentary English they had learned in school.

In Nice he met a girl his age and carried on a passionate if disjointed love affair—the ship was anchored off the Riviera only three times in six months. Her name was Claudia, and Jackie was in love, really in love, for the first time in his life. Much of what went on between them took place on a blanket on the beach at night. Nothing about it was original.

"Let me."

"No."

"Why not?"

"I don't want to."

They could hear the sea in its short rush over the stony beach. "Don't you love me?"

"I do love you."

"Well then?"

The usual dialogue. In time it became moans and heavy breathing. When the inevitable conclusion at last was reached, much the same words spilled forth again, though with a different intonation.

"Oh I love you, Claudia, I love you, I love you."

But the ship was rotated back to America. As it passed through the Straits of Gibraltar Jack stood on deck with tears running down his face, weeping for his lost love. He was not yet twenty years old.

From then on he could think only of being transferred to the *Salem*'s replacement. He had to get back to the Mediterranean, back to Claudia, but how?

It was at this time that he learned another valuable lesson, one that would stand him in good stead when he became a cop. More than a lesson, it was one of the primary rules of life, and the New York Police Department, he would find, even had jargon for it. Jackie needed what cops called a hook, or a rabbi. Without a rabbi, cops said, you can do nothing. With one, the sky's the limit. And a rabbi was precisely what Jackie had, though at first he was too young to realize it.

The flagship had carried a number of small boats, one designated the officers' launch, another the captain's gig, and a third the admiral's barge. All were made by Chris-Craft, all were similar in appearance, power, and function. Jackie was part of the crew of the admiral's barge. He stood on the prow during docking maneuvers and handled the mooring lines. The admiral himself usually went ashore by helicopter, and Jackie rarely saw him. The barge was for his wife and other guests who came aboard. The admiral, whose name was MacMahon, was not about to risk wrecking his career by airlifting civilians in his helicopter, something Jackie realized only much later.

One day in rough weather MacMahon's wife fell into the sea while trying to climb from the barge onto the boarding ladder. The barge was bounding up and down. The landing was sometimes underwater, sometimes six feet in the air. The admiral's wife, once she went overboard, was in considerable danger of drowning. She was in even more danger of being crushed between the boat and the hull. Jackie ran along the gunwale and dove in on top of her. He bore her down, down, down, she fought him all the way, down under the launch and up the other side, where both were hauled aboard again. Admiral MacMahon called him into his cabin and thanked him. Mrs. MacMahon was sitting there wrapped in a blanket, her hair still in rattails, looking numb. She thanked him too. Afterward the admiral bumped him up to third-class petty officer as fast as regulations allowed and put him in command of the barge under whatever officer had the duty that day. Jackie thought the admiral would have made him captain of the ship if he could; MacMahon was a man who really liked his wife. She followed the ship all the way around the Mediterranean. A number of wives did. Jackie had her aboard the barge many times. He landed her and other wives and many dignitaries all along the different coasts. He loved that job. He loved handling that boat. Then the rotation orders came, the launches were stowed, and they started back across the Atlantic, away from the Mediterranean, away from Claudia.

Before leaving the ship at Norfolk the admiral called Jackie over, shook hands with him, wished him luck in life, and offered help if the boy should ever need any. He offered to help get Jackie into the Naval Academy, if he wanted, or into officer's school. Jackie wanted only to talk to him about Claudia and to beg him to arrange for reassignment to the new Mediterranean flagship, but the admiral was so old, fifty at least, and had so many stripes, that he didn't dare say anything at all.

Instead Jackie put in for transfer through channels, but months went by and nothing happened. He wrote to Claudia frequently, and she wrote back, though presently her letters became sparse.

And then one day he ran into Mrs. MacMahon in the street. She was very kind and asked how he was doing and he blurted out the whole story. She said she would speak to her husband. Three more months elapsed before he suddenly found himself transferred to the USS *Newport News* and on his way back across the Atlantic for a second tour in the Mediterranean. He commanded the officers' launch this time, and the disjointed love affair with Claudia resumed. At first there was the same passion between them as before. Then it seemed to wane. On her part, not his. She wouldn't go to the beach with him at night.

"Why not?"

"We go too fast," she said. "You want too much."

She had another boyfriend, it seemed, a lieutenant from one of the cruisers. A shipmate reported having seen them together in a bar.

During the flagship's final visit to Nice she wasn't even there. This time as the ship's prow nosed out into the Atlantic rollers Jackie merely stared glumly back at the receding coastline. There were no tears. His future was somewhere else, not there.

His enlistment was running out, and he let it. His French experience had soured him on the navy too. He took his discharge papers and went home to his grandparents' house in Larchmont but spent most of his time in New York. He was thinking of going to college, although at twenty-one he felt too old for it. He was not working, he was lonely most of the time, and a friend told him to take the police department exam—he could retire on half pay after twenty years and they would credit him with the four he had already served in the navy; sixteen more years and he would have a pension. He had nothing better to do, no idea what he wanted to be when he grew up, so why not? Besides, a cop's life was disciplined, paramilitary, and to a youth who had endured institutional discipline most of his life it promised to be congenial.

Along with thousands of other young people, mostly whites, some blacks and Hispanics, a few women, he took the exam, finishing with an extremely high score. The NYPD happened to be expanding at that time, so within two months he was in the police academy.

He was assigned to the 112th Precinct in Queens. Forest Hills. Low apartment buildings, whole streets of one- and two-family houses with small lawns. A low-crime precinct but with plenty of bored housewives calling 911 for no reason. He patrolled those streets for two years, a footpost at first, then a seat in a radio car. He intervened in family fights, raced cardiac cases to hospitals, and once delivered a baby. It was a precinct of burglaries, assaults, some drug dealing. Not much chance for a cop to distinguish himself.

He met a woman who worked on Wall Street who set about to improve his mind, actually enrolling him in Queens College one day and telling him about it afterward. She was several years older. She made him arrange his classes around his police schedule. He did not move in with her, for she seemed to want to hold him at arm's length. She once took him to Hawaii. Everything was prepaid, or else she paid for it secretly. He tried to pay his share but couldn't. He began to feel like a kept man. Patrolmen got paid so little, she explained. The precinct had basketball and softball teams and he played on both and afterward sat in bars swilling beer with his teammates. Often she accused him of liking his police buddies more than her.

The love affair ended, and his college career as well, when he got into the shootout. The shootout changed his life in every way.

The call came over the radio just before eight P.M. Central's matter-of-fact voice: "Report of a ten-thirty-three, armed robbery in progress. Two men. A liquor store." Central gave the address. "Which car responding? K."

Which car? A call like that, every car in the precinct would respond. Cars from neighboring precincts would respond. You had to get there fast to have any chance of getting in on it.

Police Officer Dilger and his partner had just come off meal period, and it was Jack who happened to be behind the wheel, half alert, a cardboard container of coffee in his hand. The coffee went out the window and he had the car in gear and leaping across the intersection in an instant. He put the flashing lights on, but not the siren. He didn't want to scare the perpetrators off, he wanted to catch them in the act.

He was three blocks away, two, turned the corner, and there the perps were, running out of the store. He jammed on the brakes and was out of the car before it had stopped sliding.

Bullets came flying toward him.

He crouched down behind the wheel well as he had been taught and fired shots of his own. Three of his bullets, the autopsy showed later, went into the chief perpetrator's head and chest. The fourth shattered the liquor store's plate-glass window. It collapsed in a million crumbs, and this amazed Jack. Everything about the shootout and its aftermath amazed him. The second perpetrator immediately threw down his gun, screaming: "Don't shoot, man, don't shoot."

Now, it must be understood that very, very few cops ever discharge their guns on duty throughout their entire careers, and although cops themselves seem to regard these very rare shootouts as a kind of sacred rite, a passage by fire, this was not the attitude of headquarters. Quite the opposite. By now people of color constituted fifty-one percent of the city's population. Headquarters did not want cops on the force who through accident or design were prone to shoot people, especially if they happened to be black people. A dead white perpetrator was cause for far less alarm. If a dead perpetrator was black, as this one was, demonstrators sometimes— it happened more and more often, in fact—took to the streets. Demonstrations had a way of turning into riots, meaning cars on fire, rioters killed, cops wounded or killed.

Headquarters wanted more than proof that a shooting was legally justified. It wanted all doubts removed about the cop in question. Might he have fired out of mindless panic? Had he tried every other means before resorting to use of his firearm? If not, then the department had best get rid of him fast. Could the shooting be a personal matter, a settling of accounts? Same thing. Perhaps he was a trigger-happy racist, an assassin with a badge. Even if the cop was eventually judged to have acted properly, still there was a cloud on his record. A single shootout was one more than the norm. Let there be another and alarm bells would ring all over headquarters.

As soon as superior officers had arrived on the scene Police Officer Dilger's gun was taken from him, ostensibly to be checked by ballistics, but it was not immediately given back. Officer Dilger himself was told to report tomorrow morning, and all subsequent mornings, to the Chief of Operations, and the days began to pass and he sat on a chair and was given nothing to do—well, one afternoon they did ask him to stuff some envelopes.

The shootout meanwhile was the subject of four separate investigations—by local squad detectives, by Internal Affairs detectives, by detectives from the Chief of Detectives' Office, and by still other detectives working for the district attorney of Queens County. On the fourth day Jack himself was thrown before the grand jury, where he testified for two hours, knowing full well that the jurors might choose, following his testimony, to indict him for homicide in one degree or another. He could not be sure going in that this would not happen. Instead, as he left the hearing room several jurors stood up and applauded.

Partly this was because the chief of detectives had by then linked the two perpetrators, one dead, one incarcerated, to over twenty stickups, including two murdered shopkeepers, during the past eighteen months. Single-handedly, it seemed, Police Officer Dilger had put an end to a crime wave.

The following day Jack was called to headquarters, where the police commissioner himself promoted him to detective and pinned the gold shield on his breast in front of television cameras. The police commissioner was new, and to be effective he needed to increase his stature as quickly as possible within both the city and the department. He needed as much publicity as possible and he needed it fast. It was his deputy commissioner for public information who had suggested the promotion ceremony, saying: "We have nothing else going this week, and you'll get plenty of ink."

Jack Dilger, now a detective, had learned still more of life's important lessons. Like all lessons they were both general and specific, and their importance didn't entirely sink in at first. They were these. Only a few cops each year get into shootouts; some of those who do, lose; and some of those who win get indicted.

It was best to stay out of shootouts.

Also, people promote you in life not so you can get on television, but so they can.

He had been very, very lucky on all counts here.

He was assigned to the 19th Precinct detective squad on the Upper East Side, the so-called Silk Stocking District, probably the richest precinct in the city. It too was a low-crime precinct but with this difference: it was home to most of the diplomatic missions to the United Nations, and what those people might be up to—illegal but protected by diplomatic immunity—was probably beyond his powers of imagination. There was nothing he could do about this. Or was there?

His first job was to develop sources of information, and he walked along stepping into bars and stores, introducing himself. He would give his big grin and hand out his card. Something happens, they see or hear anything, he told them, call the squad room directly, ask for him. No need to go through 911. If he wasn't there, leave a message and he'd get back to them.

This led to his answering very many useless phone calls. But some good ones too.

And he began to cultivate doormen, if they spoke English, especially those who stood in front of buildings housing diplomatic missions. He tipped them in advance, five dollars of his own money—ten, maybe, if the guy looked promising—and said there was more where that came from. Because doormen saw and heard things. People tended to treat them like Old World servants. That is, when entering and leaving past them, or waiting under the awning for cabs or limos, people spoke in front of them as if they weren't there.

Just call him directly, he told them.

He was trying to build a career, but it was slow.

Detective Dilger's first view of Flora had been through the window of her shop. He was twenty-four at the time, still new in the precinct, still feeling his way as a detective. He had been strolling up Madison Avenue. Having noticed her he went in and handed her his card. He liked what he saw: the sleek figure, the blond hair, the high cheekbones and blue eyes. She saw his interest in her at once, and her defenses came up. Immediately he told her he was working on a robbery farther down the street. This calmed her. Had she seen anything? What kind of robbery, she asked, what was he looking for? A cop could get talking with any woman. See how she reacted to him. No fear of rejection, if he did it right. With Jack fear of rejection was real. Though tough on the outside, the toughness did not go all the way through. Perhaps he had been batted around too much as a boy.

He took her to dinner at a restaurant cops went to, for she was such a swell-looking girl that he wanted to be seen with her. Cops came over uninvited from the bar. They were hanging over the table, wanting to be asked to sit down. He kept fending them off. He learned Flora was from Kansas City, had majored in decorative arts in college, and had become apprenticed to a decorator. At present she was a sort of junior partner in a firm. He did not know what this meant but figured he would find out later. She lived by herself in a studio apartment not far away.

And she was divorced, she said.

This shocked him. It gave him confidence too, for divorced women were said to be easy. He figured that by midnight they would be in bed together, and it would be glorious, and as he walked her home his hopes were high.

But she smiled sweetly and kissed him good night at the door.

It took him weeks. She alternately drew him on and held him off. Some nights she wouldn't stop talking. Other nights she wouldn't talk at all. She invited him places. She also broke dates at the last moment. She sometimes called him up at the precinct to tell him one zany thing or another. She was exasperating. She was delightful.

Finally he gained access to her small apartment. Entering it he noted nothing out of place, no unwashed dishes in the tiny kitchen visible through a half-open door, no bras hanging over chairs, no toiletries on the bathroom sink, and this surprised him, for she seemed to him a woman who operated on whim, who seldom thought things out. Although she was his age, there were college pennants and travel posters on the wall, and a big teddy bear on top of a dresser. Her bed was a convertible sofa that they pulled out together, between kisses. They undressed each other in the light coming in from the street. Then they were in bed. He found her uninhibited, inventive, at times almost insatiable. Her face got red, and her chest between her delicious breasts. He thought her gorgeous.

Sitting on the edge of the pulled-out bed, she watched him get dressed. She had been celibate a long time before tonight, she confessed. Not once since her divorce.

"Not once?" he said.

"No."

"Why is that?"

"Well . . ." she said, and tears came to her eyes, which he did not understand.

He was so surprised he said: "Why me?"

She did not answer then, and when he would ask again later she only made jokes: she had been seduced by his beautiful pectorals, or his big brown eyes.

She came over and tightened his tie—the dress code for detectives called for coats and ties. Her tears had stopped. She was wearing a long T-shirt by then, nothing else. He felt her fingers on his throat. She apparently had no intention of asking him to stay the night, and he did not ask to stay, though he wanted to.

So he kissed her and left. In the street he stood breathing deeply, listening to the night noises of the city, pleased with himself, pleased with her. Then he took the subway home.

He adored showing her off. He would take her into the station house and the other detectives would crowd around and stare. She would sit on a desk with her legs crossed. The bad language would have stopped completely. Hardened detectives would fall all over each other trying to fetch her a chair. It was comical. They would stare at her elegant clothes and the way she wore them. She had a way of looking cool, which Jack alone knew she wasn't always, and she would focus on their faces, on their words until they fell silent, having lost the connection with what they were saying. When he would report for duty the next day they would rag him and demand to know what he had ever done to merit such a lady. It was extremely flattering.

Flora liked showing Jack off just as much, or so it appeared to him. She took him into the decorating world, dragged him to soirees, to vernissages. Her own personal detective. Perhaps she felt she was causing people—men and women who could help her career—to look at her in a new light. She introduced him to decorators, who looked at him and then at her and nodded approvingly. Many of them were homosexuals; some were even effeminate. She would stand with her arm around Jack's waist, beaming, and she almost seemed to be saying: gnash your teeth all of you, this man here is a real man. And as soon as he would take her home and they had pulled out the sofa bed she was all over him, as if to make him prove how much of a man he was, which he was only too happy to do.

He found bedtimes truly marvelous. "Are they all like you in Kansas City?" he asked her once, and she laughed. He wanted to go to bed with her every time he saw her. She had only to look at him in a certain way and he became eager. He could not keep his hands off her. In public they were seen to touch each other frequently. In private she rationed him. Sometimes he would kiss her once and she would throw herself on him, tell him he was the greatest lover who ever lived, and make him feel for a time that this was true.

Other nights she would be coy. Though smiling lovingly up at him, she would draw her finger down the buttons of his shirt and shake her head no. She would laugh at the perplexed expression on his face. "Use that thing too much and it will break," she said once, laughing, and she led him to the door. There she kissed him once and closed the door on him. He wondered if she expected him to throw her down on the floor and practically rape her. Was that what she wanted? But if he tried it and it wasn't what she wanted she would get really mad, he wouldn't know whether to go on or to stop, and he might lose her for good. So he smothered what was left of that night's sexual arousal and walked across to the subway and went home.

There came the first night she let him stay over. When he woke up in the morning he found her standing naked in her tiny kitchenette making coffee. She looked a little white, sexually spent, as was he.

"Is it really true that I was the first since your divorce?" he asked her.

"Oh yes."

"But, well, making love—you seem to enjoy it." She was spooning coffee from the can into the pot. He stood beside her, his hand on her bare bottom. An intimate moment, not a sexy one.

"With you I do." She was his friend and she happened not to have any clothes on. She put the pot on the stove.

"So how do you explain it?"

She shrugged, and her breasts swayed. "I was off men, I guess."

"Because of your divorce?"

"Don't psychoanalyze me, please."

"It's just that I want to know everything about you."

"The divorce was unpleasant. All divorces are unpleasant. There's nothing further to talk about." But immediately she softened her rebuke, smiling up at him. "And you can take your hand off there too."

"Off where?"

A week later, circling in on the same subject, he tried again.

"How old were you when you got married?"

"Eighteen."

"That's very young."

"I agree."

They were walking home from a movie, holding hands like teenagers, walking slowly as if to make the date last as long as possible.

"Were you a virgin?"

"Practically."

They went into her building past the doorman and into the elevator.

"How long were you married?"

"Four years."

"That long?"

"Yes."

At midnight Jack was going to have to go to work, for at this time detectives still worked midnight tours every third week. "How old was your husband?"

"When we married? Thirty-two."

They left the elevator and she let them into her apartment.

"What was he?"

"Him? Lawyer."

"What kind of lawyer?"

That part of her life was none of his business, she told him firmly, she was not going to talk about it. She would not even look in his direction, and when he persisted with his questioning they had a fight, their first.

He made one other try to worm the details out of her, with the same result, so he stopped.

At work he broke his first big case.

Someone fired shots at night from a rooftop into the lighted upper floors of the Israeli mission, killing one clerk, wounding another—an international incident in the making. While the FBI pored over intelligence reports of militant Arab groups, Detective Dilger began canvassing his doormen in the approximate line of the shots. If the shooter had access to a rooftop there was a doorman down below who had let him in the door, presumably because he knew him, at least by sight.

One of his doormen sent him to another some distance off, who sent him to a third. In an hour he had the right doorman, who remembered the dark-skinned youth, a recent addition to the building's staff, who had come to work earlier that day with a long package. Jack raced to the shooter's furnished room but missed him, then to JFK Airport, where, two hours later, he arrested him as he was about to board a flight for Cairo. Within two days he had the whole conspiracy.

However, he had had to break a date with Flora to do it. He had never called to tell her he couldn't meet her. He had forgotten the date and her completely. When he did call to apologize she wouldn't talk to him. He tried to explain but she hung up. He went around to her shop but there were customers present. He phoned every day. She still wouldn't talk to him. Finally he waited outside until she closed the shop, and took her hand and started to explain about the case.

With pedestrians passing on both sides, she hugged and kissed him. "Your picture was in the paper today," she said. "I was so proud. I showed it to everyone. I'm so happy for you. What are we going to do to celebrate?"

At the time he met her, Jack lived in a rented apartment in Queens, a walkup, lots of rooms but not much in them. Flora went "Ugh!" the first time he took her there, and only stayed with him there one or two nights. She wouldn't move in with him. Her studio apartment was on East 79th Street, a luxury building and a chic address, though a tiny place. "Too small for two," she said. Though he came to know it well, they continued to live apart.

That winter they went to the Caribbean for a week, and Flora met a man named Paul something on the beach. From Iowa. At first Paul's girlfriend was with him; then she went back. Flora didn't exactly flirt with Paul. Wearing a bikini that didn't hide much, she sat beside him in the shallow water all one morning, the water lapping over their thighs. Jack was snorkeling a short distance out. Though ostensibly searching for pretty fish, he kept looking up, looking back at the two of them in such rapt conversation.

"What was so fascinating about the guy?" he asked when they got back to their room.

She removed her bikini bra. "Come to me, lover," she replied.

When making love she could be playful, she could be feverish. That morning she was a little of both. Afterward they went to lunch.

The next day they got into their rented car and drove to a far corner of the island.

"Where are we going?" asked Jack.

"Someplace Paul told me about," said Flora, who was driving. She had steered down a dirt road. Having come to the end of it, a clearing that contained a number of cars, she parked and they got out, and as she led the way downhill on a narrow path, Jack could hear the sea beating.

At the bottom of the path was a small crescent beach and a dozen or more people, all nude.

"Well," said Jack. "Well."

"Come on," said Flora. "Let's go swimming."

She kicked off her sandals. She was wearing a sundress, which came off over her head. Underneath she wore panties only. She stepped out of them.

Jack, who was a bit dazed, was a little slower. He was peering all around. He had never been to a nude beach before. Neither had Flora, so far as he knew. There were people in the water, people sunbathing, people walking around, all of them without anything on. There was a reef offshore and the sea crashing against it sent spray six feet high. Inside the reef the water was calm, and of an exceptionally transparent blue.

As he began to get undressed he heard Flora say, "There's Paul now. I thought he might be here."

The man lay on his stomach a little way off, a pile of clothing beside his head, white buttocks in the air. Jack watched Flora go over there and stand above him.

Paul must have felt her shadow. Rolling onto his back he peered up at her.

She stood with legs apart. He must be looking straight up into her crotch, thought Jack, watching. Furthermore, she knows it.

Paul sat up, then stood up. They stood talking and gesturing at each other with smiles and great animation, bare chests a foot apart.

A hot wind blew in from the sea.

Jack couldn't hear what was said, but he saw Paul reach down for a bottle of what was presumably suntan oil. He appeared to be telling her that she better put some on or she would get burned, and he held out the bottle. But she refused it, and then what Jack considered an incredible thing happened. She turned, offering Paul her back. He poured oil on his hand and began transferring it onto her. He patted her with it all the way down to her buttocks.

Flora now turned to face him. Although he again held out the bottle, Flora again refused it. Jack saw her laugh and say something. After a momentary hesitation, he poured more oil into his cupped palm, and then, as if it were the most natural thing in the world, he began working over her front. He rubbed oil onto her abdomen, her upper chest, and finally her breasts. His hand smeared them around.

What am I supposed to do, thought Jack, create a scene? Stripping off the last of his clothes, he strode down to the water, high-stepped through the shallows, and plunged in. He swam out to the reef, swimming as hard as he could. When he got there he hung on to something and peered out to sea. The urge to turn and look back was enormous. He did not do it. After a time, he ducked his head into the water again and swam back just as hard.

When he came out of the water Flora was standing there with Paul, a yard of air between them, both of them pretending they were fully clothed. As was Jack, for that matter.

"I'm going back to the hotel," he told her. "You coming with me or staying?"

"Jack—"

"Suit yourself," he said.

Back at their pile of clothes he gave himself a cursory swipe with their towel, dropped it back onto the sand, then stepped into his underpants and trousers. Carrying his shoes and shirt, he started up the path to the car. He was climbing away from the beach when he realized that Flora was scurrying after him. Turning, he saw she had put her sundress back on. She was carrying the towel in one hand, her shoes, panties, and handbag in the other.

She reached him as he was sliding into the car.

"Jack, what's the matter?" she said. She was slightly out of breath.

"I decided I didn't enjoy watching you flaunt your cunt at the world."

"I wasn't flaunting anything at the world."

"No, just at some guy you don't even know."

"I'll flaunt my cunt at anyone I please."

"You do that, but leave me out of it."

They rode in silence back to the hotel. The flowering bushes, the scrub brush passed to either side of the road. Occasionally they could see the sea. They came down the hill to their hotel. Jack parked, got out, and strode toward their room, paying no attention to whether she followed or not. He had shoved the key into the door when he heard Flora behind him.

"I didn't mean to make you jealous," she said, hugging his back.

"I'm not jealous."

"It's just that . . ." And she tried to explain. She had never been nude on a beach before, she said, and Paul meant nothing to her.

Jack had never seen her this contrite.

When Paul went home to Iowa tomorrow they would never see him again, she said. So the idea had come to her to see what his reaction to her would be in such a setting. If she let him rub oil on her, "Would he, you know, disgrace himself?"

Jack said: "And did he—'disgrace himself'? as you put it." He was angry, but he was also curious.

"He started to." She was smirking. "He oils me on the left side, starts on the right, then hands me the bottle and goes sprinting down to the water and dives in. It was hilarious." She laughed.

Jack did not laugh. He withdrew the key from the lock and they moved into the room. He closed the door.

"Don't be mad at me." There had been no danger anything would happen in a public place like that, she said. But she realized now she shouldn't have done what she did.

"Next time you need something rubbed on your tits, you come to me," said Jack. Though still upset he had forced a smile. It was either smile and say something amusing or take the next plane out. What other choice did he have?

"From now on I'll ask you first, I promise."

Both made calls to New York and they stayed on an extra week. They made love every day or night, sometimes once, sometimes many times, including all through her period, which was extremely exciting, though messy, and in the morning before the maid came in Flora would spend twenty minutes washing the blood out of the towel they had put down to protect the sheet.

During these early days of their courtship Jack was becoming, as detectives go, famous.

He had been promoted to second grade after the Israeli sniper case, and he was made first grade the year after that. It was Jack who arrested a serial rapist who had had East Side women afraid to go out alone for six months. The wife of a Burmese diplomat was murdered in an art gallery; he broke that case too. He acquired such renown within the department that a succession of squad commanders proved unable to control him. If during an investigation he came across someone—a witness, a spouse, anyone—who read false to him, he would run background and credit checks, which of course he wasn't supposed to do. One of these people was wanted for fraud in three states. An easy case to make, and a good one, though not what he had started out on. He worked sometimes with a partner, usually Detective O'Malley. More often he worked alone. If what he was doing was against regulations or illegal he always worked alone. He tried to concentrate on cases that were in some way glamorous.

One day another doorman called him: his super had found something curious in the basement storeroom and didn't know what it was or what to do. Jack knew what it was the moment he saw it, and also what to do next. Someone had attached an illegal wire to the phone box. Someone else had backstrapped the tap and was tapping the tapper. He saw that both taps—the second wire passed through the wall into the adjacent storeroom—were down near the end. He gave the super a hundred dollars, told him not to worry, he would take care of this matter, and settled down to wait. The first man into the basement, who pretended to be a tenant, was an FBI agent. The second one, an hour later, was dressed like a plumber, complete with logo on his breast pocket; he turned out to work for the CIA. The phone being tapped belonged to an attaché in the Russian mission who was carrying on with a woman not his wife. The FBI was hoping to turn the attaché. The CIA didn't care about turning the attaché but wanted to know what the FBI knew that it didn't. In those final days of the Cold War multiple taps by different agencies on the same line were not uncommon. The trouble here was that neither agent had a warrant. Both taps were illegal.

Jack had held the FBI man, handcuffed to a pipe, for an hour. Now he held them both.

"Idiots, cretins," he raged. "I ought to lock both you jerkoffs up."

He didn't. He made them disconnect their equipment and let them go, and now he had two agencies, or at least two agents, in his debt. Later he became known as the detective with the best FBI contacts in the department. And if he needed illegal gear, sophisticated listening devices, and such, the CIA guy was sometimes able to lend it to him for short periods. For instance, he came to believe that a Pakistani with diplomatic immunity was involved in drug smuggling. Precinct detectives were not allowed to work drug cases, but Jack went into the man's apartment from its fire escape and planted one of the CIA's bugs. He was never able to make arrests, but seven Pakistani diplomats abruptly flew home and did not come back. He then gave the case to the DEA, but they never did anything with it.

By then Jack and Flora were living together, more or less. Sometimes at night they watched television together, sitting on the sofa bed holding hands, just like any married couple. They would have dinner on the small table under the window: usually grilled meat or fish, new potatoes or home fries, frozen vegetables. Flora, though her repertoire was limited, liked cooking for Jack, liked playing house for a man; and Jack liked, for the first time in his life, the feeling of having a home of his own, sort of, to come home to.

Flora still did things that were unpredictable and sometimes zany. One day she bought two expensive new lamps for the apartment, spending every cent of cash they had on hand. Jack had to go out and borrow money from Detective O'Malley to get them through the next week.

Another time she looked up from the magazine she was reading to say: "Jack, do you think Elvis Presley is really dead?"

"Yes, Flora."

"How can you be sure?"

"Because when someone's dead, you can tell."

"A lot of people don't agree with you, according to this."

In taxicabs she would sometimes snuggle up to him, other times stare out the far window ignoring him completely. Twice she decided she didn't like the taxi they were riding in; she jumped out at the next red light and flagged down the one behind it, leaving Jack to explain and to pay.

One day she said to him: "I want to have a baby."

"Sure," he said. His grin came on. "I'm willing to do my part."

"You already have," she told him.

He had imagined this was a subject they would talk over. Decide when. Maybe even pick out names.

"I stopped taking the pill and I'm pregnant."

He said: "Oh."

She said she had forgotten to take the first two pills that month, so she decided she wouldn't take any, see what happened.

"What did you think would happen?" said Jack.

"I guess you're right."

She began to talk about having the baby, it would be a girl, and—

"I think we should get married," Jack interrupted.

"You don't have to," said Flora. "Single mothers are quite common right now and—"

"Suppose I want to?"

"Do you? Want to, I mean?"

"I also think we should do it before you show."

They were married in the Little Church Around the Corner, Flora's idea, though Jack agreed to it. Her parents came from Kansas City, her father to give her away for the second time, and many others of her family and friends as well. Jack had felt obliged to invite only his grandparents; he had no one else. Except for Detective O'Malley he chose not to ask any cops. For one thing they might snicker at the setting, and for another he did not want to put them to the expense of having to buy gifts. The church was the one old-time film stars used to choose. It was famed in song and story, though these songs and stories were well out of date now. A wedding there was probably the ideal of every midwestern girl growing up, the epitome of romantic New York.

To Jack it was the epitome of kitsch, a New York word, probably of Yiddish origins, a word with mocking overtones, but when he pointed this out to Flora, suggesting they have a quick civil wedding, she overruled him, saying no, she absolutely wanted to be married in church, marriage to her was sacred, and this particular church would be nice for her parents and friends. Flora's first marriage had taken place in Kansas City, and he received the impression that she wanted to make sure news of her second one got back there. A famous church might help. Perhaps she wanted the news to reach her first husband. Jack still didn't know anything about him, or about her divorce.

And so on the appointed date the ceremony took place, followed by a reception, and Flora in her flowing white dress played the virgin all day.

Their honeymoon was three days in a hotel room at the edge of the ocean out at the end of Long Island at Montauk Point, and in bed in the dark that first night Flora said: "Oh, Jack, I love being in bed with you."

But the next morning she was sick, and after that she was sick every morning. He would wake up to the noise of her vomiting behind the bathroom door.

Then, when she was four months along, she began to bleed. The bleeding did not stop. Jack wasn't there at the time. He came home after a midnight to eight A.M. tour and found her on the floor with blood all over the rug. He wrapped her in a blanket and rushed her to the hospital in a taxi. By the time he got her there she had no pulse and he thought she was dead. On no sleep at all he stood beside her bed for the rest of the day. When she came awake it was dusk and he was so relieved that tears came to his eyes.

"You have two pints of my blood in you," he told her. "We're really married now."

She stayed a week in the hospital, and afterward no longer talked of having a baby. She was no longer as avid sexually either.

Flora's father died suddenly, and they flew at once to Kansas City. Since the deceased was only fifty-six, the funeral was a very sad affair. The next day Flora wanted to go back to the cemetery. Jack took her out in a taxi and stood with her over the fresh grave. "He was so good to me," she said, and began to weep.

Jack had never mourned his father. He had hardly known him.

"During the divorce especially—he was so good to me, so good."

Jack had been too young to know what death was, or that his parents weren't coming back.

"You met my ex-husband yesterday," Flora said, weeping.

He shook his head. He had met so many people yesterday.

"The tall, thin man in the blue pin-stripe suit." She kicked at the dirt over the grave, while tears ravaged her mascara.

And that was when the story, or at least most of it, at last came out. Her husband, that tall, thin, sexy-looking man given to pin-stripe suits, had turned out to be gay, she said. She hadn't known, had never guessed. Their honeymoon had seemed to her normal, although at eighteen what had she known about honeymoons, and the first months after that had seemed normal as well. Maybe he was a little less ardent than she had expected. But his attentions had steadily fallen off. She had thought it must be her fault, whose else could it be, he just didn't find her attractive. To get him interested in her again, she had tried everything she could think of: elaborate dinners, surprise gifts. She changed her hairdo, doused herself in perfumes, bought ever sexier nightgowns. Nothing worked. Inwardly she was in a state of despair. Outwardly the marriage looked fine. She made sure it did, told no one, sought help from no one.

"Four years?" said Jack, holding her.

She was weeping harder now. "Four years, yes."

Her self-esteem had all but disappeared. She told of bringing home a pornographic video. Maybe that would get him aroused. Half laughing, half blubbering, she described how her husband in his pin-stripe suit sat through the film to the end.

"That didn't work either."

Jack held her. Her face was radiant with tears.

Finally she had gotten up the nerve to go to her father, who, without telling her, hired a private detective.

Her husband, when Flora confronted him with the detective's report, broke down and cried like a woman. He said he had hoped that with a girl as young and beautiful as Flora his "problem" would evaporate, but it hadn't. He had wronged her, he said, he begged her to forgive him.

Jack held her close while she sobbed and sobbed.

Her father paid for the divorce, she said when she could talk again, and also provided the strength that got her through it. Afterward he gave her money to move to New York to try for a new start in life, promising also to support her as long as she needed it.

In New York she got a job all right. It didn't pay much but with the money her father sent she could live. But the doubts about herself remained, she simply didn't feel desirable to anyone. "Then you came along," she said. Her mascara had run down her face. She was wiping it off with his handkerchief. "You've never failed me, not once, have you?"

"Is that so important?"

"You have no idea how much."

He could see, after such an experience, why a supposedly hard-nosed cop, namely himself, had looked so good to her. Maybe such ardor as he had displayed then, and still displayed, was rare, how did he know? But it was nice to think that because of him she could once more think herself alluring and lusted after by men.

They stayed a week in Kansas City consoling her mother, then flew back to New York, back to work.

Her father had had a bank account in her name. As soon as this was released, she had the money transferred to New York and went out and bought a Porsche, even though they had no real use for a car, nor enough income to pay for its upkeep, and most of all no garage to keep such an expensive car in. When it was stolen off the street some months later, Jack found that she had never got around to insuring it.

When the first installment of her inheritance came through she quit her job, saying she planned to open a decorating shop with two older women. She had nothing lined up in advance and the salary she had been bringing home had been important to them, but within a week she had found an empty shop on Madison Avenue, and signed a lease, and had hired contractors to do the place up the way she wanted it. By the time this was done and the shop was opulently furnished, she had no money left. Jack feared the worst, but to his surprise the business flourished at once.

The two older women were both dykes, Jack saw. They did not like him and he did not like them. They had the talent, and Flora had the looks and the presence—not to mention the capital that had got them started. She served as the front for the other two. She was the one who charmed the clients and made the sales. Most of the new firm's clients were, of course, women. It was they who ordered the redecorating, true, but it was their husbands who paid for it. Flora was good with husbands.

She began to spend more and more time working and was sometimes not home when he was.

Well, Detective Dilger was busy too. At this time he was working on what became known as the Park Avenue Madam Case. One of the doormen he had cultivated put him on to what was going on upstairs. But how to make the case?

The post office, Jack knew, delivered mail to apartment buildings in sacks. It was up to the doorman to distribute it to tenants, and in exchange for fifty dollars this particular doorman allowed Jack to sort through the sacks each day. The madam received a good deal of mail, he saw, and not all the envelopes were well sealed. Many clients wrote ahead to set up "parties," or to request a specific girl on a specific date, and even signed their names, which made them, in Jack's view, absolute morons. Madam's client list was going to contain the juiciest names that had ever surfaced in a prostitution case. Jack had nothing against madams or prostitutes or guys getting their rocks off, but this woman's prices were the highest in the city, the moronic clients deserved whatever they got, and he soon had enough information to secure a legal wiretap on the madam's phones. Previous cases had brought him some notice, which he had enjoyed, but this case got him headlines. Admit it, he admonished himself when the investigation was complete and the arrests had been made, the idea of making celebrities squirm is not unpleasant to you either.

Flora had decided that they should buy an apartment overlooking the park, something fancy and big. By combining their two salaries they could afford such a place, she said one morning at breakfast. She wanted to be able to entertain clients: she wanted to give cocktail parties and small elegant dinners.

Two salaries. The comment annoyed him. She had taken to stroking his supposed ego when money came into the picture, but in fact the success of her business was so great that she was already making more than three times his detective's pay.

In any case, she now remarked, yesterday she had sold their apartment.

"You did what?"

"Sold it."

"Yesterday?"

"I put it on the market last week. I'm sorry, I guess I forgot to tell you. Yesterday there was an offer, and I took it."

It was her apartment to sell, her father had bought it for her, but he was so shocked he almost sputtered. "When do we have to get out?"

"Four weeks."

"Where will we go?"

"We'll find something."

So Jack went to the Building Department to a clerk he knew and pored over lists of delinquent taxpayers whose apartments would soon be sold at foreclosures. Access to such lists was restricted, but in the course of investigations he often needed information from the Building Department; he had used this clerk before and had always tipped him well. He tipped him again now, and left knowing not only which apartments would soon become available, but also which owners owed the city how much.

The best prospect was an apartment high up overlooking the park, but it was on the West Side, and when he told Flora about it, she commented that the city's rich and famous people lived on the East Side. The West Side was not chic, and she did not want to live there.

"Flora, we don't have much time."

At bottom she knew nothing about New York, except what she had been told when she first arrived, and he had to convince her that the West Side had come quite far upscale in recent years, that many of the rich and famous had moved there, especially into the buildings that gave onto the park. She was doubtful, but liked the apartment well enough when she saw it, so he began negotiations with the owner, a Wall Street type who had lost his job and been indicted over some fraudulent stock transaction. Working from his insider information Jack offered the owner enough to pay his taxes and mortgage debt plus, to make him bite, just a bit more than he would realize from a forced sale. The owner, who was awaiting trial, tried to get Jack up, but he wouldn't budge. Finally the man caved in. What else could he do? At that price the apartment was a steal, and Jack knew it, but the owner was a crook, and he had no sympathy for him.

Nonetheless, the man insisted he could not move out immediately, and it cost Jack ten thousand extra to get him to advance the date.

For Jack and Flora this meant living two weeks in a hotel, their furniture in containers in a warehouse somewhere at great expense.

Flora decorated the new apartment and they moved in and she began to throw her parties. After a while Jack tired of them, and of the people who came to them, whom he saw as too rich, too pseudo-elegant. They made him feel a stranger in his own living room. They came in two basic types. The straight ones, the businessmen, were hard-nosed and observant. Thieves, most of them. Of the artistic ones, about half seemed to be homosexuals. He had nothing against fags if they were suitably admiring and otherwise left him alone. Both groups, he concluded, had contempt for any man who would work for what detectives were paid—the grudging respect certain of them accorded him was perhaps only fear, as if he might choose to arrest them on the spot. Despite himself he came to feel embarrassed about being there among them. Whether they caused this or he caused it himself, he did not know. He did not aspire to be like any of them, and he was tired of trying to impress them.

Flora wanted him close by at these gatherings, preferably standing at her side. She was possessive, yet self-involved. More and more often he tried to get out of attending or to leave early, but she would not have it. In fact she wanted him around her at all times, except when she was working. She would get almost frantic if she didn't know where he was. She wanted to know what his duty tours would be, when he would be home. The more possessive she became, the more time he put into his investigations, and when he left work at the end of a tour he would sometimes stand in bars with other cops rather than go directly home.

He handled his share of precinct business, burglaries, stick-ups, and the like. But most of his time went to cases that promised to be big, if he could break them. These averaged out to about one a year, but he had had nothing for a while when, thanks to Flora, the Bulfinch case more or less fell into his lap.

One night in bed she told him, giggling, that Bulfinch was buying up art for Colombian druglords.

Detective Dilger was suddenly all ears.

There had been an auction at Sotheby's, Flora said.

"Sotheby's?"

"The auction house."

"Oh yes."

Bulfinch had bid for and won two impressionists, paying impressive sums. When the reporters asked whom he had acted for, he had murmured "Anonymous collector" and had brushed them off.

Flora giggled again, exactly the way Bulfinch must have giggled when he had bragged about it to her later. "You know who they were for," she giggled. "Colombian drug dealers."

Well, it was interesting information, but there was nothing Detective Dilger could do with it. No laws had been broken, at least not yet.

Flora loved gossip and loved to pass it on. At the breakfast table a few months later she reported on another conversation with Bulfinch.

"My clients down there in Colombia are badgering me to death," he had told her. "I guess they got tired of buying zoos and soccer teams. They're all so rich and what they're into now is art. They don't want to be known as killers and druglords anymore, they want to be known as art collectors. They're trying to outdo one another with the value of their collections." And probably he laughed at his own wit and fluttered his hand at her, the way he had a habit of doing.

"I got one client," he told her some days later, "wants old masters. Trouble is, there aren't any. Have to steal them, I guess. Do you know where there are any hot old masters?"

This too Flora reported to Jack, who did not conceal his reaction very well. He was startled, and it showed.

"He was kidding," said Flora.

"I'm sure," said Jack. It seemed to him that between buying art for druglords and selling them stolen art was no very big step.

Flora laughed. "He said there was no way that selling to those guys could come back to him. They have private armies. No one gets in to see their paintings but each other. You send something down there, it's as if it disappeared off the face of the earth."

"Yeah," said Detective Dilger. They sat at the table, coffee cups and toast between them, in the good-sized breakfast nook their big apartment contained. Flora was wearing a nightgown that was not quite transparent but did not need to be. Jack knew what was under it well enough, and he looked at her, at the thick blond hair, at the lips and breasts of her, at the sensitive hands that felt so smooth on his body, at the narrow waist and curved hips that disappeared beneath the table. The physical package of Flora was to him gorgeous. For a moment he felt choked up with desire for her, and he completely forgot Bulfinch.

She had changed a good deal since they met, as he had too, he supposed. At present she was almost totally focused on her business. He felt left out. She seemed to hold to a system of values which to him was skewed. Values that had no more weight than the suds on top of a glass of beer. She seemed to pretend that fads and fashions constituted truth and were important, and when he did not embrace them with her, she became annoyed at him. She seemed to believe in the glossy surface of things as she wanted them to be, and to probe no deeper, and he once told her so, which only started another fight. She was trying to run a business, she retorted, and if she seemed to reflect the world in which her business existed, this could not be helped.

Jack's own view of life was the accurate one, he told her hotly. Reality was bodies on the floor. Degradation and crime not only existed but were all around you. People sometimes murdered each other. More often they merely had their hands in each other's pockets.

As Jack saw it, his wife believed in what she imagined. He believed in what he had seen: people with bullet holes in them or their throats cut.

She began to remark more and more often that as a couple they were not well matched. He always denied it. Though cocky enough to believe she didn't mean anything serious, he became nonetheless slightly frightened. He did not want to lose her, though in truth he did wish he could get back the girl he had met and had lived with in the beginning.

She got up from the breakfast table and as she was passing his chair leaned over and kissed him, giving him a clear view down the front of her nightgown.

He held on to her hand saying: "We have a few minutes—"

She gave him a smirk. "I have to get ready for work."

He followed her into the bedroom, and in fact she got to work that morning later than expected.

Jack himself went to the station house, signed in, and then sat brooding. He wondered if having a baby might bring back their old closeness. They had talked about it, but Flora had said she was still too afraid, she had almost died the last time, maybe they should wait till next year or the year after.

Jack as he pondered was drumming a ballpoint on the scarred old desk to which he was assigned. What else might help? he asked himself. Well, they might take a long trip together, three weeks or more. Go to Europe, why not? He could show her the ports he had known in the navy. The only problem might be to synchronize their schedules, but it could be done. He would mention the idea to her tonight.

This much having been decided, he focused his mind on Bulfinch. What did he know of the man?

Well, the guy wore leather suits and blowsy sleeved shirts and had effeminate ways. But this was not important. Was the dealer capable of fencing stolen paintings—that's what was important.

Paintings were stolen all the time, and somebody fenced them. Who was better placed than an art dealer who could move them in and out among legitimate ones without arousing suspicion? A hot painting, wrapped, was indistinguishable from a legal one, was it not? Who was watching dealers closely? Who knew what was inside the wrapping?

Receiving stolen goods was of course a felony. Reselling them, the same. Was Bulfinch a criminal in his soul? Was he capable of risking jail?

In Jack's view people tended to see homosexuals as effeminate through and through: men as unlikely to commit crimes of violence, or crimes of any kind, as most women. But in his experience this was not so. Many homosexuals displayed a kind of cornered courage. They tended to despise a world that despised them, and many of its laws and regulations as well. All down through history homosexuality had been a crime, and if they had contempt for the particular law that proscribed their conduct, why should they be expected to respect all others?

Some gays were out of the closet now, but this was recent, and mostly they were the young ones. The older men had embraced their vice in secret for years—a lifestyle that was, to say the least, perilous. They had risked their jobs. In their social contacts they had risked being robbed, beaten, even killed, had risked, without even knowing it at first, AIDS. They were people who lived on the edge. A man as old as Bulfinch had lived on the edge for a long time. Certainly some homosexuals came to like danger. Lots of men liked danger, and homosexuals were men after all; they were not women. Jack could not understand homosexuality at all, but he could understand a man's need to risk something, for it was a need he recognized in himself.

So yes, if Bulfinch had decided to receive stolen paintings and then resell them to Colombian druglords, Detective Dilger would not be surprised.

That very night he followed him home from his gallery after it closed, and sat outside in his car and waited in case he came down again. Same thing the next night, and many succeeding nights: Jack waited in his dark car in the street, and if Bulfinch came out he would follow him to wherever he went, sometimes to meet someone in a restaurant, more often to one of the gay bars on Christopher Street in the Village, where again Jack would wait outside. The art dealer was unlikely to meet Colombian druglords in a gay bar. Even if he did, since he and Jack knew each other, going in after him would certainly blow the investigation, which had only just started, and probably Jack would get groped by strange men— to him, strange in more ways than one. The rest of the country and perhaps the world were beginning to accept gays and the gay life, but cops were not, and Detective Dilger was a cop.

Jack had decided to watch only Bulfinch's house, not his gallery. To sit outside the gallery all day would occupy too much time, there was no place to park, and sooner or later the dealer would spot him there, or Flora would, for her store was two doors down. Also, Jack reasoned, if Bulfinch was involved with art thieves he would receive them at home and at night. At home because people working in his gallery knew paintings and might stumble on anything stolen that was stashed there. And at night because that's the way the criminal mind worked. Criminals always felt safer at night. One had only to look at crime statistics to know that.

And so he watched Bulfinch from dinnertime on, learning his habits, learning to recognize and beginning to identify the people he met. Jack was no fanatic about it. He did not do it every night, only when he was otherwise free, and rarely on weekends. There was still plenty of space around Bulfinch, enough gaps in which to move all the stolen art he might care to, if that's what he was doing. But sooner or later Jack expected to see something. He was in no great hurry. Some cases took years to develop.

Also, Jack made contact with Bulfinch's doormen. There were four of them working the building in shifts. He introduced himself, gave them money, and asked no specific questions whatever. Great detectives were men with a number of important qualities: instinct, doggedness, bravery—but the greatest of these was patience. You had to wait. It was much like fishing: you never knew when or even if the fish would bite. You never knew if any fish were even there. You put your lines out, and you waited. In the first weeks Jack noted no paintings going upstairs, and when he finally asked his doormen specifically—being careful to bury the question among a number of innocuous ones—they hadn't seen any either.

Good, thought Jack. It meant Bulfinch never brought paintings home. Therefore anything he did bring home would probably be stolen. This was a pretty big leap of faith by any detective, but it satisfied Jack Dilger.

Why was he doing this? Why go to such trouble? Why put in so many hours and even, since the tips to the doormen had to be repeated, such expense? Well, it would be an exceptional case again, if he could make it, and he hadn't had anything big in a long time. He could see the headlines now: MADISON AVENUE MEETS THE MEDELLÍN CARTEL. It would make one hell of a splash. He would be in for another round of backslapping and congratulations, perhaps be invited to a press conference at headquarters, or City Hall. Usually nobody cared much about paintings stolen from rich collectors—the insurance company paid off, so what? But this was different, this case had what Hollywood called elements.

And he sensed doggedly that the case was there to be made. He sensed that Bulfinch was a thief who would grasp at any illegal profit that came his way, had sensed it for a long time. Perhaps this was due to something the dealer had said to Jack in the past, or something Flora had said, that hadn't even consciously registered at the time. Inasmuch as fences were paid off at ten cents on the dollar, perhaps less, the profit to be made reselling stolen art was truly enormous, and the only problem was to find a buyer, but Bulfinch had one, probably several. So if you were a crook at heart, why not? To Jack the crime fit the personality of Bulfinch, and it fit the situation.

If asked, he would have said he hated thieves, that locking them up was what he did for a living. But this case was more than theft. It was apart from all others because it touched on the world of wealth and privilege in which his wife moved every day, on the outer edge of which, as grim as a prison, stood the 19th Precinct station house. It was a world to which cops like himself were generally not admitted at all. So to nail Bulfinch would be a personal victory in a special sense: it would show Flora that there were criminals inside her own complacent circle. Jack would in a certain way blast that complacency apart. Perhaps he only wanted to make her see what life looked like from his point of view, so that their marriage would be close again. Perhaps he didn't realize what he felt.

At last one night he did see a painting or paintings go upstairs to Bulfinch. Two men pulled up in front of the building in a van, out of which they lifted a big package, heavy. A painting in a heavy ornate frame probably, perhaps more than one.

When the men had lugged it inside, Jack sauntered over and engaged the doorman in conversation. "You hear anything about any crimes lately?" he said. "Who were those guys?" And he pointed with his chin after the deliverers.

"Something for Mr. Bulfinch," said the doorman.

Jack watched the building until midnight before going home. The two deliverers came out after about twenty minutes, but Bulfinch did not appear, and nothing else happened.

The next morning Jack met with his CIA contact and arranged to borrow certain gear. "That thing costs a fortune," the agent told him. "You lose it, you pay for it. You can have it for one week. When you give it back, we're even."

Jack nodded.

"Don't call me again."

"Okay," said Jack.

At five-thirty Bulfinch closed his gallery as always and went home. When he came out again, looking freshly shaved and perfumed, Jack let him go. He waited twenty minutes lest the dealer, having forgotten something, come back; then he walked over to the adjacent building, showed his shield to the doorman there, and went up in the elevator to the roof.

He stood in the cold, starless night. It was as if he stood among cliff faces that rose up to all sides, but full of entrance holes. Multiple caves with fires burning in them that were visible from outside.

Jack jumped down onto the roof next door, Bulfinch's roof, and clambered down the fire escape two floors to the window of Bulfinch's study. He had been in the apartment often enough. He knew where it was. To the outside of the window he attached a resonant transmitter the size of a golf ball. The theory was that conversations in the room, probably telephone conversations, would make the pane vibrate exactly like the diaphragm of a telephone. The golf ball would pick up these vibrations and transmit them to the receiver on Jack's lap in his car in the street.

Night after night Jack sat listening, but there were few enough conversations with anyone. No contact was made with any potential buyer, as near as Jack could determine, though it was difficult to tell at times who Bulfinch was talking to and what was being said. Jack was evidently at the extreme range of the device.

The stolen painting, if it was a stolen painting, was still up there. Jack had not seen it go out and neither had any of the doormen, for he checked.

He was obliged to give back the CIA's gear, and because the doormen all knew him, he could not slip into the basement to replace it with a tap on Bulfinch's phone. He was puzzled that the dealer had gone out nearly every night all week and had stayed out late, leaving behind—under the bed, perhaps—the hot merchandise. Perhaps this proved he was not expecting the buyer to make contact on his home phone.

Jack realized he was spending more time in his car each day than with Flora. He decided to shift some of his attention to the gallery. The gallery was several blocks away, and he could get into its basement, for he was unknown there. He would attach a self-starting tape recorder to the gallery's phones.

And he had put on his telephone company uniform and hard hat and gone in there, not once but every two days, which had brought him this far and no further, sitting in his car about to listen to still more of the art dealer's inane conversations, the last ones now that he would have.

He guessed he had nearly two hours here, one full side certainly, and most of the second, for the machine was capable of recording the second side as soon as the first was full.

As it played out, Detective Dilger was bored, resigned to giving up the case entirely. He had never been able to think of a way to make it except with an eavesdropping device, first the golf ball, then the illegal wiretap. Lacking enough solid information to get a legal warrant, he had done what some detectives, himself included, often did—gone ahead anyway. He still didn't have enough for a warrant, and to go on with the illegal wire was now out of the question. It was simply too dangerous.

So unless there was something on this tape, the case was over.

And there seemed to be nothing. Most of Bulfinch's calls were brief conversations with restorers, framers. Or an auction was rescheduled. Or such and such a shipment would be arriving at such and such a time. In addition there was a long dialogue between Bulfinch and one of his lovers, who as it happened was on a business trip to Japan. Jack had met the man. His name was Robert something. Owned an antique shop. Tall, skinny guy with long skinny hands.

When the exchanges got sexually explicit, Jack was revolted.

The lover also said: "Did you get the call yet?"

"The call?" said Bulfinch.

"You know the one."

"No, not yet."

This might be interesting, but how was Jack to tell? Did it mean that the lover was in on this and could be arrested as an accomplice? Did it even refer to stolen paintings?

As he listened the car got very cold. He had to turn the engine on from time to time to warm it up. Now it began to rain. At first the rain ran down the windshield, and Jack watched its trails, but slowly the glass fogged over until he could not see the rain anymore, could not see anything.

As he listened, at least half of his mind was elsewhere. The segment he had been waiting for, hoping for, but no longer seriously expected, came near the end. Maybe it did. He couldn't be sure. But suddenly a man with a Hispanic accent had come on the line.

In the cold, airless car Jack had been listening by then for an hour and forty-five minutes, but instantly he was sitting up straight, as taut as if he had just been slapped in the face. Had he been so sure the voice, when it came, would be Hispanic?

"Do you have what we want?" the man said to Bulfinch.

"Yes, the product came in a few days ago."

Criminals on telephones, especially those of Bulfinch's type, always thought they were being so smart when they switched to code. Jack gave a snort that might have been called derisive. Product? An art dealer talking about paintings as product? He stopped the tape and marked the place with a red grease pencil. Most codes that came over wiretaps were homemade. As such they were obviously codes, and usually their meaning was transparent. Their principal effect was to cause whoever was monitoring the tap, who was probably half asleep and who otherwise might have stayed that way, to sit up sharply and pay strict attention to whatever came next.

Jack restarted the tape.

"We come there in two days, three days," said the Hispanic.

"We?"

"My brother come too."

"Your brother," said Bulfinch. "I see."

The Hispanic gave a brief laugh. "You don't worry."

"All right," said Bulfinch warily. "Two men maximum. I'll have someone with me as well."

"We come there with money."

"The price will be what I quoted you," said Bulfinch carefully. "This thing is very rare. There are only five of them in private hands."

"You don't mind if I see first before to give money."

"You know the address?"

"You tell me already."

"Shall we say Wednesday, about nine P.M.?"

The call ended a moment later. Detective Dilger shut off the machine and sat brooding. Today was Monday. On Wednesday Madison Avenue would meet the Medellín cartel. He had about forty-eight hours before the sale went down and he could arrest everybody. But if he wanted the case to stand up in court the arrests would have to be legal. Which meant he would have to have warrants. Warrants were going to be a problem.

Then for some minutes he sat behind the fogged-over windshield drumming his fingers on the steering wheel. Forty-eight hours. He sensed this was not enough time.

There was nothing at all he could do tonight.

He put the defroster on to clear the glass and glanced at his watch: Flora's party might still be in progress.

Starting the car, he drove to a bar he knew where cops hung out.

There followed many pitchers of beer and many stories traded with other cops—he laughed at theirs, and they laughed at his. Only occasionally did they talk of current cases, the talk becoming suddenly serious. He was working on a great one right now, Dilger told them once, his speech by then somewhat slurred. Madison Avenue meets the Medellín cartel. Depended on whether or not he could fit all the pieces together, he said. Lots of pieces on this one. The case was ready to break, but he needed warrants he wasn't sure he could get. They pressed him for details but he remembered in time that he shouldn't give any. Instead he shifted the topic and also the tone. Told about the time he was in uniform in a radio car and found the dead guy on the sidewalk with a screwdriver down his throat. Thought he was dealing with a homicide but it was only a cardiac arrest. Seems the dying man had been thrashing around on the sidewalk and somebody says: we should stick something in his mouth before he swallows his tongue: and this kindly neighborhood lady runs off and gets a screwdriver—it was all I could find, she says. It will have to do, the other guy says, and together they ram it down the guy's throat to prevent him from swallowing his tongue—which he wasn't likely to do since by then he was dead.

Jack was grinning into all the laughter, enjoying the beer, enjoying these new cop friends, from time to time remembering Bulfinch too, anticipating the pleasure of putting him and the two druglords in jail.

Near midnight he went back out to his car. The rain had stopped and the night seemed colder than ever. He realized he was staggering, and he got in behind the wheel and drove home with exaggerated care. He went in past the night doorman and upstairs to his apartment.

Though he had some trouble getting his key into the lock, he did remember to close the door softly behind him, and he stood in the dark slightly swaying. All the lights in the apartment were out, and he needed to orient himself. The light in the bedroom was out too. When he had made his way to the doorway he could hear Flora breathing. She was either asleep or angrily pretending to be. He went through into the bathroom and took a long luxurious pee, then undressed and brushed his teeth. He couldn't find his pajamas so he got under the blankets beside Flora naked. He stroked her hip for a time but she didn't respond. He really wanted to apologize to her about walking out on her party, though he had had to do it. He wanted to convince her he was still crazy about her, and sex was the best way to do this, he was sure, none better. She would see how much he desired her, and this would be proof of his love. She was lying on her side, and his hand moved to her topside breast, the only one available—she was lying on the other—and he went on stroking. But she didn't respond to this either. The nipple didn't even come up. While he was trying to work out what to do next he fell asleep.

≡ CHAPTER 3 ≡

At this time Madeleine Leclerq and Jack Dilger did not know each other, and neither could have imagined they would ever meet. Although both were detectives, they did not have much in common, for they operated in different languages some forty-five hundred miles apart, under penal codes and rules of procedure that differed in profound ways. A cop's life was a highly technical one. What counted as normal in one country was often not normal, and sometimes not legal, in the other. Even the two pay scales differed. Madeleine worked out of Nice on the French Riviera, a rich address; she found it a tough place to get by on police pay. Though she and Dilger held approximately the same rank, his salary was three times hers.

Nor were their units all that similar. She was an *inspecteur* of Police Judiciaire, the chief investigative arm of the Police Nationale. The NYPD and the PJ were not the same, particularly in their exposure to public scrutiny, and the day would come when Dilger would accuse her of working for the French secret police.

In Nice, PJ headquarters was at 28 Rue de Roquebillière, an address not listed in any phone or guide book. The PJ's telephone numbers are nowhere listed either, and its buildings, part of a compound shared with other services, stand inside a high and oppressive wall that bears no sign or identifying plaque. It is as if the PJ did not really exist, though it does.

The wall is very old—so are the barracks-type buildings inside—and its stucco veneer has fallen away in places. It is too high to scale and is topped in some places by rusting barbed wire, and in others by broken glass. There is an arched gateway in the wall with a barrier across it, and a guard booth beyond that. The barrier does hold a sign. It reads: POLICE, ENTRY FORBIDDEN. About a hundred PJ detectives move in and out each day. Beyond the guard booth stand their unmarked cars, Renaults and Peugeots mostly. Civilians do not move in and out, unless they are prisoners or, occasionally, lawyers.

Not only is there no public listing for the PJ anywhere, but the names of its detectives never appear in the press. The detectives are not allowed to talk to the press. This is the law, and it is enforced and obeyed. The result is that most citizens have no knowledge of who these detectives are, how they are controlled, what they do.

The PJ's part of the city is far from the beaches, roulette tables, and grand hotels, far also from the lurid glamour of the Riviera's past. This is the back of the town where the mountains begin to rise up on three sides, a neighborhood of housing projects, of cheap storefronts. The police compound behind its inhospitable wall fits exactly into this community as if by design, being old, dilapidated, as used up as everything around it.

Inside PJ headquarters one recognizes at once that these rooms and desks are and have always been inhabited almost exclusively by men. Everything is grimy. Often there is the noise of raucous laughter, and of typewriter keys that stick. The odor is the standard mixture: disinfectant mixed with urine, vomit, and fear, the whole heavily overlaid with stale smoke: too many men, too many cigarettes, for too many years. Cops here and elsewhere believe this odor to be unexceptional. They say it is the

odor of police stations, the same all over the world. To them this
is what crime and degradation smell like. They shrug. It is normal in every way.

This was the setting for much of the waking hours of
Madeleine's life. She too, however much she would have liked to
clean the place up, was forced to take it as it was. If you wanted
to be a cop in France, especially a female cop, there was much
you had to overlook.

On this particular afternoon she stood in front of the desk
of a man named Jacques Vossart, whose rank was *commissaire principal.* Vossart was head of the Finance Brigade, and her boss. She
was thirty-four years old and had been a police detective eleven
years, only a few weeks of it here. She had worked hard, had got
to where she wanted to be at last, but it wasn't turning out as she
had hoped.

Now, standing in front of Vossart's desk, holding a thick file
folder in her two hands, she tried to explain a case. It was one
she wished to pursue, but to do this she needed permission, and
there were reasons why Vossart might not give it.

Madeleine wore a white blouse under a black tailored suit that
was of good quality, for she had strong ideas about what was chic
and what was not, and she liked to look her best. She was tall and
slim, rounded where she should be, but her figure was anything
but voluptuous she believed, and she hated it when, as often happened, other cops treated her like a pinup. She had two other
suits at home, one blue, one pale rose, only three in all. It was not
very much in the way of rotation but on police pay it was all she
could afford. By changing her accessories she got by, she hoped,
and each night in her apartment she carefully ironed out the suit
she had just taken off, then hung it with equal care inside a plastic slip in her armoire.

The blouse she wore today had a high fluffy collar that
reached to her hair, which was dark, nearly as dark as her suit.
Her eyes were dark blue, but her color, because of certain remarks Vossart had just made, was high—higher than she wished.

She wore black shoes with medium heels, and flesh-colored hose as regulations prescribed, and she kept her legs, whenever she sat down, primly crossed.

She carried a regulation Manhurin .357 in her handbag, which at the moment stood back on her desk. She had never used it, and never expected to.

Commissaire Vossart was forty-five, a big man with a thick black mustache who was said to have keen political instincts, the keenest. If an investigation ran into political resistance he sensed this at once, gauged its strength and direction, and almost always backed off. He was a man whose discretion, the politicians believed, could be counted on. His smile showed as much tooth as a racehorse; most people found it both attractive and disarming. He had a great deal of surface charm, or thought he did. Though he too earned police pay, he wore extremely expensive suits which hid his slight corpulence, and he had moved in the best circles in Nice, Madeleine knew, for a number of years. He was president of the Opera Guild, for instance. He drove an expensive car, a Mercedes. High-ranking police officers, if they were willing to accept favors from citizens who courted them, could live quite well in France, and Madeleine knew this too.

She did not approve of Vossart's style, but it in no way surprised her.

"It's the Tontine case," Madeleine said now. "You've read the *procès-verbaux* of course."

"Did I?"

"I put the folder on your desk last night." She held it up. "This one here."

"Oh yes."

She had put it there under some others hoping he would not get to it, and she had retrieved it an hour later when he went out to meet one of his rich friends, or whatever it was he did when he went out suddenly.

"Good case," he said.

She was satisfied he had read nothing. "Then you know where it seems to have led?"

It had led directly to Sestri Brothers S.A., thought she did not say so.

"Of course," said Vossart.

Not having read the dossier, what else could he say?

On the surface, the Tontine investigation was exactly the type case commissaires like Vossart wished to make. Small-time. No political fallout at all. However, the Sestri Brothers, to whom it had led directly, which Vossart did not yet realize, made the case big-time. This could mean trouble for Vossart—trouble for Madeleine too. Sestri was one of the two biggest construction firms in the south of France. It had built the viaducts and tunnels when the *autoroute* went through. It had extended the airport runways out into the Mediterranean, chopping down whole mountains inland, trucking out the rocks and building up the floor of the sea until the extensions could be laid on top. Sestri employed thousands. For thirty years every single public works project in or near Nice had gone either to Sestri or to its archrival, some said its archconfederate, Belfontaine. This had reached the point where, when public contracts were let, other firms no longer bothered to put in bids.

Madeleine had not intended to mention her case's connection to Sestri unless Vossart did, but at this point in the interview she lost her nerve. She could deceive him now easily enough, but when he found out he would explode. She said hesitantly: "The Tontine case has led us, I suppose you could say, toward Sestri Brothers."

"Sestri?" Vossart said in a startled tone.

"Well—"

"Sit down, let's talk this over."

Madeleine sat. "I mean, Sestri is probably a false trail." The words came out too fast, and she tried to force herself to slow down, to add as lightly as she could: "But it would be derelict of us not to check it out, don't you think?"

"You won't find anything against them," said Vossart firmly. "They're good people."

"I'm sure you're right." She was sure of no such thing. In fact she was sure of the opposite. With the connivance of City Hall, Sestri had been gouging the taxpayers for years, and beginning tomorrow, if Commissaire Vossart let her go forward, she would find the documents to prove it. What the fallout would be after that was not her affair.

"We really," she said, "should perquisition at Sestri's as soon as possible."

"To perquisition you need a *commission rogatoire*."

"Yes, and I have one." When she thrust the document across the desk to him, he put it down unread. They all read the same and he had seen thousands.

He said: "You're way ahead of me."

"The *juge d'instruction*," said Madeleine, "signed it for me, you see."

"Which judge?"

The judge was a woman. Madeleine gave her name, Madame Ardois, and saw Vossart frown. More and more magistrates were women now, and evidently Vossart did not approve of any of them. Principally, Madeleine thought bitterly, because they could not be relied upon to behave like men.

"The two of you cooked this up," said Vossart. "Girl to girl."

"Judge Ardois wanted to do it," said Madeleine defensively. "I couldn't stop her." Not true. Upon learning that the case led to Sestri, the judge too had backed way off. A *commission rogatoire*, she had said at first, was out of the question.

Madeleine had had to argue hard.

Now, instead of responding, Vossart stood up, came around the desk, and stood over Madeleine's chair. He was encroaching on her space but she did not look up. He was a man who disapproved of women only professionally. On a more basic level he seemed to imagine himself irresistible to whichever of them crossed his path, including her. Perhaps even especially her. He had a wife and children at home. She knew this, and he knew she knew it, but she had felt the sexual pressure from the first day.

"If I perquisition and don't find anything against the Sestris," she said, "they're in the clear. More importantly, so are we."

She felt Vossart's hand lightly brushing her collar.

"No one would be able to accuse us of favoring the Sestris." She added nervously: "And burying the case."

When she turned her head to glance up at him, his hand brushed her cheek. She hated this, but it was her doing, not his. She would go that far, a single turn of the head, to get what she wanted, no further. However, when her gaze dropped again to her lap she saw that her knuckles gripping the dossier had turned white.

"Nice blouse," Vossart said, fingering it. "Silk?"

"Nylon, I think."

He went on fingering it.

"To do even a reasonable search," Madeleine said, "I'll need a minimum of about six extra detectives. That's really what I've come in here for, to ask you to assign me the men."

"Feels like silk to me."

"Sestri's has five floors of offices. It's a big place. I'll need help."

She wanted the six extra men, and she wanted Vossart to stay away from her, and she waited.

Madeleine Leclerq was born in Nice and grew up in an apartment on the Avenue Felix Faure. Her father was a yacht broker, her mother a court clerk at the Tribunal de Grande Instance. She had a brother, Alain, who was eleven years older and who became an army officer.

Since both her parents worked, she was put each day into a *crèche maternelle* beginning when she was two and a half years old. That first day, she was told later, she began to howl as the door closed behind her mother, and she continued without stopping for four hours. The nuns had to phone her mother to come and get her.

She grew into a rather stubborn young woman, not always a lovable trait, and she sometimes wondered if this early experience was at the root of it.

She graduated from the lycée at the normal age, passed her bac, and was sent by her father to work as an au pair in England. He wanted her to learn English, as it would help her if she took over the yacht brokerage one day.

In England she was on her own again, each day trying to fathom a foreign country. She was not quite eighteen years old. She lived in a third-floor maid's room in a Victorian house in Bexhill-on-Sea and took care of a boy, four, and a girl, two. The parents treated her well except that the father, an estate agent who seemed middle-aged to her, caught her in the hallway one night and tried to feel her breasts and kiss her. She slapped his face and squirmed away and after that feared for her job. But nothing happened. He behaved as if nothing had ever happened, so she did too. She lost her virginity to a waiter in an ice-cream parlor who was nice to her, and who used to take her walking along the boardwalk on her nights off. She was glad to get rid of it. Now she could do what she wanted.

When her father died suddenly she came back to France. Her brother left the army and took over the yacht brokerage. Her own job seemed to be to take over her mother. That September she entered the university at Nice, but two years later quit without getting a degree; school wasn't what she wanted. Still living at home, she considered becoming a government functionary: good pay, long vacations, absolute tenure, early retirement. It happened that the test for police detectives was being given at this time, and women were suddenly being accepted into the service. The police slogan had even been changed. Instead of "A Métier for Men" it had become "A Métier for the Future." Almost as a whim she decided to take the test, which she passed easily. She never realized then how passionate she would become about the job and the life, how much she would come to love the constant surprises, the crises dealt with, the confrontations every day with the best and the worst in human behavior. She never realized a lot of things, one of them being that the Police Nationale had no great interest in women, whose numbers were restricted by law. The female quota was ten percent. In response to pressure from women's groups this number would inch up in years to come, but would never exceed twenty percent.

Madeleine went through the national police school near Lyon, nine months, finding the bookwork easy and the field-work not much harder, for she was a big girl, as tall as many of the men, and had always been athletic. She came out second in the class, and at the end there were five posts open in the Police Judiciaire. These elite posts were supposed to go to the top five graduates, were they not? So of course she would get one of them.

She didn't. All five went to men, and she was assigned to the Youth Brigade in Lille, a factory town up near the Belgian border, where she had never lived and knew no one. The Youth Brigade, she thought bitterly, was all they thought female detectives were good for.

In her new job she dealt mostly with children beaten or burned or sodomized by their parents; or with runaways, or with child prostitutes. But detectives on the Youth Brigade, who were mostly women, were also borrowed by the Sûreté Urbaine, or by the Police Judiciaire whenever important cases occurred that required extra manpower. In this way she got to peer into all the ferocious corners of human conduct: stabbings, shootings, over-doses. Little by little she learned the tricks of the trade, which were different for a woman than for a man. She learned to flat-ter male colleagues to get assigned to cases that interested her; and at crime scenes, where there were often cops present from competing units, she learned to flatter the substitute prosecutor so as to get the case assigned to whatever unit she was with that day. She saw clearly that some cops were venal men, that at times there was money to be made, but this was no temptation to her personally, for nobody offered anything to the women, of course. At Christmastime she watched male colleagues taking home boxes of foie gras, cases of champagne. It was not necessary for her or the other women to decide whether to accept these gifts or not, as they weren't offered.

Within six months she had seen it all, or so she told herself, including the suicide of another cop.

Later, when she and Jack Dilger had met, she mentioned this suicide, and he was surprised. "You mean French cops eat their guns too," he said.

"He didn't exactly eat it," she had said irritably, giving Jack a look. At this point she barely knew him and he irritated her much of the time. He thought America so special a place that human beings were different there. To a Frenchwoman this idea was offensive. She felt so much older and wiser than he and was so annoyed at him that she kept the rest of the suicide story to herself. Why describe something that had marked her forever to someone too dense or unsophisticated to understand?

The colleague who shot himself had stuck the barrel in the folds of his ear and the bullet had gone straight through and out the other ear, taking a bit of brains with it, not much. There had really been a minimum of mess, compared to other suicides she would observe later. A minimum physically speaking. Emotionally, intellectually it had been another story, for she had had lunch with that particular detective that very day. Furthermore, the later investigation uncovered no irregularities in his professional life, nor in his personal life either. At lunch he had not even seemed particularly depressed. He had recently flunked the exam for promotion to commissaire, and he had had a fight with his wife, but with the dessert, she remembered, he had told a joke. After the dessert and the joke she had gone back to work, whereas he had rented a cheap hotel room. Evidently he had sat there an hour. Then he had "eaten his gun," as the American put it.

How do you begin to understand something like that? How do you force your mind to let it go, to chew on something else?

The incident had taught her what human brains look like leaking out onto the floor, but nothing else whatever. All the rest was incomprehensible.

As she became friends with a number of the other women with whom she worked, she learned that they had become cops for a variety of reasons. The police service was like a gigantic flea market: there was something for everyone. One woman saw the career possibilities; she planned to take all the tests and move upward in rank. Another wanted to succor people in trouble; she could as easily have become a nun or a nurse. A third was divorced and looking for a new father for her child. Still another woman, also divorced, had joined hoping to meet men, lots of men. To all, the job had seemed to promise equality with men, an idea they soon got over. "We'll always be marginal here," one woman told Madeleine once.

Men to Madeleine were the problem. The Youth Brigade shared quarters with a number of other police units, all of them dominated by males. Men to whom female cops were either sluts or lesbians. One or the other. To date a fellow cop—any fellow cop—made you obviously a slut. Refuse them all, which was the course Madeleine chose, and the rumor spread through all of the units that you were a lesbian.

But who else did a young woman meet in this line of work except other cops? Criminals, of course. Distraught victims. Occasionally a magistrate who was invariably married. Madeleine became sex-starved. When she went home to Nice from time to time, her mother told her she had become closed in on herself, that her job was making her hard.

Finally, almost as a form of self-preservation, she married a detective in the Anti-gang Brigade. He was good-looking, he could often make her laugh, and she convinced herself she was in love with him. Marriage would put an end to the slut/lesbian rumors, and with two salaries she could live in a better apartment.

The marriage lasted a bit over two years before her husband got promoted to commissaire. The promotion carried with it a transfer to Strasbourg on the German border—a transfer for him, not for her. It meant lots of long, lonely cross-country drives, and although they staggered along for a while, that was the end of that particular marriage.

For five years she worked in the Youth Brigade in Lille. She thought she'd never get out of the one or the other, but one day she was called to a hospital where a baby lay bloody and howling with his sex cut off.

She faced a grim father clenching and unclenching his fists, and a distraught mother who maintained that a rat had gotten into their apartment and into the crib with the infant. They were Algerians who lived in a run-down housing project in the worst of the city's slums. Most of the building's inhabitants were other Arabs.

Cops, Madeleine knew, had no use for Arabs, whom they blamed for most of the city's crime, France's crime.

From the hospital Madeleine went to the housing project. She went in the entrance door and the odors struck her face like a physical assault. She almost couldn't breathe: unwashed bodies, urine, feces, stale cooking. The place was crawling with cockroaches and, yes, there were rats. She saw several outside, and another inside. They were big, and obviously they were brazen.

In the apartment the mother pointed out a rat hole in the baseboard.

Madeleine didn't believe the story, and after that couldn't let it go. She spoke to the surgeon who had sewn up the infant; what kind of wound was it, could a rat have done it? She might have filed the case and forgotten it. She couldn't forget it. When her superior assigned her to other cases she continued on this one on her own time. She read everything she could find on rats, spoke to scientists who worked with rats, specialists on rat deportment, so to speak. Could a rat castrate a baby? Well, yes, technically. Was it likely? Not likely, no. Had they ever heard anything like that before? She telephoned every expert on rats she could find, one of them as far away as the University of California. She interviewed neighbors, co-workers, dozens of people in all. Slowly she learned of a festering family feud between the father and the husband of the mother's sister. She found witnesses who could put the brother-in-law close by on the night of the incident, and then one who had seen him in the building on the same floor. It was enough to arrest him and search his furnished room. In a drawer beside the pallet on which he slept she found a pair of surgical scissors filed razor sharp, for which he could offer no explanation.

She put the brother-in-law in *garde à vue*. Under the law prisoners could be held for forty-eight hours without charges and without access to a lawyer. They could be questioned nonstop hour after hour. They could call for a doctor if they wished; that was all.

For forty-eight hours she pounded on the suspect until finally he confessed. He hated the father, he said; what better way to get even with the father than to cut the sex off his infant son.

Madeleine's doggedness, the hardness and clarity with which she had approached the case, won her an official commendation, and then a transfer to Paris, where she worked on the Criminal Brigade out of the Quai d'Orsay. And she worked hard, trying to prove her worth to the men, being careful to show no reaction to bloody corpses, being first to pick up the stretcher at times, doing without complaint all the dirty jobs the men wished to avoid.

It was in Paris that she completed her studies for a DES in economics, for she had decided that she wanted the Finance Brigade. Finance was the elite of the elite, the best job she could imagine. Furthermore, female detectives were more easily accepted in Finance than in most of the other brigades, and there was not as much harassment—this was what other women had told her. In Finance the male cops found you useful. After all, women were said to be good with figures, were they not, and in Finance there was rarely any shooting, meaning a cop didn't have to worry about a woman failing to cover his back. And finally, women were useful when dealing with magistrates and other lawyers, more and more of whom now were also women.

To Madeleine, Finance seemed somehow clean. For years she had wallowed in the gutters of life. She had had enough of all that. She wanted to get away from blood and gore, from people who committed crimes out of viciousness or desperation or stupidity. She wanted to go after educated men who operated out of greed. To her, white-collar criminals were the superstars of the criminal world. The least of them was capable of stealing more in a week than any ten stickup men in a lifetime, and to nail such people would be a real pleasure.

With the DES she now had the credentials for the Finance Brigade, she already had the requisite seniority, and finally the assignment came through. Now if she could just get Nice as well. Among the other emotions tormenting her at this time was a slowly burgeoning homesickness. Nice was home. She wanted to go home.

She had met a young lawyer, and after a time they moved in together. His name was Luc Queron, he was from Nice as well. After they had been living together about three months Luc decided to quit his firm, transfer to Nice permanently, and go into partnership there with two other lawyers.

This caused Madeleine to renew her efforts to be transferred to Nice herself. She could not claim personal hardship, for she and Luc were not married, and in fact the police service was opposed to irregular liaisons. The regulations against them were strict, for it was said that they reflected discredit on the service itself. Some months passed, Luc had been all that time in Nice alone, but at last the transfer went through. Two days later she reported to the Rue de Roquebillière and introduced herself to her new boss, Commissaire Vossart.

As she handed her credentials across the desk, he glanced up in surprise, either not expecting a woman, or not wanting one, or both. "So what am I supposed to do with you?" he said, his tone halfway between exasperation and a snarl. Perhaps he was only showing off for his entourage, for there were several men in the room. For a time he stared at her in silence. A very long time, it seemed to her. Finally he appeared to decide that he liked what he saw. His exasperation turned into a grin, or perhaps a leer. "I know what I would like to do with you."

Madeleine wanted to say: You are chief of the Finance Brigade and I am a detective. I am not your lover or your whore. I have many years police experience and a DES degree in economics. I am not a teenager impressed by your rank. My job is to lock up white-collar criminals, as is yours. My job does not oblige me to listen to your adolescent humor.

Frowning, she only stared at the floor.

Whereupon Vossart's brusque manner returned, and he ordered one of the other men to find a desk for her.

She sat at this desk for two weeks with no one coming near her. Then Vossart wheeled a cart over and started dumping out dossiers. There must have been fifty of them. The top of the desk couldn't hold them all. They were sliding off and she was lunging for them.

"These just came over from the *parquet*," said Vossart, ladling them out. "See if anything looks interesting." As he strolled away she heard him laugh and say to someone: "That will keep her busy for a week or two."

The *parquet* was the prosecutor's office. The dossiers related to suspected stock swindles, questionable bankruptcies. The complainants would be disgruntled investors, or else pious employees who had decided to come forward. In each case the prosecutor's men would have made a preliminary inquiry and would have found the charges credible enough to send them to the Finance Brigade for investigation.

Madeleine formed the dossiers into neat piles and started

through them. The trouble was, complainants usually waited a considerable time to complain, and more time usually elapsed before the prosecutor's men got around to each case. This could happen because there were too many cases, or because men were sick or on vacation, or because a specific case looked "sensitive." Sensitive meant that an elected official was involved, or a major contributor to the party in power, or a company employing many workers who, in the event of a successful prosecution, could be thrown onto the street or the dole, thereby creating social unrest. The prosecutor worked directly for the minister of justice, who was a politician appointed by the prime minister. He had to get permission from the minister to open cases, and he did what he was told or was removed. So from his point of view some cases were better off buried. He didn't need to bury them completely, for that could create social unrest too; one merely sent them forward late. The statute of limitations on white-collar crimes was only three years.

Some of the dossiers on her desk, Madeleine saw, had lain in a locker somewhere for years. Several would be over the limit before any meaningful investigation could be done. Others were over already.

She found three cases that looked promising and at the end of the day handed the dossiers and her report to Vossart.

"Finished already?" he asked skeptically.

It made her explain herself, defend herself, even as she offered to work on one of the three cases herself—the one that looked to be the most promising to her—the Tontine case. For already she saw that the Sestris might be involved.

According to the complaint as sent over by the *parquet*, substantial sums of money, more than seemed justified, were passing through Tontine's small firm with offices on the Rue Trachel in the back of Nice. The case had caught Madeleine's attention because Tontine was mentioned in two of the other dossiers she had looked at. In one of them she had found a request from the Marseilles PJ, dated almost two years previously, asking Nice to look into Tontine for them. Marseilles had been investigating the bankruptcy of a publicly owned company and had found big bills from Tontine for "feasibility studies" and "cost analyses" and although the company was going bankrupt, these had been paid.

But Marseilles's request had either been buried or misfiled. As nearly as Madeleine could determine, no investigation of Tontine had been done by Nice then or ever.

"So can I keep the case?" she had asked Vossart.

She didn't explain what it was about the case that had excited her, and she kept her face blank.

After glancing into the dossier Vossart had said: "It won't amount to anything."

"Even so, it's a start for me."

"I'll think about it."

Two more weeks went by during which she asked him again several times. Finally he came out of his office and dropped the dossier on her desk, saying: "Okay. Sure. Why not?" Perhaps he figured it would get her out of the building for a few days, out of his hair. This was what she hoped. But as he looked her up and down, his eyes lingering on her breasts, she saw that she was wrong. More likely he figured she now owed him something. Giving her the case was a favor that she would have to pay back. As if to confirm this fear, his racehorse grin came on and he said: "You and I must have a long talk. What are you doing tonight?"

"Working on this," she said, attempting to look preoccupied by the dossier in her hands. "I want to do well."

But ultimately she was forced to lift her eyes. His teeth still showed, but now he nodded his head as well. "Another time, then."

As if, having established the ground rules, he now could wait.

This was the start of the case that seemed to lead to Sestri Brothers S.A.

Vossart also assigned her a partner, and not a good one, or so he thought, deliberately not making it easy for her. The partner was Inspector Bosco, a short bald man who was near retirement age and who, it was said, was content to sit in cafés sipping black coffee or red wine while others did the work. But Bosco was the only detective in the building who had been friendly to her so far, had even invited her home to dinner to meet his wife, and as the Tontine investigation began she saw that he was willing to work as hard as she was.

They began interviewing potential witnesses, spending a week on it, then switched their attention to Tontine personally.

They found he had no staff except his wife, who was on the payroll, and a few Algerians whom he sometimes hired out to construction sites. His offices amounted to two rooms over a bakery. He owned the bakery and always had. That's what he was by profession, a baker. Although he supposedly did feasibility studies and cost analyses for construction companies, he had no engineering credentials at all. Yet he had sent forward these enormous bills. They totaled millions of francs. The couple had two cars. The wife drove a Jaguar, and the baker a Porsche.

So Madeleine went back to the prosecutor's office, where she spoke to one of the substitute prosecutors, a tall gangling kid fresh out of law school. Without consulting his superior, who might have seen where the case was heading, who might have urged caution and deliberately slowed it down, the young substitute agreed to open the standard "information against X," and to consign the case to a judge, Madame Ardois, as it happened. Within a day Madeleine had her *commission rogatoire*, and nobody as yet suspected where she sensed the case would go.

The *commission rogatoire* was the central judicial document of any case. It ordered investigators to "open an inquiry, to interview all useful persons, to proceed to all searches, seizures, confrontations, and requisitions useful to the manifestation of the truth." It was an extremely broad warrant without which a detective could do almost nothing. With it his powers were almost unlimited.

The next morning Madeleine and Bosco waited double-parked outside the bakery in an unmarked car. People went in and came out again, buying bread. It was a cold gloomy morning. She could see their breath as they came out clutching the long crusty loaves. The bread would be fresh from the oven and hot, and Madeleine imagined she could see the heat coming off it, which of course she couldn't. Each time the door opened again the hot bakery breath rushed out at her and made her hungry.

From her preliminary inquiry, Madeleine knew that the entrance to Tontine's upstairs offices was through a door in the back of the bakery, but neither she nor Bosco knew what he looked like, so they watched this door through the plate glass. Almost two hours passed before a man entered, did not buy bread, shook hands with everybody, then went through the door in the back. "It's him," muttered Madeleine.

In an instant they were out of the car, through the bakery, and behind Tontine on the stairs. "Police," Madeleine told him, showing first her tricolor police card, and then the *commission rogatoire.* "We have an order allowing us to perquisition your offices."

They sat the former baker on a chair against the wall and started through his drawers and files. For a time he tried to bluff it out. He was an honest businessman, had broken no law, they would find nothing incriminating. Shortly after that he stood up and announced they could search all they wanted, but he was leaving.

"Sit down," shouted Bosco, "or I'll handcuff you to the chair."

"The law says you must be present for the search," said Madeleine.

From then on he looked more and more miserable. Madeleine had gone downstairs to the bakery and come back with a cardboard carton—it was already half full of documents.

After two hours they broke for lunch, the three of them sitting at a table on the glassed-in terrace of the brasserie on the corner, the two police officers ordering omelettes and sharing conversation, laughter, and a bottle of rosé, while Tontine beside them said nothing and ate nothing. He said he wasn't hungry.

Back in the offices above the bakery the search for documents continued. By then it was clear that Tontine's money came from a number of sources, though more from Sestri Brothers than anywhere else. Madeleine had found duplicates of the bills he had sent out, always for "feasibility studies" or other nebulous work, but nothing to justify them, no blueprints or plans or even work orders, not a single voucher for salaries paid. His bank statements showed that he deposited all checks received from the Sestri Brothers, or whomever, to an account in his wife's name at the Banque Lyonnaise on the Rue de la Liberté, and that as soon as the check had cleared he withdrew the money in cash. What he may have done with this cash was not apparent.

About three P.M. there was the sound of footsteps outside the door—Tontine's wife coming upstairs from the bakery. She came in wearing a mink coat and seemed surprised as she glanced all around. She too was made to sit against the wall, where her gaze moved in great agitation from her husband to Madeleine and back again.

And about an hour after that, Madeleine told them they were both under arrest. Bosco handcuffed them and they were taken back to the Rue de Roquebillière, and put into *garde à vue*.

Locking the wife in the cage to cool, Madeleine started in on the baker. After the routine opening questions, date and place of birth, civil status, etc., Madeleine and Bosco took turns pressuring him, a cross-examination that went on hour after hour. They caught him up in many lies; otherwise he admitted nothing.

His wife, meanwhile, remained in the vomit-encrusted cage until three A.M. and no one went near her. Her mink coat had been taken away from her. She was wearing only a thin wool dress and about ten P.M. the heat had gone off in the building and she had begun to shiver. Separated from her husband, alone with her fears, a jail term staring her in the face, she broke down almost as soon as Madeleine ordered her brought out. Within ten minutes she had told all she knew. Each time the Tontines received a check, she sobbed, they kept a commission and sent the rest of the money in cash back where it came from.

It meant that the firms, and the biggest offender was Sestri Brothers, were now in possession of vast amounts of cash that did not have to be accounted for, and on which taxes did not have to be paid, cash that had been stolen, in effect, from their stockholders and also from the pockets of all taxpayers. Company officers could use this cash to give unreported bonuses to themselves, or else they could use it to bribe elected officials so that public works contracts would continue to fall their way.

Which did they do? Madeleine wondered. Bonuses or bribes? Probably both.

She had stumbled on a nest of white-collar gangsters who corrupted politicians and in turn were protected by them, and among the side effects, if she could clean this nest out, would be the making of her reputation here, and possibly even throughout France. The next morning early she took Tontine and his wife over to the Palace of Justice where Judge Ardois indicted them both, also signing an order consigning them to preventive detention until trial.

Madeleine now asked for a new *commission rogatoire.* A carefully directed, full-scale perquisition of Sestri's offices was what was called for next, she said.

Madame Ardois frowned. The public prosecutor would have to open a new information first, she said, and she doubted he'd do it—certainly not without phoning Paris and the minister of justice for permission. Obviously this was a politically charged case. The minister would not want to take any chances. Probably he would order the prosecutor to give the case—French law enforcement had a phrase for it—a first-class funeral.

"Then it's up to you," Madeleine said stubbornly.

"Up to me?"

"To make the prosecutor see that he has to open a new information, that he has no choice."

"And how do I do that?"

"You start by dialing his number and talking to him," said Madeleine stubbornly.

Madame Ardois laughed.

She herself—all judges—had permanent tenure and thus could ignore the wishes of anyone. Judges were immune to the orders of the minister of justice; they could stand up even to the president himself. But it was not a good career step to do so. Madame Ardois, who had no desire to make powerful enemies, told Madeleine that they did not have much on Sestri Brothers S.A., the testimony of one weeping wife was all. It was a rich and successful firm. It employed more than five thousand people, and it was heavily connected politically. Most dangerous of all, this case might lead straight to City Hall.

But Madeleine kept arguing.

Finally Madame Ardois did phone the prosecutor's office, and now Madeleine had a stroke of luck—whether good or bad remained to be seen—for the prosecutor was not there. He was in Paris for some meetings and would be gone all week. The same substitute with whom Madeleine had already dealt had taken the call, and when Madame Ardois asked that a new information be opened, this young man asked for time to think it over.

"Now he's phoning his boss in Paris," she said when she had hung up. "You'll have your answer in an hour, and it will be no."

But the substitute was unable to reach his superior in Paris. He was new, inexperienced, and originally from Lyon, not Nice. Unaware of the wealth, power, and political connections of Sestri Brothers S.A., he saw no reason why Judge Ardois should not have a new information opened, if that's what she wanted.

"Commissaire Vossart's pretty cozy with the powers that be in this town," Madame Ardois commented later in the day, as she handed over Madeleine's new *commission rogatoire.*

"Yes," Madeleine said, "I've heard that too."

Legally Madeleine had all she needed to go forward. But on a practical level she still needed permission from her boss, Vossart.

"Good luck with him," Madame Ardois told her, and showed her out.

Now Vossart stood beside her chair fingering her collar, hardly listening to what she had to say.

"I'll need six extra detectives to search the Sestri building properly," Madeleine said again. She believed she needed ten, but had not dared ask for so many.

Commissaire Vossart gave up fingering her collar and re-treated behind his desk, where he sat smirking.

"You and I will have a party yet," he said, and again showed all his teeth.

"Sestri's is big, five stories, twenty or thirty offices. Even with ten men—"

"A legs-in-the-air party."

It made her eyes drop. I will not be intimidated by this man, she told herself, and forced them up again. "Does that mean I get the men?"

He laughed. "You can have two."

"Two?"

"With you and Bosco that makes four. I'm shorthanded this week."

Was he trying to hobble the investigation?

"Which two?" she asked him.

"Take Mayotte and Cenis." He was still smirking.

"Fine," she said. "Two, then."

She realized it was late in the day, she added, but she wanted to serve the *commission rogatoire* immediately, begin the search at once. This would catch the Sestris by surprise, and—

"Tomorrow," said Vossart.

"I realize we would have to work all night. But I think it's the way to go."

"Tomorrow," said Vossart again.

The smirk was gone. She could not read his face. She said: "Tomorrow may be too late."

"If they're guilty, the incriminating documents will be there. If they're not, they won't. What's the big hurry?"

"But—" People could try to conceal their emotions but the mask was always thin, and most times it was transparent. She said: "Can I ask why?"

"Tomorrow."

"All right," she said, and started for the door.

"Sooner or later we'll have that party," he said to her back. "I'm looking forward to it." And she heard him laugh again.

His laughter seemed to blossom, to follow her down the corridor to her desk, though of course it didn't. From her desk she couldn't hear it at all.

She sat staring at the wall. She had met a certain amount of sexual harassment at every stop on her career, but it should have stopped by this time. Vossart was proof that it hadn't. Nothing she had experienced in the past seemed to her as threatening as what she was being subjected to by this man now.

On her way home, unable to help herself, she drove past Sestri Brothers S.A. The lights were still burning on the high floors, and she wondered about this, and in fact it worried her. Perhaps, as in most big firms, the younger executives stayed late just to prove how eager they were. There was no reason for her to suspect anything else, she told herself.

She was driving her small Renault, which was six years old with many thousands of kilometers on its clock. Near her building she found a place to park. Walking back, she passed a butcher shop still open, with chickens roasting on spits in the glass oven just inside. After hesitating a moment she went in and bought one for supper.

Once inside her apartment, she hung up her suit inside its

plastic bag, stepped into jeans, pulled on a sweater, and was standing at the sink washing vegetables for a salad when Luc came in. She thought of telling him about Vossart, his unwelcome touches, his double entendre remarks, today's invitation to a legs-in-the-air party. But she found she could not talk about any of this. Luc was a man of medium height but heavily muscled from lifting weights. For a lawyer he had always struck her as somewhat hotheaded. She thought of him as older than herself in some ways, much younger in most others. Actually, he was two years her junior. If she told him how much Commissaire Vossart upset her, she could not be sure how he would react or what he would do, and if he went raging into Vossart's office, Vossart would deny everything, and after that simply get rid of her. She would find herself back in the Youth Brigade with most of the other female inspectors.

She let Luc kiss her under the ear, and he hung around her, pulling off his tie.

"What's for dinner?" he said.

Inside its insulated bag the roast chicken was still hot from the spit. With kitchen scissors she sliced it in two. The potatoes she had sliced up earlier were frying lightly in olive oil. She made a salad of *mesclun* and sliced beets. She brought everything to the table in their living/dining room, and Luc carried in the basket of bread and the wine.

Over dinner she told him with some excitement that she had finally got her hands on a big case, maybe a gigantic case. Tomorrow she and three other detectives would hit a place that didn't expect to be hit. She thought they'd find all kinds of things. Even the mighty would be shaken, she said, the top echelons of the city. She would probably be interrogating prisoners for the next forty-eight hours, so he shouldn't expect her home. If she got home at all it would be only to shower and change her clothes, and—

But Luc had thrown down his fork. "We have a dinner date tomorrow night."

"Oh," she said, remembering it for the first time.

"I expect you to be there."

They had been invited to a restaurant by a client Luc was wooing. "I forgot," said Madeleine. "I'm so sorry."

"So cancel your goddam raid."

"I can't."

"It's important, Maddie."

"I'm terribly sorry, I can't. You're a lawyer. You know I can't."

They argued—he aggressively, she increasingly on the defensive, until finally Luc grabbed his coat and stormed out of the apartment. Madeleine moved food around with her fork for some minutes, then got up and carried both plates to the kitchen. She put a soup dish facedown over Luc's, for he might be famished when he came in. Her own half-eaten dinner she swept into the garbage.

After that she washed her face again, brushed her teeth, put a nightdress on, and sat up in bed reading. When it was late she turned the light off—tomorrow was going to be a busy day. Luc had still not come home.

≡ CHAPTER 4 ≡

The building that housed Sestri Brothers had once been a luxury hotel. Its former lobby, which now served as a reception room, had impressed clients in Queen Victoria's time, and still did, for it was as big as a tennis court, its ceiling was delineated by heavily encrusted moldings, and from its walls hung paintings that dated back two hundred years or more. From the antique reception desk, which might have come out of the Chateau de Versailles, carpeting radiated out toward what had once been ballrooms.

The receptionist was a girl of about twenty, rather pretty. She wore a navy blue dress that fitted her well and that looked expensive to Madeleine, who glanced at it only long enough to note that it was also a uniform, for the words FRÈRES SESTRI S.A. were stenciled above the left breast.

The detectives, all four carrying briefcases, showed their police cards.

"Take us to the executive offices," ordered Madeleine.

"May I ask whom you wish to see?" said the girl courteously. She was still smiling, proof that the nature of their visit had not yet registered.

"You didn't understand me," said Madeleine. "Take us there at once."

The girl glanced from one outstretched police card to the other, from one face to the other, and began visibly to tremble.

"But—but—you can't—I have to announce you."

She had reached for her telephone console, but Bosco put his hand over hers. "That won't be necessary, chérie."

The idea was to surprise the executives, perhaps to find on their desks something they didn't wish found.

"Let's go," said Madeleine. "What floor is it?"

"They're—they're on—four," stuttered the girl.

"Relax," said Madeleine, "it's got nothing to do with you."

The birdcage elevator would take only three passengers. Madeleine and Bosco crowded in with the girl, who was still trembling, while Mayotte and Cenis ran up the stairs.

As it turned out, the receptionist was almost the only one in the building who did not expect them. With a sinking heart, Madeleine recognized this almost at once.

They came off the elevator and were joined by the two other detectives, who were somewhat out of breath, and a man came out of the corner office and said: "Can I be of help to you?" There was a secretary outside his office, and other secretaries sitting at desks, any one of whom could have performed this function. The man was in shirtsleeves. He was small, slim. His tie was carefully knotted, his hair perfectly cut. He looked perfectly groomed as well, and Madeleine imagined she could smell his cologne from where she stood.

He was smiling.

There was a monogram, BS, on the man's pocket: Bruno Sestri, obviously, and under the circumstances he ought not to be smiling.

Madeleine identified herself and her three companions. "Yes, I've heard of you," he said.

Heard of her? How could he have heard of her? If he had heard of her it was because someone had told him she was coming.

Sestri shook hands with the other three detectives too, then led the way into his corner office, where Madeleine produced her *commission rogatoire.*

He took it. "Sit down, make yourselves comfortable," he said, and began to read. This visit from four police officers appeared not to shake him at all. Madeleine's heart had already plummeted a long way down. We're not going to find anything, she told herself. They've probably been up all night shredding. Whatever we might have found is gone, and what will this do to my career?

Sestri tossed the document back across the desk. "No problem," he said.

Somebody had sold her out, and Madeleine asked herself who. It could have been almost anybody, someone from the prosecutor's office, or Judge Ardois's office, even someone from her own office—Commissaire Vossart, for instance.

What difference did it make who?

She was ashamed to look in the direction of Bosco or the other two detectives.

"Where would you like to start?" said Sestri.

"You can start by calling your executives in here and instructing them to cooperate with us in every way."

"Of course," said Sestri.

"When you tell them," said Madeleine, "be sincere."

"Certainly," said Sestri. "You're welcome to look anywhere you want. We have nothing to hide."

He sent for the executives, six men in shirtsleeves who entered one by one until they had formed a semicircle in front of Sestri's desk.

"Cooperation," Sestri told them, "that's the name of the game." He did not wink as he spoke. He didn't have to. The tone of his voice was the wink.

"You understand," added Madeleine hurriedly, "that to hide or destroy any item is a criminal offense." A short speech, but a sign of weakness on her part, and she wished she had not made it.

All the executives nodded. All were blank-faced. If her visit worried any of them, this did not show.

"Where can we work?" asked Inspector Bosco.

Sestri pointed toward a conference room across the hall.

"All right," said Bosco, "have them bring us all financial records for the past three years."

"Three years," said Sestri. "That will take some time."

"Do you have a shredding machine?" Madeleine asked him.

"As a matter of fact, we do."

"Show it to me, please."

He took her down the hall to the stockroom.

The usual stockroom: boxes of stationery on shelves, boxes of ledgers, a row of technical manuals. A counter bearing an espresso machine and cups. A heavy-duty fax. A large copier, of course. And the shredder. Beside the shredder was a bin the size of an oil drum, and it was nearly full. Madeleine dug her hand in and stirred the shreds around.

"A business like this generates an enormous amount of paper," said Sestri.

Madeleine could have sworn he was smirking.

"You'd be surprised how much," said Sestri. "We shred nearly every day."

"Did you shred last night, by any chance?"

"We may have."

She returned to the conference room. The detectives were seated and men were carrying in cartons, file drawers, and folders in loose unstable piles, and setting them down on the table. Before long the tabletop had disappeared under them.

None of the men looked a bit nervous about what the detectives might find. They got rid of everything incriminating last night, Madeleine told herself. They are confident there is nothing left.

"Show me the other offices," she said to Sestri.

They walked down the hall. The office adjacent to his own, Sestri pointed out, belonged to the firm's general manager. Next to him was the chief financial officer. The accounting department was farther along. His brother Jean-Pierre had the other corner office, but it was empty. There were two smaller offices for the two wives, who were also officers of the company; these too were empty.

"Where is your brother?"

"Skiing in Courcheval with his wife."

"How long have they been gone?"

"They took the late plane last night, as a matter of fact."

"I see," said Madeleine. She could picture it, or thought she could. Having been tipped off, they had spent time shredding. After the shredding the two brothers had talked it over, maybe with their wives present, maybe not.

"Are you considered the suave brother?" said Madeleine.

"Suave?"

"I'll bet you are," said Madeleine.

"I don't follow you."

Either he considered himself the suave brother or was so considered by the others. Perhaps both. He must have promised them he could handle the Finance police, and they had left him to do it.

"Are you the chief executive officer? You're not, are you? The chief executive is your brother Jean-Pierre. So what does that make you?"

"I still don't follow you."

"Suave," said Madeleine. "That's what it makes you. And your wife, where is she?"

"She didn't come to work today," said Sestri.

"Why not?"

"Woman's problems. You should understand that only too well."

"Should I?"

"You being a woman."

"Please call your wife and tell her to come in."

"Is that really necessary?"

"I think so, yes," said Madeleine, giving him a brilliant, inappropriate smile. "How soon can she get here?"

The absence of the brother and the two wives seemed to her the only promising note so far.

"And call your brother as well. He'll have to come home at once, I'm afraid. I want him here by this afternoon."

"But that's impossible, he's on the slopes skiing—"

Wherever he was, Madeleine doubted he was on the slopes skiing. "You didn't understand me. I said I want him here this afternoon."

She led the way back into the conference room. "Why don't you sit there?" she said, indicating a chair against the wall. "Maybe you can help us find what we're looking for."

"And what is that?"

But Madeleine didn't know. "You can use that phone there to call your wife and your brother."

"In view of your lack of consideration toward me and my family," Sestri said, "you can't expect any consideration from me toward you." His former affability was entirely gone. He gestured toward the loaded-down table, at the four detectives watching him. "You're on your own. Go to it."

"Make your calls," she ordered him. They would be hours slogging through all those dossiers, and in the end, she feared, would come up with nothing, or very little. But she was determined to go forward, however long it took, determined, according to the jargon of the Finance police, to drink the chalice to the dregs.

Just then Sestri's secretary stuck her head in the room to announce that the minister was on the line from Paris.

"Minister?" said Sestri.

"The minister of the interior."

Madeleine grimaced. So, she noted, did Bosco. The minister of the interior was, in effect, her boss—he was the boss of all

French police forces except the gendarmerie, which was a branch of the army.

"Bonjour, Monsieur le Ministre," said Sestri into the phone, but after that he called him by his first name, and even called him *tu*, which meant they were or had been intimates. Probably the minister had no idea that Sestri Frères was under investigation; he certainly did not know detectives were in the room listening to one side of this conversation. It was a social call, nothing more, and no doubt it had been arranged by Sestri in advance. Madeleine realized this. No doubt it was meant to intimidate her; she realized this too. Nonetheless, it worked, had done its job. If I find nothing, no evidence of wrongdoing, she thought with some bitterness, I am in trouble.

For the next hours Sestri fidgeted on his chair, or paced, or smoked. Madeleine's three detectives smoked also, and the room filled up with bad air, so that several times she went out in the hall just to breathe. All over the building employees were standing in their doorways, talking excitedly, wondering what was happening. Meanwhile, two young clerks kept bringing in new files as they were requested, and boxing and removing old ones. Sometimes Sestri was questioned about certain documents, contracts, work logs. Or executives were called in and questioned, or asked to find one document or another.

At midmorning Sestri's wife arrived, a short woman wearing green trousers and a navy blue blazer. She was beautifully coiffed. Madeleine, who supposed she had just come from the hairdresser, made her sit in the chair next to her husband. Hour after hour she sat there looking distressed, waving smoke away from her face.

At noon the detectives sent one of the secretaries out for sandwiches and beer. She seemed a cheerful young woman, always ready to smile. Well, she wasn't the one being investigated. For her it was almost a day off. Although she didn't understand in the slightest what was happening, she sensed that for today at least there were new bosses; the Sestris had been superseded by four detectives. This was exciting, and she was enjoying it.

She brought the sandwiches back and handed them around: baguettes sliced down the middle, both sides plastered with butter with, inside, a single thin slice of ham; and beer from the Alsace. The detectives ate and drank, they smoked until the ashtrays were full, and they continued to pore through dossiers. Madame Sestri's face showed boredom and distaste. Sestri's showed boredom and anger. He kept throwing out acid remarks, which the detectives ignored.

Bosco caught Madeleine's eye and gestured toward the hall. Obviously he had found something. The two of them stepped outside, where Bosco started to speak.

But they had been joined immediately by Sestri, who stood close, a threesome.

"Please go back inside," Madeleine told him.

He stood his ground.

"If you don't mind," she told him.

"You heard her," said Bosco.

When he had gone, Bosco showed what he had in his hands. "This is the original of Tontine's most recent bill," he whispered. "Note the date. And this is the accounting entry showing payment of the bill. Note the date."

"Looks like they paid the bill before they received it," said Madeleine.

"Right. They wrote out the false bill later to justify the payment. It confirms Madame Tontine's testimony. They willingly paid money for work that was never done. We can arrest him on this alone."

Madeleine shrugged. It was something, not much. "Until we find proof that the money came back as cash," Madeleine said, "and until we find out where it went after that, we don't have a case."

She called Sestri out of the conference room and confronted him with the paid bill and the accounting entry. "You paid for a feasibility study," she told him. "You paid Tontine good money for it. Where is that study?"

Sestri smiled confidently. "We decided not to use the study. Probably we then shredded it. No sense keeping stuff like that around."

"I see. You paid him for studies and consultations altogether seven times over the last three years. We can't find any of those studies."

"We must not have used any of them. Probably got rid of them all."

The three stood in the hall, Sestri smirking, Bosco looking grim. But Madeleine had noticed something else about the bill she held in her hand. "This was produced by a typewriter, not a computer," she told Bosco.

He said: "I noticed an old typewriter in the stockroom."

"So did I. Come with me." And she led him into the stockroom.

After hesitating a moment, Sestri followed. As she rolled a sheet of paper into the old typewriter, she glanced over at Sestri. His brows were knitted together and for the first time, Madeleine thought, he looked concerned.

She typed out the same lines as those on the bill.

The lines matched. It would take blowups and an expert to prove it in court, but both detectives were satisfied.

Bosco gave a low whistle. "You sent the money to Tontine," he said to Sestri, "then typed out the bill Tontine should have sent you. You kept the original and sent the carbon to Tontine. That's fraud, wouldn't you say?" He looked Sestri up and down. "You got problems, pal. You got serious problems."

But to Madeleine it still didn't seem like much.

Late in the afternoon they found more. First the petty cash accounts surfaced, one folder swimming amid so many. It was Madeleine herself who glanced into it, not expecting to find anything significant. Bills for paper clips, probably. Instead she saw that from time to time the petty cash fund had received enormous influxes of money, followed by equally enormous expenditures. Yes, there were bills for paper clips, but the account had been used also to purchase earth-moving machines and to pay subcontractors. Were these bills real or fictitious? Under the circumstances it was possible that neither the machines nor the subcontractors had ever existed.

But proving it was another thing.

Turning toward Sestri on his chair against the wall, handing him the dossier, Madeleine asked why the petty cash account was paying major bills.

"As if I pay attention to petty cash," he snorted. He was the one who ran the company, he declared importantly, almost beating his chest as he said it. He was involved in deals worth millions and millions of francs; he did not concern himself with petty cash.

"These sums are not petty," said Bosco.

All four detectives were watching Sestri carefully.

"Not to a cop, maybe," said Sestri. And made the word *cop* sound like an insult, and he flung the dossier back on the table.

It was the wrong response. The relationship between policeman and civilian is not a balanced one. The policeman is almost always in a position to cause the civilian expensive problems. Accordingly, to make a cop or cops angry is a mistake. This had never been more true than with these cops now, as Sestri was about to find out.

By then the perquisition had lasted more than eight hours. Dossiers in their boxes and drawers, in their half-collapsed piles, still covered the table. The cops were tired. Their attention had long since begun to flag. They were almost ready to give up, at least for the day. But when the petty cash file came flying back onto the table, their faces darkened, they began to mutter, and they dug into their work with renewed determination. Only a few minutes more passed before Inspector Mayotte came upon a second accounting ledger, this one labeled INTERIOR CASH DISBURSALS.

"Interior cash disbursals," said Mayotte, and he laughed.

As the ledger made its way around the table everyone began smiling. It showed large sums moving in and out of the building without explanation.

The chief accountant was called for. He looked scared. No, he said, he didn't know where all that cash had gone. He didn't know where it had come from either. He believed it came from Switzerland, or perhaps Luxembourg. He kept glancing in the direction of Sestri, who watched him with cold hard eyes.

There were notations beside each withdrawal. Was that a code of some kind? he was asked. The accountant seemed more and more frightened. Code? Absolutely not. But he had forgotten what the notations might have meant.

Another hallway conference conducted in whispers.

"That code is the key to this whole case," said Madeleine.

"About now I'd give my teeth for a drink," said Bosco.

"We should stop for the day," said Mayotte.

"We have to break the code," said Madeleine.

"We're exhausted," said Bosco. "We should stop."

"We'll send the employees home," said Madeleine. "We'll keep the executives and the chief accountant."

Outside the windows it was night. They heard the noise, the occasional horns of the regular evening traffic jam.

"We'll search the offices," said Madeleine. "Find the code and the case is over, I'm sure of it."

Madeleine took Sestri into his office and started through his desk. While he stood indolently against the wall she read his personal letters, studied his phone logs, his appointment calendar, his address book. There were photo albums, mostly his wife and children. In the back of one album were Polaroid photos taken obviously some years ago. His wife nude. Himself nude with an erection. Both of them nude in an embrace. Madeleine studied Sestri until he seemed to blush. A moment not of sexual complicity but of intimidation.

There was a safe. She made him open it, reached deep inside, and found more photos: more nudes. Not his wife this time.

"Interesting," said Madeleine.

But she found no code.

The other detectives had searched other offices. All four met in the hall.

"Searching the wife's office was a waste of time," said Bosco. "She's supposed to be the personnel director, but if you ask me, it's a no-show job."

"Defrauding the stockholders of an extra salary," commented Mayotte.

"A big salary," muttered Bosco.

"These people disgust me," said Mayotte.

They were having the normal police reaction to people who spent more on a suit of clothes than they earned in a month, but who had to steal besides.

The building was quiet. It felt empty, though it was not. The executives and the chief accountant were still there, each alone in an office wondering what was to happen next.

Madeleine was suddenly furious. "We arrest them all," she decided. "We take them back to the Rue de Roquebillière and throw them in the cages."

"Are you sure that's wise?" said Bosco.

As an officer of Police Judiciaire she was empowered to do it, and she no longer cared whether it was wise or not. "See if their memories improve," she said. "See how many of them can stand up to forty-eight hours of questioning."

"How many people are you talking about?" said Bosco.

Madeleine named four of the executives they had interrogated so far, then added: "And the wife, and the chief accountant as well."

A forty-eight-hour interrogation was an ordeal for both sides. "There are only four of us," said Bosco quietly.

"Only three of us," said Madeleine, who was fast calming down. "Someone has to wait here for the brother." Having been contacted, the brother was supposedly on his way back to Nice. "We can't have him come in here in our absence and make things disappear."

"Three inspectors to interrogate six prisoners," muttered Bosco gloomily.

On a sudden hunch, Madeleine said: "Seven, I think."

"Seven?"

Present all day, hovering on the periphery of the perquisition, had been a woman about Sestri's age, his private secretary. Although all other employees had left the building she was still there, hands fluttering, as the prisoners were rounded up and brought into the conference room.

Madeleine had been introduced to her at some point. Mademoiselle something, not madame. Not married, and one could see why. When faces were handed out Mademoiselle had had bad luck. Her nose was long and broad, her lips thin. She did have nice eyes, and though past the bloom of youth, a nice figure. Throughout the day she had offered to fetch things for Sestri or place calls for him. She had seemed to be trying to offer what comfort she could. Nonetheless he had snapped at her often enough.

Madeleine had been vaguely conscious of her all along, and without realizing it had sensed something else too—the woman had seemed almost in love with Sestri. Was she perhaps more than a secretary?

Madeleine said to her now: "Tell me your name again, mademoiselle."

The woman looked surprised to be singled out. "It's Georgette Icart, madame."

Madeleine said: "You'll have to come along too, I'm afraid."

"Me, Madame l'Inspecteur?"

"You'll be spending the next forty-eight hours with us, I'm afraid."

The woman blanched.

"If you don't mind," said Madeleine.

99

"Wait a minute," said Sestri. "Just wait a minute."

Madeleine sent for a van. When it came the prisoners, five businessmen and two chicly dressed women, were herded inside and made to sit on benches. There were grills on the windows, and the doors were locked on them.

The van proceeded to a part of the town none of the prisoners frequented and that some had never been in before. The Rue de Roquebillière came into view. The wall around the police complex made an impact on all of them. There could have been no stronger symbol. The barrier was raised and they were driven inside into a world no longer theirs. During the next forty-eight hours they would be without influence or power of any kind. Food would be brought to them from time to time, sandwiches only, unfortunately; they could not be permitted cutlery lest they do themselves harm with it or employ it as a weapon. Belts, ties, and shoelaces would be taken away from them. They would sleep on the floor or sitting up against the wall.

The prisoners, having been placed in cages apart from one another, were brought forth one by one to answer the preliminary questionnaire: name, date and place of birth, followed by names, dates and places of birth of parents, wives, husbands, children, etc. It was long and humiliating, as it was meant to be, and when it ended, the individual being questioned, who all along had been requesting information about his status, was locked back up again, still without any answers.

When all the questionnaires were filled out, the detectives went out to a restaurant, where they sat over aperitifs and talked about how the interrogations should proceed. Who to take first, what questions to ask, who seemed most likely to crack? The restaurant was comfortable and well appointed, and the owner gave discounts to cops. Finally they ordered dinner. They took their time about it. They lingered over dessert, over coffee. They had, literally, all night.

This was known as letting the prisoners cool. It was the way the job always began.

Back at her desk again Madeleine phoned Commissaire Vossart at home informing him of where the case stood as of this moment. She should have done this at once but had put it off until now.

"You did what?" Vossart said. "You did what?"

She had seven people in *garde à vue*, she repeated, and—

"You arrested Bruno Sestri without informing me first?"

Madeleine felt herself begin to sweat. Yes, and she had seized and placed under seal a great many compromising documents, and—

"I'll be right there."

"Vossart's on his way over," she told her colleagues after hanging up. "Bring out Sestri."

She judged him the least likely to make admissions. Nonetheless he was the prisoner she wanted to be interrogating when Vossart arrived.

In a few minutes the commissaire entered the room. Dressed in khaki pants and a leather jacket, he was grim-faced and did not greet her. He did, however, nod briefly at Sestri, who nodded back, a slight smile on his face. They know each other, Madeleine observed. They may not be intimates, but they move in the same circles.

She had questioned Sestri gently up until then, and continued to do so. After about ten minutes, Vossart signaled Madeleine to follow him out into the hall.

"You're not going to get anything out of him," he said. "You'll have to let him go. The judge will never indict."

Madeleine saw that Vossart was much too careful a man to risk interfering with the judicial process at this stage.

"Sestri's guilty of major, major fraud," she said.

"Prove it."

"We can't question these people efficiently. We're too few. We need extra men."

Vossart shook his head disgustedly, and without another word left the building.

Madeleine reentered the room, and in the face of Sestri's half smile, went back to work. This time her voice was harder, her questions accusatory. But she got nowhere. He claimed ignorance, blamed bad bookkeeping, admitted nothing. It was, she told Bosco later, like trying to pull worms out of his nose.

One after another Sestri's executives were brought forth and questioned. Sometimes two or three interrogations proceeded in different rooms. The detectives were tugging at threads, any one of which might have unraveled the case, but it wasn't working.

The heat had gone off two hours ago. In the interrogation rooms, not to mention the cells, it was getting cold.

At midnight Inspector Mayotte came in with Jean-Pierre Sestri and his wife, who had tried to slip unseen into their offices. Mayotte had been waiting for them in the dark. "You should have seen their faces," he said, and laughed. "If they had just gone home they could have slept in a bed tonight."

Instead they would be spending the night in a cell. Madeleine looked into their cold, surly stares. She sat down behind her typewriter. She said: "Last name, first name, date and place of birth."

When the questionnaires were filled out, she ordered them locked into separate cells.

At four A.M. Madeleine halted the interrogations and called in the uniformed cops who would watch over the prisoners until morning. The uniforms would escort them to the toilet one by one, then back to the cages. Keys would turn. They would be locked in for the night. A few hours ago they were upstanding citizens. Relaxed. Free. Now they were none of those things. It was unthinkable. The long night loomed. The penitentiary loomed.

Outside it was cold and raining. Madeleine and the three detectives paused under an overhang and watched the rain coming down through the streetlights. The city sounded empty. The rain fell.

They were hungry, frustrated, exhausted.

Bosco put his arm around Madeleine's shoulder. "Don't be discouraged," he said. "It's always that way the first night. Tomorrow will be better."

"Let's see what a night in the cells does for those self-important bastards," muttered Mayotte, looking up into the rain.

"Eight A.M. in the annex," Madeleine said. The annex was a bar called the Fig Tree a block down the Rue de Roquebillière. It was where PJ detectives met to discuss cases, evidence, leads. Its name came from the fig tree growing up against its front window. But detectives always referred to it as the annex.

They ran for their cars.

In front of Madeleine's apartment house cars were parked solid on both sides. The street was narrow. On one side the cars were parked half on the sidewalk. She drove around looking for a spot, found one two blocks away, and ran back through the rain, which by then was coming down hard.

She came into her apartment as silently as possible, taking her shoes off in the hall, moving forward without turning on any lights, so as not to wake Luc. Then she realized he was not there. Switching the light on, she saw that their bed was not only empty but had not been slept in.

She hung up her clothes, washed her face, brushed her teeth.

Luc might still come home. Perhaps he had stayed out with friends because tomorrow was Saturday, and he could sleep late. She, of course, could not. It would be better to sleep on the sofa, leaving him the bed for whenever he came in, lest she awaken him when she got up. She got a blanket out of the chest under the window, set her alarm, put the lights out, and lay down on the sofa under the blanket.

≡ CHAPTER 5 ≡

The Art Squad was two detectives in a small office in the police academy next door to the ballistics lab. The two men were small and thin, one bald, the other balding, both wearing ties and vests, their jackets hanging neatly in the closet behind them, most likely, both of them immediately hostile to Jack Dilger.

"You got something," said the first detective suspiciously. His name was Creed. "Whatdya got?"

"I merely asked if you have a list of recent art thefts," said Jack, "going back a year, maybe two years."

"You're a precinct detective," said the second detective, whose name was Ahearn. "Art theft is our department."

"Do you or don't you have a list of recent thefts?"

"You better tell us what you got," said Creed.

"I don't know what I've got," said Jack. He was wearing a sports coat and tie, well within the dress code for detectives, and he tried to look earnest. "I'm trying to find out if I have anything at all."

"Why'd you come here?"

"I happened upon some information about a guy," said Jack.

"There may be nothing to it. I thought I should try to find out a few things before I get to pissing in his beer."

"Somebody told you something," said Creed in a cold flat voice. "Who?"

"And what?" added Ahearn.

"An informant told me something," said Jack earnestly. In the NYPD, if you wanted to keep something secret you credited it to a confidential informant. It was like the secret of the confessional. It was a way of putting up a wall no one could get through.

"What's his name?"

"You know I can't tell you that. His name is confidential."

"This informant, what did he tell you?" pursued Ahearn.

"Oh, for chrissake," said Jack, his earnestness fading. "Do you have a list or don't you?"

There was a long hard silence during which the two Art Squad detectives eyed Jack, and he eyed them back.

Finally Ahearn said: "We do have such a list. We can give you a copy, on one condition."

"Sure," said Jack, and his pleasant smile came on again, "whatever you say."

"If your information checks out and you want to go forward with it, you come back here first and we go forward together."

"Sure."

"You agree?"

"Yes, certainly," lied Jack, still smiling.

"Give him the list," said Creed to Ahearn.

Ahearn got it out of a drawer, went out into the hall to Xerox it, and came back and handed the copy to Jack.

There were three pages and Jack thumbed through them. Each stolen painting was listed by artist, size, owner, and assigned value.

"Those prices may not be real," said Creed.

"For the most part they represent what the owners are trying to hit up the insurance companies for," said Ahearn.

Some of the artists' names Jack recognized. Picasso, for instance. Most he did not.

"What you have there are only paintings stolen locally," said Ahearn.

"If the art was stolen elsewhere," said Creed, "it won't be on there."

"Stolen art is easy to transport," said Ahearn. "It moves around a lot. What's on there could be anywhere by now."

"And stuff stolen elsewhere could be floating around New York," said Creed.

Jack looked up from the list. "Are any of these paintings rare?" he asked.

"All paintings are rare," said Ahearn pompously. "Each one is unique."

"As you would know if you knew anything about art," said Creed.

Jack ignored the insult. "I mean really rare. Only a few in private hands. Say, five in private hands."

Ahearn shrugged.

Jack decided he had asked enough revealing questions of these two jerkoffs. He stood up. "I'll get back to you," he said.

"See that you do," said Creed.

The bell over the door tinkled as he entered Flora's shop. She was on the phone and a woman was seated beside her desk as well. Her two partners were not present, and Jack moved back and forth, making a show of admiring some of the painted statuary that people seemed to buy from her, he had no idea why. Two enormous ceramic Dobermans, for instance. They stood to either side of a wrought-iron love seat with chintz cushions.

His wife, still on the phone, kept glancing at him as if afraid he might do something dangerous.

"I'll be with you in a moment, sir," she called out.

"No hurry, madam," said Jack, meaning the opposite. She was wearing gray trousers and a blue blazer over a pink blouse buttoned at the throat, and he hoped she would understand that for him this errand was urgent. Except for the list in his hand he had gained no ground so far. And time, as he had known since last night, was his enemy.

Finally Flora hung up. But the customer seated beside her desk wanted to order, it seemed, darling bathroom towels to go with her darling bathroom wallpaper, and Flora seemed totally concentrated on this nonsense. As she listened she kept smiling and nodding until finally Jack began signaling behind the customer's head, quick circular motions of the hand that meant: wind it up.

He waited with increasing impatience until at last his wife led the customer to the door. But the woman kept stopping beside this item or that, Flora listening and smiling all the while, the woman always gushing about how darling everything was, she wanted to buy absolutely everything.

The glass door closed behind her.

"Do you know who that was?" said Flora.

"No."

"She was one of the people who pay the rent on the apartment you live in."

"Terrific," said Jack.

"I mean, you were very rude."

"Rude?" said Jack. "She didn't even know I was there. Take a look at this."

The list that he handed her she tilted sideways so that it caught the sunlight coming through the door.

"Do you recognize those artists?"

"What is this, stolen art?"

"Do you recognize the names?"

"Most of them," said Flora, walking back to her desk. She put down the list so as to reach for an envelope, which she waved at him, saying: "The airline tickets came."

He stared at her absently, then remembered. The day after to-morrow they were to fly off on vacation together. First stop

Paris. How could he have forgotten? The answer was that they had made their plans months ago, after which Flora had changed the dates so often, accommodating this or that decorating contract, that at times he had ceased to believe in the trip at all. He had completely lost track of the date.

However, he now had other plans. In two days' time he would not be on an airplane with her but in arraignment court with two Hispanic druglords and her friend Bulfinch. Perhaps with the lover, Robert, as well.

"I'll take care of those," he said, accepting the envelope from her.

"Two more days," said Flora. "I'm really looking forward to it, aren't you?"

Instead of answering, Jack kissed her lightly on the lips. "Is there any artist on that list whose work is so rare that there may be only five of his paintings in private hands?"

Flora studied the pages again, thumbing them back and forth. "I can't be sure, but I don't think so."

"All right," said Jack. And then after a moment: "Who do you know at the Met?"

At the Metropolitan Museum of Art Jack was led into a bare unadorned conference room and left there. Time went by and he fidgeted.

At last the door opened again and a man and a woman entered. The woman was about fifty, short and dumpy, her hair in a bun. The man was about the same age and looked like a banker. In fact he was the museum's head of security. His name was Baker, and Jack knew him to be a former deputy chief in the NYPD. Though they had never met, Jack knew him by reputation: a by-the-book officer who had moved through the police bureaucracy to headquarters and stayed there.

Baker said in a cold voice: "May I see your credentials, please?"

"Sure thing, Chief." Jack flipped open his shield case and showed it to him. "You want my fingerprints too?"

"Usually," said Baker, "I deal with Detective Creed."

"This time, Chief, you'll have to deal with me, I'm afraid."

"Or Detective Ahearn. I'll call them later, check it out."

"Fine, you do that."

Baker said: "Do your superiors know you're here?" Clearly he sensed they did not.

However annoyed he felt, Jack flashed his big grin. "Why don't you call them too, check it out?"

Baker eyed him coldly. "I've heard stories about you."

"You mean about my devotion to duty, Chief, and my drive to put perpetrators behind bars where they belong?"

Baker did not grin back.

"You have a right to remain silent," said Jack. "If you cannot afford a lawyer—"

The woman had been looking from one man to the other, probably wondering why there should be a turf battle here in this museum. She said: "How can we help you, Detective?"

Addressing her directly, Jack said he was trying to identify a stolen painting that was about to be sold. The artist's work was so rare there were only five or so of his paintings in private hands. Since the seller dealt primarily in old masters, probably the artist had lived and worked two hundred or more years ago.

Jack had not mentioned Bulfinch's name.

"That's all you have?" said the woman.

"Yes."

"It's not much."

"I know."

Baker said: "And your information is from?"

"A confidential informant, Chief."

"Can you be more specific?"

"No, Chief, I can't, sorry to say."

"I see."

"I'm hoping," said Jack to the woman, "you can tell me what's been stolen in the last year, two years perhaps, that might fit such a description."

And he waited.

There had been burglaries, the woman conceded. At the Philadelphia, for instance. But only three Impressionists were stolen. Also a major theft from the Getty while it was closed for repairs. The woman was able to recite from memory the works stolen. Impressionists and Post-Impressionists mostly. Nothing that resembled what Jack was looking for.

"What about thefts from private collections?"

There had been a number, and she described them. "An oil man in Houston lost a Georges de la Tour," she said. "That might fit your description."

"Who's George whatever-his-name-is?"

"There are two de la Tours, actually. French. The one I'm thinking about died around 1650. There are only a handful of his works in private collections, I believe."

"And one was recently stolen. You got a picture of it?"

They did not. But leaving the suspicious Chief Baker behind, the woman did take him up into the galleries, where she showed him a work by Georges de la Tour: a girl holding her hand in front of a candle, the light turning her fingers almost transparent.

"This one is called *The Night Lesson*," the woman said. "The one stolen in Texas was similar. It's called *The Candle Bearer*."

"What would such a painting be worth?"

"Plenty," the woman said. As she studied the painting she said musingly: "De la Tour is a bit obvious, don't you think? Always the candle."

"If you're appealing to the criminal mind, the more obvious the better."

"I suppose so. He's always been very popular with the public."

After a moment she said: "I don't see how you could sell a painting like that. It's too well known."

"Depends who the buyer is," said Jack.

"Do you think the de la Tour stolen in Texas is the one you're looking for?"

"Hmm," said Jack, and he thanked her and left.

The armored steel door opened, and Jack passed through into the waiting room. Across was a receptionist sitting behind thick bulletproof glass. He went over to the glass, gave his name, showed his credentials, and signed in. After that he waited patiently for a time, remaining seated, looking over the same battered magazines one might find in a doctor's office. He was on a high floor of the building on West 57th Street that housed the New York offices of the Drug Enforcement Administration, and the wait was beginning to be a long one.

Detectives attached to the 19th Precinct now worked nine-hour days, four days on, two off, and Jack that day was on the chart for a four P.M. to one A.M. tour. Whatever the liberties he accorded himself, and was accorded by the squad commander, he was at least supposed to sign in and out on time. At this moment he was supposed to be there, not here, for it was already well past four. It seemed to him that the quickest way to lose his freedom of action was to ignore the few constraints that his superiors still tried to impose on him.

Time continued to pass, and still he progressed no farther than this bank vault of a waiting room. By now he was pacing, all the time eyeing the second steel door, which would permit entrance to the DEA's inner offices.

There came a loud buzzing noise, followed by the heavy movement of sliding bolts, and the door beside the receptionist's window at last swung open, disclosing a man in shirtsleeves whose name Jack knew to be Jeffers.

"Sorry to keep you waiting," said Jeffers.

"Yeah."

"We've had a busy afternoon here."

"That's the way it goes, some afternoons."

"Something I can't tell you about, sorry to say."

"Yeah," said Jack.

"It's about some Chinese guys. In Hong Kong. We just arrested them."

"Maybe you better not tell me any more," said Jack, and he followed him down a hall past cubicles, and finally into a big office with a view. There were plaques on the wall and flags behind the desk.

Jeffers, who was head of the Colombian desk of the Intelligence Division, sat down and put his feet up. He said: "Now I'd like to see your shield and ID if I may."

Though surprised, Jack showed them.

Jeffers gestured toward his telephone. "I had your supervisor on there a while ago. Lieutenant Connor. He didn't know you were here. Didn't know what you could possibly want here."

"It's something that only just came up," said Jack.

"If it's about drugs it's ours. Except for street enforcement the NYPD is out of the drug business. Or hadn't you heard?"

"If a precinct detective stumbles onto something, he should check it out, don't you think?"

"Yes, and whatever he finds should be turned over to us immediately. We have a joint task force operating out of this office. City cops, state cops, and our agents. You may know some of the city guys on it. Good detectives, some of them. So what do you have?"

"I'm not sure. A lead on something, maybe."

"Come on, come on."

"I'm trying to identify two brothers, drug traffickers who may be trying to buy stolen art."

"To do what with it?"

"Keep it in their houses, I suppose. Isn't that what they do down there? Show it to their peers. Lord it over their peers."

"Colombians?"

"I think so."

"Makes sense," said Jeffers. "Who's going to bust into their houses and accuse them of hoarding stolen art?"

"Right," said Jack. "It makes sense."

"Are you sure they're Colombians?"

"Yes, of course," Jack lied.

"From Medellín? From Cali? Where?"

"That I don't know, I'm afraid."

"Just that they're brothers and they're in the market for stolen art?"

"Right," said Jack. "There can't be that many brothers have their own organization or are high enough placed to be in the market for million-dollar paintings."

"Oh no? All those mutts are related down there. They're all brothers or cousins or uncles of each other."

"Well," said Jack, "how about putting me on to some likely possibilities?"

For a minute or more, Jeffers sat with his eyes fixed on Jack, and he neither moved nor spoke. Finally his feet came down to the floor. "Let's get the books out," he said.

There were loose-leaf notebooks and leather-bound albums, many of each, page after page of photos and résumés, representing years of work by Jeffers and his subordinates. Every Colombian trafficker that the agency had managed to identify was represented in those pages, and the two men pored over them.

"Two unknown brothers buying stolen paintings," said Jeffers. "That's a real puzzle you've handed me. A real puzzle."

Despite himself, or so it seemed, Jeffers had become interested in the challenge, and as they moved from book to book he sometimes read from the résumés, sometimes mumbled aloud.

"They're all collectors," he said once. "What don't they collect, that's what you should ask yourself." This was followed, as he turned more pages, by a litany. "Soccer teams, zoo animals, cars, antiques, horses, wines, weapons. Don't forget the weapons. You name it, they collect it. Paintings, of course, why not,

they're so rich. My sources tell me they buy up one lousy painting after another. They've got money, you see, but no taste."

"This particular painting would be of museum quality," said
Jack, "if my information is correct. And the brothers are buying
it themselves, not through agents."

Jeffers said: "Here's two brothers known to collect paintings,
the Ortega brothers." But he added: "No, that won't work.
They're both in jail under the amnesty program down there."

Among the major traffickers there turned out to be fewer
brothers than Jeffers had supposed, and an hour later he offered
only two names: "The Quintana brothers or the Zaragon brothers. They're the most likely."

"Who are they?"

"The Quintanas are former truckers."

Jack had been making notes. It seemed unlikely that former
truckers would know enough about art to want to judge personally what they might be buying. They'd have someone buy it
for them.

Jeffers was reading the two résumés, comparing one to the
other. "Also," mused Jeffers, "the Quintanas are older, been
around longer. They should already have all the art they need."

"And the Zaragons?"

"The Zaragons come from a somewhat better family. Their
father was a horse breeder, it says here. Colombian walking
horses—that's a special breed. The sons delivered horses to
clients in various countries."

"And set up a network of cocaine dealerships along the way."

"Apparently," said Jeffers. "The Zaragons are just coming into
their own as major traffickers. According to this the older
brother, Jorge Zaragon, is the brains of the outfit. He's about
forty-two. Has a big art collection and supposedly is quite serious about it. The younger brother, Victoriano Zaragon, is
twenty-five, twenty-six. Half-brother, really. Different mother.
Killed a girl when he was eighteen and went on trial, but the
judge was found dead in an alley, it says here. Principal witness

then disappeared. Never been indicted since. People come up against him have a way of dying. He's the muscle of the organization. You need someone knocked off, he's the one you go to."

"Tough guy."

"Goes nowhere without one or more bodyguards. Runs a string of whorehouses on the side. Is said to be his own best customer."

"Got a photo of him?"

Jeffers tossed it across the desk. "Somebody shot him in the head a few years back but it didn't go through. Left a nice scar, though."

Jack studied the mug shot. The scar started near the top of the forehead and went sideways up into the hairline.

"Is either of them under indictment here?"

"If they were here and we grabbed them, I'm sure we could think of something."

Jack stood up. He had needed a name with which to go forward, and now had one. The name Zaragon would do.

"Thanks," he told Jeffers, offering both a smile and a handshake. "I'm late for work."

As he started to the door, Jeffers said to his back: "If this leads anywhere, I want to be in on it."

"It would be a great collar, wouldn't it?" said Jack over his shoulder, and he went down the hall and the receptionist buzzed the door open for him. He crossed through the bank vault of a waiting room and out the second steel door to the elevator, and then down to the street and across town to his station house.

In law enforcement you did not share if you could help it. Agent Jeffers had no illusions on this subject and did not expect to hear from Jack again. Accordingly, even as the detective was striding out through the reception room, Jeffers had called in two other agents, instructing them to set up a surveillance outside the 19th Precinct station house and to tail Jack wherever he went. However, they were to be discreet. In law enforcement discreet usually means that the assignment is illegal or unethical or both, that the supervisor absolves himself in advance of any connection to it, and that any cop or agent who gets made is on his own.

As Jack entered the squad room and signed in, Lieutenant Connor came out of his office and said: "You're late."

"Sorry, Lieutenant, I was working."

"Yes," said Connor. "I had some phone calls. Including from headquarters. They're pulling the plug on you, Dilger."

"Plug?"

"As of today this prima donna shit ends."

"I was at the DEA," Jack said.

"You were at the DEA, you were at the Art Squad, you were at the Met. You think I don't know where you were?"

Jack said nothing.

"From now on you're just another member of this squad," said Connor, looking grim. "You don't initiate cases, you do what you're told. You work on what I assign, and nothing else."

Jack said: "When does this start?"

"Right now."

When Jack did not reply, Connor said: "I got my orders, and now you got yours."

"I think I go on vacation the day after tomorrow."

"So what?"

"I put in for it long ago. I think tomorrow's the day. Look it up."

Connor went into his office and to his desk. Jack followed him. "It was approved before you got here," Jack said.

Connor closed the folder.

Jack said: "I want to finish this case I'm working on before I go."

Connor looked up at him. "What case? Whatdya got?"

According to one of his informants, Jack answered vaguely, a famous painting was about to be sold to a Colombian drug trafficker.

"Which trafficker?"

Connor, Jack judged, did not need to know any more than he knew already. "I'm not sure."

"Who's the seller?"

"One of these Madison Avenue gallery owners," said Jack.

"Shipping a painting to South America is not illegal," said Connor.

"I know."

"Unless the painting is stolen."

"Right."

"Is it stolen?"

"Your guess is as good as mine," said Jack.

"Or if the buyers are wanted and they come here to get it."

Jack said nothing.

"Big-time drug guys," said Connor. "They're not here, are they?"

"I have no idea."

"Who are they?"

"I'm not sure."

"Fuck this shit," said Connor. "This is a busy house, I'm shorthanded, and I have things for you to do, starting with that liquor store stickup on Lexington Avenue and Eighty-fourth Street."

The result was that Jack spent the rest of the tour on precinct business.

The two federal agents had taken up position in their government car partway down the street from the station house and they remained there except when tailing Jack elsewhere, and they gave their verbal report to Jeffers the following morning. First, they said, they tailed Dilger to Lexington Avenue, where he and his partner, name unknown, entered a liquor store, remaining inside for some time. When the detectives came out they moved only as far as certain of the adjacent stores, staying inside each a much shorter time.

The agents then tailed them back to the station house. There was, however, a stop on the way: the partner double-parked outside a travel agency on 86th Street, into which Detective Dilger stepped briefly, but he came out again waving what appeared to be a travel folder. By interviewing the clerk later the agents were able to determine that the subject had changed the dates on some airline tickets. The significance of this was unknown to them.

The agents again took up position outside the 19th Precinct station house. Many civilians entered during the hours that followed. Some might have been detectives, or cops going up to their lockers to change into uniform to go on duty, and some might have been witnesses or complainants who had business with Detective Dilger and his partner—the agents were unable to determine this.

Shortly after ten P.M. Detective Dilger reexited the station house accompanied by the same detective as before, and drove to Third Avenue, where both men exited their department car and went into a diner. The two federal agents sat quietly for a time watching the diner's steamed-over plate-glass window, but they were famished themselves, not to mention bored, so one of them went into the diner and ordered sandwiches and coffee to go. From the counter as he ordered, and from the cash desk as he paid, he had been able to observe Dilger and the other detective eating dinner at a booth in the back. Dilger appeared to be talking urgently. The other kept shaking his head as if he didn't like what he was hearing.

The man was Jack's sometime partner, Detective O'Malley, but to the two federal agents discreet meant discreet, and to them his name remained unknown. The subject of the detectives' dinner conversation remained unknown also.

In fact Jack had been trying to persuade O'Malley to hit Bulfinch's apartment with him tomorrow night; O'Malley didn't like the idea at all, and he had reasons.

At one A.M. Detective Dilger exited the station house for the final time, and the federal agents tailed him home. From the street they could not see if any lights showed in his apartment, which, they were able to ascertain, was on the sixteenth floor. But it was so late they assumed his wife had been asleep for hours and that he got into bed without waking her.

All this information was received by Jeffers when he came to work the next morning. The two agents promised to put it all in the written report they would prepare later, but Jeffers told them not to bother.

No report? the agents asked.

You just made one, said Jeffers. Yesterday while suffering a fit of pique he had ordered two federal drug agents to tail a police detective at taxpayers' expense, and he did not want a piece of paper floating around that would attest to this.

Should the surveillance be continued today? the agents asked.

Just forget the whole thing, said Jeffers.

At that same hour Jack was seated in the office of an assistant district attorney named Hobson. He was trying to persuade Hobson, whom he had known for some years, to go before a judge for search and arrest warrants on Bulfinch. But Hobson had listened to the whole of Jack's recitation without moving in his chair and without changing the expression on his face.

"Would you mind running that by me again?" he said. This was his entire reaction.

His voice charged with as much confidence and enthusiasm as he could put there, Jack went through the case a second time. He was like a salesman trying to make a sale, but Hobson did not appear disposed to buy.

"The painting is by Georges de la Tour," Jack said. "De la Tour was a—"

"I know who he was."

"The painting is called *The Candle Bearer*. I spoke to the owner last night. It was stolen from his house in Houston two and a half months ago. I have the date. I have his description of the painting. I have its measurements. I have its insured value, which is five-point-six million."

"A figure no doubt many times inflated," commented Hobson.

"The buyers are believed to be the Zaragon brothers, Jorge and Victoriano. The DEA has them in fourth or fifth place in volume of cocaine exported to the U.S."

"Are they wanted in the U.S.? Is there a federal warrant out for them? Has there been an indictment?"

"No indictment as yet, unfortunately. But if I lock them up we should be able to hold them until trial, and by then the DEA promises to come up with something."

The detective waited for a reaction from the prosecutor but there was none.

"At present," said Jack, "the painting is in Bulfinch's possession in his apartment."

"And you have all this from an informant."

"Most of it. I myself saw the painting go into Bulfinch's building. The doormen assure me it is still there."

"It went in unwrapped."

"Well—"

"If it went in unwrapped," said the prosecutor dryly, "I'm surprised you didn't make your arrests then and there."

Jack was silent.

"Who's the original informant?" said the prosecutor.

"I can't divulge that."

More silence. Hobson sat hard-faced, Jack grinning with false confidence. "You know me," said Jack. "We've done cases together before. You can believe what I tell you. It's a great case."

Hobson behind his desk said nothing.

"Madison Avenue meets the Medellín cartel," said Jack. "Headlines? You think that won't make headlines?"

Hobson began rapping a pencil on his knee.

"The law calls for specificity and freshness," said Jack. "The affidavit has to have both, and I've given you both."

"And a lecture on search warrant law as well," commented Hobson.

There was another long silence. Finally Hobson said: "I can't ask a judge for a search warrant on this."

"Sure you can."

Hobson shook his head. "Not on what you've told me."

Jack feigned incredulousness. "Why not?"

"Because the warrant would not be on the home of some dope dealer but on Bulfinch, who is a prominent, taxpaying citizen."

"Who is a crook."

"Maybe so, but he has no previous record except as a taxpaying citizen."

"The stolen painting is in there."

"And if it's not in there? Or if it's some other stolen painting than the one you put in the warrant? Then where are we? If the warrant is defective, the arrest would fall through and he could sue the city for millions."

Jack started to speak, but Hobson cut him off. "You have no hard evidence to support what you have told me. No photos, no direct testimony, no wiretap evidence—"

"Well, it's true there's no wiretap recording," lied Jack.

"I don't see how you can be so sure this case is what you say it is."

"I'm sure."

"A wiretap order," mused Hobson, "is not as hard to get as a search warrant. I could possibly get you a wire."

A wiretap order required two sworn affidavits totaling about forty pages. "I wouldn't look forward to the work involved," said Hobson, "but it's a possibility." Once the affidavits were prepared Hobson would have to find a friendly judge and hand-carry all that paper to him. The judge would have to read it, or at least scan it, after which he might or might not affix his signature. If he did sign the order, the tap would then have to go in. The entire procedure would take probably two days. Maybe more.

"But there isn't time for a wire anymore," said Jack impatiently. "The sale goes down tonight."

Hobson shrugged.

"I'm begging you," said Jack.

"Also," said Hobson, "affidavits for warrants are supposed to be signed by commanding officers. Captains or above. The higher the better."

"My squad commander is a lieutenant."

"Get the lieutenant to sign it, and we'll see."

Jack doubted Connor would sign it. "He's off today," he said. This was true and would permit Jack a certain freedom of action today and tonight, but was otherwise irrelevant.

"Go to his house. But even if he signs it, I don't think so."

"There isn't time. The sale is tonight."

Hobson shrugged. "Sorry," he said.

In Jack's bedroom were two closets, one his, one Flora's, and hers was the one with the safe built into the wall. Every master bedroom in this building had its closet wall safe, the principal purpose of which, Jack liked to joke, was to make the apartments' owners feel even richer than they actually were. Now he made a path through her dresses to reach it. A small spotlight shone on the dial.

After pulling open the small door, Jack peered in at envelopes containing insurance policies, deeds, and other documents, and at leather boxes containing Flora's jewels, none of which had been presents from anyone earning detective's pay. He had given her a gold wristwatch once, and although she had gushed over it, he had never seen her wear it. After that he confined his gifts to sweaters, lingerie, and things for the house.

The safe was small and deep. Unable to see what he was looking for, he reached in until one by one his hand contacted three of the five guns he owned. The fourth was in his locker at the station house, and the fifth in its clip-on holster on his belt.

He laid the extra guns on a newspaper on the lace coverlet

atop the queen-sized bed and studied them a moment, the way a man might lay out neckties to decide which one to wear. There was a Ruger Security Six that had set him back over five hundred dollars some years ago. There was a .25-caliber automatic, which he always thought of as a ladies' gun, for it was slimmer than a pack of cigarettes, almost as light, and fit into the palm of his big hand. Being so easy to conceal, it had its uses, and he fondled it now, but then put it down. And finally there was a nine-millimeter Glock whose magazine held fifteen rounds.

This was the gun he left lying on the newspaper. Wading back through Flora's dresses he pushed the others into the safe and closed the door; but before spinning the dial he hesitated. Boxes of bullets of various calibers were in there too, and because he had no spare clip for the Glock, he considered grabbing up a handful. But loose bullets made for a strange bulge in the pocket, for even stranger noises when one walked through a room, and they weighed more than change. Fifteen bullets should be more than enough for Bulfinch and the two Colombians. And a shootout, if one happened, which he did not expect, would happen fast. He was never going to have time to reload a clip anyway.

Turning in the closet, nosing out from among the dresses, he found himself confronting Flora. Her face looked angry, closed up tight.

He guessed he knew why, and felt suffused by guilt.

"Gotta go, Babe," he said, and he picked up the gun on the bed and rammed it down behind his belt in the small of his back.

"There are people waiting for me," he said into her silence. He was folding up the newspaper. "And also people who don't know they're waiting for me."

He was wearing baggy corduroys, scuffed work boots, and a leather jacket. As he tugged the jacket down to conceal whatever might show of the Glock, he expected her to ask for details. But she didn't, which meant she was really mad.

Instead she preceded him down the hall. She was marching, not walking. In the living room she lifted an envelope off the mantelpiece.

"What's this?"

"Those are the tickets for our vacation." He had dropped them there a few minutes ago.

"You've changed the dates."

"Something has come up, Babe, a job I have to do first. A very big case. The outcome of which may surprise you, by the way."

Her face was as grim as he had seen it lately.

"Thing is," he explained hastily, "I can't possibly leave tomorrow. I'll be in court tomorrow. I'll be a week just doing the paperwork on this one." His voice was purposely cheerful, the better to ride over her mood, surely a temporary one, if he could find the right words. "We'll just have to put our vacation off about two weeks, much as it distresses me to have to do it."

"It," she said, "distresses you."

"Sure does," he said. "But I was able to change the reservations, no problem there."

She did not respond.

"It's going to be a great trip. I'm looking forward to it."

She began straightening some knickknacks on the mantel, not looking at him. Speaking to her back, he launched into a kind of guilty sales pitch, announcing the attractions they would admire on their trip: Paris, the Eiffel Tower, the Louvre, the great restaurants.

Flora spun around. "The Eiffel Tower is not what this trip is about."

"We can skip the Eiffel Tower," he said.

"Try to put this marriage back together again. That's what it's about."

It was the first time either of them had put it in those words.

"It's a great marriage," protested Jack. "I love you, you love me, what more do you want?"

He heard her begin breathing through her nose. Always a bad sign.

She said: "And don't talk to me with that stupid accent."

"What stupid accent?"

"That stupid New York street accent."

"That's where I'm from, the New York streets. Originally, anyway."

"You put it on when you want to."

He hadn't really put it on at all. It had come on because in the face of her hostility he was so nervous. "It's the way I talk, Babe."

"You think it makes you sound tough."

"There was a song once," said Jack. "Something about the streets of New York. It goes . . . " He began humming. "Something like that."

Flora, who must have come here directly from her shop, wore a rather tight, satiny dress that was dark green in color and that caught in odd ways the light from the lamps. It accentuated her bosom and the mound at the front of her skirt. It seemed to make her eyes look green as well. Different greens, but the same tone.

"You like to sound like all your stupid friends."

He laughed, trying to make the laugh genuine.

"And the clothes you wear," she said.

Jack looked down at himself. "I'm going out to make an arrest."

When making arrests, most detectives ignored the dress code. No one enjoyed getting suits ruined or paying expensive cleaning bills.

"I buy you nice clothes and you won't wear them."

"A man as handsome as I am," Jack joked, "if I wore them too much people would think I was a hit man or a pimp." But the joke sounded thin even to himself.

Flora said: "People look at my husband and think—"

Jack resumed humming, nervously chasing the half remembered tune. "I've almost got it," he said. And then: "But that's not quite it."

At that moment the service doorbell rang, a muffled noise because it came from the kitchen. Flora went through to answer it, and while she was gone Jack turned, looked out the picture window that overlooked Central Park, and wondered what to say, what pose to strike, when she came back.

It had snowed earlier in the evening. Below him the Sheep Meadow was smooth and white under the moon. The paths were white too, but the cars had turned the park's roadways into ribbons of slush.

From up here it was a strange-looking park. A park entirely walled in by lighted buildings, some of them taller than this one.

Trailed by one of the building's handymen, Miguel or whatever his name was, Flora returned to the living room.

Though on the sixteenth floor the apartment had a wood-burning fireplace, and as Miguel shuffled forward it was seen that he bore a load of logs over his shoulder.

Jack remembered the first time he had shown Flora this apartment. "Isn't this some place?" he had said to her. "I mean, isn't it?" And he had watched her smile come on, and when the owner left the room for a moment they had hugged each other.

She wasn't smiling now.

Having lugged the logs as far as the fireplace, Miguel knelt to build a fire, crumpling up newspaper, laying sticks on top. This was part of the evening ritual all winter, as ordered by Flora. In the morning Miguel would come back to remove the ashes, or else it would be one of his colleagues, Julio or Diego.

"Maybe we'll go down to the Mediterranean." Jack was trying to think of something to say to soothe his wife, get her out of this mood she was in. "The French Riviera. I was there in the navy; you'll like it there."

Directing her voice toward the handyman, Flora said: "Later, Miguel."

The kneeling Miguel glanced up in confusion. Didn't get her meaning or, like everyone else, didn't like his routine spoiled.

"Mañana," Flora said to him. "Out." Her purse stood on a

sideboard beside the jade figurines she had bought several years ago, and she reached into it.

"We'll go down to Villefranche," Jack said. "It's the most beautiful spot on the coast."

Flora was handing Miguel a tip.

"The cliffs, the sea." Jack was addressing his wife but remembering the time he had spent there. Which had included Claudia. "It's so beautiful. You'll be amazed."

They heard Miguel go out the service door.

"Wait till you see it," said Jack. "We'll have a nice time."

"We're not going."

"Sure we are. We take off in two weeks, I promise."

"I've hardly seen you these last two weeks. The last two years, in fact. What are you offering me, more of the same? The trip is off." His wife's exasperation had escalated into anger. "Every time I plan anything you're not here. I've had enough."

And she began a speech. It was a long one, and by the end had turned ugly. She couldn't postpone, she told him. She worked too. She brought in the money in this marriage. It was she who paid for this nice apartment, and—

Here she stopped herself before something came out that was uglier still.

Her vacation started tomorrow, not two weeks from now, she concluded, and turned her attention back to the jade figurines.

Jack had come up behind her. His hands were on her satiny dress, moving her shoulder pads around, moving toward the essential her. "All you have to do is change your dates a little," he coaxed, breathing the words into her ear.

She shrugged him off.

"You can do anything you want," he said soothingly. "You own the goddam shop."

"You have such a nice way of putting things. I don't own the goddam shop. I'm a goddam partner in the goddam shop."

"Same thing."

"You have no idea of the work I had to do to clear these three weeks, how much I had to rearrange—"

Jack's voice went as seductive as he could make it: "Babe, Babe—"

His wife turned on him in fury. "If the vacation is off, so is our marriage, which was a mistake from the start, if you ask me."

Changing tactics, Jack tried soothing her with charm, but that didn't work either, for she interrupted him.

"You're never home, always breaking dates."

"Babe, Babe."

She was not shouting. Her voice had gone low and cold, and she told him they either left tomorrow as planned or the marriage was over.

Jack laid the airline tickets on the mantel. "We'll start our vacation two weeks from now," he promised her. "Take off into the wild blue yonder. Paris, the Eiffel Tower, the Riviera." He approached her, until their faces were a foot apart, Flora glaring up at him, and then tried to kiss her, but she jerked herself out of his arms.

"How's this for an idea?" said Jack. "We could compromise. You go, and I'll meet you there in a few days." And he added with a grin: "We'll meet at the foot of the Eiffel Tower."

"That would be quite an interesting vacation for me," said Flora, "sitting somewhere waiting for you."

"It's only a few days," protested Jack.

"No, you're wrong there. It's tomorrow or nothing."

He gazed at her; she gazed at him.

"I can't," said Jack. "Much as I want to. Much as I really want to."

"I'm not threatening you. Tomorrow or never. A simple statement of fact."

"This job has to be done tonight," pleaded Jack earnestly. Again he waited for her to question him as to what the job might be, but again she did not do so. "I don't have any choice. There's nothing I can do."

She shook her head slightly. "You don't understand, do you?"

"I gotta go."

Before she could move her face out of the way, he leaned quickly forward, gave her a kiss on the corner of the mouth, then started down the hall toward the door. There was a briefcase on the sideboard, and a package, wrapped, leaning against the wall close to the door, and he picked up both on the way out.

In the corridor he rang for the elevator.

She closed the door behind him. No slamming. She did it almost gently, and he took this for a good sign.

The elevator came. The walls of its cabin were paneled in walnut, like a library. It was driven tonight by Pierre, a light-skinned mulatto from Martinique. That is to say it was an automatic elevator, but Pierre pushed the buttons which caused it to stop on one floor or another. He wore a blue uniform with shoulder boards and piping, but in the confines of the cabin no cap, and after greeting Jack by name spoke of the weather in his funny accent. He said it was cold but clear, or something like that. He was difficult to understand and Jack, who was brooding about his wife, was not paying much attention.

The lobby, which was illuminated by brass sconces, was paneled in the same polished walnut, and there were cut flowers on sideboards, and as Jack crossed toward the door his work shoes rang out on the marble floor. There were two doormen on duty at this hour. They wore uniforms similar to Pierre's but including braided caps as well, and they too saluted Jack, and called him by name.

"Evening, Mr. Dilger."

"Taxi, Mr. Dilger?"

He shook his head no. With one of them holding open the door, he strode out of his wife's elegant building, and perhaps out of her life as well, though he was not willing to believe this yet. He would get around her somehow. Nonetheless he was worried.

129

✳   ✳   ✳

Behind him, Flora had gone to the telephone and dialed her lawyer, Gartner.

There was a pause when he came on the line. "Hello," he said into the silence, and then again: "Hello."

Finally she responded. "I want you to file for divorce," she told him.

Now it was his turn to fall silent. "You'll feel differently in the morning."

Her hand was sweating and felt stuck to the receiver. "He's an impossible man."

"What grounds?"

"Find one," she said, and hung up.

The car was waiting on the park side of the street, double-parked, pointing uptown, Detective O'Malley behind the wheel. It was O'Malley's personal car, a red Toyota. Nobody wanted to use an obvious police vehicle for a job like tonight's. Jack opened the back door and got in. "Let's go," he said curtly.

O'Malley drove up to 81st Street, where he was held up by the light. Both men were silent. But as he turned down into the transverse and crossed Central Park, O'Malley said over his shoulder: "I don't feel good about this."

Jack said nothing.

"What's in the package?"

"Something we might need. Maybe, maybe not."

O'Malley was forty-four years old, which in the police department counted as middle age. Over the years he had worked on some big cases, including the Drake Hotel jewel robbery and the bombing of the Iranian mission. He was a slow-moving man with a potbelly. His paperwork was always up to date. He was an excellent interrogator and a strong witness in court. He was patient on stakeouts—his partners sometimes remarked that he had an iron ass. He had never fired his gun on duty, and did not expect to start tonight. He tended to admire and come under

130

the sway of more dynamic detectives, one of whom was Jack Dilger. Dilger seemed to possess instincts he himself could only envy.

O'Malley was a follower, not a leader. After a moment, without turning from the wheel, he said: "I don't see what we can do without a warrant."

"Just drive."

"We really should have a warrant."

The car came out on Fifth, and O'Malley turned downtown. He said: "What did your wife say about the change in your vacation plans?"

"She threatened to divorce me."

O'Malley's head turned sharply. "Does she mean it?"

"No," said Jack. "Don't be silly."

The two men had worked together off and on for six years.

"I wouldn't blame her if she did divorce you," O'Malley said with a laugh.

"She'll get over it," Jack said. He was thinking it out. "I'll make it up to her, buy her something, take her out to dinner."

"She's a nice lady. I like her."

"How's Paula?"

Instead of answering, O'Malley only grunted. Paula had been nagging him to retire and get a better job for some time. He was a first-grade detective, meaning that he received lieutenant's pay. This was the pay scale on which his pension would be based when he put his papers in. But he and Paula had two sons in college, he was heavily in debt, and the outside world was scary. He did not know what, if anything, he would be able to find out there.

To O'Malley it paid to humor wives. "Look," he said, "maybe we should just forget about tonight, and tomorrow you take her on vacation as planned."

"Can't. Gotta lock up her friend." Then he added, as if considering this complication for the first time: "I wonder how she'll react when I lock up her friend."

"You can be very exasperating to people sometimes," O'Malley said, and lapsed into silence.

A few minutes later they passed in front of Bulfinch's gallery, and O'Malley pulled into the next bus stop and parked, and a man came out of a doorway and got into the back beside Jack. This was Brock, a newly made detective just assigned to the 19th squad.

"He's still in there," Brock reported.

"Anybody else go in?" asked Jack.

"Since he closed up at five-thirty? No."

All three of them peered across at the gallery. Spotlights shone on the paintings behind the grillwork in the two display windows. The interior of the gallery was dark, but light showed in the back where the office was.

"Did you get the search warrant?" asked Brock.

"No."

"What?"

"He did not get the warrant," said O'Malley.

"Then we can't go in there. We can't do anything."

The two older detectives did not respond.

"We can't, can we?"

Brock was twenty-five. He was tall and skinny with a long nose and straight blond hair that was always in disarray. He did not have enough confidence to buck the older detectives, and tonight, however much he protested, he would in the end obey whatever orders they gave him.

"We could take them in the street, I suppose," suggested Brock.

Jack said: "You mean with all three of them standing on the curb trying to flag down a cab, the painting propped up between them? I don't see that happening, do you?"

There was silence in the car.

"Bulfinch is the one I want," said Jack. "If we take them in the street, we might get the two Colombians, but we wouldn't get Bulfinch. Probably not the painting either."

Brock thought about this.

"I don't see them leaving with the painting," mused Jack. "They'll look at it, pay for it, and leave. It will be sent to them."

"Most likely," said O'Malley.

"If they don't have the painting, what do we arrest them on?" said Brock to Jack.

The gallery was behind them. They were watching it in the mirrors.

"Bulfinch will ship it to them later," said Jack. "He's shipped enough stuff down there in the past."

"So what do we do?" asked Brock, perplexed.

"Let me give it some thought," said Jack, and he slouched down in the backseat and pulled his cap over his eyes. "Wake me up if you see anything."

"You are the calmest guy," said Brock.

Jack's second gun was digging into his hip. He shifted it and shifted himself, getting comfortable.

The three men sat in the car twenty yards past Bulfinch's gallery and on the opposite side of the street, Jack and Brock in the back, O'Malley having moved to the passenger side in front, and they waited. Only O'Malley was easily visible from the street, and he could be mistaken for a man waiting for the driver to come back to the car. The driver would get in behind the wheel and drive him away.

At last Bulfinch came out of the gallery. They saw him lock the door and begin to walk briskly up Madison Avenue. He passed their car without noticing it and they watched his figure as it diminished and finally was obscured by other pedestrians.

"His apartment is up that way," said Jack. "He's going home. Follow him."

O'Malley slid behind the wheel and put the car in gear. They went up the avenue in the bus lane, moving slowly, maintaining a half-block distance behind Bulfinch. As they turned the corner they saw him nod to the doorman and enter his building. A bit farther on O'Malley pulled in beside a hydrant, slid over into the passenger seat again, and adjusted the car's side mirror. Now he could see the building entrance with the doorman standing out front.

A man and a woman got out of a cab, talked to the doorman for a moment, and went in.

"Tenants," said O'Malley.

A man pedaled up on a bicycle, removed boxes from the basket, and went in.

"Chinese takeout," said O'Malley.

"We're looking for two guys," Jack told Brock. "One of them carrying a suitcase full of money. Let me know when you see them." And he slouched down in the seat and again pretended to doze. "The two guys come," he murmured, "the doorman will have to go inside to announce them." He was working out what he was going to do. "If my information is correct, it will be a while. About nine, I think. Wake me."

During the next hour a number of people entered and left the building. From their behavior O'Malley made all of them to be tenants, and each time said so aloud.

The three detectives were waiting for something they knew was coming and were on their nerves, even Jack, who was still pretending to doze.

When it was nearly nine o'clock, he sat up again: "Any time now," he said.

"We got no warrant," said Brock nervously. He took his gun out and checked to see that it contained its full complement of bullets.

"I don't think you'll need that," said Jack.

"Those drug guys like to shoot."

"No one ever gets shot over stolen art," said Jack. His grin came on and he added: "But if you should have to shoot, for God's sake don't shoot the Georges de la Tour."

"I don't feel right about this," said O'Malley. "Not at all."

"Put bullets in the painting," continued Jack, "and that guy in

Texas will start a lawsuit you won't believe. You'll be penniless the rest of your life."

It was banter at which no one laughed. It made them, if possible, even more tense.

"We'll take them in the street," stated O'Malley after a time. "We have no choice."

"No," said Jack, "upstairs in the apartment."

"Without a warrant we can't get into the apartment."

"Trust me," said Jack.

"Not legally we can't."

"Trust me."

"I'm not going in there without a warrant."

"Bulfinch is going to invite you in," said Jack. "You won't need a warrant."

"I don't see that happening," said Brock.

"You'll get the case thrown out of court," said O'Malley, "and you'll get us all in trouble. You'll get us kicked off the job."

"Everything will be legal," said Jack. It had grown stuffy in the car. He rolled his side window partway down.

"There'll be plenty of money in that suitcase," said Jack. "Try not to put any bullets in the money either."

The tension was in their voices, even Jack's, and it was rising.

"Legal or not legal," said Brock, "if this case is what you say it is, it's too big to do by ourselves. We should have a boss here."

The other two were silent.

"A captain," said Brock. "A lieutenant. At least a sergeant. What we're not doing is, we're not covering our ass."

"We'll get medals," said Jack. "Madison Avenue meets the Medellín cartel meets the NYPD."

O'Malley's misgivings were even stronger than Brock's, but he was swayed by Jack's confidence. Jack evidently knew something O'Malley didn't. If Jack was right, if they made the case, it would be talked about for years. It was a case to go into retirement on.

O'Malley was still weighing the pros and cons when a van came into the street and double-parked in front of the building.

"It may be them," said O'Malley.

Two men got out. They looked to be the right age and fit the general description, and one carried a suitcase. They spoke to the doorman, who led them toward the building. The one carrying the suitcase was straining slightly, meaning the suitcase was heavy.

"It's them," breathed O'Malley.

"There's a guy still in the van," said Brock. All three detectives had swiveled in their seats and were peering out the window.

O'Malley said: "The van must mean they're taking the painting away with them. Good, now we can grab them in the street."

"Upstairs," said Jack.

"In the street," said O'Malley. "I'll settle for the two Colombians."

"I want Bulfinch."

"It's not legal," said Brock.

Jack was studying his watch. "Five minutes to let them get up there. That's about right, don't you think? The five minutes is up."

He took a cellular phone out of his briefcase, dialed Bulfinch's number, and when the dealer came on the line identified himself.

"Oh yes," said Bulfinch.

"Herb," said Jack into the phone. "I need to ask you a favor."

"I'm a bit busy right now."

"We got a painting here. Supposed to be a Van Gogh. I need an expert to tell me if it is or it isn't."

"Tomorrow—"

"It has to be done right away. You're my only hope."

"I have people here right now and—"

"It will only take a minute," said Jack. "Time it takes to say yes or no. I'll be right up."

Before the dealer could respond, he disconnected the call.

They had with them two radios. One was on the front seat

beside Detective O'Malley, the other went into the pocket of Jack's leather jacket.

"We go upstairs," Jack said to his two partners. "You two hide in the stairwell. You have one radio, I have the other. I ring the bell. The perpetrator opens the door because he knows me. I flash my Van Gogh." He gestured at the package in the floor-well beside his knees. "I go in."

"Is it really a Van Gogh?"

"It's wrapped, he won't know the difference."

"What is it?"

"Something my wife had on the wall. Once inside I recognize *The Candle Bearer* by Georges de la Tour, which I happen to know is stolen. How's that for probable cause? I key the radio and call you in and we lock them all up. Easy as pie, and legal besides."

"Suppose you do get into the apartment," said O'Malley skeptically, "and the painting is not in plain view? Maybe it's in the bathroom or under the bed. What then?"

"What are you, a lawyer?"

"There goes your probable cause."

"Why don't you leave the legal distinctions to the lawyers?" said Jack. "By the time you get in there it will be in plain view."

The others remained silent.

"Let's go," Jack said, and the interior light came on as he opened the door and stepped out onto the street. Moving the radio to his back pocket he pulled his leather jacket down over it and reached back inside for Flora's wrapped picture.

The other two followed him down the sidewalk. As they came abreast of the double-parked van, Jack said to Brock out of the side of his mouth: "Get the plate number on the way by." The driver appeared to be a burly man in his twenties with scar tissue over his eyes. He glanced at them, then looked away. "If he's still there when we come down with the others," muttered Jack, "we'll arrest him too."

As they turned into the building, Jack saw that the doorman on duty was one of the ones to whom he had been giving money.

"These men are with me," he said to him, and led the way inside.

The doorman hurried after them saying: "I announce you. Who you go to see?"

"We won't be long," said Jack.

He and the two detectives stepped into the elevator, he pushed the button for Bulfinch's floor, and the door closed on the doorman.

Out in the street, the driver had got out of the van. Standing beside it he lit a cigarette. He stood there thinking hard, and when the doorman reappeared, ambled over to him. "Who were those guys just went in there?" he said.

His authority having been flouted by Jack and the other two men, the doorman was already in a somewhat shaken state. And he was immediately afraid of this tough-looking hombre who was speaking to him in Spanish with an accent he could not quite place.

The doorman said he didn't know two of the men, but the third one, the one he did know, was a policeman.

As soon as he heard the word *policía* the driver ran past the doorman into the building. He was running for the elevator with the doorman running after him, calling out: "Wait, wait, I have to announce you."

The three detectives had come out onto the upstairs corridor, where they located the stairwell door without difficulty and without speaking. O'Malley and Brock stepped into the stairwell, and the door closed.

Alone in the corridor, Jack patted his two guns and his radio, took a deep breath, and then, still carrying the wrapped package under his arm, walked forward and rang Bulfinch's bell.

He heard the spy hole open, and grinned into it, attempting to give Bulfinch confidence.

The door opened a crack, exposing a longitudinal slice of the art dealer's face: one eye, a nose, part of the mouth and chin.

"I told you," Bulfinch hissed, "I'm busy, I have people here." A single drop of sweat appeared at that part of his hairline Jack could see. It popped out as if by magic, then began its long slow roll down his forehead. "I can't help you right now."

Jack perceived the art dealer's fear and read it accurately. If the men behind him realized there was a cop at the door . . .

"Herb, Herb," Jack said, "I need that favor. Ten seconds of your time." He pushed forward, meaning to force the door, but it came up short against the chain.

Frustrated, Jack waved his package. "Is this or isn't this a Van Gogh? That's all I need to know."

On the art dealer's face was a mixture of anxiety and indecision. Plainly he wanted to get this over with. "Open the package."

"I can't show it to you like this," said Jack. "Open the goddam door."

In the hall behind Bulfinch a man appeared briefly. Jack caught only a glimpse of him, then he was gone. Short. About forty. Fit the description of the older Zaragon brother. Wore an expensive suit. People do not necessarily resemble their mug shots but Jack saw a match. Or thought he did.

He heard Zaragon's voice. If it was Zaragon. "Some problem?" the voice said.

Bulfinch gave a frantic glance over his shoulder. "I'm taking care of it."

To Jack, he said: "You can't come in. I have people here."

"You come on out here, then."

Driven by a number of imperatives, Bulfinch chose to deal with what seemed to him the most urgent of them, which was to get this interruption over with. Slipping the chain, he prepared to step out into the corridor.

The package under his arm, Jack brushed past him into the foyer. He saw Zaragon, if it was Zaragon, duck back into the living room. Jack followed, with Bulfinch behind him wailing: "I told you not to come in."

The other Zaragon brother, the young one with the scar, had been standing at the window looking out. He turned sharply as Jack entered the room. The Georges de la Tour, Jack saw, stood in its big frame leaning partly against Bulfinch's fake fireplace. If it was the Georges de la Tour. Its face was to the wall. So much for swearing in court that the stolen goods were easily identified and were "in plain view."

Jack stepped over, grasped the frame, and dragged it partly away from the wall, tilting it to see what it was.

This brief view was enough for Jack, who dropped Flora's package on the sofa, yanked out his Glock, and announced: "You're all under arrest." He gave his big grin. "The charge is criminal receiving." His grin might have been called salacious, for he was riding an almost sexual high. "Plus whatever else I can get you on. For instance, got any fake passports, anybody?"

He could not help laughing.

Nobody else laughed.

"Get over there beside the window. Hands on the wall." He was one man against three and so could not toss them for weapons just yet. His partners would have to do that. With his free hand he withdrew his radio, brought it to his lips, and keyed it. "Come on in here, guys." And he waited.

In a moment the bell rang.

He did not believe Bulfinch could be armed. "Herb, go open the door for my friends."

The other two detectives came in pushing Bulfinch ahead of them at gunpoint.

"Is that the stolen painting?" said Brock. He went over and looked at it.

Shaking his head, O'Malley threw a disgusted glance at Jack. The glance read: how are you going to claim that thing is in plain view?

"Toss those guys," Jack ordered his partners.

It all happened very quickly after that. The van driver, whose name was Vargas, came off the elevator, rushed in through the open door, gun in hand, saw all the other guns, and started shooting. He was an ex-boxer, once middleweight champion of Colombia. Later it would be found that he was traveling on a Panamanian passport, false of course. He had been the bodyguard of the younger Zaragon for six years. Zaragon paid him well, ensuring intense loyalty, and went nowhere without him. He had sharp instincts, was quick sizing up situations, was very, very quick with his hands, and he had never minded assignments that involved killing people.

When the shootout started the odds were even, the detectives might have thought, if they had had time to think at all. Assuming one counted Bulfinch as a neuter, it was three against three, no advantage to either side. But Vargas's eruption into the room occurred with what amounted to blinding speed. In an instant he was there, flame spouting like flowers from the barrel of his gun. It was so shockingly unexpected, and was accompanied by such deafening noise, as to tilt the odds sharply in one way only.

An instant after that the odds got worse, much worse. Vargas's weapon was a Mac 10 set for automatic fire. For as long as he held down the trigger it would spew forth bullets. He might as well have been wielding a machine gun. He fired at Jack first and hit him, and then at Brock, who had only half turned from Georges de la Tour's *The Candle Bearer.* The first or second shot caught Brock beside the right ear and came out the other side of his head. That bullet and the next ones, together with bone from Brock's skull, slammed into the mirror over the mantel, and shattered it, which sent its glass showering down. Brock himself fell so fast that Vargas's next bullets missed him, but did pierce the painting. In fact they stitched it. Bullets put out the candle and the eyes of the girl holding it, then struck and smashed up the marble fireplace against which the painting was partially leaning. The marble broke into fragments that splattered back into the 350-year-old canvas, tearing it to shreds.

Not even a second had passed, but one detective was dead, the painting was irretrievably ruined, and Vargas was still shooting, his bullets searching out Detective O'Malley, who had dropped to the floor. Cushioned by his big belly, O'Malley had begun firing back. His weapon was a Smith and Wesson Chief, a snubnosed .38 revolver, five shots, what cops always referred to as an off-duty gun, and he emptied it in the direction of Vargas. Sailing wild, one bullet struck Bulfinch in the knee, and he went down screaming. Of the other four, two tore through Vargas's clothing and two hit him in the chest. His gun fell from his hand, he too went down, and about sixty seconds later he died.

Both Zaragon brothers, meanwhile, had turned from the wall and produced guns of their own. There was only one target in view, Detective O'Malley, whose gun was now empty and useless, and in a rain of bullets they executed him.

After that there was silence in the room. The two brothers ran frantically about. No one survives a shootout without an immediate emotional reaction. At least momentarily they did not know where to go or what to do. For as long as this panic lasted they were intensely vulnerable. They had forgotten Jack completely and when they saw him force himself to one knee they failed to react fast enough. Jack's face was white. He had two bullets in the abdomen. His trousers were so soaked in blood they seemed to weigh a ton, as if he had lost control of his sphincters, and he was so weak he could barely raise the hand that held the gun, or after that pull the trigger. He got off only one shot. It struck the older Zaragon brother in the face, bringing forth an instantaneous gout of blood. The younger brother, Victoriano, fired back repeatedly. One bullet went through Jack's colon, another broke his hip, and a third tore off one ear so that it hung by a flap.

That was the end of the shootout. It had lasted less than a minute—according to police statistics quite long for a shootout involving cops, most of which terminated in under two seconds. The expenditure of bullets was also far greater than what was considered to be the norm: more than twenty shots fired; in the past less than half that number would have been expected. The explanation lay in the new machine pistols which were proliferating; more and more criminals had them, kept them set on fully automatic, and were in the habit of spraying bullets. Most authorities considered that the old statistical norms were now well out of date and needed changing.

There was blood all over the carpet, all over the scattered bodies. Victoriano Zaragon, the only man standing, had no time to gloat, if that was what he was of a mind to do, for almost at once he heard sirens in the street. It was the sirens that put him into a state of almost preternatural calm.

He checked to see that his brother was indeed dead, then stepped over and nudged Vargas's body with his shoe. Vargas seemed dead too. Zaragon didn't care whether he was or wasn't. Vargas had failed them. Stooping, he retrieved the keys to the van from the bodyguard's pocket. Lastly he checked the gun in his hand: one bullet remaining. Good, he thought, and walked over to Bulfinch, who was still writhing and moaning on the floor, and fired it into his head. Either deliberately or by accident the art dealer had led him into a trap and deserved no better.

Dropping the empty gun onto the carpet, he went out into the foyer, where there was a mirror on the wall. In it Victoriano Zaragon, twenty-five years old and still alive, examined himself carefully. There was no blood on his hands or face or suit, or at least none that he could see. He was not wounded. Nothing showed.

So he went out of the apartment, slamming the door behind him, and in the corridor outside rang for the elevator and then waited for it, apparently calm. Having left behind all the guns, he was unarmed, but guns were not going to help him now. He had abandoned also the suitcase full of money. Money was not going to help him either, there was plenty more where that came from, and its weight would slow him down.

As he waited for the elevator he noted that some doors in the hall were ajar. Eyes stared at him. He ignored them.

At last the elevator came. He stepped inside and rode down to the lobby. He was crossing the lobby—unhurried, the very picture of the consummate young businessman—as two cops came running in past him, trailed by the wildly gesticulating doorman.

Zaragon stepped outside into the cold clear night. He could hear more sirens, which meant that additional cops would soon arrive, and he moved out between two parked cars, climbed up into the van, settled himself behind the wheel, and drove away.

≡ CHAPTER 6 ≡

She awoke at daylight after just under three hours' sleep, and began groggily but carefully to dress. Luc had not come home. Standing in bra, half slip, and slippers, she ironed the blouse she would wear that day, and the pleats in her skirt. She dressed, arranged her hair. She put on just enough makeup, not too much, plus a dab of perfume under her arms and between her breasts.

By the time she met her colleagues in the annex just after eight A.M. she looked dressed to go out on a date. The four of them sat around a small table beside the bar. She drank two cups of café au lait and ate two freshly baked croissants as they talked of what the day might bring.

The three men had dressed with similar care: dark suits and ties, fresh white shirts. She could smell the aftershave on each of them, and she noted this approvingly. The prisoners would have slept in their clothes in cages, those who had slept at all. Dirty, uncombed, the men unshaven, they would have watched the day come up through bars. They would have had to wait their turn to be taken to the toilet, some of them perhaps protesting to the uniformed men that they could wait no longer.

Now they were to be allowed to admire the detectives' clean and well-pressed clothes, to sniff their varying scents. The contrast was designed to humiliate them, demoralize them further.

At the counter the four detectives paid their bill, then walked across to the police compound. Upstairs they settled themselves at their desks, got themselves ready.

One by one the prisoners were brought out. Each was asked how he or she had passed the night. Comfortable enough? Warm enough? Were there any preexisting medical conditions? Did anyone want to see a doctor? The *garde à vue* still had many hours to go, they were reminded. There were still two whole days to get through, and another night—this last was said with false sympathy. Yes, I know, the nights are long. Is there anything you'd like to tell us? No? Then it's back to your cell, I'm afraid. We'll speak to you again later.

In the night in the dark they would have considered their situation. By now even the Sestri brothers would be scared. These people in no sense thought of themselves as criminals. Psychologically they were not prepared for the way they were being used. They found themselves facing jail—they were already in jail. It was incomprehensible. It was socially and intellectually beyond acceptance.

Bruno Sestri, when called forth, seemed to be looking around for Commissaire Vossart. Perhaps one or two of the others were too. However, Vossart was absent.

But he had not sent extra men to help with the interrogations either. During the morning the four detectives muttered about this. It was obvious to them that the bosses didn't want the case broken. Which meant that unless they broke it, and fast, they would find themselves in trouble. Such pressure as this none had faced before, but its effect was to force them to press on. There was nothing else to do. It was too late to turn back.

Madeleine and Bosco brought forth the chief accountant while, in another room, Mayotte and Cenis interrogated the general manager.

From time to time each pair of detectives could hear the raised voices through the wall.

The chief accountant was a forty-two-year-old salaried employee, not an executive. He had a wife and four children and lived in a small apartment in a working-class building near the soccer stadium. The business suit in which he had slept was badly rumpled. It was badly cut and a poor fit as well, proving, if proof were needed, that he was not well paid.

Madeleine asked if the company owned a safe-deposit box.

The accountant swallowed hard, said yes, and when she asked, he named the bank.

She pursued him. "Do you have access to that box?"

He nodded glumly.

Madeleine stood up. "Let's go see what's in it, shall we?"

"We?"

"You and me, monsieur, you and me."

"Well I—" The accountant had begun to sweat.

"On your feet."

Being without a belt he was obliged to grip his pants to hold them up. "The box, well, it's—well, empty."

"Empty?" Madeleine sat back down again. "Please tell me the story."

Bruno Sestri, the accountant said, had suggested that he empty out the box and put its contents somewhere for safe-keeping.

"When was this?"

The answer was late in the afternoon of the day before the raid. "I work for him," the accountant said. "I have to do what he tells me."

"Why do you think he wanted you to empty out the box?"

"I don't know."

"Somebody tipped him off that we were coming. Is that the reason?"

"I don't know," said the accountant miserably.

"What was in the box?"

"Some papers and—and some cash."

"How much cash?"

"About a million francs."

Madeleine wanted to whistle, but kept her face blank. "A million francs. Which you put in a safe place. Where?"

"In—well—in the trunk of my car."

"That certainly sounds like a safe place to me," Madeleine said gravely. She felt suddenly giddy. The case was going to break after all. She was sure of it, and almost laughed.

The accountant's car was parked inside the Sestri compound. Madeleine sent Inspector Mayotte to fetch it.

An idea had come to Madeleine. An executive who engaged in dishonest practices as a matter of course, even if warned that a perquisition of this kind was coming, could not afford to shred everything incriminating. Businesses ran on paper; the dishonest aspects ran on paper too. Without records a business like the Sestris' could not continue to exist. To have shredded every false invoice, receipt, and ledger would have been a form of financial suicide.

Therefore the Sestris would have saved piles and piles of incriminating documents, at least a suitcase full, most likely. They would have ordered someone they trusted to put the suitcase somewhere for safekeeping, Madeleine believed. But who? Where?

She decided to play on the notion that the secretary, Georgette Icart, was perhaps the lover or ex-lover of Bruno Sestri—that her role in the company was more than it appeared.

And she ordered her brought forth.

Georgette looked even plainer now than last night. She was certainly more bedraggled.

Madeleine wasted no time with her: "Two nights ago Bruno Sestri sent you out of the building with a packet of documents to put somewhere for safekeeping. Where are they?"

This was a bluff. But cracking the accountant had given her

confidence and from the expression on Georgette's face she knew she had guessed right.

"The documents," said Madeleine impatiently. "Where did you put them?"

In each of her interrogations up to now Georgette had defended her employer as an honest man. Her plain face had grown hot with rage at Madeleine's suggestions to the contrary.

She attempted to muster this same rage now, but there was a difference of tone, a lack of righteousness and force.

"I'm waiting," said Madeleine.

"I don't know to what you might be referring," said Georgette.

Madeleine picked up the woman's coat and tossed it at her. "Put that on."

"Where are we going?" Her voice had got very small.

"To search your house, that's where we're going."

"By what right?" she demanded weakly.

"My *commission rogatoire* says to search 'in all useful places.' "

"But—"

"I think your apartment will prove useful, don't you?" Madeleine took her roughly by the arm. "Let's go."

Georgette lived in a building with balconies in Cimiez, Nice's best quarter. She must spend all her money on rent, Madeleine supposed, as they entered the rather splendid lobby. It was a finer building than Madeleine's. Up here on the hill even a small place would cost plenty. Was Sestri paying part or all of the cost?

The apartment was a studio, Madeleine saw as Georgette unlocked the door. There was a tiny kitchen off to one side, and a single main room with a pull-out bed. Bedclothes trailed on the floor, and there was soiled clothing on the chairs and the one table.

"All right," said Madeleine roughly, "where is it?"

She watched tears come to Georgette's eyes. In a moment she was sobbing.

"Tell the truth," said Madeleine. "It will soothe you."

The documents were in the refrigerator, two six-inch thicknesses of manila envelopes. Georgette handed them over, then stood at the window looking out, sobbing loudly.

Madeleine opened an envelope and quickly paged through it. She found a listing of bribes paid to city officials. Names, dates, amounts. Even comments scrawled in the margins, such as: "Reliable." Or: "Can't be trusted." Or in one case: "Greedy."

The handwriting would no doubt turn out to be Bruno Sestri's.

"This precious boss of yours," Madeleine said, looking up from the documents, "made you part of a criminal conspiracy, but neglected to tell you so. How nice of him." And then in a harsher voice from which all trace of sarcasm had vanished: "He's a thief and a corrupter of city officials. If I were you I'd shift my devotion to someone else." She thrust the documents back into their envelope. "Let's go."

Back at the Rue de Roquebillière Madeleine huddled with her colleagues. Mayotte had driven the accountant's car into the police compound and parked it downstairs. He had come into the room lugging an attaché case full of money, and a manila envelope containing documents. The money had to be counted and placed under seal and she set Mayotte to doing this while she and the other two men combed through first the accountant's documents and then Georgette's. Both batches were rich. They not only showed cash money going to city officials, but even identified who should be approached to make sure the money got to the right official: a kind of who's who of the city's bagmen. Some of the bribes appeared to have been paid in exchange for inside information on competing bids on construction projects; and some were not even in cash. In one case a swimming pool was built beside the villa of a city counselor who apparently lost his nerve midway through the transaction. He actually paid a few thousand francs toward the cost of the pool, then demanded and received a bill marked paid in full.

Bosco laughed when he came to this document. "How much do you figure a swimming pool costs?" he asked the others.

"Not less than a hundred and fifty thousand francs," said Mayotte. "I know that from a case I had last year."

"I can get you one for a tenth that," said Bosco with a dry laugh.

Among the documents out of the accountant's car was one that broke the code to Sestri Brothers' petty cash disbursals discovered earlier. The firm's petty cash, it now appeared, had financed an avocado farm in California and a radio station in Nice; "petty cash" had been wired in substantial amounts into bank accounts in Uruguay. There was more, but this alone caused the detectives to look at each other in stunned silence, for the petty cash fund seemed linked to the mayor himself. He was known to own avocado farms in California and to spend a great deal of time in Uruguay at Nice's expense, supposedly spreading the fame of Nice there so as to attract Uruguayan tourists, while also being on the lookout for singers for the Nice opera; as for the station, Radio Baie des Anges, which belonged to the mayor's party, having supposedly been paid for with party funds, it now seemed to have been financed by money extorted from construction firms that did business with the city, one of them Sestri Brothers. Radio Baie des Anges played music from time to time. Mostly it specialized in news reports and interviews that favored the mayor while vilifying opponents, and during electoral periods it was used almost exclusively for campaigning.

If Madeleine and her team could substantiate all or even some of this, the mayor, even though he was not mentioned anywhere by name, would go to jail, as would most of his administration. He had been mayor more than twenty-five years, and his father, whom he had succeeded, for an equal length of time before that. The two of them had run Nice as they pleased, the son even more high-handedly than the father. Now in his mid-sixties, the incumbent mayor did not spend much time in Nice anymore.

It was clear from the documents that all these sums ultimately got added on to projected constructions; and the taxpayers footed the bill. Madeleine marveled that such documents had not been shredded. But subjects not only felt obliged to keep certain documents. They also seemed to feel confident they could be safely hidden. Even subjects like the Sestris, who had been warned that the Finance Brigade was coming. She had seen it happen again and again.

The detectives clustered around her desk discussing in whispers what their next move should be. The prisoners were in their cells, none within hearing; the whispers were due to awe at the number and incendiary nature of the documents they had found. All they needed now was to substantiate them.

They would have to grill the prisoners all night until someone cracked.

But it was hard for them to concentrate on what needed to be done next, for gradually they gave way to glee. What they saw most graphically was that they were in position—or soon would be in position—to bring down a thoroughly corrupt administration.

"The guy's been mayor twenty-five years, and looting the city all that time."

"He was immune."

"No one could touch him."

"No one but us."

"A bunch of ordinary detectives."

"Who else was there?"

"No one."

"Us or nobody."

All these lines were spoken in almost matter-of-fact tones. They were all trying to repress what they felt. They were professionals, after all, and the job wasn't done yet. They went out to lunch at the annex, where they shared two carafes of Côte de Provence. Under the circumstances it was enough to make them all a little dizzy.

"He's going to feel us closing in on him."

"Probably."

"When he does, do you think he might try rough stuff?"

"What kind of rough stuff?"

"You know," said Bosco, "rough stuff."

"No, of course not," said Madeleine.

"He might," said Bosco, the oldest and most experienced among them. "When he realizes how close we are, he might. Or someone who works for him might. If he falls, they all fall. And he's never been challenged before. We don't know what he might try. What they might try."

"That woman had the casino," Mayotte noted, "she disappeared."

"The Casino de la Méditerranée," said Bosco. "Never to be seen again."

"Oh, I don't think the mayor had anything to do with that," said Madeleine.

"Maybe, maybe not."

"From now on," said Bosco, "better watch where you're walking."

Madeleine felt a sudden slight chill. "You're exaggerating, I'm sure."

As they started back to the compound Bosco said to Madeleine: "Are you going to call Vossart?"

She looked at him. She was not afraid of the mayor or the mayor's henchmen, or so she told herself. Commissaire Vossart, however, was another story. But her chin came out and she said: "I don't think so, no. Let him call me."

Both knew that commanders expected to be kept informed every step of the way, whatever the case. This would be particularly true of Vossart now.

Bosco said: "Are you sure that's wise?"

Madeleine shrugged. "That's the way I'm going to play it." Then she added: "Let's take the secretary and the accountant first. They're the weakest and the most compromised."

They broke the accountant down quickly. He was asked about his wife, his children, his future, then about the documents. There were no overt threats, but the threats were there. Confronted with the documents, his denials ran dry. At the end, the sweat pouring off his face, he was babbling, offering details they hadn't known or even suspected.

It took three hours for Bosco to get it all down in a *procès-verbal*.

However, the accountant was too frightened to implicate anyone but himself.

"Frightened of what?" Bosco demanded harshly. "Of losing your job? You've already lost it. The whole company is going down the tubes." Bosco had been a cop a long time. He saw life as a cop. To him, five-thousand people out of work meant little or nothing. "Are you physically frightened? Did someone threaten you?"

To the end the accountant would name no one else.

By then Madeleine was interrogating the secretary, who proved much harder to crack. The hours in her cell had had a reverse effect on Georgette—it had given her time to fabricate a story, and she stuck to it. She hadn't known what was in those envelopes, had often been given material to take home for safekeeping, she couldn't even remember who had given her those envelopes or when. She demanded to be released at once.

Madeleine was obliged to take her back over the same lies five, ten, twenty times, repeatedly tripping her up until the poor woman couldn't remember what she had previously claimed. She burst into tears again, and then at long last began telling what she knew. It was not, unfortunately, very much. Confronted with one document after another, she sometimes seemed shocked. Other times her eyes filled with tears and she shook her head hopelessly.

She too, although she signed the *procès-verbal* when Madeleine had typed it out, refused to accuse any member of the firm of wrongdoing, particularly her boss. "Bruno Sestri is an honest man," she kept insisting. Her tears were real, and so perhaps was her faith in Sestri.

All this time Madeleine kept expecting each moment that Commissaire Vossart would call, though he did not; or suddenly appear, but this did not happen either.

She also phoned Judge Ardois at home, asking for a meeting: "We need to talk, madame." And she offered to come to her house.

Madame Ardois refused, saying she was with her children, it was Saturday afternoon and she did not work Saturdays. Besides which, she never did business at home.

"But in two hours I need to get the *garde à vue* renewed." The forty-eight hours was not automatic. It had to be renewed after twenty-four—usually only a formality.

Madame Ardois sighed.

"The law says—" said Madeleine.

Madame Ardois sighed again and agreed to come in to the Palace of Justice.

They met at six P.M., Madeleine having slipped away from the Rue de Roquebillière, where Bosco was hammering without much success at Bruno Sestri.

In her ornate, high-ceilinged office, wearing slacks and a wool shirt, Madame Ardois received Madeleine with bad grace, and she hardly brightened when she saw the amount of evidence Madeleine and her team had already put under seal.

"You have the secretary and the accountant cold," Madame Ardois said.

"I know that." Madeleine had expected a different reaction, a smile at least, perhaps a congratulatory pat on the back, woman to woman. Madame Ardois must realize from personal experience how alone and beleaguered a woman in law enforcement felt. And when had any female detective ever brought down a company as big and as corrupt as Sestri Brothers?

Madame Ardois appeared to see the case not from the point of view of a woman, but only as a lawyer. "You don't have the Sestris or the other executives yet."

"Give me another twenty-four hours and—"

"Without some admissions from one of the Sestris you don't have much of a case."

"They're all crooks."

"You'd finish up with just the accountant and the secretary. Would that satisfy you?"

"No."

"It would probably be better to be satisfied with just those two. Lock up all those executives and the company will go bankrupt."

"Good," said Madeleine. She too tended toward the cop's view of life.

"Throw a lot of innocent people out of work. Have you thought of that?"

But finally Madame Ardois renewed the *garde à vue*. She was obviously nervous, but she did it, and Madeleine hurried back to the Rue de Roquebillière, where Bosco met her in the hall as she was taking off her coat. He was getting nowhere with Sestri, he said. "My relationship with the guy has deteriorated totally. You try him."

"We'll try him together."

Together they did no better. Even with the incriminating documents thrust into his face Sestri denied all knowledge of wrongdoing. He had the entire company to run, he insisted, and had left the details to others.

"Why don't you quit lying to us," said Bosco. "Your brother ran the company, not you. He was the chief executive officer, not you."

This was Bosco's luckiest shot so far. He had finally made Sestri angry. "My brother is an asshole," Bruno Sestri snapped. In French: *trou du cul.*

"That's your brother Jean-Pierre you're talking about?"

"That's right, and if you believe he could run a company, any company, you're an asshole too."

"I don't understand," said Bosco, who understood perfectly well.

His brother had the title because he was older, but was a figurehead, Bruno Sestri said, and then he lapsed into silence.

Another hour passed, two. Madeleine had sandwiches and beer sent in from the canteen downstairs, everyone ate standing up, and the interrogation continued. Midnight approached. The detectives drank innumerable cups of coffee. Finally they had Bruno Sestri thrown back into his cell.

"Another night in a cell will soften him up," said Bosco. "Tomorrow we'll crack him."

Madeleine no longer believed it. She was jumpy from all the coffee, and nearing exhaustion besides. She said: "Let's try the brother."

Jean-Pierre Sestri was led in. He was five years older, taller than his brother, thinner, with less hair, and by now badly in need of a shave. He was wearing the after-ski outfit in which he had been arrested and in which he had slept, but he looked presentable still, far less rumpled than his business-suited brother.

He took a seat across Madeleine's desk and from behind her typewriter she talked to him gently for a while about skiing and about his children. A son had been killed last year in a car crash. His daughter was married and he had two grandchildren.

Then: "Your brother says he is the one runs the company, not you."

"I know he thinks that."

"He called you a figurehead."

"My brother said that?"

"He said worse."

Jean-Pierre Sestri smiled. "What did he say?"

"That you were an asshole." She watched him carefully.

Jean-Pierre Sestri frowned. "Probably because I told him not to get in bed with those politicians. The amount of money they extort from businesses like ours—"

"Do you want to tell me about it?"

"You go along with them or you don't get the contracts. They suck the life out of us. It's been repugnant to me from the start."

"But not repugnant to your brother?"

"Him too. He's managed to adapt better than I."

"Do you want to tell me how it's done?"

"No."

"You have an opportunity to put an end to it all, if you wish."

He gave a brief laugh. "Tell me how."

She showed him the documents seized from the secretary's apartment and from the accountant's car.

As he scanned them, he said: "Whoever put this stuff on paper, and then saved it, he's the asshole, not me."

"Did you ever see those papers before?"

"No."

"But you did know about it all?"

He shrugged.

"Whose handwriting is it, your brother's?"

He shrugged again.

"As of now," she said, "the case will all land on the accountant and the secretary."

"They'll go to jail?"

"Unless whoever is responsible takes the responsibility." Madeleine watched him carefully. "So far your brother has denied any responsibility whatsoever."

He sighed.

Suddenly Madeleine realized why Bruno Sestri had stayed to face the police: not because he was the suave brother but because he was the hard one. The man across the desk from her seemed to be struggling with his conscience even as she watched him.

"You can let your employees take the rap—"

"Or I can go to jail for them."

"You may go to jail anyway. Under French law the chief executive can be held responsible in cases of bribing public officials."

He gave another dry laugh. "But my brother claims the chief executive is him."

"Legally, though, it's you, isn't it?"

When he made no reply she said: "The administration in this city is thoroughly corrupt, and there are many cities like it in France. You have a chance to change that."

"How?"

"You tell what you know. And if you will stand up and do it I'll stick by you every step of the way. I'll make this into a case no one can bury, no one can stop."

They talked for the next two and a quarter hours. Madeleine spoke of conscience, responsibility, honor. At length Sestri began to respond. At times the discussion became philosophical. Madeleine never threatened him, never raised her voice, never made false promises. Inspector Bosco, who was present throughout, rarely spoke. Three o'clock in the morning was the best hour to get admissions out of prisoners; every PJ cop knew that. A witching hour of a different sort. But this time when the witching hour struck Jean-Pierre Sestri was not quite there, so Madeleine gave him his belt and shoelaces back, Bosco loaned him a razor, and when he came back from the bathroom they took him out to an all-night restaurant on the Avenue Felix Faure, where they shared a late snack and a bottle of wine.

When they came back to the Rue de Roquebillière he began to talk. Bosco at the typewriter could hardly keep up with him. Jean-Pierre verified most of what was in the documents already seized. There was no such thing as sealed bids on city contracts, he said. The contractors were told what to bid, and they were told how high a bid was needed to win. City counselors and adjunct mayors were regularly paid off—one paid them what they asked or one did not get the contract. Sometimes what they wanted was not money at all, but a swimming pool, or something of that nature. Sestri Brothers regularly added the cost of the bribes into the final contracts, so yes, it was the taxpayers who paid, of course it was. Donations to campaign funds were added into the public works contracts as well, meaning that the taxpayers were supporting candidates whether they wanted to or not.

No, he could not personally testify to seeing money put into the mayor's hands, but other officials came to him or his brother often enough saying: "This is what the mayor wants."

He knew for a fact that Nice's other major contractor did the same.

The *procès-verbal* took two hours to write and ran fourteen pages. Jean-Pierre Sestri signed it and was put back into his cell.

In the parking area outside, Madeleine stood beside Bosco saying good night. The sun was coming up by then. Bosco embraced her, kissed her on both cheeks, and whispered in her ear: "Congratulations. You did a beautiful job."

She watched him drive off, then looked up at the building she had just come out of and thought of the Sestri people in there trying to sleep on benches in cells.

It was six A.M., the hour of the milkman and the cop. She was entirely happy, though a bit ill at ease as well. She thought that being a cop was the most beautiful and disgusting profession in the world.

She drove home, where she found Luc in bed asleep. She was overjoyed to see him there, and she shucked off her clothes and pounced on him and woke him up. He did not seem to mind. Her body felt flayed when he had finished with her.

She pulled a nightdress on, set her alarm, and got into bed on her side.

"You just nailed somebody, didn't you?" Luc said.

"Hmm," she said, and fell instantly asleep.

The alarm woke her three hours later. Luc was gone. No note, nothing. She washed, dressed carefully, and drove back to the Rue de Roquebillière. Bosco was already there. He was sitting at his desk doing nothing at all, apart from drumming his fingers on the desktop from time to time, and as she came in he gestured with his chin in the direction of Commissaire Vossart's office. Madeleine understood this to mean that Vossart was in there, that he was studying the evidence they had placed under seal, and the *procès-verbaux* that the prisoners had signed. As chief of the Finance Brigade it was his right to do this. They could only wait until he was ready. If his door had been open she might have gone in and directed him through the documents and listened to his comments. But the door was closed, so she hung up her coat and sat down at her own desk across from Bosco, and they gazed at each other without speaking.

The other two detectives straggled in, and when the closed door was pointed out to them, they too sat in silence at their desks.

Since it was Sunday the big room had not been cleaned. It was littered with empty bottles, sandwich wrappings, dirty coffee cups, overflowing ashtrays. It reeked of stale smoke. After a time Madeleine got to her feet and began to clean up. She emptied the ashtrays into a plastic bag and tied a knot in it. She swept the bottles and wrappings into a basket. She collected the cups and saucers and carried them out and rinsed them and left them to dry.

When she came back Vossart was standing in his doorway, the various dossiers under his arm. He was wearing a designer jogging suit and sneakers. His hair was slicked down. He was clean-shaven, his mustache neatly trimmed. He did not smile, nor did he greet anyone. Instead he walked over to Madeleine's desk, deposited the dossiers on it, and said:

"An exercise in futility. You're wasting your time. Everybody's time."

"I beg your pardon," said Madeleine. The pile of dossiers that he had just put down was many inches thick, a leaning tower of Pisa though less stable, and Madeleine suddenly had to lunge forward before the pile spilled onto the floor.

"Your case is not going to stand up."

"Is there something we've missed?" said Madeleine.

Vossart had a copy of the *Nice Matin* under his arm, and he waved it. "Your case hasn't reached the paper yet. With luck it won't. That's one good thing."

161

With that he strode out of the room and they heard him leave the building. No one spoke. Madeleine went to the window and saw him get into his car and drive away. His car was a Peugeot 605, the biggest the factory made.

She went to her phone and dialed Judge Ardois. "We need to talk."

"Look, it's Sunday."

"In a few hours the *garde à vue* comes to an end. I can't hold these people forever."

Madame Ardois sighed. "I can meet you in my office in an hour."

Madeleine carried the dossiers over to the Palace of Justice. Madame Ardois was a small woman, not much over five feet tall. This Sunday afternoon she wore a black cocktail dress and high heels. Half-glasses clung to the end of her nose and she read the documents Madeleine had put before her. "Well," she said as she read. "Well, well, well."

When she saw that Madeleine was still standing, she gestured toward a chair and said cordially: "Please sit down and be comfortable. You must have been up all night."

After a few minutes she looked up. "You've done a grand job," she said. "I should have told you that yesterday. You really have. No man could have done it better."

A somewhat annoying comment even when coming from another woman. But Madeleine took it the way it was meant and smiled.

Madame Ardois put the dossiers down. She had already received numerous phone calls about the case, she said, all pressuring her to quash it. She hadn't quashed it and now, seeing how strong the evidence was, she was angry enough to charge all eight prisoners with abuse of confidence, mismanagement, and bribery of public officials, and to indict them, and to order seven of the eight held in preventive detention to await trial.

"We have to leave one of them out there to run the company

or it will collapse," she explained. "Throw a lot of people out of work. The question is, which one?"

Madeleine argued that Jean-Pierre Sestri should go free pending trial. It was Jean-Pierre Sestri who had put conscience and courage first and had provided the testimony that broke the case open. "Whereas Bruno Sestri is still stonewalling us."

But Madame Ardois ruled against this suggestion. "The law says the chief executive is responsible, and that's Jean-Pierre Sestri."

"But he's not. Bruno runs the company."

"But technically it's Jean-Pierre, so he'll have to be the one to go to jail. His crooked brother I'll have to leave in control of the business, unfortunately."

"That's really too bad."

"It's worse than too bad. It will be a year before the trial starts. The good brother goes to jail and the bad one spends all that time going around town spreading lies about you and me, you can count on it."

Madeleine bowed her head and acquiesced.

The next question was: where did the case go from here? Both women agreed that it led not only to City Hall but into the mayor's office. The mayor's bagman, according to the evidence developed so far, was most likely a city counselor named Derobert. Therefore Derobert, Madeleine urged, should be the next target. However, Madame Ardois suggested caution. "City counselors are elected officials. Go after one of them, and the whole political establishment will rally around."

Madeleine was silent.

"There are special laws to protect elected officials," said Madame Ardois. "Adjunct mayors, however, are appointed, and you have one of those—Grosjean, is that his name?—who's apparently in this up to his armpits. Let's take it one step at a time. Tomorrow morning I'll ask the prosecutor to open a new information that will take us as far as Grosjean. Maybe the politicians will decide to sacrifice him. Let's try to nail Grosjean. After that we'll see."

Madame Ardois showed Madeleine out. "Congratulations again," she said. "You make me proud to be a woman."

"Thank you." Madeleine was grinning with confidence and pleasure.

"We really are just as good as they are."

"Better," said Madeleine.

That night over dinner with Luc in a restaurant she described what she had done. She was proud to be seen with him, imagining how much other women must envy her. He had dark curly hair and nice hands. He really is a good-looking man, she told herself as she spoke.

The restaurant was called Coco Beach. It was just past the Nice harbor, set into the cliff above the sea. A strong wind was blowing outside, and they could look down and watch the waves smashing onto the rocks. While waiting to be served they sipped their wine and munched on the crusty bread and she told him everything about the case, alternately laughing and beaming.

She expected additional praise but did not get it.

Instead Luc began to look troubled. "Have you thought this out?" he said. "I see problems ahead."

"What problems?"

"You're going after powerful men."

"They're crooks."

Luc frowned. "If you see life as simply as that—"

"This entire administration is crooked."

"—you're not going to go very far in your career."

"My job is to put crooks in jail."

"You really ought to try to get along better with people."

"What does that mean?"

"People who can help you."

"Not with crooks."

"The men you're going after will see how close you are, and one way or another will move to stop you."

"Are you saying," Madeleine scoffed, "that they'll shoot me?"

"No, but only because they don't have to." Luc was toying with the stem of his wineglass. "There are plenty of legal ways."

"Like what?" she demanded.

Sitting across the table from her, he was not dressed like a lawyer, for tonight he wore a tweed sports coat and a shirt with no tie, but he fixed her with a lawyer's eye. "I haven't researched it, but people like that can always find something." And he started to give her a lecture on the political facts of life. In national elections the mayor could deliver Nice. In the national assembly on important issues he could deliver his own vote and a number of others. Paris was not going to let the investigation go forward.

"How can they stop it?"

"There are ways."

It was enough to ruin Madeleine's dinner. With her ebullient mood gone, fatigue set in quickly. She was yawning before the main course was served, and later fell asleep in the car going home.

In the morning, almost as soon as she reached her desk, the phone rang and it was Madame Ardois. She said she had just spoken to the public prosecutor, who seemed agreeable about opening the new information against Adjunct Mayor Grosjean. He had promised to call back within the hour.

"That's good news," said Madeleine, though she feared it wasn't. And although they chatted amiably for a moment before ending the conversation, she sensed Madame Ardois feared the same.

For even an hour's delay meant that the decision was being chewed over by others: by the prosecutor himself or, worse, by the minister of justice in Paris.

That first hour passed, and then a second hour. In fact Madame Ardois did not call back until three in the afternoon, by which time Madeleine knew that the news would be bad.

The public prosecutor, Madame Ardois reported, had declined to open any new information at this time, citing an insufficiency of evidence.

"The evidence," said Madeleine, "is overwhelming."

"What can I say?"

"Paris ordered him to quash it."

"I don't know."

There was silence on the line as Madeleine digested the harsh dose.

"Something worse may have happened," said Madame Ardois. Madeleine braced herself.

"He's informed the court of cassation that he should have bucked the case up to them immediately as mandated by law, but failed to do so." The court of cassation was the next highest court.

Madeleine sensed what was coming, and dreaded it.

Madame Ardois said: "When an investigation develops evidence sufficient to indict an elected official, the public prosecutor must forward the case immediately to the court of cassation. It's in the code of penal procedure."

Madeleine had begun to feel sick inside.

"Articles 681 and 687. The court of cassation then assigns the case to some other jurisdiction. Far from local passions and pressures, as the saying goes."

"It's not our case anymore," said Madeleine in a dull voice.

"The prosecutor has called the court's attention to the fact that he didn't notify them immediately," said Madame Ardois. Her voice had got so small Madeleine could barely hear her. "The court may be obliged to throw the case out completely."

Madeleine found herself arguing fiercely that this interpretation of the law was ridiculous. The elected officials named by Jean-Pierre Sestri had only been accused. Nothing had been verified. No other evidence had been developed to bolster the accusation against them. No official faced indictment as yet. There was not nearly enough evidence for an indictment, the case was not nearly at the indictment stage, and—

"I'm sorry," said Madame Ardois. "I'll keep you informed."

*   *   *

Three days later the court annulled the case. The prisoners were ordered released, and the evidence against them—the documents and money that had been seized and placed under seal—returned. When Bruno Sestri came around to the Rue de Roquebillière that same day it became Madeleine's job, because no one else wanted to do it, to hand the seized material over to him. He made her place its substantial bulk into a rather big suitcase.

Of course it would be possible to do the entire case over, provided the public prosecutor would agree to open a new information, which was doubtful. But that suitcase full of incriminating documents would not be left around to be found a second time.

"Thank you," Sestri said to Madeleine, and he closed up the suitcase. "Very kind of you." And he left the building smirking.

Madeleine seemed to have lost the power of speech. In Sestri's presence she had hardly spoken a word. She had been unable to think of anything to say.

The next day the judge's syndicate lodged an official protest, but no one else did, and not one word of the case ever reached the public press. The former prisoners, for obvious reasons, did not contact the press, and the police and judicial personnel were not permitted to. This was the law. Madame Ardois was bound by the secret of the instruction, and Madeleine and her team were subject to the obligation of reserve, which bound all cops; for a cop to speak of a case publicly was grounds for dismissal, and in some instances for criminal prosecution.

≡ Chapter 7 ≡

Two days later, when Madeleine returned from lunch, Bosco looked up from his desk, gestured toward Commissaire Vossart's office, and said: "He wants to see you."

She went along the hall. Vossart's door was open. There was a pile of folders on his desk and he was turning pages so intently that he didn't see her in the doorway. Or pretended he didn't.

After a moment, Madeleine knocked on the doorjamb. "You wished to see me, monsieur."

In the police world commanders were usually addressed as *patron*, or "chief," though not by Madeleine, who considered *monsieur* sufficient.

"Ah yes," he said. "Come in, madame. Please close the door."

Madame? She was already alarmed. In the past he had called her Madeleine, or even Maddie, often enough, and although this had annoyed her, she missed it now.

As instructed, she swung the door closed. There was an empty chair in front of his desk, but he did not ask her to take it.

"I have some rather bad news for you, madame."

He sat back with his hands behind his head and surveyed her

for a moment. "You're being transferred out of Finance, I'm afraid."

Madeleine said: "I'm being—" and stopped, unable to continue.

"The word just came down."

She peered at the wall behind his head: a movie poster of an actor pointing a gun, a tattered flag recovered from some now-forgotten demonstration when he was a young detective in Paris.

"Evidently the direction feels that your talents are better suited to the Youth Brigade."

When Madeleine did not respond, he added: "You should fit right in there. Lots of other female officers there."

He seemed to be waiting for her to say something, but she could not.

"You're very good with runaway children, I'm told. That sort of thing. As I understand it, you are."

To his credit, he seemed embarrassed. "This was not my decision," he said into her continuing silence. "Not at all, I want you to know. But the direction—for whatever reasons the direction feels . . ."

The direction. No specific person was to blame. In English he might have said: the powers that be. If you don't like it, take it up with the direction. Take it up with the powers that be.

It was all Madeleine could do to keep from pleading with him. Finally she managed to say: "When does this take effect?"

"At once, I gather. Take your time. If you're out of here by this afternoon, that will be soon enough."

He came around the desk and stood with his hand out. In a daze she took it. In a daze she turned and left the office. She heard Vossart close the door behind her.

Out in the big room sat a number of detectives, some on the telephone, some studying dossiers. Numbly she moved toward her desk.

Only Bosco was watching her. He said: "What did he want?"

She only shook her head.

Bosco saw that something had happened. Coming over to her, he grasped her shoulders. "What was it?"

"I've been transferred out."

"Oh, Maddie." His arms came around her and for a moment she buried her face in the neck of this short, middle-aged, honest detective. She wanted nothing so much as to burst into tears.

But not here. Not in front of men. She shook Bosco off, picked her purse off the desk, and strode toward the women's toilet. There she spent five minutes washing the hand that had shaken the hand of Vossart, but whatever felt stuck to it would not come off. Finally she looked at herself in the mirror and with that the tears came. She gave in to them for a few seconds, then washed and dried her face and marched back to her desk, where she telephoned the man to whom Vossart reported, Commissaire Divisionaire Demalet, the overall chief of the Nice PJ.

"What's it in reference to?" asked the secretary who came on the line.

"He'll know," said Madeleine grimly. She intended to demand an interview and an explanation.

But the divisionaire refused to see her, or even to take the phone.

The next day she addressed herself to her union, which went by the rather grandiose title of Syndicat National Autonome des Policiers en Civil. The union lodged the strongest possible protest with Demalet and with the direction in Paris, but it went unanswered.

Judge Ardois wrote a letter protesting the removal of officers who were still involved in important cases, and the removal in particular of an officer as brilliant as Inspecteur of Police Judiciaire Madeleine Leclerq.

This letter too drew no response.

Rather than report to the Youth Brigade she took a week's leave, but spent most of it by herself because every time she tried to speak of what had happened she felt a deluge of tears coming on.

It was for this reason that she did not immediately tell Luc. Before she told him, she wanted to be sure she could control herself. She wanted to tell him matter-of-factly, as if it weren't important. She wanted his sympathy, yes. She wanted him to hold her and soothe her and tell her it was all right, yes, but she judged in advance he would find tears unattractive, perhaps even repugnant.

Well, sooner or later he had to know. Finally she told him. Four days had passed. She waited until dinner was over, until she had cleared the table and washed the dishes and left them to dry. By then he was seated on the sofa in pajamas and bathrobe reading through material out of his briefcase.

She sat down beside him and when he took no notice she placed a hand over whatever he was studying. She said: "There's something I have to tell you."

He looked at her quizzically.

She took a deep breath. "I've been fired off the Finance."

He frowned.

"I've been transferred back into Youth."

As she spoke these words she felt the tears coming on anyway, and she struggled to repress them.

Though it was clear that Luc recognized the depth of her suffering, he did not commiserate with her as she had hoped, did not take her in his arms. Instead he shook his head with impatience, or annoyance, or perhaps disgust.

"You can't say I didn't warn you."

Madeleine, still trying to hold back tears, peered off into a corner.

"This is exactly the type thing I expected," said Luc. "You're an inspector. You're not even a commissaire, but you had to take on the big boys all by yourself. That was bright. That was really bright."

Madeleine had her voice under control, or nearly so. "I wasn't alone. The prosecutor had opened an information. A judge had been assigned. I was clearing everything with her."

"Two women against the power structure," said Luc. "If it wasn't so tragic I'd laugh."

"The evidence in the case was overwhelming."

"And where is that evidence now?"

Madeleine said nothing.

"What else did you expect, for God's sake?"

"I expected to put those people in jail."

"If that's what you truly believed, you're not as bright as I thought you were."

His reaction had made Madeleine sullen. "What do you think I should do next?"

"Take your medicine in silence, and if the Finance is what you really want, then slowly work your way back."

"It took me eleven years to get there the first time."

"Yeah, well—" Luc went back to his studying.

For a time she continued to sit beside him, brooding. Finally she said: "I'm thinking of going public."

That caught his attention. "Public?"

"I'm sure I could find a reporter or editor who would love to hear about the case and what the politicians did to it."

"You would accuse the Sestri brothers of crimes?"

"Not just them."

"Who else?"

"City Hall, maybe."

"It's against the law. You're an officer of Police Judiciare. You have an obligation of reserve."

Madeleine shrugged.

"You start talking about the case publicly, you'll certainly lose your job," said Luc. "You may go to jail. And if you accuse City Hall of something you may wind up in a box. That's a mean bunch of boys over there."

Madeleine stood up and walked into the other room. As she got ready for bed she found herself banging things around. By the time Luc came in the light was out and she lay in a fetal position, facing away from him, curled up tight.

They haggled by telephone over where to meet. Madeleine did not want to be seen visiting a man in his hotel room, or even entering a hotel alone. It might give someone the wrong ideas. She did not consider herself a prude, but she cared about her reputation. In fact she wanted to avoid meeting a man she didn't know in a hotel room, period. He might feel it gave him the right to try something, which could be embarrassing.

A café or bar was out. She could not afford to be seen with this particular man in public at all. Nor could she invite him to her apartment lest Luc walk in. A meeting in some other town was no better. Detectives from Nice's various PJ brigades worked all the towns along the coast. They were observant, curious men who, in addition, had informants everywhere.

Finally, when a hotel room seemed the only possibility, she stipulated the Negresco, Nice's most splendid palace. I might as well get an hour's luxury out of this, she convinced herself. Besides which, the Negresco was so expensive that no cop was likely to be in there casually.

So on the appointed day she walked into the hotel and crossed the grandiose lobby, which was two stories high and crowded with clerks and bellboys, the clerks in cutaways, the bellboys dressed like pashas. All were eager to help her, though she needed no help. Ignoring them, looking neither right nor left, looking for all the world like a call girl, which was exactly the opposite of the impression she wanted to give, she reached the elevator.

It rose to the fourth floor, and she got off. Her heels rang on the parquet flooring. She found the door, glanced furtively up and down the corridor, which fortunately was empty, and knocked. As soon as the man opened to her she sprang inside, nearly knocking him down.

"Alain Duhamel," he said. He was immensely fat and had his

hand outstretched as well. She saw that she was taller than he was.

"Madeleine Leclerq." He had thick fingers, and a meaty palm.

"Please come in," he said.

She was barely able to get by him.

The room was big and airy, for the French windows stood open onto a big balcony. Beyond that was the sea. She moved past the bed and looked all around. She was very nervous. "Nice room," she said, and immediately cursed herself for the platitude.

"I was about to order lunch from room service," said Duhamel. "What will you have?"

Madeleine could never have afforded Negresco prices and had hoped to be offered lunch. But now that she was here she wasn't a bit hungry. She said: "A sandwich, maybe."

"How about a filet of sole?" Duhamel said, adding apologetically: "I have to watch my diet."

Duhamel was a reporter for *Paris Match*, the biggest-selling magazine in France. *Match*, Madeleine reasoned, could afford to buy her a lunch whether she ate it or not. Let Duhamel put it on his expense account. "A filet of sole would be fine," she said.

"With maybe some oysters to start. No calories in oysters."

"Sure."

"With maybe a bottle of Meursault. I like a good Meursault, don't you?"

He's trying to put me at my ease, Madeleine told herself. Which was impossible, under the circumstances. She went out to stand on the balcony. It was a warm day, though not yet spring. There was so little wind that the sea was smooth as a plate. Most of it was very blue, but it had rained hard the day and night before, and there were great brown stains where the rivers came out.

Behind her she could hear Duhamel ordering lunch. When he had finished she went back inside, opened the attaché case she had been carrying, and handed him three pages stapled together.

"Here's a brief résumé of the case. Once you have read it, I can show you verifying documents."

But Duhamel put the pages aside. "We'll eat first, work later," he said. "So tell me about yourself. How old are you, are you married, do you have children?"

Well, she was thirty-four, she told him, divorced, no children. She would like to have children someday, she told him. And there was someone in her life right now whom she cared for, so maybe children would work out. Duhamel wasn't even prodding her for such information. She was so nervous she was babbling about herself, without even being asked. This was not at all the impression she wished to convey.

"And what about you, monsieur?" she made herself say. "Are you married?"

Duhamel, it turned out, was not only married but had already fathered seven children. Since she could not imagine a woman going to bed with a man so fat, this information struck her dumb.

Watching her shrewdly, Duhamel said: "I can see why you might want to tell your story, but why did you decide on me to tell it to?"

She had picked his byline off an article in the previous week's issue, knowing nothing about him, and had phoned him. "I knew you by reputation, monsieur," she lied.

He nodded, evidently pleased by her response.

There was a knock on the door and a waiter came in wheeling a table which he set up near the window. The Dover soles lay under silver domes, and the oysters on their platter sat on beds of ice. The waiter opened the Meursault.

The wineglasses were big and thin. Duhamel swirled the first dose around in the bowl, sniffed it, and finally drank. When he nodded, the waiter poured wine into both glasses.

Finally the waiter withdrew, and they started in on the oysters.

"So why did you become a cop?" asked Duhamel conversationally.

She tried to tell him how she had taken the police test almost on a whim, then became passionate about the job. The constant surprises. The crises dealt with. The best and worst in human behavior. She was babbling again.

She made her mouth close and stay closed.

Duhamel did not appear interested in this type of talk anyway. He asked how long she had been a PJ inspector, he asked about the quota for women, he asked about job-related sexual harassment.

She was there to talk about the Sestri case, not sexual harassment. She shouldn't be talking to him at all. The possible consequences to herself were incalculable.

"You married a cop?"

"Who else was there?"

He interrogated her skillfully all through lunch. Talking about herself was bad. She was afraid she was coming off as just another disgruntled woman. And yet she couldn't seem to stop talking.

She had no appetite. She ate several of the oysters, only toyed with the sole. Almost without realizing it, she did drink her share of the wine. It made her somewhat dizzy. There was a silver thermos on the table, and when at the end of the meal Duhamel filled the tiny cups with strong black coffee, she sipped it gratefully.

Finally the fat journalist threw the tablecloth up over the dishes, pushed the table aside, and without leaving his chair reached for the three-page synopsis on the bed. After reading it, he asked to see the documentation, and Madeleine lifted the dossiers out of her case and handed them to him.

He said: "Why don't I just glance through this material? Then we can talk."

She went out onto the balcony again and studied the sea.

When she came back inside she saw that he had not moved from his chair, but that his tape recorder was now in his lap and he was pushing buttons.

She reached across him and turned the machine off. "No tape recorders," she said.

"We're dealing in very sensitive matters here," he said. "I need to prove to my editors not only that I have talked to you, but that everything I will write is accurate."

"No tape recorders," insisted Madeleine, and they argued about it for some minutes, but she knew from the beginning that she would give in, and ultimately she did. *It's far too late now to try to protect myself,* she thought, and she watched him pushing buttons to get the machine started again.

When it was rolling he said: "You said over the phone that you had had to give all the evidentiary documents back. So these are copies. Is that correct?"

"Obviously."

"Who made the copies?"

Madeleine said nothing.

"Did you make them?"

Her eyes on the tape recorder, Madeleine again said nothing.

"You can probably be prosecuted for making them," said Duhamel.

"In your article," said Madeleine, "I'd appreciate it if you simply wrote that they came into your possession."

"Why did you make them?"

"I didn't say I made them."

"Let's assume for sake of argument that you did. Why would you have done that?"

"I think it's safe to say that whoever copied those documents did so because he or she was afraid all along that what has happened would happen."

Duhamel said curtly: "And what exactly has happened, according to you?" Although he had maintained a genial manner all through lunch, this had suddenly vanished, and Madeleine was surprised.

She said: "A week ago the case was reopened. There was a second perquisition at Sestri Brothers led by Commissaire Vossart himself. Some documents were seized and two employees were indicted and put into preventive detention."

Duhamel said: "A secretary and an accountant, as I understand it. Case closed."

"Case closed," said Madeleine. "Yes, I'm afraid you're right."

"And you think there's more to it than the two rather minor employees?"

"You've just looked through the evidence," said Madeleine impatiently. "What do you think?"

"Why should you care?"

"Well, I care."

"The secretary and the accountant, they're crooks, aren't they?"

"Yes, they're crooks. But they're not the main crooks." It was like trying to explain something obvious to a child. "They don't deserve to take the rap alone while their bosses get off scot-free."

"It's the principle of the thing with you? Is that it?"

Madeleine shrugged.

On the journalist's lap the tape continued to go round and round.

"So you call me. You want to publicize the case. For you it's a big risk. But you want to take it. I still don't understand why."

Madeleine said nothing.

"You're getting even with someone," said the journalist. "You're settling accounts with someone. Who?"

Madeleine ignored the question entirely. The room's floor-length window was still spread wide. Through the bars of the balcony she could see sailboats barely moving on the bay.

"One of the Sestris? The mayor? One of the mayor's men? Who?"

The man's cynicism made her angry. "That's ridiculous," she said hotly. "I didn't know any of the Sestri people until the day I arrested them, and I don't know the mayor or any of his people at all. There are no accounts to settle."

"So what's your motive? Why'd you call me? If it isn't publicity or settling accounts, what is it?"

Madeleine said nothing.

"You're trying to make a name for yourself. Want to go into politics, is that it? You're trying to use me and my magazine. We make you famous and you get elected."

Madeleine stood up, yanked the documents out of his fat hands, and rammed them into her attaché case. "The interview is over," she said. "Sorry to have wasted your time. Sorry to have wasted my time too." And she started for the door.

He jumped up and blocked her way. For a man of his girth he was very quick.

"You don't expect me to believe you're risking your career— and a good deal else—on a matter of principle."

Madeleine had reverted to sullenness. "If that's the way you prefer to see it."

"You could go to jail."

"Please get out of my way."

"All right, then. We'll start over on that basis. I had to try to be sure. Please sit down."

After that the interview went better. He started through the documents page by page asking pertinent questions to which she gave pertinent answers. When occasionally he asked for her opinions or interpretations she declined to give them. "Stick to the documents," she said. "Leave me out of it."

After almost three hours, three changes of tapes, they had come to the end of the documents, and Madeleine rose to go. "I'll take my documents back now," she said.

He sat with the dossiers in his lap and made no move to hand them over. "I have to keep them, I'm afraid."

"No you don't."

"Unless I can show them to my editors," said Duhamel coolly, "they will refuse to publish the article. You don't want that, do you?"

When she did not reply he said: "They're safe with me. No

one else will see them. No one will ever know where they came from."

"I'll bet."

"You can trust us. We know how to protect our sources."

Again they argued and again she knew in advance she would lose.

As he showed her to the door, Duhamel was effusive in his praise and gratitude.

She left the room without looking back.

But the day was not quite over. She prepared a simple dinner, lamb chops, rice, a beet salad. As she was serving it Luc asked casually—too casually—what she had been doing in the Hotel Negresco that afternoon.

She glanced up in a kind of guilty panic. Evidently Luc saw principally the guilt, then ascribed her panic to the fact that he had caught her out.

"Having a tryst with a lover I don't know about?" he said casually. Too casually.

"Who saw me?"

"That's not the question. The question is, who were you meeting in there?"

"Who saw me?"

"A friend of mine saw you. Who were you meeting?"

"An informant."

"What was his name?"

"That's not your business."

"I think it is, under the circumstances."

"You think I was meeting a lover?"

"It's possible."

"I don't have lovers."

Luc seemed to force himself to calm down. When he spoke again it was with a lawyer's excessive reasonableness: "Don't you think you should answer my question before this thing blows up all out of proportion?"

"No I don't." He could not really believe she had taken a

lover, she told herself; they may have been having their problems lately, but things were not that bad between them.

However, the roughness of his questioning had made her stubborn. Let him think what he wanted. If she told him the truth they would have an even bigger row.

The result was that they finished the meal without speaking another word, after which Luc got up and went out, still without a word. By the time he came home Madeleine was in bed asleep.

In the morning she got up and went to work at the Youth Brigade as on any other day, and began to wait for whatever would happen when the *Paris Match* article appeared.

≡ CHAPTER 8 ≡

The first time Jack Dilger opened his eyes his wife was standing beside the bed looking concerned, which caused him to realize that he wasn't dead, which he had thought he was. He was glad to see her and squeezed her hand, or tried to. But he had been deep in a warm, painless dream from which he was unwilling to come totally forth, and his eyes closed again.

During his brief consciousness he had been vaguely aware of how uncomfortable he was. His nose and throat felt raw, and something was making him breathe faster than he wanted. His penis felt raw, and his arms seemed lashed to the bed. He much preferred the dream and in a moment was back in it, swimming along half a mile underwater in a sunlit sea, with no necessity to breathe at all.

The next time he woke up the room was full of uniforms, cops he had never seen before, who looked not so much concerned as cross. This too he realized vaguely. There was much braid, so they had rank, but he was unable to decide why they were there or what their presence might mean.

He tried to say: "What happened?" but swallowed half the sounds. He was understood anyway, and one of the men began to tell him what had happened. But it was too complicated and he did not really want to know, and so decided to go back to sleep again, trying and failing to recapture the old dream. He was vaguely conscious that their voices continued on. This was what was keeping the dream away. They seemed to be asking him questions. But he didn't feel like talking anymore, and so didn't, and after a while the voices stopped.

During the following day he woke up three times for brief periods, and each time there was a cop in the room. Not a boss, an ordinary cop, the same one all day.

"Where am I?" he asked this man.

He was in Bellevue, he was told. "Downstairs they were sharpening their knives for you."

Downstairs was the city's principal morgue, and even in his present condition Jack realized this. "They'll have to wait," he managed to say, the feeblest of jokes, and went back to sleep.

The next time he came to, he pressed for more answers.

"The cops that brought you in thought you were dead," said the cop beside his bed. "That's why they brought you here, probably. Because of the morgue. Save themselves the trouble of moving you."

Jack tried to digest this information, but it was hard to do. The doctors must be giving him something, for he felt almost drunk.

"They got you out of their radio car and onto the table and you did die," the cop said.

"Nothing to it, dying," said Jack, another feeble joke.

The cop beside the bed had been there for days and in all that time hadn't said ten words to anyone who spoke English. The interns and nurses who came into the room were all foreigners. He wanted to talk. "The doctors brought you back to life," he said, but Jack was asleep again.

The next morning he asked what day it was, and the cop told him. "You were in a coma for a month."

But again Detective Dilger, who didn't want to hear any more, had gone back to sleep.

Whenever he woke up that cop or another was in the room. "Why are you here?" he managed to ask. He was afraid they had been ordered to tell him nothing. "Am I under arrest?"

"I'm supposed to keep the press off you." The cop seemed to be trying to decide how much to say. "They had a circus, those guys. Funerals for the dead cops. The politicians making speeches. The commissioner nearly got canned. You were lucky to be out of it."

In the dimness of his mind Jack was aware of the irregularities he had committed; perhaps he had been dreaming about them. "What were they saying about me?"

The cop said airily: "The bosses were trying to explain you for days."

Jack made an effort to grasp what this might mean. Would he be brought up on charges? If not by the state, then by the department? He doubted he had come off a hero. What was his future to be?

But it was too much for him, and he went back to sleep.

The next day there was a different cop, who was a good deal more blunt. "You didn't come off very good," he said. "I think they're going to try to fire you off the job."

They were interrupted by a doctor who came in and took the tubes out of Jack's nose. His throat felt burned but he reveled in the taste of the air as he sucked it in and out, and for a moment forgot his other concerns. The air tasted suddenly fresh to him, as fresh as autumn or spring. It tasted the way air tastes when you have been swimming and you burst to the surface gulping and gasping.

"Has my wife been around?" he asked the cop when the doctor had gone out.

"She usually comes at night."

Jack was beginning to fade again.

"You got guys guarding you around the clock," the cop said. "It's not just the press the bosses are worried about. The way I heard it, Intelligence picked up some information."

This was important. Jack tried to take it in.

"Maybe off a wiretap, how should I know? Those Colombian druggies put out a contract on you. It's only normal. You cost them two men and a lot of money. Do you know how much money was in that suitcase?"

"Money," said Jack, trying another feeble joke. "Since I've been on the job I've never taken a dime."

"The bosses don't care about you personally," the cop said. "They don't care about any of us. They just don't want anyone coming through that door and blowing you away while you're their responsibility."

Jack did not want to ponder this. He wanted to go back to sleep.

"Once you're out of the job," the cop said, "they won't care what happens to you."

He was merely articulating the street cop's cynical view of the police brass. But it was a view every cop shared.

"You should ask someone what it's all about," he advised.

But who could Jack ask? Needles nailed his arms to the bed, and he was awake enough to realize what his future would be.

The day after that he ate solid food for the first time. Hospital food, but to him delicious. Because of the needles the cop on duty, a new one named Jimmy, fed him. This bothered him, and the cast bothered him. He was in plaster from knees to ribs. He guessed the drugs were being withdrawn, for he was in increasing pain. And he must be losing weight because he could feel the points of his bones against the cast.

Flora came bringing flowers; it was the first time she had come while he was awake. She gave the cop on duty, it was still Jimmy, a look which he didn't understand at first. Finally he left the room saying: "I'll be out in the hall."

When he was gone, Flora draped her mink coat over the other chair and sat down beside the bed. She said: "You have two pints of my blood in you now, so we're even."

He said: "Hold my hand."

Her fingers twined in his on top of the board. "You gave us

quite a scare," she said. After what seemed like a long time she said: "There's something I have to tell you."

A silence followed which he felt obliged finally to break. "All right, what is it?"

"I did something."

"What did you do, Flora?"

"They told me it might be six months before you came out of the coma. You were dead on the table, did they tell you that? They said you might not come out at all."

"So what did you do, Flora?"

"I sold the apartment," she said after hesitating.

This wasn't so bad. He could live without the apartment.

"I did what I thought had to be done," she said.

"You planning on moving back to the Midwest, or what?"

"No, of course not." She was wearing tight slacks and a tight blouse. She looked very good to him. She looked delicious to him. "I'm buying another one on the East Side. The East Side is nicer, don't you think? It's more, well, me."

From her manner he sensed there were other surprises to come. He said: "What else?"

"Well—"

"I'm not sure this is going to be fun to hear."

She looked at him and her mouth moved but no sounds came out. Watching her, he thought of her as he sometimes had in the past during one of their fights: a spoiled girl child from the Midwest pretending to be a sophisticated New York business-woman.

"I'm sorry about your friend Bulfinch," he said into her silence.

"I guess he was mixed up with all those people."

"It wasn't me who brought them into his living room."

"He wasn't really my friend." She gave a shrug, shrugging off the former friendship. "Are you the one killed him?"

"Me? No." Whatever else she might be about to tell him was serious, he decided.

"You have to admit," she said finally, "that our marriage had not been going so great."

"Sometimes it went fine."

"Not recently, though. You have to admit that."

Jack watched her.

"I was very angry at you that night. I mean, how was I supposed to know that an hour later you were going to get shot?" She hesitated, as if trying to phrase what she would say next. "Five minutes after you went out that door I called up Gartner."

Jack recognized her lawyer's name. He looked down at their fingers laced together and sensed what was coming.

"I mean, we did talk about divorce before this thing ever happened to you, did we not?"

"No, I don't think we did."

"Well, it seemed like a divorce was what you wanted, canceling the vacation and walking out on me the way you did. I naturally assumed you didn't want to stay married to me."

Jack said nothing.

"And when they told me you could live for years and never come out of that coma, well, I—" She stopped.

"You what, Flora?"

"I let the paperwork go forward."

"The paperwork?"

"I mean, I wasn't abandoning you. You had already abandoned me. This coma thing. I mean, what else was I supposed to do?"

Once again Jack was amazed at women—this woman, anyway—their facility at turning reason back on itself in order to justify whatever conduct they had decided on.

"Gartner had already filed," Flora said.

"For divorce?"

"Yes, divorce."

They looked at each other. Finally it was Jack who looked away. And then to his shame he felt tears in his eyes that he could not wipe away because his arms with the needles in them were strapped to boards. So he closed his eyes and kept them that way.

"I mean, if you were going to be in a coma for months or years there wasn't any point staying married to you. Jack, are you listening to me?"

His eyes came open and he nodded.

"I mean, you wouldn't have known the difference."

To his relief his voice, when he spoke, sounded okay. "My coming out of the coma was a bad break for you, I guess."

She was immediately wary. "What do you mean?"

"Well, suppose I contest the divorce? A wounded hero and all that."

"We don't actually have to get divorced. We can talk about all that when you're better."

"Maybe I'll go back into a coma." And he grinned at her.

"Now you sound like your old self again." She bent over him. "What can I do for you? Can I plump up your pillows? Would you like a cold washcloth on your forehead? Would you like me to get you something to eat or drink?"

Tears, once she had gone, came to his eyes once more. They were tears not of self-pity but of frustration. He was nailed to this bed as if to a cross, and would be for weeks to come. How long he did not even know. He could do nothing to alter or control any part of his life. He was at the mercy of whatever anyone wanted to do to him.

Some detectives from the precinct came. They brought him a box of candy and spoke sorrowfully of their dead comrades. Though he held himself responsible for the deaths of O'Malley and Brock, they did not seem to agree. As they described the funerals, the investigation, his guilt was so strong it was difficult to keep silent, and he was glad when they left.

Now he began to get out of bed each day, an orderly and whatever cop was on duty lifting him out and setting him down in a chair. Sitting was painful. Each day he stood it for longer

188

and longer periods, before asking to be lifted back into bed again.

He measured his progress in pain. He got so he could hop to the bathroom on one leg, but peeing on one leg was impossible and he had to sit down like a woman.

Flora came at the same hour nearly every day. She brought fresh fruit, which he ate, and the newest best-sellers, which he didn't read. She would sit and prattle about her new apartment and how she planned to furnish it. He came to know the date she would close on it. Unfortunately she would have to carry two apartments for a while, for the closing date on the old one was much later.

"That's good for you if we get divorced," she told Jack. "When you come out of here you can live in it until I close, and by then you should have your feet under you."

Obviously, she was used to the idea of divorce. During the weeks he lay in the coma, she had had time to get used to it. He, however, had not.

He didn't know what she actually intended, what she might be thinking. He was afraid to ask her because from this bed there was nothing he could do to influence her one way or the other.

"I thought I might live in the new one with you until the divorce comes through," Jack teased.

She said doubtfully: "I don't think that would be legal, would it?"

She was too easy to tease. But if she intended to go through with the divorce, why did she continue to come to see him?

He looked forward to her visits more and more. It gave him pleasure to look at her in her tight dresses. He liked her smile, her voice, her pleasure in the gossip she recounted. He realized she still liked to excite him—that's what the tight dresses were for—and that therefore her feelings for him must be as confused as his for her.

It seemed to him that if he pushed for answers to the questions that tormented him she might not come back.

When she was not there he played gin rummy with whatever cop was on duty, often for hours at a time. The cop would sit facing the bed. He would have his coat off, his gun hanging down beside the chair, and Jack would ask himself: suppose somebody came through that door shooting?

If it happened, it would all be over in a second, and he knew this. The cop would not have time to draw his piece. He wouldn't have time even to throw in his hand.

As if to prove the accuracy of this thesis, a process server appeared in the doorway one afternoon. The cop hardly had time to turn around.

"Are you John F. Dilger?" the process server cried.

Without waiting for an answer he flung an envelope onto the bed, and just as quickly was gone.

The envelope contained legal papers relating to the pending divorce; they, and the manner in which they were served, shattered certain of the illusions that had been holding Jack together.

One: if the Colombians had truly put out a contract on him, and if they chose to murder him in his hospital room, a single cop on duty beside his bed was not going to save him.

And two: for all her nice smiles and tight dresses and cheerful chatter, Flora fully intended to go through with the divorce.

When she turned up an hour later he thrust the envelope at her saying: "What the hell is this? Is there some reason you couldn't hand it to me yourself?"

She was immediately and intensely apologetic. She had known nothing about serving papers on him, she said, it was her lawyer's fault. "Now I know why all you cops hate lawyers," she said.

"Yeah," said Jack, his face like stone.

"Oh Jack," she said, and bent over the bed and kissed him.

The next day he was visited by an assistant district attorney and two detectives from the Major Case Squad. They took him over the shootout and he told what he could remember, after which they showed him photos. He identified Victoriano

Zaragon as the man who had shot him, and the assistant DA said: "Are you sure?"

"Somebody shoots you," commented Jack, "you tend to remember his face."

"Good," said the assistant DA. "The doorman identified the same photo, so we got the guy good."

The two detectives said nothing. Jack didn't know either of them. "There may be a legal problem though," said the assistant DA. His name was McCauley, and he was very young. His hair was slicked down, he was trying to grow a mustache, and he wore a three-piece suit.

"Legal problem?" said Jack, playing dumb. "I don't understand."

"How did you know the painting was in there?" said one of the detectives. Both detectives were in their forties. They had been around a long time and would know when they were being lied to.

"Information," said Jack.

"From a confidential informant?"

"Right."

"But you didn't have a search warrant," said young McCauley. "So how did you get in?"

"I knew the guy personally," said Jack. "He invited me in."

"With a hot painting and two Colombian drug dealers in the room?" scoffed the same detective.

"No," said the young assistant DA hastily. "It's possible. I'll accept it."

"A good defense lawyer will blow your case out of the water," said the detective to McCauley.

"Whose side are you on?" said Jack.

"All right," said McCauley. "He invites you in, you see the painting and try to make your arrests, and the shooting starts."

"That's correct," said Jack.

"But all the cops I've interviewed so far have testified that the painting, what was left of it, was facing the wall. So how could you have known what it was?"

"It was facing out. I put it back facing the wall after looking at it," said Jack.

"Before or after you got shot?" scoffed the detective.

"Must have been before," said Jack.

"Yeah," said the detective.

"What can I tell you?" said Jack, and he began smoothing out the sheet beside his hand.

"You'll have to testify under oath to the grand jury, and also later at the trial, if we ever catch the guy," said McCauley.

"No problem," said Jack.

"You'll be the principal witness. We'll indict him for murder and attempted murder, and seal the indictment. Zaragon himself won't even know about it. He'll be walking around down there thinking he's in the clear, and we'll have their cops grab him." The young assistant DA was beaming, as if all these steps had now become automatic. "Then we extradite him. For drugs Colombia would never give him up. For murder they will."

"Will they?" said Jack.

"You betcha they will."

"If you fail to seal the indictment," said Jack, "or if word of what's in it gets out, the principal witness's life won't be worth much, if you ask me."

"Don't worry, we'll seal it," said McCauley.

"Did you hear anything about a contract on me?"

"No, I didn't hear anything like that."

"Why am I being guarded around the clock?"

"The district attorney ordered it. It's a formality. You're our only viable witness against Zaragon."

"What about the doorman?"

"That guy."

"I thought he identified Zaragon too."

"Well, he doesn't really know what he saw."

"So the DA ordered me guarded around the clock as a formality."

"As I understand it."

They left shortly afterward, and the cop on guard that day, Jimmy, came back into the room.

"What did those guys want?" he asked.

Jack told him the gist of it.

"So when they question you under oath, what are you going to say?"

"The truth, of course," said Jack, grinning smugly. "I'll tell it exactly the way it happened."

But he sobered up a moment later. "Did you hear anything about a contract on me?"

"One of the cops told me there was one. I don't know whether there's any truth in it or not. You know how cops talk."

"See if you can find out for me."

"Sure. I'll ask around."

The next day two other detectives came. One worked for the chief of detectives, the other for the chief of Internal Affairs. Both were sergeants. Jack did not know them. They told the cop on duty, still Jimmy, to wait in the hall, which made Jack immediately wary. He was sitting in the chair by the window. The two sergeants identified themselves without offering to shake hands, and one of them then walked over and closed the door.

At first they were both solicitous.

"How ya feeling, fella?"

"They're taking good care of you here, I hope."

Jack remembered the day Flora had come to tell him she was filing for divorce. He watched the two detectives as warily as he had watched his wife.

"You all squared away with the grand jury?" the first detective said.

"The assistant DA said you were squared away," said the second detective.

"What's this all about?" said Jack.

"I envy you, at your age retiring on three-quarters disability for life."

"Do you know how much money that adds up to, guy?"

"And disability's not taxable either."

"Most cops would give their teeth to be in your spot."

Jack's eyes were swiveling from one to the other. "Who said I was retiring?"

"I thought you had decided to put your papers in," said the first detective.

"I thought it was practically done," said the second detective.

"I'm not disabled," said Jack. "I'm going to be fine."

"You were shot up pretty bad."

"Yeah, well, I'm almost ready to walk out of here."

"I could have sworn it was already decided. Your papers were practically in already."

"Why don't you tell me why you're here."

"The reason I thought it was already decided," said the first detective, "was, our bosses were talking. My boss said to his boss that he had never seen such a mess as the one you put the department into."

"Yeah, I happened to hear that conversation too," said the second detective. "They blamed you for the two cops getting killed."

"Yeah, they cited a number of procedural irregularities. I don't remember what—illegal wiretap or something. Breaking and entering. You'd know better than I."

Still watching them carefully, Jack nodded. A young assistant DA maybe couldn't see the irregularities, or didn't want to, but any cop could in a minute.

"My boss said if they kept you on the job there'd be another shootout someday with maybe some more cops killed."

"Evidently the commissioner was talking about it too."

Jack could no longer tell which detective was from Internal Affairs and which was from the chief of detectives. Did it matter?

"My boss said the department couldn't afford any more shootouts."

Jack had had his two shootouts. That was the quota. He was in a business where two strikes was out.

"Mine said the next one would be even harder to explain."

"You two should take this show on the road," said Jack. "You're real good at it."

"And that painting that got shot up. The guy who owned it is suing the city for five-point-six million. The lawyers say the city will have to pay."

"The dead art dealer's family is suing the city too. The dead drug dealers' families are not—at least not so far."

Jack said: "Do you know anything about a contract on me?"

"Contract?" said the first detective. "No, I didn't hear anything like that."

"How about you?" Jack asked the other one.

"Nobody told me anything about a contract."

It was harder to find someone willing to take a contract on a cop than on a private citizen, Jack realized. On the other hand Zaragon was already involved in murdering two cops and putting bullets into Jack himself.

"So what are my alternatives?" said Jack. "Three-quarters disability. Or what?"

The first detective said: "My boss wanted to bring you up on charges and fire you off the job. You wouldn't get anything."

The second detective said: "My boss was feeling more softhearted. He said you intended to put your papers in and they should let you do it. Spare the department all that additional trauma."

"My boss wondered if the commissioner would go for it."

"My boss said he thought he would."

"I see," said Jack. "And that's the deal you were sent here to offer me?"

"Deal? Who said anything about a deal?"

"Our bosses told us to go up to the hospital and see how you were feeling. So what shall we tell them?"

An orderly came into the room carrying a plastic cup with pills in it. "Time for your medication," he announced cheerfully. He handed the cup to Jack and poured out a cup of water and handed him that as well. The two detectives watched silently.

"So I guess you're going to put your papers in, right?" said the first detective. The orderly was still in the room, a big black guy grinning pleasantly.

"I'll think about it," said Jack.

"I wouldn't think too long."

He waited until the two detectives and the orderly had all left the room, then flung the pills against the wall. He drank the water, then crushed both cups in his hands and sat with his jaw clenched staring out the window.

The police surgeon and the cop on duty came into the room simultaneously.

There were a number of police surgeons, who were physicians in private practice who had agreed to devote a certain amount of time, not very much, to the police department. In exchange they got to carry a badge and ID card and in theory this made them immune to traffic tickets. When a cop got shot, one or another supposedly supervised his treatment, usually from a distance.

Jack had seen this particular surgeon, whose name was Dr. Aker, several times already. Now he came into the room humming, as he always did, then made a show of studying the chart on the end of the bed, as he always did, then came over to the chair and made a show of taking Jack's pulse, also as he always did.

"I hear you're putting your papers in," he said. He was studying his watch while holding Jack's wrist.

"Who'd you hear it from?"

"They want me to estimate when you can leave the hospital."

"I see."

"When you are fit enough to leave the hospital, they can separate you out."

"And when will that be, in your opinion?"

The doctor dropped Jack's wrist. "Pulse is strong," he said.
"About a month, I should say."

"How about tomorrow?"

"I wouldn't recommend it."

"It's settled, then," said Jack. "Tomorrow."

"You can't even walk, man."

"I like wheelchairs. You should try them sometime. They're a
great way to live."

"You would need someone to take care of you."

"My wife," said Jack. "She's a trained nurse."

"Well, if she's willing to take care of you."

"She's looking forward to it," said Jack.

"I suppose I could prescribe some pain pills."

"Good, you do that."

"That's about all you'll need at this point."

"One other thing. See if you can get me back my guns."

"That's not exactly my department, Detective."

Ballistics had them, probably, Jack decided. They would have
picked them up at the crime scene and test-fired them to match
against any other bullets they recovered.

"Also we could send a therapist in to see you every day," the
police surgeon said.

"Thank you."

"All right, I'll arrange for you to leave tomorrow."

Victoriano Zaragon was in Medellín and he had problems.

The original members of the Medellín cartel had been killed
by the police, or were in jail, every one. This had left a void, and
Jorge Zaragon, a small trafficker at the time, had moved quickly
to fill it, taking over existing networks, penetrating new ones,
hiring and expanding on all sides. The market, though already

enormous, was growing every day, he used to say. There were fortunes to be made.

He had organized his business along the lines of major corporations, setting up divisions for manufacturing, marketing, distribution, finance, and legal matters. At the bottom of each division were the growers, lab workers, couriers. At the top were some of the best brains in Colombia: lawyers, accountants, chemists, bankers, some of whom had already worked for his predecessors and were by then well compromised. None had criminal backgrounds. Most considered the work they did to be ethically neutral. All stayed well away from the violent aspects of the business.

Jorge Zaragon, once he had got it all organized, had stayed even further away. He had served as a kind of chairman of the board. He had directed policy, and worked at expanding his art collection.

There was still another division, this one composed of strong-arm men and killers, which reported directly to Jorge's much younger brother, Victoriano. Running a major narcotics operation was not a job for the squeamish. Discipline, both internally and externally, had to be enforced. Whether it was associates or rival traffickers who got out of line, Jorge never flinched from the type of discipline that he was sometimes obliged to order. Victoriano, who carried out these orders, sometimes personally, became feared and hated not only in Medellín but all over Colombia. This was partly because the bombs and the bullets sometimes brought down buildings or bystanders, and partly because he seemed to enjoy his work so much. People said someone would kill him one day. But he moved amid bodyguards and operated under the protection of his brother, and so far it had not happened.

Victoriano had quit school at sixteen. As a boy he had liked to ride his motorcycle at great speed up over the mountains to the capital. Usually he was accompanied by a rising young boxer and street thug named Vargas, his pal and hero, on a second bike, that same Vargas who later became his chief bodyguard and who was to be killed in the shootout in New York. The two youths would sometimes give rides to Indian peasant girls they passed along the way and, if the opportunity presented itself, would rape them under the trees before speeding on.

In Bogotá they would make the rounds of the whorehouses. Victoriano liked whorehouses, and when he was older and working for his brother, he bought some in Medellín and also in Bogotá. It was his habit to try out all the new girls. He also liked to throw orgies. He would invite a dozen or so pals his age and four or five whores. Score was kept, performances cheered. Who did what to whom how many times. Indefatigable as teenagers. The idea was to wear the whores out, make them weep for mercy, cause them to walk bowlegged for a week. Older brother Jorge did not approve of the whorehouses or orgies; he considered it draining in time and energy, and a possible weakness that rivals might find and exploit. But he was unable to dissuade the boy and finally left him to it.

One night one of the whores caused a brawl. She insulted Victoriano, or he thought she did. He was high on his own product, and so perhaps imagined it. In a rage he began beating her. He beat her badly. This was in the reception room with other girls and patrons watching. One of the patrons, a textile manufacturer, pulled a gun—in the violent Colombian society nearly everyone is armed, even reputable businessmen. There was a shootout in which no one was hit but Victoriano. The bullet caught him in the head, producing the scar near his hairline that he still wore. By the time the police came he was on the floor bleeding profusely. The next day the girl died.

He was in real trouble now, indicted for murder, but the presiding judge got killed, and his successor dismissed the case.

Jorge had got him out of it, so it was okay, except that when released from custody he had to listen to Jorge's furious tirade. He was to lay off crack. He was to sell the whorehouses at once. The motorcycle too; he couldn't be protected on a motorcycle.

If he didn't do these things the money stopped and he could get a job. Jorge also talked to him like the older brother he was. Victoriano didn't need whorehouses to get women, Jorge said. He was young, rich, handsome. Women would think him dangerous as well—that always turned them on. Buy a Ferrari to take them around in. Buy them jewelry, he could afford it, they liked that too. Kiss their hands. Treat them like ladies. Remember the manners his mother had taught him. If he did all this, he could get any woman he wanted.

Accompanied by Vargas, Victoriano lay in wait for the businessman who had shot him—the man was found some days later, all his fingers crushed and his penis in his mouth. No suspect was ever arrested.

Victoriano did buy a Ferrari. He also began studying the old black and white movies that were still playing in local movie houses—Colombia never received movies when they were new. He studied people like Ronald Colman and William Powell. Gregory Peck was more up to date; he was suave too.

In Colombia girls of good family were still almost cloistered. Still, there were plenty of actresses, models, showgirls available, and he found that the hand kissing and jewelry worked. He liked to give necklaces in long velvet boxes. Liked to watch the girls'— most of them were women—eyes widen. He rarely got rough with them. Rarely had to. Of course he still visited whorehouses occasionally, either because no girlfriend was available or because a murder he had ordered or taken part in had left him in a state of high excitement that could be relieved in no other way.

On the night of the shootout in New York it had been too late for Victoriano to catch a plane to Colombia, and by morning he was afraid the airports might be watched, so he had taken the precaution of driving the van to Washington. It took him five hours. From there he hoped to catch a flight to Miami and then Bogotá. But he didn't like the look of National Airport either. Too many men standing around who could be cops. Getting back into the van, he drove on. In Miami he decided against a direct flight, flying instead to Panama, and only then to Bogotá, where at last he boarded the air bridge to Medellín.

He had made it home, where he believed no one could touch him, but it had taken three days. With Jorge dead, he had, as he saw it, inherited the organization. It was his by right. His job was to make everyone know this, to take immediate control.

But in the last three days someone else might have tried to move in ahead of him. There could be plots. He might already be marked for assassination.

He began a series of meetings. He sat at the head of the big table and the accountants, chemists, bankers, marketing experts, transportation and electronics experts, and all the rest came in and reported to him. All were much older men than himself, and he had trouble understanding what they told him. After a time he gave up listening. His brother had employed hundreds of people Victoriano had never met, and he had been unaware of most of the intricacies of the business. Now, instead of listening, he postured. Future decisions were to be authorized by him personally, he said. When he gave orders they were to be obeyed instantly and without question. Also, he issued threats. Failure would not be tolerated. Disobedience would not be tolerated. He stopped short—barely—of promising to have anyone who crossed him murdered. But the men seated around his conference table got the idea.

These meetings took place on Jorge's ranch outside of Medellín. Victoriano gave orders. Often they were conflicting orders. He played a role for which he was not suited. Don't bother me with details, he told men who protested. Do what you are told. Men came and went. Victoriano was suspicious of them all. He felt himself a virtual prisoner on the ranch, unwilling even to go into the city. Until he could surround himself with new bodyguards he could trust, he could go nowhere. He went more than a week without a woman. He considered himself highly sexed; a day in which he did not have a woman was to him a wasted day. Finally he had one brought to him.

By that time he had received the first of a number of telephone calls from New York from his lawyer there.

The lawyer, formerly an assistant DA, was one of the city's most prominent defense attorneys. His client list read like a who's who of mafiosi, drug traffickers, and crooked politicians. Using skills honed at public expense, he got most of them off, and he banked fees. From the Zaragons, beginning several years ago, he had accepted a huge yearly retainer, and for this, plus his usual hourly rates, he defended such of their employees as got arrested. He was also in the habit of passing on to them—no extra charge—whatever information he picked up around the courthouse: planned drug sweeps, new police tactics, the progress of investigations.

Now he told Victoriano, with whom he was dealing for the first time, that a major investigation was in progress in New York. He spoke carefully, not wanting to excite or affront his new employer. In a quiet voice he explained that although police officers were slaughtered regularly in Medellín, and even in Colombia as a whole, New York considered the killing of even a single cop to be the heaviest of crimes. In the present instance it was not one dead New York cop, but two, with a third on life-support and probably dying, plus a dead art dealer. So the present investigation was truly gigantic.

He knew Victoriano had had nothing to do with the case, he said smoothly, but since Jorge had died in that same shootout, he thought he ought to pass on news of the investigation. The police had a partial description of the shooter from a witness or witnesses and were distributing an artist's sketch. And, er, well, Victoriano's own name had been mentioned.

"Come down here," Zaragon said into the phone.

"No can do," the lawyer said. "Too busy."

"I said come down here."

"Better if I stay here, keep track of what the cops are doing."

Zaragon, fuming, hung up.

Witnesses, the lawyer reported a day or two later, had described a van in the street, and a van had been found in Florida that could be the one. There must be a thousand detectives working on the case, he added. The FBI had been called in and was helping. In New York and elsewhere scores of Colombian citizens had been rounded up and questioned. The press and TV could talk of nothing else. The entire NYPD seemed to be concentrating on this one case.

"Get down here," Zaragon said. "I want to talk to you."

The lawyer protested that he was too busy with other cases, but Zaragon interrupted: "You got a wife? You got kids you want to see grow up?"

From the other end of the phone came a horrified silence. When the lawyer finally spoke, his voice came out as no more than a whisper. "I'll be there as soon as possible," he said.

He was met at the Medellín airport by Victoriano's men and driven to Jorge's outlying ranch. The place was a mansion, he saw. Guards all around it.

Zaragon walked him up alongside a pasture in which horses grazed. It was a day of low-hanging clouds. The grass was wet and very green. When at last they were out of sight of the house or any possible listeners, Zaragon quizzed him about American procedure, American law, and the lawyer understood that the man beside him was the shooter every cop in New York was looking for. He had already guessed as much. If I asked him, he'd probably brag about it, the lawyer thought. But it was better not to know, and so he asked nothing.

The dying cop was the only one to be afraid of, the lawyer said. Apparently there was no other evidence that would stand up. But if the cop lived and could identify the shooter—whoever he was—a case could be made.

Both men were silent for a time. If the dying cop identified Zaragon, the weight of the United States government would come down on the politicians in Bogotá. The lawyer knew it, and so did the young man beside him. In Colombia, prosecution was nothing to fear. Witnesses were regularly bought off or killed. Judges the same. But if the shooter got extradited to America, prosecution would not be a joke.

"What about extradition?" Zaragon asked.

"For the Americans to extradite someone," the lawyer explained, "just showing an indictment is not enough. The Americans would have to go before the Colombian courts and outline their entire case, showing what proofs, what witnesses they had. The Colombian judges would have to be convinced that the case against this someone—whoever it might be—was airtight, or almost airtight, or they would refuse extradition."

He saw that extradition was what worried Zaragon. Certain members of the original Medellín cartel had been extradited to America, were in jail there now, and they would not ever get out. Zaragon himself could not be extradited for narcotics offenses, for he was protected by recent changes in Colombian law. After many bombings and murders, Zaragon's predecessors had succeeded in convincing their lawmakers that the existing extradition law, which offered up narcotics traffickers to American justice, was against Colombian sovereignty and must be repealed. The frightened lawmakers had repealed it, and much of the killing had stopped.

However, murder was still not a protected offense. Especially the murder of American police officers was not protected.

"The case against whoever killed the two cops, as I understand it," the lawyer said, "rests on the testimony of the third cop, this Detective Dilger. Without him they got nothing. But he's got a machine breathing for him."

"The person they are searching for could send men up to New York," said Zaragon.

The American received the impression that this had already been done, and the idea chilled him. He wanted only to continue receiving his retainers and fees, and otherwise to be left alone. He did not want to be party to another murder. "It would only draw attention to that person," he said.

"Send men into the hospital," muttered Zaragon.

"Not a good idea. The cop is going to die anyway. It's a miracle he's stayed alive this long." And he gave Zaragon an inappropriate grin.

The young man stared at him until the grin disappeared and his eyes dropped.

"I think they have him guarded," said the lawyer.

Zaragon turned and walked down toward the house. The American had to hurry after him. "Besides," he said to his back, "they may have other witnesses."

Zaragon stopped and looked at him. "Who?"

"Well, I heard there might be others."

He looked into Zaragon's face and did not like what he saw there. "Well, the doorman, for instance," he mumbled. In trying to protect one man, he had just signed the death warrant of another. To his horror he realized this. But the damage was done; he did not know what to say that might undo it.

Men had come out of the house to meet them. "Take him to the airport," Zaragon ordered, and walked away.

Within the hour, without having been offered so much as a cup of coffee, the American lawyer was back on the air bridge to Bogotá.

About three weeks later, wishing he had never accepted any retainer, he took a roll of quarters and went out to a pay phone and dialed Medellín.

"I may have made a mistake," he said when the expected voice came on the line. "That detective has come out of the coma. It now looks like he may not die. In fact he may recover."

At the other end, silence.

The American gave a broken chuckle. "Yeah, he may even testify before the grand jury."

After hanging up, Zaragon turned toward men in the room with him and gave orders more explicit than those he had given before.

≡ Chapter 9 ≡

*P*aris *Match* comes out each Thursday.

Before work Madeleine double-parked in front of the newspaper kiosk at the edge of the public gardens and bought a copy. The magazine's cover showed the mayor of Nice, who was surrounded by other officials, cutting a ribbon opening a school. The headline read: NICE THE CORRUPT. And inset was a photo of her—the mug shot off her police card. They must have got it from her union. In the photo she looked like a criminal, which in a sense she now was.

She stood on the curb in the early morning light and read the story, and when she finished she stepped between the bumpers of parked cars, bent over, and vomited onto the street.

When the retching stopped she glanced guiltily around, but there were no pedestrians at that spot so early in the day, and the cars moving by in the street paid her no attention. Opening her handbag, she dragged a handkerchief out from under her gun and wiped off her mouth and then her shoes. There was a litter basket nearby into which she threw the handkerchief.

After locking the magazine into the trunk of her car she drove to work.

She was supposed to be investigating the case of a brutalized child. There were phone calls to make, interviews to set up, forms to put in order, but she was unable to concentrate on any of it. She kept waiting for a copy of the magazine to appear in the room. After about two hours one did. Denise Potier, an inspector with whom she sometimes worked, came into the office from outside. Her movements as she approached Madeleine were furtive.

"Have you seen this?" she whispered, spreading the mouth of her handbag. She had the magazine folded in half in its depths.

Madeleine could only nod.

"What ever possessed you?" Denise whispered.

Madeleine shrugged, gave a half smile, and pretended to be concentrating on her forms.

Later that copy, or others, began passing from hand to hand. There was much whispering back and forth as well. The reaction of her colleagues was almost amusing. Either they would not look at her at all or could not look anywhere else. Apart from Denise, no one came near her. It was as if she had a communicable disease.

She had never in her life felt more lonely.

After lunch Commissaire Lamartine, the woman for whom they all worked, called her in. Standing before her desk, Madeleine felt as nervous as a schoolgirl. This woman had been kind to her in the past, but now her face was hard.

She said: "I don't presume to know why you felt obliged to do what you did. I've never worked in the Finance. I don't know how they do things over there. But you may be in serious trouble. I don't know what I'm expected to do. I'm awaiting instructions."

Often after work some of the women would meet in a certain café. It was five or six blocks away, well out of the police orbit, a nice enough café where they would sip aperitifs and talk everything out. Much of it would be shop talk: victims, suspects. Sometimes they talked about the men in their lives: husbands, boyfriends, bosses. These meetings were important to all of them. But tonight when the office closed the other women did not invite Madeleine along, and she did not presume to join

207

them. After they left without her, she went downstairs and outside and got into her car and drove home.

Luc was waiting for her.

Grabbing her arm, he virtually threw her against the wall. He had the magazine rolled up in his hand, and he stabbed her with it. "Are you out of your mind?"

She had been hoping for sympathy, not a physical assault.

"Just what the hell got into you?"

"It was the only way I could think of to make the justice system do what it is supposed to do."

"And who appointed you to that job?"

"I swore an oath eleven years ago, and—"

"No, you went on an ego trip."

"I didn't."

"You accuse the Sestris of crimes. Do you know how many subcontractors are dependent on the Sestris?"

"No."

"About sixty. Do you know how many people the Sestris employ?"

"No," she shouted, "and I don't care either."

"You accuse the mayor and most of his administration of selling contracts, accepting bribes."

"I accused him of nothing. Monsieur Duhamel wrote the article, not me."

"It's clear where Duhamel got his information from, though, isn't it?"

"If that's what you want to read into it, go ahead."

"It's what everyone will read into it," Luc snarled. "If you couldn't think of yourself, at least you might have had a thought for me."

"I don't see where that article has anything to do with you."

"It has everything to do with me."

"It doesn't mention your name."

"You attacked the entire establishment in this town. You challenged everyone in Nice who has money, power, the same people I'm trying to cultivate. You compromised my entire career."

"I compromised my own career, not yours. Which I have a perfect right to do."

"And you're taking me down with you."

When he got into a temper like this she felt like his mother. He ought to be spanked. Not being big enough or strong enough to spank him, she could only stand there and absorb his abuse.

"When you attack the establishment you attack my clients, my potential clients. I'm trying to get a law office started. I'm barely hanging on here. Who's going to come to me now? Tell me that. Who?"

"You're exaggerating."

"Everyone knows we live together." He pointed toward the telephone. "People call you on that line. My line."

"Who called me?"

"There must have been five calls since I came in. I told them wrong number."

"You didn't even get their names?"

"I don't care what their names are," he shouted. "When you commit an act of supreme irresponsibility I get blamed. You think I don't get blamed?"

She would like to have known the names. Surely some of the callers approved of what she had done. Some of them might have been important men, able, and perhaps even willing, to support her position when the police establishment came down on her, as it surely would. From now on she would have to keep track of the names, for she was going to need allies, and where else could she get them? "If there are other calls when I'm not in," she said coldly, "I'd appreciate it if you would take down the names."

"I don't want people calling here and I won't take their names."

"I live here too," cried Madeleine.

"I know," said Luc, "and I wish you didn't."

"Beautiful," said Madeleine, "really nice."

"As far as attracting new clients, forget it. After this no one will come near me."

Obviously he believed this. Maybe it was true. For a moment she felt sorry for him but he continued to abuse her and this emotion passed.

"You've ruined me."

"If I've ruined anyone, I've ruined myself."

"I'll have to go somewhere else, start all over."

Name-calling began. He called her arrogant, stupid.

She called him overbearing.

He called her a selfish bitch.

"Let's both lower our voices," she said.

But the argument degenerated further. Even harsher words came forth.

The result was that Madeleine made her bed on the couch, where she lay awake and worried about her job, about Luc. Would she lose her job? She could do nothing about that, but she could patch it up with Luc. She hoped she could. Maybe she could. Unless they had truly said unforgivable things to each other. But they hadn't, had they?

Perhaps the breach was truly unmendable. What would she do if it was?

In the morning she made the coffee and sat with it at the table, but Luc drank his standing up, mostly in the bathroom while he shaved, then left the house without speaking to her.

The story had been all over the television news shows last night, apparently. She hadn't watched any of them, but this morning her name was in front-page headlines in the *Nice Matin,* and the Paris papers as well. She didn't read any of the stories, but the headlines were so big she couldn't miss them.

At work her phone never stopped ringing: journalists mostly. She declined all requests for interviews. Other calls were from politicians representing opposition parties who, as they congratulated her, were perhaps only seeking to exploit her for their own purposes. She took down their names. She was glad the case had come to public attention, she told them, and she hoped now that justice would take its course. Since she was not attached to the Finance Brigade anymore, she added, it was up to others to take over any future prosecutions.

It was a way of telling the politicians that she herself had withdrawn from the controversy. It was up to them now.

By withdrawing, she had decided, she might possibly save her job.

At lunchtime she went to see her brother, Alain, who was still running the yacht brokerage agency at the port of Beaulieu. Though Alain was so much older she nonetheless felt close to him. In any case, he was all she had left of immediate family.

But Alain was not in his office. An employee told her he was out in the marina somewhere.

She found him standing on the stern of a yacht that was moored between two others, stern to the quay.

"My sister, the star," he called out when he saw her, and he jumped off onto the quay and embraced her. "I've been reading about you. I never knew a star before." And then after a moment: "Are you in trouble?"

She shrugged. "Too early to tell."

"You don't look happy."

"Actually I'm more worried about my relationship with Luc than anything else."

"Luc," said her brother. Madeleine knew Alain had never liked Luc.

"Things are not going so well between us just now."

Her brother did not know what to say, apparently, so he gestured toward the yacht he had just left. "What do you think of her?"

Yachts did not touch her life in any way. "It's pretty enough, I suppose."

"She's yours for five million."

"Francs?"

"Dollars. Belongs to that actor plays a detective in the movies.

Englishman, I forget his name. Wants me to sell it for him. Doesn't have a word of French. We talked sign language." He waved his hands in both directions. "Nearly every boat in this marina is for sale. Rich owners never use them. They get tired of paying the upkeep."

Madeleine was looking for solace, not a lecture on yachts. Her brother saw this and put his arm around her. "Come on," he said, "I'll buy you lunch."

He walked her along the quay to where the restaurants were, a whole row of them with tables out front facing the yachts. They sat down and she put her sunglasses on.

Afterward Alain walked her to her car, where he embraced her again. They had not talked of Luc at all. "I'm here if you need me," her brother said.

That day and in the days following, encouraging things happened.

The press and TV stuck with the story: that there was major corruption in Nice, that the mayor was possibly involved, that for political reasons Paris was trying to protect the mayor, ignoring criminal activity by him and those around him. Reporters were out verifying the details divulged by Madeleine. Other reporters demanded interviews with major political figures, most of whom refused. Television viewers watched footage of government ministers ducking away from cameras; some were almost running.

As early as the second day the mayor of Nice, who was among those who refused to be interviewed, left for California with his much younger second wife. According to a communiqué issued by his office, this was a vacation that had been planned for months. In California, of course, reporters could not find him.

The prime minister departed for Africa on a tour of France's former colonies. His office too issued a communiqué, according to which the trip had been planned since last year.

Opposition deputies raised embarrassing questions in the national assembly, and when the government ignored them, they demanded that the government resign. The government did not resign, and the embarrassing questions went unanswered all week. Finally, selected ministers agreed to appear on talk shows, where they continued to ignore the questions while vilifying a certain female inspector in Nice, whom they did not name and who, they said, after being transferred out of Finance for incompetence, and possibly while suffering from female problems, had made wholly unsupported charges.

It made Madeleine cringe to hear herself described in this way.

However, the ministers were paired most times with opposition deputies who shouted down such arguments, defending Madeleine by name and demanding that the discussion stick to the issues she had raised. Most of the exchanges were vituperative, and on one program TV viewers were treated to an unexpected spectacle: the two gray-haired men rose up and started punching each other. Cameramen and electricians had to run into the picture to separate them.

Madeleine, though still making no statements or appearances herself, was becoming known throughout the country. She began to hope that when she appeared before the council of discipline—which would certainly happen soon—this might help her.

At home she continued to sleep on the sofa. Whenever Luc was there she was smiling and friendly enough, ready at any time to kiss and make up, willing to accept any overture that he might make. But he would have to make it, not her. However, no such overture occurred.

The day came when she was officially suspended pending the disciplinary hearing; Commissaire Lamartine relieved her of her gun and police card. Madame Lamartine was very nice about it, it wasn't her doing, she said, the orders had come from Paris. With the gun lying in plain sight on the desk between them, the two women even chatted awhile.

Madeleine didn't mind losing her gun, was glad to be without it in fact. But the police card was another matter, because it meant she was no longer part of something she had loved. She left the building extremely upset. Would she ever again set foot inside a police enclave?

She fixed herself dinner. There was no one to talk to about how she felt, and in bed on the sofa she couldn't sleep. She could have used a little loving. A few caresses would have helped, a tender word, the weight of a well-loved body on top of her, and especially the pleasant physical depletion that sometimes followed. That was what sex was for, and it was what she needed. But Luc wasn't even there.

As it happened a little tenderness was what Luc needed that night too. An important client had taken his business and walked out. The struggling new firm could not afford a controversial lawyer, Luc's partners had told him. Perhaps he ought to think about making new plans for himself. He came home very late, drunk, or pretending to be drunk, yanked Madeleine's bedclothes to the floor and, still fully clothed himself, pushed her nightdress up to her neck. It was the opposite of tenderness. She had been sound asleep, and at first scarcely knew what was happening. Then she clasped him to her thinking in her confusion: good, now maybe we can love each other again.

But he spoke not a word. When he finished he simply got off, zipped himself up, went into the bedroom, and closed the door.

In the morning when he came out to the living room he was dressed in a lawyer's three-piece suit and was carrying a small suitcase. The suitcase caused Madeleine's stomach to give a sudden lurch, as if she knew what was coming.

She herself sat at the table in bathrobe and slippers sipping café au lait from a double-sized cup.

"Would you like a cup of coffee?" she offered.

"No thank you. I don't have time."

She stared into her cup. She thought he might make some mention of last night, but he did not.

He said: "You're not going to work today?"

"No. I've been suspended from duty."

"Since when?"

"Yesterday."

He nodded. At least he didn't tell her it was what she deserved.

"I had some bad news yesterday too." When he didn't tell her what it was, she knew worse was coming. She waited.

Some seconds passed. Finally he said: "This isn't working, is it?"

She knew what he meant without being told, but decided to force him to say the words. "What's not working?"

"You and me."

"Look, I'm suspended now. Whatever harm I may have done your practice, that's the end of it."

"I'm not so sure."

She wasn't going to help him say what he evidently meant to say. She waited for him to get it out—his decision, whatever it was.

He said: "I think it would be better if we ended it."

"What are you trying to say, Luc?"

"I've got a case in Aix. I'll be tied up there the rest of the week. Now that you're not working, perhaps it would be a good idea if you used the time to find a place of your own."

And there it goes, she thought. All those nights sleeping in the same bed, all those meals shared, all that laundry done, all those birthday presents searched for. Finished. All over.

"You want me to move out?"

He was still standing there holding that stupid little suitcase. "You must feel it isn't working as strongly as I."

After a moment she said: "I never thought it was permanently not working." This was as far as she would go, and she watched for his reaction. She wasn't going to beg him.

He shook his head. "It isn't working. You know it isn't."

"Do you have somebody else, Luc?"

"Of course not."

She didn't know whether to believe him or not. "I wouldn't be surprised," she murmured half aloud.

"What did you say?"

"Why don't you move out and I'll keep the apartment?"

"It's my apartment," he said. "It was mine before you came down here. The furniture is mine. It's convenient to the courts."

This was all true, unfortunately. She decided not to torment him further. "I'll try to find a place."

"Yes, that would be best."

"I'll try to be gone before you get back."

"No hurry," he said hurriedly.

"I thought you said you wanted me out when you get back from Aix."

"Well, if it's convenient."

"Convenient," said Madeleine.

He came to the table and bent over and kissed her on both cheeks, kissed her good-bye apparently, the way any Frenchman would have kissed good-bye the wife of an acquaintance. Shake hands with the man, kiss the woman.

She did not kiss him back.

"Well," he said, "so long."

Then he was gone.

Madeleine, sipping her coffee, thought: I'm thirty-four years old and no closer than I ever was to a home of my own, a husband I can care for and care about, children. Somehow she had got her priorities wrong. When, how? What was she supposed to do now? Her career down the drain too, most likely.

She got dressed and went to see her brother. Alain owned an extra apartment upstairs over one of the warehouses on the port. It was very small. In summer he was sometimes able to rent it out. Perhaps he would let her use it for a short time—just until she got her life in order again. Her brother also had a small truck. Perhaps he would lend it to her, and one of his men to help, for she wanted to carry away the few pieces of antique furniture that had belonged to their mother. She was not going to leave them to Luc. Her furniture and her clothes, her hair dryer and her steam iron—that was all she would be able to save from this relationship. It wasn't much.

She was determined to have moved out of Luc's apartment by the time he got back from Aix.

Two weeks passed. The mayor of Nice returned from California and was able to laugh off the few questioners who met his plane. The charges this female inspector had made against him were all silly, he said. She must be going through the change of life.

The prime minister returned from Africa and when he stood up in the National Assembly and was asked about these same charges he replied that he had been away and had no firsthand knowledge of anything. He then proceeded to announce new economic measures to help France's former colonies. There were journalists present looking for a story. Since this was the only one available to them, they went with it, and it made headlines the next day. And why not? The charges Madeleine had made had led nowhere so far; she and they had begun to seem like old news.

Madeleine, having moved into the tiny apartment above the warehouse, had gone out each day looking for a job, which she did not find. By then she was interested in survival, not bringing down any particular politician, and she did not even realize the story was over. She had made no effort to keep it alive, had supposed it would stay alive by itself. It hadn't. Nor could any enterprising journalist now find her. She had no office. Her new apartment had no telephone. In effect, no one knew where she was. Without realizing it, she had become unreachable.

It didn't matter. The hubbub had died down. The journalists of France had gone on to something else.

Whereupon the minister of the interior made the mistake of ordering the Police Judiciaire to convene the council of discipline board that would hear evidence against Inspector Madeleine Leclerq on the charge of lack of respect for the obligation of reserve. She had breached the secrecy of an investigation. This was a charge of extreme gravity, and a trial date was set. Madeleine was notified, and so were the media.

It reawakened the entire case. Journalists suddenly remembered that the Sestri brothers, the mayor, and most of the mayor's administration had been accused of corruption and the case had been buried; all these accusations were still unresolved.

Madeleine's hearing was to be held in a conference room on the top floor of the so-called Hotel de Police, on the Avenue Foch. On the appointed day a mass of journalists and news crews waited on the sidewalk out front, fifty or more people in all.

Upstairs in the conference room the eight judges took their seats. Four of them represented the administration in Paris: two prefects, one subprefect, and one commissaire divisionaire of police. The other four judges were detectives assigned to the hearing by the police unions. Since the unions had already announced their formal support for suspended inspector Madeleine Leclerq it seemed she could count on four of the eight votes in advance. And she was not, after all, a corrupt cop. Quite the contrary. She was an honest cop who had denounced official corruption. Therefore she and her lawyers were extremely hopeful. If the hearing ended four votes to four she would probably escape any sanction, for it seemed unlikely that the minister of justice, who would be the final authority, would choose in such a publicized case to overrule the council of discipline. He might order a slap on the wrist, but would he dare pronounce the ultimate penalty, which was dismissal from the service?

This seemed unlikely.

And so the hearing began. One of the prefects sat as president of the council. The *Paris Match* article was entered into evidence. Commissaire Vossart testified as to the events themselves and as to the character of the defendant. The defendant was energetic and honorable, he said, but too emotional (as female inspectors often were, he noted), and likely to rely more on "female intuition" than on time-tested detectives' tools.

Cross-examined by one of Madeleine's two lawyers as to the truth of allegations of corruption contained in the article, Vossart hedged. No corruption had as yet been proven in a court of law, he said.

Now it was the turn of Madeleine's witnesses. All three of the detectives who had worked with her testified to the facts and details that their investigation had uncovered—the truth of the *Paris Match* article. Bosco then announced that it had been an honor for him to work beside Inspector Madeleine Leclerq. This statement made Madeleine want to weep with pride and gratitude, but it brought a frown to the face of the president of the council. Next came two deputies to the National Assembly, both of them members of the opposition party, who spoke on Madeleine's behalf. It was indeed ironic, they said, that representatives of a corrupt administration should sit in judgment of an honest police officer.

Madeleine herself then spoke. She did not deny being the source of the *Paris Match* article. She did not deny having failed to respect the obligation of reserve. All this seemed to her beside the point, she said. As an officer of judiciary police she had sworn an oath to seek the truth in all investigations to which she was assigned. In this one she had found proof of massive corruption by construction firms and by the Nice administration. To manifest the truth took precedence over the obligation of reserve, she said. She had had no choice, once the politicians had conspired to suppress the truth, but to make that truth public. Her honor as an officer of Police Judiciaire demanded no less. Her honor as a Frenchwoman demanded no less.

She had been more eloquent than she knew, and her side applauded when she sat down.

The eight judges retired to deliberate.

In less than an hour their verdict became known.

There exists in France a long tradition in certain kinds of de-

219

liberative bodies, today's kind for instance, of something called the "preponderant vote." Which is to say that in case of a tie, the vote of the deliberating body's president counts double. The preponderant vote had fallen into disuse in recent years and had not been employed in a police disciplinary case in a long time.

The vote of this particular council of discipline ended in a four-to-four tie, whereupon the president resurrected the principle of his right to preponderant vote. By a vote of five to four Madeleine was convicted. Conviction brought with it an order stripping her of her faculties and privileges as an officer of Police Judiciaire.

The court was adjourned.

But the administration had reckoned without the cries of outrage this would provoke in the press—the outrage of Madeleine as well. With nothing now to lose, and no other calls on her time, ex-Inspector Madeleine Leclerq decided to make herself available to interviewers.

French television viewers at this time had access to about ten channels, depending on location, for some emanated from neighboring capitals: Luxembourg, Monte Carlo, Brussels, Geneva. Madeleine appeared at least once on every one of the ten, sometimes in the middle of the noon or evening news broadcasts, sometimes on talk shows. Sometimes she appeared alone, sometimes in the company of opposition deputies who praised her; and there were occasions when she appeared on the same channel twice in one day: one program invited her back three straight days, and she accepted.

The country boasted also innumerable radio stations; she appeared on most of the important ones, and on all of the major call-in shows. She gave interviews to all of the national newspapers, and to the *Nice Matin* of course, and also to any magazine journalist who asked.

Her face and voice became well-known throughout the country.

In all of these interviews she stuck to the evidence she had uncovered. She added nothing, invented nothing. She resisted drawing conclusions or giving opinions. She didn't have to; the media people did it for her. "The government is covering up for a corrupt administration in Nice," they would say. "Why is the government doing that?"

But she would only smile sweetly and make no answer.

Obviously they wanted to hear her denounce people as thieves and swindlers. When she wouldn't, they did.

"How can you not denounce these people," they would demand, "in light of the evidence you have presented?"

"It was my job to present the evidence to the *juge d'instruction*," she would say. "From there it should have gone to the *parquet*, and then to trial. There would have been a legal verdict. All that has been short-circuited. Evidently there is to be no trial. Therefore I leave each of you to form your own conclusions, decide on your own verdict. If the evidence convinces you that certain members of the Nice administration are crooks . . . " And with a smile she would stop.

There were invitations to appear before town meetings, student groups, bar associations, police conventions, conventions of magistrates. Most of these she accepted, asking in return only the cost of her plane ticket and the night's lodging.

As a result media interest in her did not die down.

The mayor of Nice was unworried, or so he claimed. He saw her as a canary out trilling—and trilling and trilling. The image was an old one, but it satisfied him. It was how he described her one day to a man named Delmas, a childhood friend and the most trusted of his adjunct mayors. He said that if he just went on laughing her off, she would eventually go away. He had been mayor so long that his hold on Nice was solid. He could not be hurt by a defrocked detective who was a woman to boot.

But more and more he realized that her song was being heard. If she kept on he risked losing the support of Paris. It became impossible to laugh her off any longer. If Paris cut him off his exposure would be real. The police might dare to come after him. A serious investigation might be opened.

This could happen without warning. The police would sense very quickly that they were no longer under any restraint, and if this happened teams of judiciary police would descend on the homes and businesses of those closest to him. There would be perquisitions all over the city. He wouldn't learn of it until it happened.

What would they find?

There was too much out there.

Having come to this realization the mayor became worried. At a meeting of his top aides he was heard to mutter that he wished someone would "get that woman off my back."

Delmas, who was present at this meeting, had been appointed an adjunct early in the mayor's first term and had held the post ever since. It was his job, he believed, to put into action every mayoral whim, to divine what the mayor wished and do it.

There were ways to arrange what he believed the mayor wished now. All it took was access to one or two tough young men willing to take on dirty jobs for a price. For a man of Delmas's rank this represented no problem at all.

The mayor's party had clubhouses throughout the city. Money from campaign contributions, and also from the type of kickbacks of which the Sestri brothers were accused, was regularly funneled into them. This money, some of it accounted for elsewhere, some of it not, was in cash—stacks of bank notes that were held in the clubhouse safes for use as needed. The cash kept the clubs open, kept the party cadres happy, and during campaigns it paid the workers who handed out tracts, pasted up posters, and cheered the mayor's speeches—those same workers who sometimes tore down the posters of opposition candidates or started the riots that broke up their rallies.

The mayor by no means kept every franc that came into his hands. Staying mayor for twenty-five years cost plenty.

Delmas went into one of the clubhouses. Having found the

man he wanted, he said to him: "The *patron* wants that woman silenced."

"Silenced?"

"Yes, and do it quietly."

It made for a kind of pun, and they both laughed.

"Quietly?" the other man said.

"You know. The press shouldn't find out about it."

"It will cost money."

Delmas shrugged.

"The going rate. You decide."

"Half down, half when it's done. Does that sound about right?"

"Whatever you say."

The other man was younger than Delmas, only about forty-five. It was understood between them that he would not do the job himself but would pass the contract on. If he wanted to keep a commission, that was up to him.

He said: "It will take a little time to set up."

"Quickly," said Delmas. "Quickly and quietly."

"Okay," said the other man. "Consider it done."

They shook hands, and Delmas left.

The contract was already well outside City Hall, already several levels below the mayor. Legally speaking, it could be traced to him only with difficulty. It would drop down two more levels before being put into action, and by then would not be traceable to him at all.

Madeleine became used to giving autographs after her public appearances, sometimes a lot of autographs. She liked that part of it, but when people began recognizing her in restaurants and coming over to talk to her, she felt she had gone far enough, too far perhaps, and she stopped. She retreated to her room above the warehouse, and her public life was over, or so she thought.

But by then it was too late.

≡ CHAPTER 10 ≡

The body cast encasing Jack had been whittled down several times already. The next morning it was reduced further, after which he was lifted into a wheelchair and rolled to the elevator. On the ground floor he was rolled out to a police van and loaded aboard. But instead of being taken directly home he was driven to the courthouse on Centre Street and wheeled into another elevator for the trip up to the courtroom in which the grand jury was sitting.

He was sworn in by McCauley, the young assistant DA he had met previously, and asked to state his name, rank, and employer for the record.

And on a specific date, McCauley asked him, did something unusual occur?

Jack, who hated these legal formulas, said: "It certainly seemed unusual to me at the time." He looked up into the faces of the twenty-three grand jurors sitting in a kind of amphitheater.

"And what was that unusual event?"

"I got shot."

"Did you get shot more than once?"

"Five times," said Jack. "Bang, bang. And then bang, bang, bang."

"Just like that?"

"Just like that." He had refused to take the pills the police surgeon had prescribed, and the pain was making sweat stand out on his brow.

"And were you able to recognize your assailant?"

"I had expected to meet a narcotics trafficker named Victoriano Zaragon. I recognized him from photos I studied before the meeting and I verified his identity from other photos I studied afterward while I was in the hospital."

"And on that specific night, did a firefight break out?"

"Yes."

"And were certain of your partners killed?"

"Yes, two of them."

This grand jury had already heard testimony from the doorman, from the department's various forensic detectives, and from whomever else the young prosecutor had decided to have testify. There was no cross-examination in grand jury hearings, and a simple majority was sufficient to indict.

Only a few more questions followed. After making his responses Jack was wheeled out of the courtroom by McCauley, and into an anteroom. There he closed his eyes and concentrated on his pain. McCauley had gone back into the hearing room, where he would review the evidence and would ask the grand jury to indict Victoriano Zaragon.

In a short time he came out. "They're voting now," he said.

Almost immediately the door opened again and the court clerk came out with the official notice that the indictment had been voted.

"So much for that," said McCauley with satisfaction. He was clean-shaven again. He must have given up trying to grow a mustache.

He was young enough to imagine that an indictment was a triumph.

"Just see if you can keep it sealed until we catch the guy," said Jack in his wheelchair. "I'm a sitting duck here."

The police van took him home and Jimmy, the cop on duty that day, wheeled him past the doormen into the elevator. The doormen were running alongside the wheelchair asking what they could do for him. Jack was in such pain that it was hard to accord them even a smile.

Upstairs he saw at once that little furniture remained in the rooms. The place smelled musty, unlived in. Jack wheeled himself from room to room. Flora had left him one armchair, a TV set on the floor, the table and chairs in the dinette, and, in the bedroom, the big bed. He opened the two closets and peered inside. Flora's was empty. In his own hung his clothes the way he had left them.

"Where's your wife?" inquired Jimmy behind him.

"She'll be along later," lied Jack. "Would you do me a favor? Would you go out and buy some things for me?" He made a list: bread, butter, canned soups, hamburger meat, a few other things. His cooking repertoire was not very broad. "Get me a bottle of bourbon too."

While Jimmy was gone he rolled himself over to the window and looked down on Central Park.

There was a car parked in the bus stop below with three men in it, all Hispanics. Jack couldn't see them. From the wheelchair he could not see directly below the window at all. In any case, from this height the car would have looked no different from any other car.

He rolled himself into Flora's closet and opened the safe. There were no dresses to push aside to get in there. The closet was empty and so was the safe. His other two guns were gone. In some confusion he glanced all around the room and it was then he noticed the papers on the counterpane. He rolled over to them and saw they were receipts for his guns signed by the department's chief clerk.

It meant that during his hospital stay, probably while he was in the coma, the police department had sent someone here to collect his remaining guns. He fingered the receipts. There was one for each of them: the two from the safe, the two he had been carrying that night, even the service revolver from his locker in the station house.

He had no guns left, and did not like the feeling.

The doorbell rang and he went to it.

"Jimmy?" he called through the door.

"Yeah, it's me."

Jimmy came in carrying the grocery bags. In the kitchen he put things away. When he finished he handed Jack his change. "I don't like to leave you alone like this," he said.

"My wife will be along any minute."

"You sure?"

"Absolutely." Jack forced himself to give a big smile. "You go on home. Thanks for everything."

Jack wheeled himself down the hall behind him, and when the door closed threw all the bolts. He then forced himself to stand up. Again the beads of sweat popped out on his brow. The desire to sit down was immediate and almost overpowering. Nonetheless, he pushed the wheelchair away from him and made his way, one step at a time, back to the same window as before, where he stood with his jaw clenched staring down at the park. It began to get dark. He watched the lights come on.

When he heard keys turn in the front door, he froze. Automatically he reached for his hip where his gun should have been, but wasn't. He was worse than unarmed, he couldn't even run.

High heels went tap-tap on the parquet floor of the entrance hall, and he heard Flora's voice. "Jack? Are you home, Jack?"

She came into the vast, empty living room saying: "Ah, there you are." And then: "Why didn't you tell me you were being discharged today? I went all the way to the hospital and you weren't even there."

She was carrying food, which she took into the kitchen and began to prepare. Unwilling to let her see him in a wheelchair, he followed on foot, standing beside the stove for as long as he could stand it, watching Flora's hands slice up vegetables, listening to Flora's chatter without hearing a word. At last she turned toward him, saw his face and said: "You're in pain."

"It's not so bad."

He let her help him sit down at the breakfast table. "I wouldn't mind a drink," he said, tight-lipped.

"If you're taking pills you shouldn't drink."

"I'm not taking anything."

Her face full of concern, she fixed a bourbon on the rocks, which he sipped gratefully. He could smell and hear the steak broiling, and was grateful for that too. He had been fed through a needle for weeks, and after that had come more weeks of hospital food.

The steak, when finally he cut into it, fulfilled all his expectations. They sat opposite each other at the breakfast table and Flora chattered and Jack ate this first good meal in so long and tried to concentrate on it, but the pain got in the way. He cleaned his plate and mopped up with bread because he knew he had to eat if he was to get strong again, but when he had finished he forced a smile he could not maintain and said: "And now, if you don't mind, I'd like to lie down for a moment."

"All right, I'll go."

"I don't want you to go."

She followed him into the bedroom and helped him onto the bed, where he lay drained by the pain. It seemed to have emptied out the last of the energy with which he had started the day.

Flora had sat down on the edge of the bed and was holding his hand, and in a moment he felt a bit better.

"There's something you forgot to tell me," he said.

"No, I've told you everything."

"About my guns."

"Oh, that," she said airily. "They knew what they were looking for. They had the right serial numbers and everything, because I checked them. So I handed them over. I left you the receipts, did you see them?"

"You might have told me."

"It didn't seem important. Anyway, you're not going to be needing guns anymore."

"Maybe not."

"I left you the airline tickets too."

"The trip to Paris we never took."

"They're in the bedside table."

Jack took the tickets out of the drawer and looked at them.

Wearing the same concerned expression as before, Flora said: "I don't think you're going to get up again tonight, are you?"

"I don't think so."

"Would you like me to take your shoes off?"

"Yes."

She pulled them off, and they dropped with a thud on the floor.

"Your trousers too." Flora always said trousers, never pants.

"Sure."

He hiked his hips up slightly and she pulled his pants off.

"Well, well," she said, "what have we here?"

"Sorry," said Jack.

She stroked him.

"Hmm," said Jack.

She stood up. She was wearing a midwestern girl's idea of Manhattan chic, high heels, jeans, and a maroon cashmere sweater. He knew it was cashmere because he had just felt it. She lifted first one heel, then the other, removing the shoes. The jeans dropped to the floor too and she stepped out of them.

"If I hurt you, just say so and I'll stop," she said.

Her knees were beside the body cast, and as she worked he pulled the sweater up over her head and then undid the bra so that it hung. He felt the sweat pop out on his brow again, but not from pain this time, and despite himself he cried out: "Flora, I love you."

"I love you too," she said, though in a less passionate tone of voice.

When they were finished he found that the airline tickets lay beside him on the bed, and he pointed them at her and said: "Let's take this trip together."

Wearing nothing, she picked up her bra and bent forward to hook it on.

"Can't," she said. He could not see her face but she seemed to be smirking, as if she were in on a certain joke and he was not. "We have to get divorced."

He watched her pull her panties on, then step into her jeans.

"How do you feel?" she asked.

He said: "Glad to know the thing still works."

She smiled. "I thought you might have been worried about that. Did I relieve your mind a little?"

"Flora—"

"I'm a pretty good mind-reliever, wouldn't you say?"

He reached for her hand.

"I'd better be going," she said.

This statement hit him hard, cold water to the face. He wasn't going to beg her to stay. "When you go out," he said, "be sure to lock all the locks."

He listened to be sure she did this, then again picked up the airline tickets. After studying them a moment, he dropped them into the drawer of the bedside table.

His wife came to see him regularly after that, sometimes cooking dinner, which they would eat together, but there was no return to the bedroom. He did not ask, though he wanted to, and she did not offer, though he wanted her to.

The therapist came every morning for a week until Jack dismissed him, saying he could do the exercises by himself; he didn't want the therapist to see how bad the pain was. The cop Jimmy came by occasionally. The police chaplain, Monsignor O'Hare, came once, and the police surgeon twice. Jack was always careful to know who was at the door before he opened it. Some detectives from his old precinct came, the first time paying a social call, the second time to tell him that the doorman to Bulfinch's building had been murdered.

"Van drives up in front," one of them said. "Guy gets out with an Uzi, we think it was an Uzi, and empties it into the poor fucking doorman."

"The only other direct witness," murmured Jack.

"Yeah, we thought that too."

"Poor guy," said Jack.

"He caught about ten in the gut, and one final one in the ear."

"To make sure," said Jack.

"We should have been guarding the poor fucker, but nobody ordered it."

The second detective, who had not yet spoken, said: "When you go out, you better watch out for yourself."

"Yeah," said Jack.

The police department van drove him back to Bellevue, where the last of his body cast was removed, and from there to head-quarters at 1 Police Plaza, where he was led first to the pension section on the tenth floor and then down the hall to the chief clerk's office. In both places he signed papers, and the chief clerk asked him to turn over his ID card and shield, which he did.

Now officially retired from the police department, he asked for a pistol permit and the return of his guns.

"I don't have your guns," said the chief clerk, who was a civilian employee, not a cop, "and I've been told not to issue you a pistol permit."

"What?" cried Jack. "What?"

Almost all cops when retiring were routinely issued permits, and almost all kept their guns. To walk about armed had become, for most of them, an emotional necessity. In addition, most daydreamed of intervening as a civilian in a stickup or some other crime in progress and becoming a hero one last time.

In fact the city liked the idea of all those extra guns out there. It made for a kind of unpaid auxiliary police force.

"If you want a permit and your guns," said the chief clerk, "you better go see the chief of detectives. His office is on thirteen."

In a rage Jack went up there. The door to the chief's private office was closed, and it was guarded by a captain and two lieutenants whose desks were placed just in front. When Jack tried to brush past them, they jumped up and stood in his way.

"Wait a minute, fella."

"You can't go in there, Dilger."

Jack was walking with a cane by this time. When he began screaming and flailing around with his cane they all scattered and he started for the chief's door, which, however, suddenly opened, and the chief stood there.

"Come in, Dilger," he said courteously. "What seems to be the trouble?"

"You know goddam well what the trouble is. I want a pistol permit and I want my guns."

"Well, as a matter of fact the mayor would prefer it if you weren't armed."

"The mayor?"

"Someone higher than me, in any case."

"There may be a contract out on my life."

"Who told you that?"

"A little bird told me."

The chief looked thoughtful. "Nothing that we take seriously."

"What if I take it seriously?"

"Let's not exaggerate."

"What about the doorman? They blew away the poor fucking doorman."

"We believe it's unrelated. That guy was into drugs, or some goddam thing."

Jack's vision was clouded by tears of rage and frustration. "They put about fifteen bullets into the—"

"The department's position is that being as you're disabled, you don't need a gun. There's always the possibility you might do yourself harm. Become depressed because of nagging pain or whatever, and do yourself harm. Or do someone else harm. The department's position is you shouldn't have one."

The chief of detectives went on speaking in a courteous, even voice, but Jack no longer heard him. No longer flailing his cane, no longer screaming, he felt the police department had condemned him to death and he was speechless.

The van took him home. He stood on the sidewalk between the van and the entrance to his building and eyeballed the street. He spotted the car parked in the bus stop half a block uptown. There were three men in it. It was too far away to be certain, but they could have been Hispanics.

Jesus, he thought, as an instantaneous sweat broke out on his back and began to run toward the band of his shorts. Never before had the desire to live burned this strongly within him. In the past he had loved taking risks, but the terrible pain he had suffered, and now this day's events, had broken his nerve.

Shaken, he stood in the lee of the van and was ashamed to realize he was sopping up the security it represented. For as long as it remained in place he was safe, and when it drove away he wouldn't be. The Colombians could make their try at him with impunity. They would move with some caution imagining him still a cop, still armed. This lack of knowledge on their part was the only security he had left. It wasn't much and it wouldn't last.

He went upstairs and telephoned the faithful Jimmy, asking him to come over as soon as possible.

"What for?"

"I need a ride to the airport."

"Where are you going?"

"I don't know yet." He knew, but didn't want anyone else to know, not even Jimmy.

"It will take me a while to get there," said Jimmy.

"Wear your uniform," Jack said.

"What for?"

"Please."

While waiting he got together his passport and credit cards, and packed a bag. The airline tickets were still in the drawer beside the bed, New York–Paris round trip. He put both in his pocket.

On the way to the airport, to be sure they were not being tailed, he had Jimmy square two different blocks twice each. At the airport he changed his destination from Paris to Nice, paying a surcharge, turned in the second ticket, then sat amid the milling crowds feeling safer than he had for days. Already no one knew where he was.

The flight took off on time.

Eight hours later he got off into the bright Mediterranean sunshine and rented a car, and drove along the seafront into the city, reacquainting himself with scenery he had not seen since he was in the navy.

His plan was to find a room, then try to make contact with people he had known in those days. It wasn't much of a plan, but for the moment it was all the plan he had or needed.

There was no contract out on him here.

≡ BOOK II ≡

≡ Chapter 11 ≡

Beaulieu-sur-Mer, seven miles east of Nice, thirteen miles west of the Italian frontier, is one of the smallest of the Riviera towns, and some say the most chic. The promenade above the small sand beach is in two levels, almost a park, and is shaded with palm trees and flowering bushes. Tucked in at either end are intimate but extremely expensive hotels. Across the street is a small jewel of a casino dating from the end of the last century with, beside it, surrounded by hedges, the Tennis Club de Beaulieu, eight red clay courts. The town itself, caught between the sea and the mountains, consists of two or three streets lined with art galleries, antique shops, and real estate agencies. There is an elegant little railroad station which dates from the last century also—one can imagine horse-drawn carriages waiting for the travelers who got down here. At the back edge of the town the Maritime Alps rise sharply. They leave room for a few posh villas; after that the cliffs climb almost straight up.

The lower corniche road winds through the town, and where it exits at the other side there is a U-shaped yacht harbor. Along the harbor's long side stand restaurants with tables out front, plus the various warehouses and businesses that service the yachts. The harbor itself is so crowded that not much water can be seen. There is a wide central quay off which extend narrower quays, four in each direction. They stick out like fingers, and to them the yachts are moored side by side, stern to the quay, two or three hundred of all sizes. Above their decks the sky bristles. From the sterns miniature gangways extend toward the quays, most of them raised up and hanging in the air, the drawbridges of modern times.

Water, even water as densely packed and as sheltered as this, moves. The yachts move too, perpetually rubbing their jowls one against the other.

The yacht owners are all rich, some are famous as well, and most are absent. On the bigger yachts live hired sailors who are mostly young, blond, and bronzed; their job is to keep the yacht ready to put to sea, in case the owner comes around and wants to. On the smaller yachts there is usually nobody. Most of them, big or small, are for sale; yacht ownership is evidently not as much fun as people sometimes suppose. The yacht brokerage business, including the one that had been in Madeleine's family for two generations, is not constant. In good times it is good; in bad times it is nonexistent.

On this particular morning Madeleine came down from her room above the warehouse, entered her brother's storefront office, and found him in conversation with a tall thin man who did not look healthy and who was leaning on a cane. For a man her own age to look that unwell surprised Madeleine, and she wondered what was wrong with him.

She hung back listening to the conversation, which was conducted in a mixture of execrable English by her brother and equally execrable French by the other man, until her brother turned to her in exasperation and said: "Will you please give me a hand here?"

Madeleine laughed and stepped forward. "Can I help?" she asked the other man, obviously an American.

He glanced at her sharply. "You English?"

"No. I'm French."

"You sound English."

It pleased Madeleine that she could pass as an Englishwoman. "I lived there for a while," she said. "This is my brother. What was it you were trying to tell him?"

It seemed the American wanted to rent a boat and knew more or less what he wanted. No, he said in response to her question, he had no boating license yet but supposed he could get one. She judged partly from his words, mostly from his manner, that he had not much money either. He was not overbearing. She had translated for yacht buyers before, and the rich ones showed it. This man didn't want anything exotic. He wanted to be able to sleep on it and go at least as far as Corsica—maybe even farther, he said, sticking close to the coasts, of course. He said he had already looked for such a boat in Nice and Villefranche. Nice had turned out to be a commercial port, cargo ships and car ferries. Villefranche had nothing that suited him. Now he was here, working his way down the coast, still looking.

He said he had some idea of hiring himself out to tourists for day trips: fishing, sightseeing, snorkeling. It was a way of making a small living.

Madeleine was skeptical.

He turned to her and a rather big grin came on. "You don't approve?"

"This part of the Mediterranean is pretty well fished out," said Madeleine.

"Sightseeing, then."

"There are big boats operating out of Nice and the other cities with whom you'd have to compete."

The American's grin began to look forced. Turning back to Alain he said: "Do you have anything to rent or not?"

"Tell him," Alain joked, "there are three things no Frenchman ever lends: his wife, his boat, and his pen."

"Tell him I said rent, not borrow," answered the American sharply.

Alain showed him three boats, the first one an ex-fishing

trawler, rusty, half rotted out, but cheap; the American gave it only a glance. The next prospect was a so-called cigarette boat that could make fifty knots an hour. The purpose of such a boat, the American commented, was to attract the attention of girls, and the customs police. If he wanted to go into the smuggling business, it would be wiser to use something a bit less obvious.

Smuggling? Madeleine glanced at him sharply.

The third boat was a twenty-four-foot cabin cruiser built in Norway. It had two 110 Volvo Penta motors. Though ten or more years old it looked from the quay to be in pretty good shape. There were two bunks inside the cabin, and the stern banquettes could be rigged into a third; one would sleep out in the air with an awning overhead. There was a tiny galley, a chemical toilet, a hot-water heater and, in the hold, an oversized water tank which would make freshwater showers possible, though one would have to stand on the foredeck and use a hose.

Alain judged the boat's top speed at about fifteen knots. Now price was discussed, with Madeleine translating.

They had spent most of an hour moving from one to the other of the widely separated boats, walking slowly so the American with his cane could keep up. Now suddenly he sat down on a bollard.

"I'm sorry," he said, "I need to rest for a moment."

He was sweating, though it was not a hot morning, and looked more haggard than ever.

"You're not well," suggested Madeleine.

"I'll be fine in a minute."

She waited for him to explain himself, but he did not do so. Alain, who had been several steps ahead, continued on to his office.

The American looked across the harbor at the row of restaurants. It was hard to see them through all the masts and awnings. Mostly what could be seen were the tops of the umbrellas that stood above the tables out front.

"Are you busy?" the American said. "Could I take you to lunch?"

Madeleine on this day was in no mood to get mixed up with another man, neither this one nor any other.

"And then after lunch," he said, forcing the same big grin as before, "we can see about me renting that boat we just looked at."

How badly did her brother need the commission? In her present state she saw men as threats. Did she owe it to Alain to be nice to this one? But a man this ill did not seem threatening. And she had eaten too many meals alone recently.

"Sure," she said to him, "why not?"

As they made their way around the harbor she dawdled. Nonetheless, it was hard for him to keep up.

"You're in pain," Madeleine said.

"It comes and goes. It's not so bad."

"Your hip, is it?"

"I'll be fine in a few days."

When they were seated the American ordered a bottle of Rosé de Provence, and when it was poured held his glass up to the light so that they could admire its color. "Nice," he said, and smiled, and for a moment she saw what he had looked like as a child.

"Are you on vacation?" she asked him.

"I don't know. Maybe I'll stay awhile. Maybe not."

"What sort of work do you do?"

"I was—I had a government job."

She looked at him. When he said nothing further she said: "But you don't have it anymore?"

"Retired."

"You're pretty young to be retired."

He said: "Hmm." She watched him study the color of his wine.

He was being closemouthed because he was still worried about being tracked down, but she didn't know this. He didn't want anyone to know who he was, and that included this young woman.

Madeleine thought him merely rude, and it made her persistent. "Were you in an accident?"

"Something like that."

"Accident in the workplace?" she probed.

He laughed. "As a matter of fact, yes. Let's order." He studied his menu. "What's this?" he asked, pointing to a line on the menu.

"Grilled sardines. You eat them with your fingers like corn on the cob."

"That's for me, then." And he smiled. He really had a very nice smile.

They sat outdoors under the umbrella on a pleasant sunny morning and looked across at the yachts. "And you," he said, "what sort of work do you do?"

"I'm between jobs right now." She could be just as closemouthed as he.

"But you do work?"

"Oh yes."

"What kind of work?"

"I've moved around a lot, Lille, Paris, here."

"I see."

Over lunch they talked of language, and of boats—impersonal subjects—and the conversation went better. When she told him she had learned English as an au pair girl in England, he asked what parts of the country she had seen and what she had enjoyed most about her time there. He seemed genuinely interested in her answers, and she gained confidence. She knew she looked nice today. She had slept well for a change and looked healthy. Her hair looked nice, and she had on nice earrings just peeping out underneath.

He hoped to see England one day, he said. So far he knew only the Mediterranean, and he described things he had seen in Greece and Turkey while in the navy.

They had become like singers working over the introduction to a love duet. They were nowhere near the melody yet, and there was some doubt they would ever reach it.

He ate his grilled sardines as she had suggested, picking the flesh off the skeleton with his teeth, and they both sipped their rosé, and he asked if she knew boats.

Her father had had the brokerage before her brother, she told him, and they talked of boats in general, and boating here off the coast. She told him old stories of smugglers just after the war when France was short of everything, when American cigarettes were coveted above all others and men loaded cases of Chesterfields and Lucky Strikes aboard disused PT boats in Tangiers, and ran them across the Mediterranean and offloaded them in the night.

"Today it's not cigarettes but drugs, I imagine," he said, and for a moment they were perhaps close to admitting to each other that they had been police officers. If they had pursued the subject of drugs this might have happened.

But the topic switched back to yachts. She told him of storms, and of million-dollar yachts that had piled up on the Riviera rocks. She told of people who had disappeared off yachts, and of famous wild yacht parties of the past. Sometimes she made him laugh. In any case, the strain was gone from his face.

"You know the waters around here?" he asked.

"Yes, of course." As a girl she had been on and off pleasure boats constantly.

"Do you think your brother would let you and me take that Norwegian boat out for a trial run this afternoon?"

An hour later she steered the boat out of the marina. They stood behind the windscreen, their rumps against the high chairs, and when they were clear of the breakwater she pushed the throttles forward until she could feel the wind against her sunglasses, the wind in her hair. The water was very flat, and overhead there were small puffs of clouds moving east toward Italy.

She drove them over toward the Cap Ferrat and slowed, and they cruised slowly along the long craggy cape admiring the big villas, the occasional big estates. There were other boats anchored close to the cliffs, and people were swimming or sunbathing, and a patrol boat manned by two uniformed gendarmes and flying the French flag moved by, the gendarmes studying them for a moment.

When the patrol boat was gone the American leaned close and shouted into her ear. "How closely do they patrol this coast?"

The question stopped her. She had been enjoying the freedom of the open water, the wind, the slight bounce to the boat. Suddenly she was thinking like a cop again. "Are you thinking of smuggling something?"

Now he looked suddenly wary too.

But after a moment his grin came on and he answered jokingly: "I don't know. Have to see what comes up."

The American never took the helm, though she offered it to him, and presently they returned to Beaulieu. She steered slowly, carefully into the harbor, nosing in among all the parked yachts, until finally she backed into the slot they had come out of an hour before.

In Alain's office the American signed papers for the boat and wrote out a check in dollars. Madeleine, who still had not been told his name, leaned over his shoulder to read it off the check. Now in her head she was no longer obliged to think of him as The American, but could address him as Monsieur Dilger if she wished.

"Sorry that my check's in dollars," he said. "I haven't had time to open a bank account here yet."

They all stepped out of the office onto the harbor front. There Alain shook hands with him, so Madeleine did too. She watched him hobble off toward his rented car, still knowing nothing whatever about him. Of course he knew nothing about her either.

The next day he moved his belongings aboard the boat—from Alain's doorway Madeleine watched him do it. He had been living in a cheap hotel in Nice, she learned later, but from then on that twenty-four-foot boat was home.

She herself flew to Le Mans all expenses paid to address a convention of judges. Again she told an audience how she and her former colleagues had proven that elected officials were demanding bribes in exchange for the awarding of municipal contracts. For as long as those officials in Nice, and others like them in other cities, were protected by the government in Paris, she declared, the police could do nothing. Her audience of magistrates represented the next rung above cops on the judicial ladder, but they were lawyers and had tenure, and it was up to them to force into existence the changes that were needed. She urged them to try.

She received a standing ovation and for a heady moment was able to believe herself important in the political life of France. But the moment passed. She still had no job, no prospects of a job, no husband or lover to come home to, nor any prospects of same, and there was still no active investigation into any of the corruption she had uncovered in Nice.

The next morning she caught the same plane back.

As she was getting out of her car in front of the warehouse she noticed Monsieur Dilger coming out of the small grocery a few doors down. He was carrying a sack of provisions and making his way slowly in the direction of his boat. Though still limping he was without a cane this morning.

She greeted him in French. "Bonjour, Monsieur Dilger."

"Hello, Maddie," he said. Maddie? She was aware that Americans tended to call everyone by first name, but the French were more formal than that. Maddie, indeed. Not even

Madeleine. French formality had not been observed and she was a bit shocked.

She told him he was looking better this morning, and commented on the missing cane.

Once again he gave her his big smile. "You're all dressed up," he said.

"I had a meeting."

They stood smiling at each other. She was wearing her black tailored suit over a rose-colored blouse, the same outfit in which she had addressed the judges in Le Mans the night before.

As they walked toward his boat she offered to carry his sack for him, but he refused.

When they came to his boat he at last handed it to her, then stepped carefully on board, using both hands to steady himself against the slight lurch of the boat.

"I'm going into Nice to the open market tomorrow," she said as he reached up for his sack. Afterward she did not understand what had made her speak. "You're welcome to come along if you wish."

"Tomorrow's Sunday."

"Well, Sunday's the day I do my marketing."

"Say, I'd like that. What time?"

She was surprised by this reaction. She was as surprised that she wanted to do things for him as she was that she wanted him to like her. "In the open market the produce will be cheaper and fresher," she said inanely. She should have just told him when to meet her and left. "And there will be more choice," she finished.

During the brief time they were together she had continued to call him Monsieur Dilger. He had continued to call her Maddie. To her surprise she liked it.

The open market in the Cours Salaya is long and narrow, rows of stalls under awnings, with cafés to both sides, the tables pushed out until there is hardly room to pass between the tables and the stalls. One enters the Cours via one of the several archways that give onto the seafront, or via the old town, for many of its narrow alleys—one hesitates to call them streets—debouch into the Cours on one side; or else one strolls in past the opera house, encountering the flower stalls first, the sun coming down through the awnings onto the fresh-cut flowers, carnations of course, but also ranunculas, anemones, roses of all sizes and colors, gladioli, tulips. The sun through the awnings onto the flowers creates multiple shades of reds, oranges, and golds, a luminous light, a kind of halo one can walk through. It creates also an almost sultry odor in which one imagines it may be hard to breathe.

Farther on the produce stalls begin, the redolence of flowers gives way to the earthier odor of fruits and vegetables, and to considerably more noise. Merchants hawk their wares, shoppers want to know where something was grown and when harvested, money changes hands. Sunday dinner is on everyone's mind. Everyone is in good humor. Jokes pass back and forth. The merchants slice open melons or pears, offering slivers to prove ripeness, taste.

Nearly everything that can be eaten is on sale, most of it fresh: live chickens and ducks; and eggs still clotted with barnyard muck; and fresh-caught fish hacked cleanly in two to show the color and texture of the flesh of both halves; and mushrooms—bins and pyramids of all types, sizes, colors; and cheeses made in local farmhouses and identified only as made from milk from either cows or goats; and olives that may be black or green or any shade in between, either pickled in brine or not; and homemade honeys and jams. The odors and aromas of all this seem to rise up into an invisible cloud trapped under the awnings.

Walking past the stalls, one becomes hungry. Shoppers pause for coffee and croissants, sitting down outside one of the cafés and giving their orders to waiters. Itinerant musicians move from café to café and afterward pass the hat, guitar players mostly, though at least one man stationed nearby grinds out tunes on an old-fashioned barrel organ, and all these songs drift out over the cafés, over the stalls. Groups of tourists wend through, guides haranguing them in whatever their native language happens to be. In addition, the nearby old town, small as it is, contains no less than seven churches, some of them almost side by side, all with belfries, and on Sunday mornings the tolling of their bells goes on and on.

Sitting beside Jack at one of the cafés, Madeleine looked out over her coffee cup and was aware that the market represented one of Nice's premier tourist attractions. Life was not a travelogue, she mused, though it sometimes seemed so, and she realized why she had brought Jack Dilger here this morning—because it gave her pleasure, she didn't know why, to show her town and its attractions to this strange man about whom she still knew nothing. Why was she so curious about him? It wasn't just the mystery of him. Every human being constituted a mystery at first, and in most cases one had no interest whatever in resolving it.

Most of the other patrons of the café sipped their coffees, ignored the view, and read their *Nice Matins*. Not Jack, who was all eyes and ears and grin. "This is really nice," he told her. "I never would have seen it. Thanks for bringing me here."

They had finished their shopping. Their sacks of groceries sat on the vacant chairs at their table. Eventually they finished their coffee, Jack left money on the table, and they got up to go, working their way out of the Cours through the people and the stalls and the flowers, Jack still limping but with no cane, and they found Madeleine's car again.

She was feeling pleased with herself and with him, but as she settled herself behind the wheel, he said: "Could I ask a favor of you?"

"Sure." When he seemed to hesitate she said: "What's the favor?"

There was someone he used to know, he said. He had been to the address but was unable to understand what was said to him.

Would Madeleine be willing to come with him now and interpret? With her help, perhaps he could locate this person.

The request seemed harmless enough, and the address was not far. They drove down streets lined with plane trees, the branches close together overhead. On a Sunday morning few other cars moved anywhere in the town.

The address was an apartment building on the Avenue Victor Hugo. In the small open cage elevator they rode up to the third floor, where Jack rang the bell.

A woman opened the door a few inches, looked suspiciously from one of them to the other, and gave a barely perceptible nod in the direction of Jack. Madeleine explained the nature of their errand, then turned to Jack. "What's the name of the person you're looking for?"

"It's her daughter," said Jack. "Claudia. I used to know her."

"Oh for God's sake," said Madeleine.

"Ask her about her daughter."

Madeleine nearly refused. But finally, with many apologies to the woman in the doorway, she complied.

The two women spoke in French.

"She says her daughter is married with three children and lives in Paris."

"Yes, that's what I thought she told me the other day. Ask if she ever comes down here."

Madeleine shook her head in a kind of disbelief, but did as asked. "She says the last time her daughter came down was for her grandfather's funeral."

"Ask if I can have her phone number."

"That's ridiculous," said Madeleine.

"Ask her, please."

Madeleine glanced at him sharply, but again complied. "She says her daughter has no phone."

"No phone?" said Jack.

"It means she doesn't want to give you the number."

"She knows me. Remind her that she does."

249

"She already told me she remembers you. It makes no difference. Look, her daughter is married and that's the end of it. Forget it."

"Ask for her address."

"She won't want to give you that either."

"Ask her."

Madeleine had become increasingly uncomfortable, increasingly annoyed.

During the brief discussion that followed, Jack looked from one woman to the other. "What did she say?"

"She said you should write a letter and send it here. She'll send it on."

"Do you think she will?"

"Are you always this obtuse?"

"You don't have to get mad at me."

"She's a middle-class Frenchwoman, her daughter is married, and she would not be likely to send on a letter that could damage or wreck her daughter's marriage. Is that plain enough for you?"

During the ride back to Beaulieu, Madeleine felt used and resentful, and would not talk to him at all. She could not believe he was as stupid as he had seemed, or else he was simply—like most men—thoughtless and unfeeling. Either way he had ruined a pleasant morning. She had had enough of him.

From time to time she caught a glimpse of his face as she drove. He was eyeballing the streets the way a cop would, and when he realized she was not going to make conversation he commenced to comment on double-parked cars. There were always double-parked cars in Nice. She scarcely noticed them anymore. Even today on a Sunday they were double-parked outside bakeries, butcher shops, cafés. Where were the cops? he wanted to know. How was such a thing permitted? Did the shopkeepers pay off the cops, or what?

These comments were rendered in a rough, aggressive tone, so that an idea came to Madeleine. However, she was in no mood to express it. She was in no mood to talk to him at all. When she let him out in Beaulieu, having driven out on the central quay close to his boat, he thanked her for a nice morning. She merely nodded and drove away.

She ran into him three days later on the escalator at the Galleries Lafayette. He took her by the arm and led her into the men's clothing section, for he had to buy some shirts and trousers, and needed her help. He had arrived in France with very few clothes, he confessed.

Her curiosity got the better of her. As he fingered garments she said: "Most people when they go on a trip pack a bag with everything they might need."

"Most people," he conceded.

"But not you." She watched him.

"I had to leave town in a hurry."

"Why was that?"

"People after me."

"What people?" she persisted.

The big grin again. "I haven't told you this, but what I am, well, I'm a gangster."

"I see."

"You can imagine all the people who might be after me."

Her suspicions hardened. No, she thought, you're a cop or ex-cop. Everything about him read cop to her. The aggressive way he carried himself, his way of eyeballing streets, the details he noticed that an ordinary civilian would not have. To another cop it was plain.

But she chose to say nothing.

Instead she stood outside the changing room, and each time he limped out and turned full circle in front of her, she either approved or disapproved of whatever he had on. Neither her former husband nor Luc had ever asked for or needed her help in picking out clothes, and she felt for a moment like an American wife.

He took her to a place he knew, apparently from long ago, the

Scotch Tea House on the Avenue de Verdun, a nice enough little place, entirely French despite its name, having nothing to do
with Scotland or Scots. She supposed he had picked it out long
ago, and again today, imagining it a place where people would
speak English.

Today they sipped tea and munched on scones and chatted of
this and that. There were no revelations of any kind on either
side, but by sharing this pot of tea a chance encounter in a department store had somehow been transformed into what was
almost a date. Whether knowingly or unknowingly, they had
begun moving forward in step. They were beginning to construct
a joint past—and the past was what made the future, theirs or
anyone's, possible.

On the sidewalk after leaving the tea shop, speaking in a low
voice out of the side of his mouth, Jack said: "There's a guy on
a motorcycle—look around real casual. See him? He's wearing
leather and leaning on his bike against the lamppost."

Madeleine turned back to Jack. "What about him?"

"You don't know him?"

"No, why?"

"Not some old boyfriend you threw over?" Jack joked.

Madeleine looked puzzled. "No."

"The other day I saw him hanging around outside that building you live in. I think it was him."

The man was wearing a motorcycle helmet. It was impossible
to see his face clearly.

Madeleine said: "I never saw him before."

"Not someone you owe money to?"

"No." To Madeleine, conscious of the important enemies she
had made, was still making, it was no joking matter.

"Could he be following you?" asked Jack. "Is there any reason
anyone should be following you?"

Madeleine felt a chill between her shoulder blades. "No," she
lied.

"My imagination, I guess."

She studied Jack for a moment, her suspicions about him hardening. Who but a cop would have noticed the man on the motorcycle? Behind her its engine started up. Turning, she watched the man steer it out into the traffic. Since there was nothing she could do about him, whoever he was, Madeleine tried to shrug him off. She had been on television—he could be a fan following her around. Or his appearance at several different points in her life could be coincidental.

Or he could be someone hired to do her harm. A possibility, sure. But the more she thought it over, the harder she found it to believe. She had been dealing with white-collar criminals. Such people could not possibly constitute a physical threat. They were rich men, and rich men were neither violent nor likely to get violent, she believed. Violence was not part of their culture.

Jack was saying something. She hadn't even heard him, and now had to force herself to listen. He was inviting her out on his boat. They could take a picnic, he was saying, swim off the boat, make a day of it.

She hesitated. She had enjoyed this past hour, but their meeting had been impromptu, accidental. To spend the day on his boat changed the rules. It would be a formal outing, a real date for the first time.

"I was looking on the chart," he said. "We can go out to the Iles de Lérins. Between the two islands the water should be calm, good for swimming."

"As a matter of fact it is." She was trying to gauge his offer, decide yes or no, and needed time. "When?" she said.

"Today, tomorrow, whenever."

A vague answer. Its very vagueness disturbed her. She not only had to say yes or no, but even pick the day. Did she really want to get involved with this man? As a girl she had been supremely confident of her sex appeal, of her power over boys and then men. But her husband had rejected her, then Luc. For the time being she had little confidence left.

She saw that he waited anxiously for her reply. His uncertainty was pleasing.

"Okay," she said.

"Tomorrow, if it's a nice day?"

She nodded.

They shook hands as the French did when concluding a meeting, and walked away from each other toward their cars. Jack was limping less every day, Madeleine noted.

As she approached the boat Madeleine wore a denim skirt and a blue blouse that matched the color of her eyes. On her feet, espadrilles. Her dark brown hair was tied back at the base of her neck. She wore a floppy white tennis hat, and sunglasses, and she carried a picnic basket in one hand and a big handbag that contained a towel, along with everything else she might need.

Coming from a different direction, Jack carried a sack of groceries with a loaf of bread sticking out the top. Inside the sack were cheeses, rosé wine, and raw vegetables. They met at the boat and as she jumped down into it, it bounced. She reached up and took Jack's sack, and then his hand as he stepped gingerly aboard.

He started the engines. After casting off the lines, she jumped down into the cockpit a second time and they moved slowly out of their berth and out into the harbor and through the alley of other boats. Engine speed being low, the noise level was low too. It was still possible to talk.

"Are you a policeman?" Madeleine asked.

He looked startled. "A what?"

"A policeman?"

Already less startled: "What makes you ask that?"

"You look like one."

"How would you know what a policeman looks like?"

"I've known a few."

"American policemen?"

"No, but I don't think the nationality makes any difference. You act like one too."

"And how do policemen act?"

"Overbearing," she said. "If I had to put it in a single word."

"Overbearing?"

"There's a certain hardness in the voice, a certain aggressiveness of manner."

"Interesting," said Jack. He steered out the opening in the seawall. There were other boats nearby, and as yet not much room. He pushed the throttles half speed forward.

Madeleine had to speak louder. "Cops recognize each other immediately. I think homosexuals do too."

"Cops and gays," he said. "That's an interesting combination."

"You know what I mean. If you're a cop, any cop, it shows."

Jack looked thoughtful.

By now she was almost shouting. "So are you?"

He gave a mischievous grin. "I already told you, I'm a gangster." They were clear of the other boats. He pushed the throttles further and the boat lurched forward.

But she was satisfied that she had guessed right.

They went out along the coast of the cape and then around it, the sun now at their backs, Jack steering due west. They were alone between sea and sky, and she realized she was more interested in this man than ever. The wind pushed against her sunglasses. She held her hat down as far as her ears. She reveled in the wind and sun, the freedom of it.

"You've been shot," shouted Madeleine. Again she was guessing. "How did it happen?"

He told her the gist of it. He told it over the noise of the engines while the boat surged across the open sea between the Cap Ferrat and the Cap d'Antibes. He did not look at her as he spoke, and by foreshortening the hospital part and glossing over the pain and suffering, he made the shootout sound almost amusing. "In the middle of all this, my wife decides to divorce me."

"How could she, at such a time?"

"I guess I wasn't a very good husband."

He did not mention that he had been forced out of the department. Madeleine found out about all that only much later. Instead he pretended that the decision to resign had been his own.

"How many times were you hit?"

"I don't really know. Five, I think."

"Well," she said, "you lived."

"The doctors did a great job. Want to see my scars?"

"Not particularly, no."

But she got to see them anyway. He was wearing a yellow, open-necked tennis shirt and green boxer swim trunks, which he now peeled down to the beginning of his pubic hair. There were only two puncture holes left. The others had disappeared in the angry red welts left by the surgical stitching.

He gave the impression that sympathy was not what he wanted, so she refrained from giving any. "Nice," she said.

He pulled his trunks up. "One of the bullets hit me in the ear, but they fixed that. My ear looks okay, doesn't it?"

"Your ear looks grand."

"You don't seem too impressed."

"I've seen bullet wounds before."

"What were you, a nurse?"

She made no comment.

"Anyway, you're not a gangster," she shouted.

"No, but I am on the lam."

"The lam?" It was not a word that an au pair girl in England was likely to have learned.

He explained about the death threats that the department pretended were not serious even after the only other witness, the doorman, had been murdered. "Believe me," he shouted, "I'm safer here. Those Colombians come after you, you don't have much chance. They have all the money in the world, and they're vicious killers. They can buy you dead, or do it themselves, as they wish."

"Yes, I know. We have them here now too."

He turned to face her. "You seem to know a lot about all this."

"My ex-husband was a cop," Madeleine said, adding in a smaller voice that was almost inaudible over the noise: "I was a cop too."

Jack stared, a reaction that was oddly pleasing.

For the time being the conversation ended there. It had been a conversation only, nothing more, and part of it, once Jack had pushed the throttles forward, had had to be shouted over the noise. Nonetheless these were revelations that had been held back long enough on both sides that the sudden giving and receiving of them now constituted an intimacy somewhat akin to the taking off of one's clothes—not shameful, certainly, but deeply personal, and both of them realized it.

Considerable time passed during which neither spoke.

The water rushed by on both sides, and the hot wind blew, and they crossed in front of Nice in its bowl of hills. From out here the city looked small, which it wasn't. Steep green hills rose up all around it. They were clotted with villas, and with the newer apartment buildings, some of them very big, tiers and tiers of balconies all the way up. Behind the already high hills, tumbling backward as far as the eye could see, stood ranges and ranges of mountains, the highest ones with snow lying across the summits as if layered on by a cake knife.

"Do you like *pigeon aux lentilles?*" shouted Madeleine.

"What's that?"

"Pigeon with lentils," she explained.

He looked surprised.

She had it in an iron cocotte in her picnic basket, she told him. She would heat it up when they anchored.

"Pigeon?" he said.

Conversation had resumed, but it was hesitant, neutral, difficult to sustain, and not just because they had to talk loudly or shout above the noise. When she was a child and a picnic was planned, Madeleine told him, her mother always prepared hot dishes. Her parents would set up a table under a tree and dine on pigeon with lentils or something similar.

He laughed. A picnic to him was a couple of hot dogs, he said. This would be a first.

Again conversation lapsed.

They closed on the Cap d'Antibes, though keeping well offshore. This was the second of the great Riviera capes, a mile-long thumb of land jutting out into the sea. Extremely expensive real estate indeed, Madeleine said. Crouched amid the palm trees and umbrella pines were luxury villas, luxury hotels. Madeleine pointed out some of the more famous ones, and he nodded, and then neither spoke for a time.

Despite the awkwardness, there was now a closeness between them that had not been there before.

After clearing the cape they could see Cannes in the distance, with the two islands offshore half hidden in a heat haze, and they began to close on them. Between them was a channel, and Jack reduced speed and drove into it, and Madeleine clambered forward. As soon as the engines shut down and the boat had stopped moving she slung the anchor as far forward as she could, dragged in the line until she felt the hooks snag, then snubbed it off.

She stood on the prow, the boat rocking, and listened to the silence.

Both islands were heavily wooded. There were no other boats in the channel, and no buildings to be seen except for the ruins of a medieval fort. There was the slight noise made by the movement of the boat, that was all.

The near island had rocky edges and tiny beaches here and there. Madeleine knew both islands from her girlhood. They were national parks, she said. The bigger one, Sainte-Marguerite,

258

the one they were anchored closest to, was two miles long, about a thousand yards wide. On the far side of it, the side facing Cannes, there was a dock where the excursion boats landed, and a row of restaurants. The island at their backs, Saint-Honorat, was only about half as big. On its far side was a monastery with working monks who prayed a lot and also produced a liqueur called Lerina that they sold to the tourists.

"All the times my ship put in on this coast," Jack said, "I never came out to these islands." And then finally, unexpectedly, without skipping a beat: "So what kind of cop were you?"

It occurred to her that he had been wanting to ask this question for thirty minutes or more, but feared what her answer would be—that she had been a clerk-typist or something similar. This would have diminished her in his eyes.

She told him she had been a member of the Police Judiciaire, and there was considerable pride in her voice, even though she then had to explain what the PJ was, the five major brigades: Criminelle, Narcotics, Anti-gang, Grand Banditisme, and Finance. She went on to describe the Finance Brigade, how it worked, what it did.

"But you're out of the police now?"

"Yes, I left a while back."

"How long were you a cop?"

"Eleven years."

"How long were you a Finance cop?"

"Not long."

"How long ago did you leave?"

"Few weeks."

"Why'd you quit?"

She shrugged.

He waited for an answer, but none came. "Sounds like you were not really a cop," he said.

She was quick to take offense. "Not really a cop?"

"You were more like the FBI."

"I gather you don't like the FBI."

"They're not cops. They're pretty boys who don't get their hands dirty."

"Well," she said, "it's true the FBI was our corresponding agency whenever an American angle was involved."

"In any case, you weren't a street cop."

Again she bristled. "I'm sure my police experiences in no way match yours."

"You were an investigator," he said. He was looking off at the bigger island, she noted. It seemed to her he was talking to himself, was not even aware of her reaction. "Being on the street is something else."

"Something else?"

He didn't get the sarcasm this time either. "Well, you didn't risk getting shot, for instance."

Remembering the man on the motorcycle, she thought: there could be a bullet with my name on it even now.

"You didn't deal with slime."

She thought: the mayor of Nice is not slime? Bruno Sestri is not slime?

She said: "This conversation is ridiculous. I'm going swimming."

Standing up, she stepped out of her shoes, shucked off her skirt and blouse, and stood for a moment barefoot in the bikini she had worn underneath. There was none of the usual shyness about displaying the flaws of her flesh. She was so annoyed at him she didn't care what he thought of her body, or of her.

Jumping up onto the gunwale she plunged over the side. The water seemed to her lukewarm, it was so clear she could see the bottom, and she began swimming toward a tiny beach between big rocks.

When she got close she saw that the bottom was studded with other big rocks and she stood up and waded carefully ashore. It was then she realized that Jack was coming out of the water behind her. She stood and shook the water out of her hair, out of her ears.

"I'm sorry if I offended you back there," said Jack.

She said nothing.

"All I meant was that there are different kinds of cops, and you were one kind and I was another."

Madeleine was swiping at the water on her arms, her stomach.

"When I was a little boy," Jack said, "I had a grandmother who was a Protestant of some kind. I told her she wasn't a Catholic. She certainly was a Christian, she said. But she wasn't a Catholic, I said. She certainly was a Christian, she insisted. I kept saying she wasn't a Catholic until finally she burst into tears."

Madeleine was hopping on one foot trying to clear an ear.

"It was a semantic problem," Jack said. "I didn't mean to offend her. Or you."

He was studying her, Madeleine saw, trying to perceive her reaction to his little story, her reaction to him.

She did not reply, was careful to give no reaction of any kind.

Instead she said: "I'm going to lie in the sun for a while. Will it bother you if I remove my top?"

"No, no," said Jack, though he sounded suddenly shocked. "Whatever you want."

So she did. She sat down, unhooked it, placed it beside her, and then lay down. It was, she told herself, a way of showing her annoyance, neither more nor less. It was a way of showing this man that he meant nothing to her.

Jack, she saw, did not know where to look, what to do with his eyes. It was almost amusing.

She lay out on the sand and felt the sun on her and closed her eyes. Topless sunbathing, to a Frenchman, would have had no significance—it was practiced on every beach in France. But it was not done in America and Jack Dilger had not seen much of it, perhaps not any, and Madeleine knew this. The stripping off of her bra became, therefore, an intimate act. And although she could deny the fact, she knew this too.

"Aren't you going to talk to me anymore?" he said.

She opened one eye and regarded him. "You're pretty white,"

she said. He was skinny too. He must have lost a lot of weight. "You could do with a little sun, I think."

"I've never liked lying on beaches much."

With her eyes closed she could hear him bouncing around in the shallow water, and then, not hearing him for a time, she looked and saw he had swum back to the boat. A little later she heard him coming toward the beach again and saw he was swimming one-handed, while holding a tray above the water with the other. On the tray stood a bottle of rosé in an ice bucket, plus two of the practical, short-stemmed wineglasses that were used on shipboard.

He came ashore carrying the tray above his head like a waiter. He said: "Would Madame like a glass of wine?"

Despite herself Madeleine found this gesture charming. She sat up and put her bra back on, then accepted the glass he held out to her. As they touched glasses she found herself smiling.

"Cheers," she said.

A little later they swam back to the boat. Madeleine dried herself off, then went below and put on dry underwear out of her handbag and put her clothes back on, and dragged a thick comb through her hair. After that she stood in the cabin at the small galley stove and reheated the *pigeon aux lentilles*, and then served it. They ate at a fold-up table in the cockpit, and finished the rosé and started on a second bottle Jack got out of his small fridge.

Later he inflated his dinghy and they went ashore and went for a walk under the trees. There were many paths crisscrossing and benches here and there on which Jack rested from time to time. They walked much of the island breathing in the scent of pine resin all the way, then found one of the restaurants on the far side and sat down and ordered tea, which was served with an assortment of pastries. Jack kept staring at her, which she liked. She knew she looked fresh-faced and healthy.

The afternoon grew late. They returned to the far side of the island, paddled out to the boat, and Jack started the engines while she stood on the prow and hauled up the anchor. Then they headed back to Beaulieu.

It took them almost two hours to get back. When they had docked and stood together on the quay, Jack said: "I don't see the guy on the motorcycle."

Madeleine had looked for him too—for any suspicious-looking man standing around.

"Did you arrest anybody lately who might be looking to do you harm?" Jack asked her.

"Maybe," she said. "I don't know."

"In general, white-collar criminals are not violent."

"No."

"It depends who, of course. And how much you have hurt them."

Or are continuing to hurt them, Madeleine thought.

"So who did you hurt?"

"Could be anybody," she said.

She had a desire to tell Jack about the Sestri case, and what had happened to it and to her. She wanted to tell him about Nice's crooked mayor, and about the speeches and interviews she continued to give, keeping the pressure on Bruno Sestri and on the mayor and his men, as best she could. But she told him nothing. She was afraid he wouldn't understand, or would belittle the case, or belittle her. Or even worse, begin to worry about her. She didn't want him to worry about her, and yet she did. She didn't know what she felt. She was thoroughly confused, so she shook hands with him and walked away down the wide empty quay carrying her handbag in one hand and her picnic basket in the other. The picnic basket was still heavy. It held the empty iron cocotte that had contained the *pigeon aux lentilles*, and also the wet bikini that had contained her.

"Remember to lock your door," Jack called after her.

≡ CHAPTER 12 ≡

The Beaulieu post office is small, a single high counter, usually with only two clerks behind it. Since post offices are also savings banks in France, the entire counter is fronted with bulletproof glass. Slots in the glass allow money, stamps, and letters to be passed back and forth, and there is a cylindrical turntable for packages.

One day a man stepped up to the *poste restante* window and asked for Jack's mail. When the clerk, a woman, requested identification the man explained in a thick Corsican accent that he was trying to pick up mail for a friend who was sick.

The woman wouldn't give it to him.

The man then retreated to the railroad station across the street, where he took up position in the parking area, leaning against the balustrade. A black and white photograph was taped inside the newspaper he was pretending to read, and he watched the door of the post office, taking note of everyone who went in or out. He stayed there during business hours for three days, except from noon to two when the post office was closed for lunch.

※　　　※　　　※

As New York law required, Jack Dilger had carried a gun every waking moment on and off duty for twelve years. When he got dressed in the morning he would put on his watch and put on his gun. He would no more have gone out without it than he would have gone out without combing his hair.

But now as he drove through the streets toward the Beaulieu post office, he was of course unarmed. Gunless, he missed its weight. It was not on his hip where it was supposed to be, which in a physical sense made him feel slightly off balance. A dozen times a day he patted himself and was momentarily surprised to find nothing there.

In an emotional sense he missed being armed just as much. Although most cops took their guns with them into retirement, some did not, knowing that for one calendar year afterward, they could get them back just by asking. Once the year had elapsed, however, there were formalities, and they were strict. To get a permit to carry was a long and difficult process, even for an ex-cop. New York's gun control laws were among the strictest in the world.

Jack had known men who retired saying they were glad to get rid of their guns, but the withdrawal symptoms became too great for most of them. Before the year was up they were back in headquarters reneging on what were probably promises to their wives, asking for their guns back, sheepishly filling out all the forms.

Of course Jack himself had not had the option. And here in France he could not legally have carried a gun anyway.

His current discomfort had nothing to do with personal security. No doubt Victoriano Zaragon would like to have him killed, but he would have to find him first, and this, to Jack, seemed unlikely. His personal security could not be better, he believed. No one knew he was here, no one could find him here, and the chances of anyone even looking for him here were infinitesimal. In Beaulieu or Nice or any of the surrounding towns he was as close to anonymous as one could get. Only Madeleine and her brother on this side of the Atlantic even knew his name.

He supposed he would get used to walking about unarmed eventually.

But it was not true that no one knew his name or where he was. Although determined to reveal his whereabouts to no one, there had had to be one exception, and then a second exception, and then after that one or two more.

As soon as he had rented the boat and moved his few belongings on board he had gone to the post office where the public phones were, and he had telephoned the pension section on the tenth floor of police headquarters in New York. He would not last long here without his pension checks, and now he changed the address to which he wanted them sent. His new address, he told the detective who answered, was: *poste restante*, Beaulieu-sur-Mer, France. He made the detective spell the words back to him.

"What's *poste restante* mean?" the detective wanted to know.

General delivery, Jack told him, and rang off. This address was vague enough, Jack reasoned, and he could count on the police department not to divulge it to unauthorized persons. In any case he had had no choice.

On a practical level, however, it was an address to which almost any cop had access. All it took was a visit to the pension section, where the cop could claim to be a friend wanting to contact the retiree. And there were at present more than thirty thousand cops.

Next Jack had phoned Flora.

Gradually he had come to terms with the idea of divorce. She didn't want him, that was that. There was nothing he could do about it from here. He still missed her, but he told himself he had started on a new life, had made a clean break with the past.

He phoned her now because—again—he had no choice. His few pieces of furniture had to be emptied out of their former apartment, his bills had to be paid.

As he dialed her number he realized that he wanted to hear how she sounded. But he cautioned himself not to expect too much, and that if he valued his security he should not give her even a hint of where he was.

When she came on the line he told her what he wanted her to do: put his furniture in storage and pay his bills. When next he called, he told her, she could inform him how much he owed her, and he would send a check. These were pretty big favors to ask, he admitted, hoping she would say they were not. But he was on the run and hiding out.

"Hiding out from me?" she said.

"No, of course not."

"Hiding out from someone. Why?"

Because he feared for his life, he told her.

It was the wrong thing to say to this particular woman, for now he had to spend ten minutes calming her down. He was absolutely safe in this place where he was, he assured her.

"How can you be positive?" she said. She was almost in tears. "You can't be positive, can you? Where are you?"

It was nice that she wanted so badly to know, it warmed him, so in the end he let her worm it out of him.

"What's *poste restante* mean?" she demanded.

At least her tears had dried, and presently he was able to hang up.

His checks came into the Beaulieu post office once a month and then had to be deposited in a bank, for it took them two weeks to clear. This meant he had had to open an account, and the banker with whom he dealt had made him show his passport. Nor would the banker accept *poste restante* as an address; Jack was obliged to give the name and quay number of his boat. So that was a third breach in his security.

He had rented a small car and of course had had to show his driver's license, passport, and credit card.

One can try to move without leaving tracks, but in modern life it is impossible. Jack had moved with utmost care.

Nonetheless, his tracks were everywhere. A corrupt or unsuspecting cop might furnish his address, either for money or as a favor. Or Flora might let it slip in conversation. Or a person with influence or money could cause a computer search of Riviera car rental companies, or of depositors in the five or six biggest Riviera banks. For a determined man to find him was no great trick.

But as he drove toward the post office that particular day Jack felt good. This was a time for healing. After what he had been through he did not mind living alone. There was less pain every day. The scars across his abdomen no longer tugged at him the way they had. His hip no longer hurt, except when it rained. He no longer limped except when tired. The weight he had lost was coming back. He was still bothered by constipation, but that seemed to be improving too.

On the minus side, he lived in a cramped space that never stopped moving, and he could say he didn't mind this, but he did. He had barely enough money. He did not speak the language and did not understand what people said to him. Any encounter with anyone was uncomfortable for him.

How he would feel about staying here once Zaragon was in custody, once all his strength came back, he did not know. In truth he was thinking no further ahead than the next few weeks.

He enjoyed being with Madeleine, whenever she would permit it, and one of the reasons was she spoke English and he could talk to her. They had shared other short voyages after the first one, other picnics, and now she no longer sunbathed topless, if that meant anything. She was as wary as a bird. He had not even touched her as yet, except to shake hands, or to pull her out of the water onto the boat. She was the wariest bird he had ever met. He was afraid if he touched her he'd scare her away. He wondered what she felt about him. He wondered what he felt about her, and what would or would not happen between them.

He turned into the railroad station, parked, got stiffly out of his car, and walked across the street to the post office. He was not at all on his guard. There was a man leaning against the balustrade reading his newspaper, but Jack never noticed him, though he passed less than ten feet away. He went into the post office and was there almost ten minutes, for other people were ahead of him in line. When he came out he was tearing open the pension envelope and pulling out his check.

By then the man with the newspaper had moved, was on the same sidewalk as Jack and pretending to stare into a shop window. Jack's thoughts as he studied his check were forty-five hundred miles away and he didn't notice him this time either.

From the post office Jack walked up to the Place De Gaulle, where there were women with baby carriages sitting on benches under the trees, and then along the Boulevard Marinoni to his bank, where he deposited his check. He then continued along the same street to the storefront studio where he was having a sign made. The sign was ready, and Jack paid for it. Almost three feet square, it read:

JACK'S CRUISES

Day Trips

See Italy, the Islands

SIGHTSEEING—PICNICS—SNORKELING

The signpainter wrapped it up, sealed it with movers' tape, and Jack carried it to his car. Hanging well back, the man with the newspaper had followed him this far, and now as Jack drove out of the railroad station the man moved to a nearby motor scooter, kicked it to life, and followed. At the yacht harbor he parked the scooter and sat down at one of the cafés. So far, all his actions had looked quite normal. Jack, who was really much better at perceiving threats to other people, Madeleine for instance, than to himself, still hadn't consciously noticed him.

As he struggled to get his sign out of the back of his car he saw Madeleine drive up and park. He stood with the wind blowing the sign against his hip and watched her coming toward him carrying a small suitcase.

He was glad to see her and supposed this showed on his face, and when she was close enough, taking a chance, he put his hands on her shoulders and kissed her on both cheeks the way the French did. He wasn't very sure of himself but thought: I'm just being friendly, she can't object to that, can she?

"Where have you been?" he asked her.

"In Lyon making a speech."

"What about?"

"Oh, just telling old war stories."

The man in the café had his newspaper out again. He seemed to be paying no attention to them, so they paid no attention to him.

"What's in the package?"

He tore off the paper and showed her.

"Maybe it'll work," she said.

"But you don't think so?"

She laughed. "We'll soon see."

She walked him out to his boat, where he propped up his sign, after which he offered her a coffee or an aperitif.

"Tea, maybe," she said.

He took her suitcase and they walked over and sat down at the same café as the man with the newspaper. This time Jack did notice him, and in a low voice in English called Madeleine's attention to him.

"Know him?"

"No. Why?"

"I've seen him around."

Madeleine said nothing, merely stared into her tea.

"I've seen him around too often."

The man with the newspaper folded it, left money on the table, and left the café. He was strolling up the quay in the direction of Jack's boat, which would be identified now by the hand-painted sign.

"Where have you seen him?"

"I don't know exactly." In fact he had noticed him outside the post office but didn't realize it.

Jack was having a physical reaction, not an intellectual one. He said: "You better tell me why you're not a policewoman anymore. And what these speeches are that you do."

He was convinced no one could have found him here. Therefore the threat, if it was a threat, must be against Madeleine.

So she told him.

When she finished he was silent for a time. Then he said: "If the mayor of a city like this is a crook, he can't be a crook all by himself. To stay in power he has to share the wealth. There have to be bagmen, front men, intermediaries, arrangers. There have to be bribes and kickbacks of all sorts."

Though obviously shaken, Madeleine tried a joke: "You sound just like a cynical cop."

"The whole administration has to be crooked," Jack said, "and you are out there in plain view making speeches, making headlines, trying to bring it down. Do you realize how many lives and livelihoods you have put at risk? How many people want to shut you up? Permanently, maybe."

"I can't see one of those guys pulling a trigger."

"So they hire somebody."

"The mayor wouldn't dare try anything."

"It doesn't have to be the mayor. It could be any of the people around him."

"Kill an officer of the Police Judiciaire?"

"That no longer describes you."

Madeleine was silent.

"You're not protected anymore, are you?" The way I'd do it, Jack thought, I'd make her disappear. Wire her to something heavy and drop her overboard. It would be weeks before it was certain she was missing and an investigation even started. The trail would be ice-cold.

"It's a big sea out there," he said.

Madeleine gave a slight shiver, and he saw that she understood him. She said: "So what should I do?"

"Are you armed?"

"They took my gun away."

"Could you get it back?"

She shook her head.

"Could you get me one?"

"No."

"You could go back to your ex-boss and ask for protection."

"Go begging to the Police Judiciaire?" said Madeleine.
"Absolutely not."

They looked at each other. Presently Jack paid, and walked
her back toward her room. When they reached the door in the
side of the warehouse she took her suitcase from him, then put
her face up to be kissed on both cheeks.

She looked so vulnerable that he wanted to grab her and kiss
her good, but he didn't do it. Instead his lips brushed her face
twice, once on each side. That much has been gained today at
least, he thought grimly.

"I'll wait down here until I see you in the window," he said.

She nodded and went into the building.

When he started back to his boat he looked for the man with
the newspaper, but did not see him. If he had seen him, what?
In New York, confident of his strength, his authority, he would
have demanded ID, demanded an explanation, perhaps thrown
the man up against the nearest wall and searched him, even
shoved him into the back of the car and dragged him into the
station house for questioning. But he wasn't strong enough now
to do it—he had lost thirty pounds and had gained back only
about half of it so far—and of course he had no authority here.

No gun either.

He thought he knew what it felt like to be emasculated.

The man with the newspaper rode the *rapide* to Marseilles,
where he took a taxi to the Café de l'Amitie on the Rue de

Récollettes. He went in past the bar. The owner sat at a table in the back, together with a number of other men. He addressed the owner as *patron* and made his report, after which the owner handed him an envelope. He should have just shoved the envelope into his pocket, but could not keep himself from lifting the flap and taking a peek. The envelope was full of hundred-franc notes.

"Go count it at the bar," said the owner sourly.

The man went to the bar, where he ordered a glass of red wine. He wanted to count the money, but when he saw the owner watching him, did not dare do so. Instead he ostentatiously put the envelope in his inside coat pocket, drained his glass, and went out.

Behind him the owner searched through his pockets for a telephone number written on a slip of paper, then handed it to one of his men. Because he assumed that all of his telephones were tapped by the police, the owner never made phone calls himself. "Tell whoever answers that the party in question has been located."

The other man was looking down at the number. "This is an overseas call, *patron.*"

"Really?" said the owner. "Imagine that."

The phone was attached to the wall behind them. The man was dialing the number.

"If he wants us to do anything," the owner said, "write down what he tells you."

It was early morning, sunny, no wind. It had rained in the night and the air was bathed clean. The sun was still low. The towering cliffs above Beaulieu stood out sharply, every color, every detail clear. The air smelled faintly of the sea, and more strongly of the coffee being brewed in the nearby row of cafés. Jack on his boat was on his stomach on the prow, his head hanging over the edge, scrubbing scum off the hull as far down as he could reach, when a man he had not seen before hailed him from the quay. The man was pointing to Jack's sign.

Jack came off the boat rubbing his hands dry on a length of paper towel.

The man's English was atrocious. Jack understood him to say he wanted to go to Corsica.

Jack was ready to take passengers along the coast in either direction, or to any of the nearby islands. But Corsica was straight out. One would be out of sight of land a long time, and in such a small boat, if the weather turned bad, it could be dangerous.

"Take a ship," Jack told him. "They have ships every day."

The company was on strike, the man said, and he took the *Nice Matin* out from under his arm and showed Jack the story.

Jack, who got all his information from the *Paris Herald Tribune*, never read the local paper. For him the *Nice Matin* was hard going. But there it was, easily translated from the French: FERRY SERVICE STOPPED.

"Take a plane," Jack said. "It's under an hour."

The man made a speech. It was mostly in French, with English words mixed in. Jack understood almost none of it. He did understand that the planes were overbooked and that the man had to be in Corsica tonight.

Jack took the newspaper from him and opened to the weather page. The forecast was at the bottom: not only the details written out, but also a map of France in color with tiny suns or black clouds over the major cities. There was a sun over Nice, and another over Corsica. So the weather looked all right.

"It'll take six or seven hours," Jack said.

The man said he knew this, but they must start at once.

"It will be expensive," Jack said. "I'll have to come back empty." And named what he considered an exorbitant sum.

The man said yes to this too.

"Half now, half when we land," Jack said cautiously.

The man pulled a roll out of his pocket and began counting out hundred-franc notes.

Folding the money, Jack put it in his pocket. He was curious about Corsica, and not at all about this man, whose story sounded reasonable to him so far. In New York a detective would have been asking himself many questions by now, some of them cynical ones. But Jack was in a country not his own that he did not entirely understand, and he was not a detective here. Corsica wasn't that far. He had been meaning to sail over there someday. Why not today, all expenses paid? Maybe Madeleine would come with him. They could make an outing of it. He had no navigation gear on board, but an island that big shouldn't be hard to find.

Having told the man to come back in an hour, he drove the boat over to the pump and filled the tanks. He filled the water reservoir too and bought charts for northern Corsica and for the harbor at Bastia, which was where the passenger wished to land.

He found Madeleine with her brother in his office. She was wearing jeans and a green polo shirt. Her hair was pulled back in a ponytail. She looked tall and slim and about eighteen years old. The French shook hands with each other every day—by now Jack knew this, but he still had trouble accepting it. So that was the first thing he had to do, shake hands with both of them—no kisses in public yet, apparently. Only then could he invite her to sail to Corsica with him.

"Corsica?" said Madeleine, hesitating. "When?"

"Twenty minutes from now. I've got a paying passenger."

"Who is he?" Madeleine wanted to know.

Perhaps Jack had expected a glad smile. All he had seen so far was a frown.

"Just a guy." He explained about the ferry strike. "We have to leave in about twenty minutes."

"I don't know," Madeleine said.

"We can sail over today, stay overnight, and come back tomorrow."

She looked to her brother and he shrugged.

"What about the weather?"

"The forecast is good."

If the weather kicked up it would be a long bumpy ride. Perhaps all she was considering was how arduous the trip could prove to be.

"Get your things."

Despite himself he had been in a state of some excitement. The idea of a day with her, the trip itself, the amount of money already in his pocket—all this had excited him, though by now it was leaking away. He wanted her to want to come with him.

"I have to go buy some groceries," he said. "The boat's at the pumps. If you want to come, get your things." And he left before she could say no.

Twenty minutes later, as he came up the quay carrying the groceries, again with the loaves of bread sticking out of the bag, she was not there beside the boat. It made him bite down on his lip.

The passenger was there, however. He was pacing impatiently. "*Allez, on part,*" he said, and jumped down into the cockpit.

Jack understood this. Shove off, it meant. Let's go. Something of that nature. But he took his time stowing the groceries. He came out of the cabin and fiddled with the controls. He kept gazing back up the quay, hoping Madeleine would appear, and suddenly she rounded the corner and he saw her.

The passenger had thrown off the lines and the boat was drifting away from the quay. He too appeared to have noticed Madeleine.

"*Allez, allez,*" he said again.

"Have to wait for my friend," said Jack, now wearing a happy smile.

The man began some sort of angry statement. Jack understood the meaning well enough: the guy didn't want Madeleine aboard.

"Tough, pal, she's coming," Jack told him.

More angry remarks from the passenger. Reaching up, Jack took Madeleine's hand as she jumped down into the boat.

She had a small bag. The passenger was standing beside a big one. Jack stowed both bags below. The passenger also had an attaché case, but he held on to that.

He was muttering darkly.

"What's he saying?" Jack demanded.

"He doesn't want me on board. He says he hired the boat. He decides who comes along. He says to give him his money back."

"He's bluffing," said Jack.

"Look, I don't have to come."

"Tell him you're my girlfriend," said Jack.

It made Madeleine smile. "I never tell lies," she said.

"Tell him I go nowhere without my girlfriend."

A half smile on her face, Madeleine said something to the man.

"I'm afraid he's adamant," she told Jack.

"Tell him to go screw himself," said Jack. He turned the key and the engines came to life.

"He says to give him his money back," said Madeleine.

Jack looked at the man a moment, then took the folded wad from his pocket and held it out.

The man stared at it a moment, then turned away.

"That's what I thought," said Jack, and he steered out through the aisle of moored boats into a second aisle of moored boats, this one somewhat wider. At the end of it was the gap in the seawall.

They came onto the vast expanse of the sea but did not feel its vastness yet. The continent of Europe, which seemed vaster still, was in plain view at their backs.

Jack stood at the wheel, hand on the throttles, with Madeleine beside him. Both wore sunglasses and squinted against the glare. The passenger sat on the banquette astern, looking angry, holding his attaché case with both hands.

"What do you make of him?" asked Jack above the noise.

"He has a Corsican accent."

"Is that significant?"

277

"Most of French organized crime is Corsican."

Jack looked at her.

"When you hear that accent you think about it," said Madeleine.

"Cops do, you mean."

"Yes, cops."

"What's his big hurry to get to Corsica?"

"He says he has to go to a funeral."

"Whose?"

Madeleine shrugged.

The Riviera towns were visible still, and the boat surged smoothly forward. Except for a slight swell, the surface was like dark blue glass into which the prow cut a perfect white V. There was no wind, no spray, and the sun was shining, though it had grown somewhat fainter. The tanks were full, both engines were running smoothly. So what could go wrong?

Jack was happy enough to look back at the passenger and throw him a smile. "Why do you think he didn't want you aboard?" he said to Madeleine.

"He wanted to be alone with you," Madeleine said.

The man's behavior seemed curious, no more. As Jack saw it, there was no way the passenger could constitute a threat to anonymous Jack Dilger, nor to Madeleine either, since he not only hadn't expected her, but didn't want her on board when she appeared. The chances were he was what he pretended to be, a businessman anxious to get home to Corsica. A funeral was as good a reason as any to be in a hurry.

Jack had the chart spread out on the dashboard. He glanced from it to the compass and back again. A course of 120 degrees should raise Cap Corse, where the chart said there were rocky islands, but also a lighthouse. That should take about five hours, maybe less. From there he could follow the east coast down to Bastia.

When he glanced around he saw that the towns behind him had already disappeared, even the biggest of them, which was

Nice, but the reassuring mountains were still there. They would disappear in time, but by then Corsica should begin to rise up out of the sea, for it had its own mountains, which, though lower than the Maritime Alps, were substantial. Probably it was too late in the year for them to have snow on them, but they might.

The day began to cloud over.

Madeleine went below to prepare lunch, slicing the long loaves down the middle, lathering on the mustard, laying out the thin slices of red Parma ham. When she came topside she saw that the entire sky was gray. She was carrying the sandwiches and glasses on a tray in one hand and an unopened bottle of wine in the other. After handing the bottle to the passenger, she dropped the folding table in front of the banquette and put her tray down. Having taken the bottle back, she pulled the cork and poured. The passenger started in on his sandwich at once, while she carried a glass of wine forward to Jack.

By then the Riviera coast could not be seen at all, and the sea was getting choppy.

"What happened to your nice weather forecast?" said Madeleine.

Jack sipped his wine and peered all around at the sky. "We're all right," he said shortly.

By the time he had finished his sandwich there were big swells passing underneath them, and the boat had begun to feel unsteady. On the surface, whitecaps began to be seen. Holding the wheel with both hands, Jack was having some difficulty keeping on course. Beside him Madeleine balanced herself by grasping the top of the windscreen. Above was a very dark sky, but the sky they were driving toward was darker still.

A little later they were in a fine mist, and the boat had begun to pitch and yaw. Leaving Madeleine at the wheel, Jack scurried about putting the canopy in place, clipping on the isinglass side curtains.

The mist soon changed to rain, a light drizzle at first, then increasingly hard.

The passenger had come forward out of the rain. He stood at Jack's elbow, and he did not look well.

"How you know where you go?" he said in English.

Jack nodded in the direction of the compass.

The man was clutching his attaché case and looking pasty. Turning, he spoke to Madeleine.

"He wants to know how long this is going to last."

"Your guess is as good as mine, pal," Jack told him. To Madeleine he said: "Any minute he's going to be sick. Better show him where the head is."

Madeleine led the passenger below. She was gone for some time.

"He's on his knees in there vomiting," she shouted when she came back.

"Weather like this is not good for repeat business," said Jack.

"I tried to help him, poor guy. He won't let go of that attaché case."

"What he's got in it, do you suppose?"

A rhetorical question. Jack was concentrating too hard on holding the boat on course to wait for an answer.

The rain drummed on the canvas roof. The sea was covered with white froth into which the rain beat like bullets. The sky had gotten very low, very black.

"Are you all right?" Jack asked Madeleine.

"I'm fine."

The wind came in gusts of increasing violence, slapping against the boat, against the curtains. It drove the rain through the seams and gaps and before long both were drenched. The wind seemed to be mostly in front, pushing them sideways, pushing them back. It threatened to split open the curtains as well. Almost certainly it was pushing them far off course, and although Jack tried to compensate, he had no way to measure its force or to know what the sea was doing. The horizon had completely disappeared. They were driving into a gray void.

The sea got steadily more turbulent. The waves were three feet high, then six. The boat felt like something that was being beaten to death. Jack had had to throttle way back. He was trying to meet the biggest waves head-on. It meant frequent turns off course, which he didn't like, but the alternative was to risk being swamped. Madeleine stood beside him, hanging on. There was so much noise they couldn't talk; even shouts could barely be heard. It took nearly all their strength just to hang on, just to keep from being thrown about.

It occurred to Jack that in a storm like this they could miss Corsica entirely. If the storm held and they missed it, the next land was Africa. There was another alternative he chewed on for a while. The Corsican coast was rocky nearly everywhere. Suppose, instead of missing Corsica, they met it head-on. They could pile up on rocks before they ever saw them.

Or collide with some other vessel; there could be other vessels out here too.

There was no radio phone aboard, no radar. Jack had never imagined a situation in which he might need a phone or radar, and he had not had enough money to equip the boat with either. He did have a radio direction finder he had bought a week ago but had not yet tried out. It was stashed under one of the bunks below. He was not even sure how it worked. Leaving Madeleine at the helm, bracing himself on whatever came to hand, he went down the three steps into the cabin to get it.

He found the passenger on his knees retching onto the floor between the bunks. He had evidently fallen into his own vomit once or twice. The door to the head kept banging back and forth, first open, then shut. There was vomit on the floor in there too. Jack closed it. In one hand the passenger held a flask of cognac. It was his own, for Jack had none aboard—it must have come out of the attaché case, which lay on the bunk behind him. Jack supposed he was trying to get drunk, which was no specific for seasickness.

"It won't work, pal," Jack muttered. The cabin reeked of vomit. Jack was furious, but for the moment could do nothing, and he had to get out into the air quick before he started retching himself. Reaching under the bunk, he grabbed his direction finder and bolted.

The DF had suction cups underneath. Jack clapped it onto the dashboard and turned it to the Bastia frequency marked on his chart, then turned the antenna until he got the strong *beep-beep* he was looking for. But it was many degrees off the compass course he had been trying to hold.

If the signal was accurate, and if the compass was accurate, they were being swept far to the west. The possibility of missing Corsica altogether had become real. He steered as best he could in the direction of the radio signal, but for minutes at a time it disappeared. Each time he lost it he began twisting the dial trying to find it again. Each time the strong *beep-beep* resumed Madeleine gave him a weak smile.

Waves spilled across the gunwales. At times they stood in water up to their ankles. At any moment seawater could leak through and short out the engines, and if this happened the seas would hit them broadside and they would be swamped. Madeleine, who knew boats, gave him a worried laugh. She was scared now. He saw this. He was scared himself. She must be exhausted just from hanging on, but did not complain, and she kept her fear to herself.

The direction signal was gone again. This time it was gone ten minutes or more. When Jack found it finally he could barely hear it over the noise, and wasn't sure it was the right one. Patting him on the back, Madeleine flashed him a weak grin. Since they could converse only by shouting, he gave her arm what he hoped was a reassuring squeeze, but just then the boat bounded sideways and for a moment they clung to each other for balance.

When the boat steadied, the embrace lingered a moment on both sides, before he let her go again.

There had been crashes of lightning for some time, but so distant they were only dimly seen, dimly heard. Now bolts of electricity suddenly split open the sky all around them. Sparks danced and crackled in the eyelets in the curtains, as if trying to start fires. The thunder was so loud and so near that it seemed to be inside the boat, and it boomed again and again. The lightning too was everywhere, each bolt igniting the bow wave, the interior of the cabin—igniting Madeleine's frightened wet face as well. Her hair hung in rattails, and when she tried to smile her eye teeth showed.

"Nothing to worry about," Jack shouted.

"I'm not worried," Madeleine shouted back.

Jack had been in bad storms before; once his ship had sailed into the edge of a hurricane. That had been a storm of monumental dimensions. Even a ship as big as a cruiser pitched and yawed, and only three sailors, one of them Jack, turned up in the mess all that day. But that experience bore no relation to this one. Someone else was captain then, not him. Now he tried to hang on to the wheel as the tiny boat bounced all over the sea, tried to keep his footing, tried to keep a course and at the same time turn into each of the monstrous waves that bore down on them. And all this time the lightning threatened to fry them. Was he scared? He knew he was, but he had too much to do to focus on fear, and that included Madeleine's.

"We'll be out of this in a minute," he shouted.

"I know."

"Five minutes at the most."

She nodded. She looked too scared to speak.

There came another peal of thunder. Branches of lightning appeared all over the sky. The small flagpole aft was struck and set ablaze. The entire length of it was on fire.

"Grab the wheel," Jack shouted, and he ran back and beat at the flames with a wet towel. As he beat the fire out the boat dove into a trough and he nearly went overboard.

He jumped back for the wheel and ordered Madeleine to go below and put on a life jacket. She came back with one for him too, and he struggled to squirm into it while still trying to steer the boat.

The wind-driven rain beat against them like nails. The seas were tumultuous, the boat riding high one moment, then plunging, its propellers giving their high-pitched whine as they churned air. Jack, still fighting the wheel, had no idea where they were, and he had become seriously worried about fuel. In this wind, these seas, the boat had used up much more than he had budgeted. There was a reserve, but they were into it, the needle still going down.

The six-hour crossing went into its ninth hour with Corsica not yet in sight. Nothing was in sight, not even the horizon. Jack was not going to see any Corsican mountains rising up out of the sea. Had he missed the huge island altogether? Even if it was still ahead, they could run out of fuel before they got there. Would the sky lift a little? He willed it to. Would he see something soon? The boat continued to rise, plunge, then rise again, propellers screaming. Occasionally he lost control, got broadside to the seas, and a deluge came aboard, while the boat wallowed sickeningly. The rain continued to beat at the canvas, beating its way inside. Jack was soaked, they both were, his arms and legs ached with fatigue, and his scarred hip and abdomen felt on fire.

"I think it's lessening," Jack shouted. He said this mostly to encourage Madeleine, but then realized it was true. The lightning still came. It was still close, still frightening, but now there were gaps, and then finally it seemed to flicker, then dim, then stop.

They waited for more in what sounded like silence, though the rest of the storm was as loud as ever. But no more lightning came.

All this time the passenger never reappeared on deck. Madeleine, who looked in on him, shouted that he was stretched out on one of the bunks asleep.

"More like a drunken stupor," Jack shouted back.

It was evening. They should have been tied up at Bastia by three in the afternoon.

About an hour later the rain finally slackened. The sky brightened somewhat. Because the seas remained high, and also to conserve whatever fuel remained, Jack continued to run at half speed.

And an hour after that he perceived far in the distance the beam of a lighthouse—its dim, intermittent sweep. He focused on that spot on the horizon for some minutes, watching for the light to sweep around again and then still again just to be sure it was not a mirage.

"Well," he said to Madeleine, "that's a relief."

He realized she too had been holding her breath.

"Yes," was all she said.

All of the tension went out of both of them, and they looked at each other and began to laugh. For some minutes they giggled like children.

But which lighthouse? Was it some outlying islet? Behind it Jack could see no lights of a town. He searched his sopping-wet chart for lighthouses and became convinced he was closing on L'Ile Rousse, which was supposed to be guarded by red granite islands. Definitely islands ahead. In this light and at this distance it was impossible to discern their color. As the lighthouse came closer the dim glow of a town appeared behind it, and he concluded that he was approaching L'Ile Rousse for sure. It was not where he wanted to be. They must have sailed all the way down the west coast of Cap Corse without ever seeing it. Bastia was on the other side of the cape over the mountains.

"Go wake up our friend," Jack suggested. Inside the outlying islands they had come into a place of relative calm.

She came back a few minutes later shaking her head. "It's a mess down there."

As they neared the entrance to the harbor, although the boat still pitched in seas far heavier than normal, Madeleine went below and began to clean up. He saw her with a roll of paper towels sopping up the mess on the floor of the head. Then she went to work on the cabin floor.

When she came topside she had the used paper towels in a plastic bucket. The passenger came up behind her. He was swiping at his face and clothes with a wet cloth, and he peered drunkenly at the moored boats all around them.

"Thish not Bastia," he said thickly.

"I'll make an adjustment on the price," said Jack. "Give me half of what you still owe me."

"Too much."

"Half," said Jack, "or I'll take you out to sea again." He laughed. The fear was over and he was giddy with relief and exhaustion. "Tell him that, Maddie. Threaten him good."

After talking to him, Madeleine said: "He says he'll write you a check."

"Okay," said Jack. He no longer cared about the money. All he really wanted was to stand on dry land again. This, he imagined, was all any of them wanted.

As they tied up to a dock a customs guard came out and stood above them and asked to see their identity cards. Jack, who had none, handed up his passport, then lifted the passenger's suitcase up onto the quay. The guard was looking over their papers. Jack lifted out Madeleine's bag, then the bucket of used towels.

The guard handed back the two identity cards and the passport. The passenger handed Jack a check. Briefcase in one hand, suitcase in the other, he staggered up the quay, and they saw him get into a taxi. Jack studied the check for a moment, then folded it into his damp wallet, which he replaced in his damp trousers. His knees felt wobbly. He supposed Madeleine's did too.

"Well, we made it," he said, and embraced her.

To his pleasure she laughed and hugged him back. "My captain, my hero," she said.

There was a refuse bin nearby. She carried the bucket over and dumped in the wadded-up paper towels. Returning to the boat, she tossed the bucket in on the deck.

"Dinner is what I want," she said to Jack. "Dinner, and then sleep."

"We could sleep on the boat," said Jack.

She shook her head. "I want a bath and I want to sleep in a proper bed."

"Okay," said Jack. "We'll find a hotel."

≡ CHAPTER 13 ≡

Having climbed into the taxi, their passenger, whose name was Cesare Bussaglia, ordered the driver to take him over the mountains to Bastia. He knew he should phone ahead, but the post office would be closed at this hour, and from a bar or hotel he might be overheard. In addition he was drunk, which might show in his voice. He could not afford to call in drunk.

"Let's go, let's go," he told the driver.

But the driver only drummed his fingers on the steering wheel. This went on for some seconds. Finally he named a price, five hundred francs.

"Five hundred," screamed Bussaglia. The boat had landed five hours late on the wrong side of the island. This was not his fault, but the men he worked for would be furious. The five-hundred-franc cab fare would be money out of his own pocket. The money he had given Dilger would not be reimbursed either, most likely, including the check he had just written, which he could not afford to stop lest it attract police attention.

"Five hundred," the driver said, "or get another cab."

There was no other cab that Bussaglia could see.

They argued, but the driver was adamant.

"All right, all right," Bussaglia agreed, for by now he was in a terrific hurry.

The driver turned the ignition key, and at long last they started off. However, they went only two hundred yards before the driver made a stop to fill up his tank. Then he went inside to pay—and stood talking to the guy for five minutes or more.

The cab was old and not in good shape, but they started up into the mountains. There was no light except their headlights. Bussaglia, who could hear the engine laboring, stared glumly out through the window. When the driver tried to talk to him, he told him to shut up. And then: "Can't you go any faster?"

The road as it climbed was thin and there were many switchbacks. Pitch-darkness. No light anywhere in these godforsaken mountains. The switchbacks were making him sick all over again.

"Stop the car," he told the driver, and got out and vomited onto the road. Wiping his mouth, he got back in, and again the cab wheezed into movement.

Bussaglia believed he had just lived through the worst day of his life, but when he thought of the men waiting ahead he decided that what was left of it would be as bad, maybe worse.

The ride took over three hours. They came down out of the mountains onto Bastia and the lights of the empty streets seemed blinding to Bussaglia.

The driver set him down in front of the Bar des Chasseurs on the Rue des Zephyrs near the old port. Carrying his big bag in one hand, his attaché case in the other, Bussaglia went in. At the bar drinking Calvados or cognac were men he didn't know. Other men played dominoes at a table to one side. He didn't know them either. And there was Musso sitting at his regular table. Musso was a huge man. He was about fifty, weighed over three hundred pounds and seldom moved from that table during business hours.

With him were three strangers. Two looked like businessmen, maybe lawyers, could be bodyguards, of course. Bussaglia had learned that bodyguards came in all guises. They sat half a pace back. He judged that they worked for the third guy, the one at the table with Musso who was much younger and wore a silk suit that cost plenty. Dressed that way he could not be a Corsican. Probably not even French. Tough-looking guy with a scar on his face.

Bussaglia wondered who he was, sitting cozy with the boss like that, guy half the boss's age but being treated with respect. He did not expect Musso to introduce him.

During the time Bussaglia approached the table Musso's eyes never left him.

Bussaglia stopped two paces away. "Where is everybody?" he said with pretended cheerfulness.

"You're late," said Musso.

"Yeah, I had some problems."

"This better be good," Musso said.

"Here's what happened, *patron*," said Bussaglia, and stopped and licked suddenly dry lips.

"I'm waiting," said Musso.

Bussaglia began to explain about the storm, about waves as high as houses, about puking into the head, puking on the floor.

"So the boat's in L'Ile Rousse?" Musso interrupted.

"In L'Ile Rousse, *patron*. Exactly right."

"But the welcoming committee was here."

"Couldn't be helped, *patron*," said Bussaglia nervously.

"Men here waiting to do the job."

"The storm—"

"And the man you were supposed to bring here is in L'Ile Rousse?"

"Exactly right, *patron*. Also there was another complication. A woman."

"A woman?"

"At the last minute she came aboard."

"There was supposed to be no one aboard except you and him."

"I couldn't stop her."

"Couldn't stop her."

"I didn't know what you wanted me to do."

"And after that you were seasick?"

"Sick as a dog, *patron*."

"Poor guy," said Musso. "Come closer."

Bussaglia moved two steps nearer the table.

Musso's meaty hand came up and slapped him in the face. Hit him so hard he almost went down. Fat as it was, the hand had moved with such speed Bussaglia never saw it. Musso screamed at him, called him a cunt, a piece of shit. All the men in the bar had turned and were watching. The other men around Musso's table—the two lawyers or bodyguards and the younger one in the silk suit—studied his reactions as if he were under glass.

Bussaglia had no reaction. He did nothing, just stood there taking Musso's abuse, his face stinging, one cheek redder than the other.

Having finally calmed down, the fat man turned to the man in the silk suit: "We'll do the job at L'Ile Rousse," he told him.

"How will we do it, *patron*?" said Bussaglia.

Ignoring Bussaglia, Musso said: "After such a storm they're not going anywhere tonight. Either they'll sleep on the boat or in a hotel. I'll send men over there right away."

Musso had spoken Italian. To Bussaglia this proved that the visitor was not French and when he murmured some response, Bussaglia realized he was not Italian either. What was he? Spanish, maybe?

Musso called him Signor Zaragon.

Italian and Spanish are close but not identical. Musso seemed to be watching carefully to see that Zaragon understood. "It's a small town," Musso told him in Italian. "Only three or four hotels. We do the job either tonight or tomorrow morning. Depends how long it takes to get men over there."

Zaragon nodded. The other two men, bodyguards or whatever they were, were not consulted and never moved.

"I want to be part of it, *patron*," said Bussaglia.

Musso looked at him until he looked away.

Musso was writing out a list of names. "Contact these men," he ordered Bussaglia. "Tell them to come in."

Bussaglia took the paper and moved toward the bar where the phone was. It was late and the men could be anywhere. Suppose he couldn't find them? Under the circumstances he had decided it was better not to ask Musso for the money he was out of pocket.

Having seen the HOTEL sign from the quay, Jack and Madeleine had walked up the street and inside. The lobby was small and not particularly clean. There was a boy in a denim apron behind the desk. The carpeting was frayed. The boy offered two rooms, each with a shower. Jack and Madeleine looked at each other. They were cold, tired, their hair and clothes still damp; they were in no mood to look any further, and when the boy passed across registration cards they signed them. The hotel had no restaurant, he informed them. Leaving their bags behind the desk they went out and walked along the sidewalk under the trees until they found a restaurant that was still open.

Some men stood at the bar. A few couples still sat at the tables leaning over tiny cups of coffee, or else snifters of what was probably Corsican marc. Local people, from the look of them. The tablecloths were paper. Those tables that had been vacated had not been cleared off.

The waiter came. The dinner hour was over, he told them curtly. When they said they'd take anything he offered, he suggested fish soup, followed by a plate of charcuterie: ham, pâté and sausage, cheese, take it or leave it. Plus wine, of course. He brought over a basket of bread, which they emptied at once.

"Were you scared?" asked Madeleine as they waited.

"Sure."

"You didn't show it."

"I was, though."

"So was I. I was terrified." She showed him a wry smile.

He took her hand, and she did not protest.

The fish soup came. It was in a tureen and steaming. Jack ladled it out. It was thick with chunks of fish. He kept refilling their soup plates until the tureen was empty. The charcuterie did not last long either. The wine was a coarse Corsican red. It made them giddy, and before long the crossing they had just made became funny. They joked about the misleading weather forecast, about the passenger vomiting all over the cabin. In their exhaustion, in the residue of their fear, they made each other laugh.

On the way back to the hotel Madeleine could not keep from yawning. "Are you in a hurry to get back home?" Jack asked her.

"No."

Maybe they could spend a day or two cruising around Corsica, he suggested. There was no point staying in L'Ile Rousse, Jack told her. There was nothing here.

Madeleine said: "We can decide in the morning."

The boy in the denim apron was on the phone as they entered the hotel. "Somebody want you, but he hang up," the boy said to Jack.

Jack puzzled over this, but only briefly. There must be some mistake, he decided. His mind was focused by then on Madeleine. He took the two keys from the boy and the two bags from behind the desk, and went up the narrow staircase behind her. He watched her hips, her rounded bottom as they climbed.

The two rooms were side by side on the same floor. Jack made a show of offering her whichever she wanted. She gave only a glance into the first of them, then took her suitcase and the key from his hands.

Now they stood smiling at each other, ready to say good night. Both had both hands occupied, neither spoke, and slowly the two smiles faded.

A peculiar expression had come onto her face, but he could not read it. It was a grave expression, certainly. This was a serious moment for her too, as was proved by the silent passing seconds, for suddenly she had to make a decision. The moment was there to grasp if she wanted to. She had only to issue the invitation. Yes or no. What did she wish to do?

It is always the woman who decides, Jack thought, and he waited. He knew she liked him. The question was, how much?

A man could fall into bed with someone for no good reason, and so could a woman. Jack had done so in the past, and perhaps she had too. In such cases what took place was insignificant, hardly even an intimacy. But if you cared for someone the act of love was a big step, for it extended forward into the future.

Could Jack now force her decision? Kiss her, see what happened? But this could spoil it all, convert whatever they were coming to feel for each other into a kind of sweaty wrestling match or, worse, into nothing at all.

She's thinking about it, Jack told himself. That's good, in a way. It means that she attaches importance to me, to us. But he knew what her decision would be before it came.

"Let's take a few days going back," she said. "We'll have a nice time."

He knew what this meant. Having managed a smile, he said: "Okay."

"I'll see you in the morning."

Her hand with the key in it pulled his head down, and she kissed him on the lips.

A moment later her door closed.

Musso's men, Bussaglia and two others, left Bastia in a white Mercedes before dawn. Jack Dilger at that time was still asleep. Bussaglia had been warned that there must be no slip-ups. The Mercedes was in good shape and the three men went up over the mountains easily enough, and then down again. Still, they had started out later than planned, and they had been delayed once en route by a flock of sheep crossing the road. While they waited for the sheep the sun climbed out of the sea and smacked the east face of the mountains full on.

Finally they got past the sheep. Even on the down side the slopes had begun to glow.

The night before, Musso and Zaragon had spent much time deciding on what orders to give. The final scenario was mostly Musso's, since he knew the terrain and Zaragon didn't. Actually there were several scenarios. The first had had to be changed because Bussaglia had been unable to locate the precise men Musso wanted, and then later it was changed again. According to the final scenario, the men in the Mercedes were to reach L'Ile Rousse just after first light, in plenty of time to wait by the boat until Jack appeared, after which they were to "escort" him out to sea, where he was to be attached to something heavy and dropped overboard. If the woman was with him, same with her. A rendezvous with a speedboat was fixed for the northernmost point of Cap Corse. The three men would transfer to this speedboat, and Jack's boat would be sent under power straight out to sea. Someone would eventually find it or ram it or it would sink. People loved mysteries, and this one would tantalize them for years. What could have happened to Dilger, or whoever had been driving the boat? The questions would go on and on but there would be no answers.

Zaragon laughed. "I like it," he said. His only regret, he added, was that he would not be there to watch. Of course, he would have to insist on proof that Dilger was dead.

"Get a Polaroid camera," Musso had ordered Bussaglia. "Take some shots of him lying there."

Bussaglia understood the importance of the order, and he nodded. However, at that time of night it took him a while to round up such a camera.

In the morning Jack woke up early and took his bag and went downstairs and paid for both rooms. The kid in the denim apron was still on duty. Jack asked him to tell Madame, when she came down, that he was at the boat.

He strolled down the street to the quay. The light was still very low, the town scarcely stirring. He passed cafés with the chairs on the tables and the waiters mopping and sweeping. The town looked much poorer than the Riviera towns. The port was poorer too, a place of rotting pilings and rusty fishing boats.

He drove his boat around to the pumps and tied up. While the tanks were being filled he went across to a café and ordered a café au lait and croissants. The croissants, still hot, were brought to him in a basket. There was a folded newspaper on the next table and he reached for it and tried to decipher the headlines. Presently his coffee came, and he dunked one of the croissants and ate it, then drank the coffee, pastry flakes and all. When he looked down the street he saw Madeleine carrying her bag and coming toward him. She kissed him on both cheeks, then sat down in the other chair. When the waiter came she said in French, "I'll have the same."

"And another coffee for me," said Jack.

They lingered over their breakfasts, talking about where they would go today.

"Want another coffee?" Jack asked finally.

"No," said Madeleine.

The register checks peeped out from beneath the sugar bowl where the waiter had placed them. Jack added them up, put down money, and they strolled over to the boat. Jack backed the boat away from the pumps, got it straightened out, and they moved slowly out of the harbor.

They were still short of the open sea when the Mercedes came fast down the main street and onto the quay, and Musso's men jumped out. Bussaglia led them along the quay to where Jack's boat had been moored the night before. As they came close their pace slowed, and they approached the mooring cautiously, hands on their guns. But they found only a gap between two other boats. In the grip of sudden immense fear, Bussaglia began running up and down the various quays thinking he had made a mistake or the boat had been moved. By the time anyone thought to glance in the direction of the harbor exit, Jack's boat was out to sea, hidden from view by the seawall. The three men didn't know where he might have gone, or when, and they stood there confused, wondering what they ought to do next.

The jutting peninsula known as Cap Corse is about eight miles wide, about twenty-five long. It has a mountainous spine four thousand feet high that runs its entire length. This spine, a tract of bare rock, is in some places several miles inland, but in others it rises out of the water, its base bathed by waves. Jack and Madeleine, sailing north close to the coast, marveled at such steepness. The first major village they passed, Nonza, seemed to them an amazing thing, being built on a spur of black rock that rose up sheer from the sea.

Beyond Nonza were no more villages for a long time. Cap Corse had been a busy place once, but the people had all left. Mountains were stepped with terraces that were no longer worked. Brush had grown up around stone farmhouses that looked caved in.

At the wheel Jack stood in green boxer swim trunks; Madeleine had changed into a bikini. It was red in color, briefer than some Jack had seen some women wear, more modest than others; later when she began to worry about the unremitting sun she put a T-shirt on over it, and that part of the equation became moot.

A corniche road sometimes appeared, carved into the mountainside high up. It looked fragile, and bore only an occasional car or truck. The coast was studded with stone watchtowers dating from the days when Corsica was a possession of Genoa. They stood above the brush like top hats.

The boat was moving slowly, close inshore, though before long the sun got hot so that Jack would speed up from time to time to let the wind blow through their hair; sometimes it blew unexpected spray all over them, making Madeleine squeal.

"Where do you want to stop for the night?"

"What are the choices?"

If they hurried, Jack said, they might round the top of the peninsula, which was also the top of the island, turn south and make Bastia, and find a hotel. But Madeleine answered that they were not really in such a hurry, were they?

So they watched the scenery pass: villages that perched dramatically on crags or that hung like birds' nests over the sea; streams that coursed down mountains, spilling at last into an inlet or cove, sometimes onto a beach; occasional hamlets inland, some of them abandoned, crouching in the folds of mountains. The broken terraces that surrounded them had once supported olive groves or vines. The steep meadows, now overlaid with brush, or scrub timber, had once fed goats and sheep. This was a land that had gone most of the way back into wilderness. For all its beauty, Cap Corse was a ruin, still alive, but barely.

The heavily indented coastline continued to pass. By lunchtime they were at Centuri, population 160, which had a pretty jetty, with a couple of sleepy restaurants overlooking it. They tied up to a dock, and Madeleine put a skirt on over her bikini; Jack donned a sweatshirt that bore the legend NEW YORK GIANTS, and they walked into the village, where they sat down outside a restaurant called the Vieux Moulin and ordered *moules marinières* and salad and bread and some local cheeses and got giddy again on Corsican rosé. Afterward they walked through the one or two leafy streets, buying food for supper, and a bag of charcoal in case they should decide to cook out on a beach somewhere, for they had noted plenty of beaches, nearly all of them empty.

When they had carried their purchases back to the boat, Madeleine untied the lines and pushed away from the dock, and they went on, cruising up the coast into the hot wind and, sometimes, into the cold spray. They had all the time in the world, they imagined. They also had each other, and this occupied them. Though neither said anything, there was now a certain tension between them, and it kept building. The hours so far had passed without a single intimate touch. At sea they did brush against one another from time to time, but in a boat that sometimes bounded about this was inevitable, was it not, and therefore meaningless. It did cause a number of fleeting glances, however, and, when the other was not looking, some intense ones.

In the afternoon they came to still another rocky inlet, this one with a minuscule beach. There were several other parked boats, and people were snorkeling over the rocks. Jack cut the engines, and Madeleine slung the anchor overboard, but Jack came forward and stood beside her studying where it had landed, not liking the look of the bottom in this place; it was too easy to imagine the boat dragging its anchor and drifting away. Finally he decided to move closer to shore, where, in addition to anchoring, he swam a rope in and tied it to a tree. The boat rocked gently, half underneath the tree, and he broke out his snorkeling gear and he and Madeleine plunged into the water and swam along facedown looking for fish.

It was during this time that a helicopter chartered by Musso flew over looking for them. Bussaglia sat beside the pilot while Musso and Victoriano Zaragon peered out the side windows. The helicopter hovered a moment over the cove, but Bussaglia did not recognize the half-visible boat, and presently the machine flew on. "They must be almost to Nice by now," said Musso to Zaragon in a curious mixture of Italian and Corsican. "I'll have men waiting for them when they land."

The younger man nodded coldly. "Just so long as it's done," he said in Spanish.

The helicopter had already made a fruitless search far out to sea, and now it turned back to Bastia.

Below it some of the children had scampered up and down

the beach shouting and pointing upward, but Jack and Madeleine, being facedown in the water, had taken no notice of it whatever.

When they tired of snorkeling, they frolicked through the shallows like children, splashing water at each other.

Later they talked to some of the others nearby, most of them foreigners: a Swedish family, an English one. Although some of the sunbathing women were topless, Madeleine's bra, somewhat to Jack's disappointment, stayed in place. The English couple offered them tea. The water was boiled on a spirit stove on the beach and served in real cups, along with rather stale scones.

They sailed on. The sun stayed hot, the sea calm.

"We're never going to make Bastia," Jack said after a time. They had spent over two hours at the beach, and by now the sun was low. He had turned from the wheel. "What do you want to do?"

"Sooner or later we have to stop."

"Yes, but where?"

"Find a place."

"Sleep on the boat?"

"If you want to." She shrugged.

"Okay," said Jack.

He began searching for a sheltered cove. He sailed into several, but then steered out again, for one was guarded by rocks that he did not want to cross and another was too big, offering no protection from any sort of storm that might blow up and send in swells; neither of them wanted to sleep in a boat that bounced around all night. A third cove already contained a boat they had not seen at first. Jack looked at Madeleine, and without a word spoken he sailed on out again.

The coast here was high and rocky, there were many choices, and at length they found a cove that satisfied them, and anchored. They had been towing the dinghy. Now they stepped down into it and rowed ashore, where they clambered up some boulders and walked into the forest. Though they walked some distance, much of it uphill, they came upon no road or habitation. In this spot the corniche road was about a mile inland, for it had left the coast to cut straight across the peninsula, and when they listened they could not hear it. They could near nothing but birds tweeting and the rustle of the breeze pushing through leaves.

There was also no beach where they had come ashore, nor was there any clearing in which they might cook or lay out sleeping bags, so they rowed back to the boat. The sun was going down and they sat on deck sipping aperitifs and watched it drop and disappear. There was a net of clouds overhead, and its filaments changed color the way a bruise does, from yellow to red to mauve to purple, streaks that changed very slowly.

When the sunset was gone and the light had turned to everdarkening gray, Madeleine ducked into the galley and put the light on to prepare dinner, grilling the steaks they had bought, mixing a vinaigrette for the salad, slicing up the bread. After opening the wine, Jack stood in the entryway watching the way her hands moved and the way she tossed her hair out of her eyes, feeling a certain hotness through his entire body.

Night fell absolutely windless. They ate dinner in the glow that the interior light threw out into the cockpit, and when they had finished they sat in the soft warm air over the last of the wine.

Finally Jack got up and got out the air mattress and inflated it.

"What's that?" asked Madeleine.

"My bed." He laid it down in the stern. He had learned long ago that women did not like to have their goodwill presumed upon. "You can have the cabin."

She watched him with a slight smile on her face. "Thank you," she said. "That's very gentlemanly of you."

They sat awhile longer in silence. "It's still very hot," said Madeleine.

"Yes, it is."

"Want to take another swim?"

"If you do."

"Is there enough water to take a shower afterward to wash the salt off?"

"Sure. You can stand on the prow and I'll hose you down."

"Okay, then." She stood up, peeled the T-shirt off, and plunged over the side. When she came to the surface she called up: "The water's warm. It's lovely. Come on in."

He stood at the rail watching her.

"It's like soup in here."

He saw her reach behind herself to unhook her top. She made a ball of it. Her legs pumped and she threw it. The soggy wad came flying up at him out of the water.

"What would be really nice would be to swim naked," she said.

"Go ahead, I won't look." He feigned putting his hand over his eyes.

It was fully dark now, but the galley lights made a small glow around the boat, and the moon seemed to be rising over the forest they had walked through a while ago.

"You sure I can trust you?"

"Absolutely."

"Okay."

Another ball of wet cloth nearly hit him in the face. He could see the whiteness of her as she swam off into the darkness.

Having stripped off his sweatshirt, he stepped up onto the rail and plunged in and swam toward the noise she made splashing. The water threw off a kind of phosphorescent glow that surrounded her face like a halo. Her hair was plastered back in a pompadour, and she looked beautiful to him. She looked as virginal as a teenager.

"Hey, what's this?" she said. She had both hands on his hips, their feet and knees bumping as they stayed afloat, and she was feeling the cloth. "It's swim trunks," she said, "and I say it's cheating."

"Come back to the boat," he said. The words came out almost as a croak.

"But we're having a nice swim," she said. "What do you want to go back there for?"

She let him pull her toward the boarding ladder. He went up first, turned, and caught her as she stepped down onto the deck—caught more by accident than design one cold slippery breast. He caught the other one on purpose.

What happened then seemed almost preordained, inevitable since breakfast. Her face was salty, her breasts too, her thighs, and her flesh was cold, though it warmed up soon enough.

The mattress Jack had inflated, the bed he had made up for himself pretending he meant to sleep in it alone, served instead for what happened now, a different purpose, the hoped-for purpose all day. Sheet tucked in at the start, pillowcase in its slip, both bodies soaking wet, this bed was rendered soon enough impractical for any use anytime soon other than the present one. The boat rocked gently underneath them, as if it were alive, though not nearly as alive as they made each other feel. Their only blanket was the stars, which they took turns looking toward but not at, neither one able to look away from whoever was on top, the face and body hovering there much closer than any star, and more real, and blotting out awareness of everything else.

They worked each other over a long time. It was quite noisy, not a bit romantic except to the couple involved, not only because of the rhythmic slapping together of bodies, but for the many grunts, endearments, and cries as well. In between there was talk in low voices, and much cuddling and silliness and giggling, the outward manifestation of the incredibly intense intimacy that both felt so strongly, and that no other human activity can provide, that may exist in life at this level at no other time.

Later, still giddy but not from wine, both of them sore in certain places, they carried the two mattresses out from the cabin, moving about unclothed in the balmy night air, for they intended to sleep the rest of the night under the stars. They were determined now to stop this foolishness and sleep. Madeleine tucked in a dry bottom sheet and tossed open a second sheet that would be available if a breeze should come up and cool off the night—they were too hot in more ways than one to need it now. Except for the stars the night had got very dark. The moon had either never risen very high or had set almost at once. They were thoroughly depleted but too happy to sleep after all. Filled with a sense of wonder, they lay half entwined and gazed up at the billions of stars they had not properly admired earlier. The emotion both felt most strongly could perhaps be called awe— not of the stars but of each other, awe in the presence of love, if that's what it was, awe at the illusion of having touched and understood another human soul.

But the word *love* was never mentioned, and as drowsiness began to overcome him Jack realized this. Love was the same every time, but different every time as well, and he was old enough to know this, as was she. Particularly it was different at different times in one's life, more rare perhaps as one got older, but less headlong, more calculating, less consuming. With age therefore love could be difficult to recognize and even more difficult to acknowledge. To acknowledge it had become disturbing, for with acknowledgment came the same obligations as always but one saw them now, one hadn't seen them earlier in life, at least not clearly. The future became the problem: where do we go from here? There was now another person to consider at all times and to protect at all costs, which meant factoring in an ownership component as well.

These thoughts became too much for Jack, and he drifted off to sleep. Madeleine did too. But the night was not over. Both slept lightly, and it was as if this were deliberate. They clung to each other, aware even in their sleep of the other body, its warmth, its fragrant flesh, the perfume and feel of someone else, aware too of the passing of the night, aware that when morning came the bright light of day might change everything. In this counterfeit of sleep any movement of the boat, any change in the breeze, would cause one or the other to stir, from which to a kind of wakefulness was the shortest of steps, and as soon as semiconsciousness was achieved there came a desire to conjoin all over again. This was enough to restart the process. Half asleep, they would begin, sometimes completing the act, sometimes not, as one or both of them fell back to sleep before completion occurred on either side.

Morning.

Jack came awake and Madeleine was standing between him and the sun. He squinted. She was washed and combed and modestly bikinied. He covered himself with the sheet and they grinned at each other, grins that turned sheepish on both sides.

Late in the afternoon they reached Bastia, a low town with mountains just beyond. There was a long high seawall that enclosed the new port. As they passed along the length of it they could see the tops of the cranes and smokestacks of the shipping inside, and the high decks of one of the ship ferries that had been stranded there by the strike. Farther on the seawall ended and a row of buildings faced the sea, overhanging a wide boulevard that ran along in front. A number of the buildings were hotels, or else cafés with tables set out, and they glided on past until they came to the entrance to the Old Port, into which they carefully steered. By then the sun was going down behind the town.

Having tied up, they walked up the street to one of the hotels and checked in. Jack took a long shower, Madeleine an even longer bath, after which they went out and strolled through the streets of the Old Town. The food stores were still open; women were shopping for dinner. Some of the other shops were closed or closing. There were many churches, some with wonderful old art inside, but these too were closing, the big exterior doors swinging shut. The streetlights had been on for some time. Jack and Madeleine had dinner in a restaurant and then went back to the hotel to bed.

They stayed in Bastia the next day too, holding hands as they walked through the narrow streets. In the open market they gazed down on the stalls and inhaled the odors of the fresh produce. They sipped aperitifs at cafés on the public squares, they entered the churches and chapels they had missed the night before. Bastia much resembled some of the smaller Riviera cities, though without the elegance and chic. Much of it was very old, not a wealthy town obviously, but an attractive place for all of that. In the afternoon they went to the boat to deposit the bags of groceries and other supplies they had bought, and Jack drove around to the pumps and had the tanks topped up, water and fuel both.

Their hotel was two blocks from Musso's bar. In the course of the day they had walked past it twice. They might easily have gone in and sat down and ordered a drink. Jack had never heard of Musso. Madeleine, who knew his reputation, would have recognized his name and possibly his face; she knew about his great girth too, though she had never seen him.

Of course Musso had never seen them either, and a drink in his bar would have been safe enough after a certain hour, for Bussaglia, the only one of his employees who knew them by sight, was gone by then, as were Zaragon and his men. They were in a chartered plane along with two other *milieu* shooters being flown across the Mediterranean to what Corsicans always referred to as the continent. The gunmen's instructions once they had deplaned at Nice were to stake out the port of Beaulieu until Jack Dilger returned. Dilger was perhaps there already. If not, it could not be more than another day or two. They were contract workers. They were to do the job they had contracted for. They could do it any way they chose, but they had to be prompt.

Musso, as he gave these orders, was seated at his regular table in his bar, and he looked around at Zaragon, who was alone at the time, and at Bussaglia and the two shooters. The young Colombian druglord was the only one who met his eyes, the other men being in rapt contemplation of the tabletop. Zaragon's eyes were cold and hard, and the fat man read in his attitude, and in that of his own men, his own considerable loss of face. Up to now the target had thwarted not them but him. By escaping, Dilger had shamed him. There were to be no further slip-ups, he told his men. That he was outraged was clear from the low, ominous timbre of his voice.

Zaragon had stood up nodding, then remarked that he would take a hotel room in Nice or nearby and wait to be notified. He had other business to transact while waiting, he added, a not very veiled threat against Musso's business future and perhaps his health.

Musso at his table watched him go.

Musso was Zaragon's distributor both for Italy and France, Corsica being ideally placed in relation to both. He had made his deal with the late Jorge Zaragon, not with this wild younger brother who understood nothing and made threats. Unfortunately, there were other *milieu* clans, mostly out of Marseilles, with whom Zaragon could make contact if he chose. This was Musso's fear: he had invested heavily in boats, trucks, men, bribes, but all was now at risk. Everything depended on his men finding Jack Dilger and fulfilling their contract.

Jack and Madeleine sailed out of Bastia, intending to cross directly to Beaulieu, where Bussaglia and his colleagues were by now set up, for they had no idea that this was what awaited them. However, it was another hot, sunny morning, and they had scarcely cleared the port before Madeleine said: "We don't really have to go back right away, do we?"

Jack turned from the wheel. Seeing her standing close in her bikini made him smile with pleasure. "I don't. Do you?"

"No."

This was not entirely true. In fact she was scheduled to see her lawyer tomorrow, for she had instituted a civil suit asking the government to show cause why her status as an officer of Police

Judiciaire should not be restored, and at this meeting they planned to discuss tactics; but she could telephone or fax the lawyer from wherever she and Jack would put in tonight. She could ask that the meeting be postponed.

Also she was scheduled to address a police group in Brest in two days' time. She no longer wanted to do that either. Well, she could phone or fax them too, making up some excuse. It was probably a good idea to lie low for a while anyway, let the noise die down. She could not be sure that anyone meant her harm; she rather doubted it, in fact. But if men she didn't know were tracking her movements this was, to say the least, troubling.

Most of all, in her present mood she did not want to be separated from Jack. She was in a mood to sail around the Mediterranean with this man forever.

"Let's just loaf for a couple of days," she suggested.

"We could go across to Italy and up the coast," said Jack. "Avoid having to cross ninety miles of open water."

Madeleine smiled. "Anything to avoid that."

And so they turned due east and made for Elba, which lies about twenty miles off the Italian coast, that same island where Napoleon was once held, and from which he escaped, sailing to the Riviera and making his way north toward Waterloo. They talked about Napoleon on the way. The house he had lived in was probably a museum now, they decided.

They saw the island long before they reached it, for its central peak rises thirty-five hundred feet out of the sea. When they came closer they noted many beaches and coves, some fronted by fine hotels. They found an empty cove and sailed into it and anchored and had a long swim by themselves, after which they tied up outside the most luxurious hotel they had seen and took a big comfortable room with a balcony that looked out onto sea and rocks.

They stayed two days in Elba, then continued east to the Italian mainland, where they began making their way slowly north, stopping for the night at Portofino and Rapallo, among other places, smoothing suntan oil on each other each morning, and sometimes soothing balms each night, eating too much pasta in pleasant restaurants, drinking a bit too much wine, living almost exclusively with the sun and the sea and each other.

Eight days out of Corsica, bronzed, happy, and at ease, they came into the harbor at Beaulieu at dusk and tied up, and Jack walked Madeleine back to her room above the warehouse, where he kissed her and turned away. The future, it seemed to him, was there between them, not like a wall but more like one of those beaded Riviera curtains that one could see through or even step through. He and Madeleine could go in any direction they chose, but would have to choose somewhere, and they would have to confront this choice before too much longer. It was not a choice he was afraid of now. After this past wonderful week he looked forward to it.

He was, as he walked along, ignoring certain imperatives. They hung like a weight on his back, and would be there to-morrow, and next week, and for a long time to come. However good he might be at pushing out of his thoughts whatever he did not wish to confront, this was sometimes hard to do. Realistically speaking, what kind of life was open to him if he stayed here? Thirty or forty years as a boat bum? Was that what he wanted? Already he was feeling the not-so-subtle pull of New York. New York was on his skin, under his nails. To him it was the focus of the world. New York was home—perhaps it was as simple as that. He belonged there, not here. New York was Flora too. In a way that was indefinable he missed her—how much he could not say, for whenever images of her came into his head he tried to switch quickly to something else.

If he stayed here he would always be a foreigner. He would not be permitted to work. He did not speak the language and he saw now that learning it would be extremely difficult and would take years. At present it required a major effort to make even his simplest needs understood. As soon as Zaragon was behind bars he could go back, if he chose. Once pretrial motions started he would have to go back, for his testimony would be crucial at every stage. Real life to him was New York, not the yacht harbor at Beaulieu-sur-Mer. Perhaps he imagined Madeleine would agree to uproot her own life and come with him. If so, he was overlooking the fact that real life to her might be the opposite.

The sun was below the seawall and the air was still—the masts were not moving at all.

One night in the dark they had spoken of the future, vaguely, and she had snuggled up against him saying: "Hush, let's play it one day at a time." Now he walked down the central quay with boats to either side, knowing nothing about killers who might be waiting for him ahead. The voyage just completed had become a romantic haze, and he was adrift in it, focused on Madeleine only, imagining or perhaps only hoping that they could play it one day at a time forever.

The harbormaster was coming toward him along the quay. "*Bon soir*," he said, when he was near, and he stopped and they shook hands.

Some men had been looking for Jack during the week, the harbormaster said.

Jack made out this much, but not much more. He could not imagine who such men could be, so perhaps he had misunderstood.

The Frenchman went on talking. Jack caught the words for "waiting near your boat," or thought he did. What could that mean? The next several sentences he did not understand at all, which he would have been embarrassed to admit, so he grinned and shook hands again.

"*Bon soir*," he told the harbormaster, "*bonne nuit*," and he moved on.

He was very happy, and as he neared the slip where the boat was moored, the problems he saw ahead seemed to him small ones. He liked living in France. He liked the sun, the coast, the sea. He liked Madeleine, who blotted out Flora. He could feel his strength coming back. His body had become tanned and his ribs no longer showed. Also, no one here was out to put bullets in him.

He came to his boat and jumped down into it.

Having watched for his boat day after day and seen no sign of it, Musso's gunmen had begun to complain. There were many phone calls to Corsica. They had begun to attract attention, they said. People looked at them oddly. The customs guards eyed them. The *mec* might never come back. Customs guards and gendarmes were around the port constantly. How long should they wait?

Victoriano Zaragon had complained also. From his hotel he too made many calls to Musso in Corsica. His voice became increasingly strident, his rage increasingly near the surface. He wanted Dilger "suppressed." An American might have said "eliminated." Where was Dilger? Why wasn't it done? How much longer was it going to take?

Zaragon was becoming frantic. He could not go home while Dilger lived, and he was worried about what might be happening there in his absence. An international arrest warrant had reached Medellín with his name on it. For a time he had hidden out near one of his jungle laboratories. Finally he had fled the country via Brazil, afraid not so much that the police would find him on their own as that one of his own men would give him up. He trusted none of his subordinates. What was happening in Colombia in his absence? He did not know but feared the worst. His control over the business became shakier every day. He had to get back, visibly take charge, but was stuck here until Dilger was taken care of.

Millions of francs of narcotics profits rode on the Zaragon-Musso relationship. But from the threats and imprecations Zaragon shouted over the telephone line to Corsica each day, this would have been impossible to guess.

Musso, who seldom left his bar and rarely left Corsica, flew to Nice and there was a tense meeting in the back of a parked car outside the airport. Where was Dilger? the young druglord demanded. Why couldn't Musso's men do what they were being paid for?

Musso's face got beet red and he was in the grip of a murderous rage. A lesser man might have strangled or shot Zaragon on the spot, but the Corsican was slightly afraid of the criminal power Zaragon represented, and at first he was trying to preserve their business relationship. Zaragon's voice became more and more shrill, his spittle sometimes crossed the two feet of stale air that separated them, and he screamed additional threats and curses. The South American was worse than intemperate, Musso decided. He had no manners at all, which meant that dealing with him would always be dangerous. Musso was past wanting to kill him. He wanted nothing further to do with him.

"You want the man killed," he hissed, "then kill him yourself," and he got out of the car, walked back into the terminal, gave orders pulling his men off the yacht harbor at Beaulieu, and flew back to Corsica.

For Jack Dilger this would mean a reprieve of some days, perhaps even more—however much time it took Zaragon to set up something else.

≡ BOOK III ≡

≡ Chapter 14 ≡

He thinks I've got an excellent chance to get my job back," said Madeleine.

Some days had passed. She had just come from her lawyer's office.

It was noon and the sun was hot. She had come aboard bearing an enormous salad bowl as a gift. Hand-carved out of olive wood, it was highly polished, beautiful. Very pleased, Jack had thanked her with a kiss.

At present, she stood in the galley preparing a *salade niçoise* to go in it. He leaned in the doorway watching as she pared the tiny artichokes, sliced the tomatoes, the hard boiled eggs, dropped in the chunks of tuna fish and the small black olives, her fingers mixing the ingredients, then pouring on the vinaigrette.

"Do something," she said. "Don't just stand there."

So Jack set up the table under the awning at the stern. He could feel the sun beating down on the awning. He could feel the heat on the canvas, and smell it as well.

Over the folding table he sailed out a red and white checkered tablecloth, on which he laid a plate of thickly sliced ham from the Pyrenees, and another of cheeses from the center of France—he had shopped at the *épicerie* on the port. There was a fresh baguette that Madeleine had bought at the bakery up in the town.

As she came out with the salad bowl she was talking about her lawyer again, and she was ebullient.

"Did you ever think about going to New York?" Jack interrupted.

"On a visit? Sure?"

They sat down. There was rosé wine in an ice bucket, and Jack poured it into the two glasses.

"My lawyer said the court might hear my case by September."

"I mean living there."

She grinned at him. "What is this, a proposition?"

"Absolutely not," said Jack. He felt a bit embarrassed, so he grinned back. "An idle question. You don't have to answer."

She was wearing a sundress today. Her arms were bare, her legs bare also, her feet in thong sandals. Her hair was tied back in a ponytail which the sun, each time she turned her head, lit up like a torch.

"No, I never thought about living in New York," she said.

"You speak the language," he pointed out.

That took the topic out of the lighthearted banter range. Realizing this was no longer a joke, she looked into her wineglass.

"You might like it."

She seemed to concentrate on the contents of her glass as if looking for answers there. "Well," she said, "I'm French."

He put his hand on hers on the tablecloth. "You could live there if you wanted."

"Are you hungry or not?" Madeleine asked after a moment. Removing her hand, she lifted servings of salad onto the two plates. She broke the bread into pieces for him, for her.

"My lawyer thinks I have three chances, in fact," she said. "First the lower court. And if that fails, the appeals court."

Jack took a sip from his glass. "And the third?"

"We wait for the administration to change in Paris."

Jack could not imagine a country where the federal government got involved in what was essentially an internal police matter, and a local one at that.

In any case, the idea of moving to New York did not appear to tempt her. At least not yet. Give her time, he thought. "Do you want to get back on the PJ that much?" he asked.

"I want to clear my name, and I want to have a solid job again." After a moment she added: "I want to do something important with my life." This statement seemed to embarrass her slightly. "What cops do is important, don't you think?" Then she added lamely: "You do, don't you?"

Jack was silent.

"Do you think what cops do is important?"

"Sure."

"So wouldn't you like to get back?"

There was no possibility of getting back, but the desire remained. It had tormented Jack for weeks, sometimes rising up when least expected, other times ringing in his ears like a tune that wouldn't stop. He kept pushing it down. In the daytime this was hard to do; alone in bed in the night there was sometimes a pain of loss, call it grief, that he could not suppress—one many times more severe than he had ever imagined. It was no good mooning about it, he kept telling himself. Getting back was not possible. He was out, and would have to settle for some other kind of life.

"What you're asking is where would I rather be," he said. "There or here?" Getting back was no more possible than trying to get innocence back. He was determined to quash such thoughts whenever they arose. "Frankly, I'd rather be here with you." He smiled at her, and for the moment at least believed what he had said was true.

Her eyes crinkled with pleasure, her teeth showed, and she held her wine up to the sunlight, admiring the color. "It's beautiful, isn't it?" Motes of sunlight danced pale pink in the glass and were reflected like jewelry onto the planes of her face.

He felt a surge of emotion that was extremely intense. Whether it was love or not, he did not know.

She smiled at him, then glanced over his shoulder and her smile faded. "Don't look now, but there's a woman over there."

"Woman?" he said, but did not bother to turn around. Jack was a man who focused on one woman at a time.

"Who seems interested in you."

In a crowded marina their privacy had been total. Jack's boat was gripped as if in a vise by boats to either side, yet both of those were empty, buckled up tight. Other boats stretched off right and left, constantly rubbing up and down on each other, all also empty. Across the narrow channel were more boats, very few of which were lived on.

But now a woman had walked out onto the quay, and their privacy was over.

"She's just standing there," said Madeleine, frowning.

Jack noticed the frown, but discounted its importance. He loved her face, which was always extremely expressive. It refused to hide whatever she felt. Her moods were always all there. It gave him pleasure just to look at her.

"Now she's walking back and forth," said Madeleine.

He leaned across the table and poured more wine into her glass.

Madeleine was once again peering over Jack's shoulder. "Who is that woman, Jack? I think she thinks she knows you."

Jack turned around. The woman did know him, and he knew her. It was Flora.

Seeing her, he jumped up as if stung. Then he jumped onto the gangway and off the boat and stood before her on the quay.

"Well," he managed. "Well, well." And then after a moment: "What a surprise to see you here!"

It was more than a surprise. He was so shocked that he found himself shaking her hand.

"You didn't give a very explicit address, dear."

His wife's hand. Wringing it.

"I mean, I've been an hour looking for you up and down these boats."

"When did you get in?" It was as if she were an acquaintance he barely knew. "Did you have a nice flight?"

She freed her hand and moved closer to the boat, no doubt for a better look at Madeleine, who was still seated at the table.

"Is this your bachelor pad?" she asked in a voice loud enough for Madeleine to hear.

The two women eyed each other.

"Isn't it a bit small, dear?" Flora said. "I mean even for one person."

Turning from Madeleine, she beamed a big smile Jack's way. "Aren't you going to . . ." evidently she sought a jaunty phrase, "pipe me aboard?"

Jack jumped down into the boat and reached up a hand for her.

"Introduce us, dear."

"Yes, of course." He had begun to come out of it. "Madeleine, this is Flora. Flora, this is Madeleine."

Two names. Madeleine's signaled nothing to Jack's wife. On the other hand, there aren't that many Floras in the world. Madeleine knew very well who this woman must be, and so was as shocked as Jack. Perhaps dismayed too. As she glanced from one face to the other she still held her wineglass, though she didn't seem to know it.

"We were just having some lunch," said Jack.

"Yes, I see."

Madeleine stared fixedly at the deck. "We were just finishing," she said.

"Would you like some lunch?" said Jack.

"I've already eaten, thank you."

"We were just about finished," said Madeleine. She began picking up dishes of uneaten food and carrying them into the galley. In less than sixty seconds the table was cleared.

"I'll see you later," said Madeleine to Jack, and she jumped up onto the quay and was gone.

He took two steps after her but was too late. After watching her departing back, his gaze returned to his wife, who had sat down on the banquette that ran across the stern.

"Where'd you pick her up?" Flora inquired.

"She works for the agency that rented me the boat," said Jack. This reply was less than complete. Less than loyal too.

"Nice-looking woman," commented Flora.

He was peering off through the masts and deck houses, watching for a glimpse of Madeleine as she crossed between the prows. He did not know what to say to Flora, and could not imagine what Madeleine might have expected from him just now.

"Where are you staying?" he asked his wife.

"At the Voile d'Or."

Jack knew this hotel, which looked down onto the tiny harbor of St. Jean Cap Ferrat, about three miles away. It was one of the most beautiful hotels in the world. One of the most costly too.

"Nice place," he said. Clearly Flora had spent money to get here and was spending much more to stay.

"It's very chic. I like it very much."

Jack found that he was suddenly ferociously hungry. He glanced at the table, looking for the food that was no longer there. "What brings you here, Flora?"

"I wanted to see you."

Reaching into the galley he brought out the plate of ham and the basket of bread, and set it down. "How's the divorce going?"

"That's what I wanted to see you about."

He made himself a quick sandwich, shoving ham inside a piece of the bread and beginning to chew. "You wanted to see me," said Jack. "What about?"

"I thought we should talk about the divorce."

"What is there to talk about?"

"Before it goes any further."

"Before what goes any further?"

"The divorce."

"Oh."

There was a long silence.

"You're looking much better," Flora said. "You've gained back a lot of the weight."

"Yes, I feel pretty good." Jack began giving himself orders. So she surprised you, so what? Put the sandwich down. This woman has surprised you since the day you met her. Decide what your attitude is to be, then hold to it. From the first day you've never known what she was going to do next. Stop being surprised.

"The air here must agree with you," said Flora.

"Flora . . ." He peered at the half-eaten sandwich on the plate, and then off through all the boats, not seeing them, trying to decide what he wanted to say.

"Do you have a car?" she asked.

"A rental, yes."

"Could you drive me back to the hotel? I came in a taxi."

Because she was wearing high heels and a dress, which was not the best garb for climbing on and off boats, he gave her his hand as she stepped onto the slim gangway and from there onto the quay.

But his boat could be seen from Madeleine's room over the warehouse, he believed. Madeleine could in fact watch him all the way to where his car was parked if she wished, so he let go of Flora, and they walked along with Jack trying to keep air between them. He glanced several times up at Madeleine's windows but did not see her. Nor did he expect to, now that he thought about it. Madeleine was a much more predictable woman. Unlike Flora, you could rely on her to be the same woman every day: she was honest, direct, responsible, frank, never flighty, never whimsical, with a good earthy sense of humor. Easily hurt as well. But there was a certain solidity to her French pride. Spying from her window on him, on them, was not the kind of thing she would permit herself to do.

His attention switched to Flora. Now that the surprise was over, he was glad to see her. In her tight silky green dress, in her spike heels and handbag that matched, she projected, to his eyes, terrific elegance, much more than Madeleine did. She had always exerted an extremely strong pull on his psyche, not to mention his libido. Her unpredictability was much of her appeal. Now here she was once more jumping into his life with both feet, and at a time when he had become adjusted to the thought that she was gone forever.

Obviously she was rethinking the divorce, perhaps had discovered that she did not want to give him up, and this was to say the least flattering, even if it threw his way a number of problems he was not anxious to confront. But it certainly was flattering. Well, he would hear her out. But he wondered if her sudden, unexpected appearance had not already cost him Madeleine. Madeleine had taken it hard; he knew her well enough to know that. In a day or a week Flora would leave and he would not have Madeleine either.

Flora got into his car and he drove out of the harbor, through Beaulieu, and out onto the Cap Ferrat. Flora's hotel, he knew, was about two miles out on the peninsula.

"Have you missed me?" said Flora. "You have, haven't you? I could tell from the way you looked at me that you did."

"Sure I missed you." And he added, because it was true: "Probably I'll always miss you."

"Always?"

"You've been a big part of my life."

"And you've been a big part of mine."

"What about the divorce?"

"I stopped it."

A few months ago he would have given a lot to hear this. Now he was not so sure. "Stopped it?"

"Put it on hold. It didn't seem fair to do it when you weren't there."

"Why not?" He was having trouble understanding whatever she was trying to tell him.

"I mean, you didn't even hire a lawyer."

"I didn't need one, did I? Unless I wanted to contest it."

"Don't you want to contest it?"

Contesting it, under the circumstances, had not been one of his options.

"If you don't have a lawyer, my lawyer can take advantage of you."

"Flora, I don't own anything anyone can take advantage of."

"That woman I just saw you with, does she mean anything to you?"

"No," he decided to say, hoping to avoid immediate complications.

He thought he saw a small smile come onto Flora's face, but could not be sure.

I shouldn't lie to her, he told himself. But the lie was done now, and to change it would require too much explanation.

Jack drove into the village of St. Jean, where he turned downhill along one side of the port, and then up onto the promontory which formed a second side. On top stood the Hotel Voile d'Or. He steered into the small parking area in front, and there he parked, a Ferrari on one side of him, a Rolls-Royce on the other.

"Nice company you keep," he murmured as they got out of the car. A hotel like this had so little to do with the life of a New York cop that it almost made him laugh. What was he doing in this place?

A valet came out and took the car keys, and they walked down the path alongside the French windows, behind which were the hotel's public rooms. There was a strip of lawn between them and the railing. Below the railing was the tiny port full of still more yachts. Ahead was a terrace with wicker tables and chairs and they sat down and a waiter came out and they ordered coffee. Jack was silent, not knowing exactly what he felt, much less what he wanted to say. Perhaps Flora felt much the same, he could not tell, but she too had fallen silent.

The view was back toward the coast, toward the towering Riviera cliffs marching east toward Italy. At the base of the cliffs he could discern the several small villages that cowered there, pinned like butterflies, the immense wall above them.

"Nice view," Flora said finally.

"Yes." The view was better than nice. It was one of the most gorgeous in the world, but it seemed to him stupid to say this. In any case, he was so troubled he did not yet trust himself to speak at all.

"How long do you think you'll stay here, Jack?"

He looked at her. "Till they catch that guy."

"Suppose they don't catch him?"

"They will."

"Living on that little boat?"

"It's a nice boat."

"It's not even as big as a trailer."

"Well—"

"Do you have enough money?"

"I have my pension."

"That isn't much."

He gestured at the hotel behind him. "Well, I certainly couldn't afford this place." He smiled and added a joke: "The prices they charge here, I'm not sure I can afford this coffee we're drinking."

"I'm taking care of the bill," she said seriously.

"I was joking."

"I'm sorry, I didn't realize."

Flora, he reminded himself, was a woman who entertained whims and obeyed them. She did not tell jokes herself and sometimes did not get those she heard. She could laugh heartily at times, but on the whole tended to seriousness. Her sense of humor, like much else about her, was not, he had learned, predictable.

"Because if you need money . . ." she offered.

"That's very nice of you."

"I mean it."

"I've been taking people out on short cruises," he lied. "For instance, I took someone to Corsica a while back. These cruises bring in plenty of extra money." There had been only the one cruise so far, and the idyll with Madeleine that followed had used up the entire profit. "Thanks for the offer, though."

Flora nodded and, biting her lip, was silent. Whatever she meant to say to him, she was not yet ready to say it.

"So aren't you lonely?"

"Not really."

"You don't speak the language here."

"No. A few words."

Toying with his coffee, he thought he should tell her about Madeleine, and even ordered himself to do so. I've found another woman, he should say.

Is it serious? she would ask.

How should I know if it's serious? he would answer.

You didn't waste any time, did you? she would say, in a hurt voice.

He had no idea how strongly Flora felt about him, and there was no need to say anything. Why take a chance on hurting her? he asked himself.

Which made him realize that he cared about this woman still, and how much. He was surprised by this realization, almost shocked.

Some people came out onto the terrace, sat down at a neighboring table, and began speaking English. The terrace and the view were no longer theirs alone. Their conversation, such as it was, would from here on be monitored.

"Let's go up to my room," Flora said. "We can sit out on the balcony and talk."

In the end they did very little talking. They came into her room and he saw that it was far bigger than his boat, bigger than two of his boats put together. The floor was marble. The French windows were open onto the balcony and he saw that the view was the same as from the terrace below except, this high up, even better.

They stood on the balcony together, hands clutching the wrought iron.

"Your idea about getting divorced," Flora said, "I thought that by now you might be having second thoughts."

"My idea?"

"That maybe you had changed your mind about the divorce."

The audacity of this woman caused him to give a dry chuckle. "Me? Changed my mind?"

"I wondered if maybe," Flora said, "you weren't as keen on divorce as you had been. Didn't want to go through with it anymore."

His mind reeling, Jack fixed on her use of the word *keen*. A midwestern word, probably. Though still part of Flora's vocabulary, it was one you never heard in New York anymore. It proved how provincial she still was. Maybe it did.

"Most of our marital problems," Flora offered, "had to do with you being a cop. You cared more about being a cop than about being my husband, right?"

She waited for an answer.

Maybe it was true. Finally he said: "I don't know."

"But now you're not a cop anymore. So those problems are over, aren't they?"

Jack was unable to answer. He watched his hand stroke the railing of the balcony.

"Your name hasn't been out of the papers since you left, do you know that?"

"No," said Jack, "I didn't. What do they say?"

"There's a lot of speculation about where you are. But I haven't told a soul. When the reporters interview me I tell them I know where you are and that you're safe, and that's all."

She was gazing out at the harbor. Jack studied her profile.

"People keep asking me what's it like being married to such a hero."

Jack was amused at her. "What do you tell them?"

"I roll my eyes and say: 'If you only knew.'" And she laughed. She had a clear, musical laugh. He had always loved to hear her laugh.

There was no awning over the balcony. The midday sun beat down on their heads.

"It's so hot," said Flora. "I'm going to get out of this dress, put on something cool, do you mind?"

She stepped back inside. "It's hot in here too."

After a moment he too stepped into the room. "Put the air-conditioning on."

"You know how I've always hated air-conditioning."

He watched her step out of her spiked heels.

"There's a great job waiting for you if you come back," she said.

"Doing what?"

"That's up to you. I just know that you're a hero and a lot of people would like to employ you."

She presented her back to him. "Undo me."

His fingers worked on the buttons down her dress. He thought it was getting steamy in this room, and he didn't mean from the heat of the day.

"So if you changed your mind about the divorce, if you wanted to go on with our marriage, well, I think I could be induced to give it a try."

Although he had known for some minutes where her peculiar logic was taking them, still he was speechless.

In bra and panties she laid a sundress out on the bed. Then she reached behind herself and unhooked her bra. "There's a built-in bra in the dress," she explained conversationally. "So I don't need to wear this anymore."

He kept his eyes down and started for the balcony, for she had stepped out of her panties too. "I'm so white," she said conversationally. "I must get some sun while I'm here, don't you think?"

She whirled around for him. "Look how white I am."

He shouldn't have looked, but did. And once he looked he had problems.

He went out and stood on the balcony, where he stared resolutely down on the harbor, trying to ignore whatever Flora was doing or not doing. There were people on some of the yachts, and others on the promenade opposite, none looking up as yet, even as Flora came out naked onto the balcony behind him. He felt her bare arms come around him and she rubbed herself on him in plain view of all those people down there.

He had perhaps known, knowing Flora, this was going to happen. Nonetheless he was startled. "People will see you," he said, and turned so fast he almost knocked her down. He had to grab her to keep her from falling. But she continued to fall backward. She fell all the way back to the bed, pulling him along, pulling him down on top of her. He was fully dressed and she was not, but this disparity did not last long.

For the first time in his life he was seduced against his will— well, more or less against his will. The French windows were wide open and the sunlight streamed in, together with the heat. It was like making love out of doors. It lasted over an hour. It was so totally unexpected that it became, in a certain sense, magical.

But afterward he took a shower in Flora's bathroom and thought of Madeleine. He scrubbed and scrubbed, especially those parts of him that had done the work, trying to scrub Flora's scent off him, in case Madeleine was waiting at his boat or he should meet her on the quay. He felt like an unfaithful husband getting ready to return home, and had trouble comprehending why this should be. He had not known Madeleine long and did not know her all that well. There had been no commitment—not spoken, not yet. Flora was the one he was married to, was still married to, was still pledged to be true to. It was absurd, he told himself. What had just happened between them had already happened hundreds of times and was of no significance. But he did not imagine this would be Madeleine's opinion if she found out. For the longest time he went on scrubbing, but whatever he was trying to scrub away remained.

After leaving Flora he drove up onto the high corniche and found a spot from which he could look down on almost the entire coast, and there he continued to brood. Below were all the tiny harbors, and the bigger harbor over at Nice, and farther on was the vast Nice airport whose runways from this distance and height seemed to reflect the sun like mirrored glass; a plane taking off looked no bigger than a fly. He watched it and brooded about Flora, about what she was offering him. He tried to deny that they had just had a delightful time together, one of the best they had ever had. Suppose he did go back to New York with her. What then? What was he doing in this foreign place anyway?

To his left was one spiky peninsula jutting out, and to his right were two more, each one two or more miles long. And in front of him in all directions was the true vastness which was the sea. Sure it was beautiful here on the coast, but beauty was not enough, if it was not where a man truly belonged. New York was where he truly belonged. Victoriano Zaragon could not remain at large much longer. New York was in his soul. Its grime had become part of his psyche. If you were a New Yorker you could scrub and scrub and never get that grime off yourself. No, he was not a cop anymore, but so what?

And he brooded about Madeleine. Why did he feel at present so unfaithful, so guilty? He was only a man and had behaved as one. It wasn't just the male orgasm that, once started, could not be stopped. A good deal of the foreplay that preceded it, once started, could not be stopped also. An imperative took over that was stronger than the will of any man. You could almost say that what had happened wasn't really his fault. It was Flora's fault.

Which woman did he love, and how much? It seemed to him that Madeleine was the one he had betrayed. That's where the guilt was. So perhaps Madeleine was the one he loved, for guilt and love were the same, were they not?

Did it have to be one woman or the other? Was love exclusive? Couldn't he love both?

Two women at once. Now, there was a true perversion for you.

What was love? A question for the ages. No one, so far as he knew, had ever come up with an answer. But whenever the subject of love arose there was a second question that also had to be asked: who could you live with in what the world calls happiness, and who not?

There were some who might have called Jack twice blessed, for he had made love with two women one right after the other. But this was not how he himself saw it.

Getting back into his car, he drove down from the high corniche to the middle one, the road dropping and twisting all the way, and from there to the lower corniche, same kind of roads, and into the Beaulieu port, where he parked his car and got out. Though he looked all around he did not see Madeleine and so he walked head down along the quay and back to his boat. He walked past her windows without looking up, knowing that she might be looking out now, this would not be spying now, it fell well within what he conceived to be her code, for she would be watching only to see when he would come back. After that, again as he conceived her code, it would be up to him to make the first move. And he would make it, but he needed a few minutes longer to be alone, to think.

When he came to his boat he jumped down into it—his hip was strong enough now even for that—and went into the galley and made himself a cup of tea, and took it out to the banquette in the fantail and sat sipping it. Often Madeleine would come by in the afternoon, he would brew a whole pot for the two of them, and they would sit sipping and talking and watch the sun begin to go down behind the Cap Ferrat. But he did not think she would come today.

About ten minutes later he did receive a visitor, but not someone part of, or interested in, his troubled love affairs. The visitor was a man, not a woman, and once he made his presence known, Jack's life, what was left of it, would never be the same.

He had noticed the man moving along the quay looking into boats, though afterward he could never be sure when he had noticed him. At what point had he felt the first vague itch that to him meant danger? At what point did the itch go into premonitions that were a form of fear—disaster on its way?

The man was wearing a white shirt open at the neck—a Lacoste tennis shirt, Jack would realize later, for he would note the crocodile over the pocket—and brown trousers with a sharp crease, and loafers. He was wearing a floppy tennis hat and mirrored sunglasses. He wasn't doing anything except looking into boats. In itself this wasn't suspicious—people did it all the time. Some people liked to gawk at yachts the way other people like to gawk at girls. Sometimes Jack even talked to gawkers, if they spoke English, and one day there had been a Danish couple he had invited aboard for a drink.

Slowly, deliberately, the man was moving into Jack's range. He was looking into each boat as if looking for one to buy. He may already have spotted Jack by then. Perhaps this was why he was so unhurried. He seemed a man with all the time in the world, but something about him had caught Jack's eye—the way he walked, the way he carried his head—something—so that Jack said to himself: I know that guy.

When the man reached the level of Jack's gangway, which was a foot wide and six feet long, they stared at each other for a time. That is, Jack stared at the image of himself as reflected in the man's sunglasses.

There was four feet of water between them. Standing on the quay the man was, of course, much higher. Slowly, dramatically, exactly like a stripper at the ultimate moment removing her brassiere, he removed his sunglasses. But it wasn't a bit sexy. Or funny either.

Jack was looking into the sardonic smile of Victoriano Zaragon.

There followed a moment of mindless, instantaneous terror. It was purely visceral, not something Jack or any man could have controlled, and it was caused as much by shock as by the realization that it was in this man's interest to kill him. He stared at Zaragon the way a soldier would stare at a hand grenade that had landed live at his feet. Did he have time to do something, or was it already too late?

"Bang, bang, you dead," said Zaragon, pointing with his forefinger.

Although it had been all he could do to keep from cringing, Jack had willed himself, as soon as the initial surprise had passed, to continue sipping his tea, to concentrate on lifting the cup to his lips. He was unarmed. If Zaragon meant to kill him now, there was nothing he could do about it. Therefore it became a matter of pride. He would die if necessary, but his hand would not shake, nor any tea spill.

"Bang, bang," said Zaragon, the stupid forefinger still pointing. And he gave a laugh that was very close to a giggle.

A moment ago Jack had had love problems, sure, but apart from that was in a state of almost total peace. He was sipping tea and his body felt good, well used today certainly, but otherwise no problems. He had rarely felt so healthy, so physically safe.

But terror had chased that moment from his head.

"You recognize me, I think yes," said Zaragon.

"I recognize you. What do you want?"

However much he had tried to hide his initial reaction, there must have been an involuntary flinch, or some other sign that Zaragon had picked up on.

"Then you know why I arrive in this place." The young man's giggle was gone, his thin smile fading fast.

Jack was sneaking glances here and there, looking for a weapon. He remembered the gaff lashed down forward. Could he get to it?

"How you not die? How I miss you? You so close that night. As close as now."

The gaff was too far away. He'd never make it.

"You kill my brother."

No weapon. Jack could throw the teacup at him. There was nothing else.

Zaragon held up both hands outward, the universal gesture of peace, though that wasn't what it meant here. In one hand he held his sunglasses, in the other his hat, both hands otherwise empty and unthreatening. He said: "Relax yourself. You not dead. Not yet. Later." And again he laughed.

Jack's eyes raked Zaragon's body, discerning no revolver-shaped bulges. The drug trafficker was apparently unarmed. Other than this Jack's mind leaped about, fixing itself nowhere.

"You know why I come here today?" Zaragon said. "So you will know I have find you. You think I not find you? I find you easy. I not kill you. Me? No, no, not me. I get someone." As he became increasingly angry, almost ranting, his English began to fall apart. "That man you take to Corsica? He supposed to do it. The sea make him sick."

The shock of this information perhaps showed on Jack's face.

"Next time you not be so lucky," said Zaragon. "Who will do it? Ask yourself. Could be anybody. I hire someone. From Nice maybe. Local talent. Good idea, no? You don't know who, you don't know when. You watch everybody. You cannot watch everybody. You worry. You die many times before you die." He began to laugh again. "Is very funny, no?" He stopped laughing and said: "Finally someone come and kill you."

Jack got up and carried his cup into the galley where, for all Zaragon knew, the weapons were. There he stood for some seconds trying to collect himself. When he came topside again Zaragon was gone. Jack spotted him striding rapidly down the quay. In a moment he had turned the corner and was hidden by other boats.

Shock and confusion were over. Jack stepped off the boat and went after him, a detective's natural reaction. Get practical. Define the problem, define the threat. Get as close as you can. Stick to him. Find out where he goes, who he sees. Collect the facts. When you have the facts you make your plans.

There was this added advantage, Jack knew: close to Zaragon, the threat was less. The safest place to be was on top of him.

On the restaurant side of the port he saw him climb into a low red sports car, an Alfa Romeo perhaps, its top down. This made Jack sneer. A nice flamboyant car, easy to tail. For such a man to drive such a car was stupid. To pretend to the role of rich tourist on the Riviera was stupid. It gave Jack something to hook into. How could he exploit it?

As soon as Zaragon turned the corner, Jack got into his own car, but when he came up onto the lower corniche he had to make a choice: east toward Monte Carlo and Italy or west toward Nice? He picked west, came out the other side of Beaulieu, and was rewarded. In places the corniche was a true ledge road cut into the cliff face and curving around each indentation in the sea. There were places where he could look across the intervening space at cars half a mile ahead.

One of them was the red car.

The road narrowed further as it filtered through Villefranche. When it came out the other side he could see the deep, horseshoe-shaped rade below with many pleasure boats close in toward shore and two cruise ships anchored in the middle with launches glued to their sides.

Ahead the road reappeared on its ledge and he looked for the red car but did not see it. He was about to pass two small hotels. He thought it unlikely that a man like Zaragon would deign to put up at either but he ducked into the first one's parking area, checked it out, then tried the other.

No red car in either place.

He came back out onto the corniche and returned to Villefranche, where he steered down the steep narrow street that drops to the Old Town and the harbor. He knew there was a row of restaurants down there along the edge of the sea, and a single hotel as well. This hotel, the Welcome, built originally during the first half of the last century, was small, chic, and famous. It was the type place Zaragon might choose.

Jack found the red car parked under the trees of the village square. It stood almost at the hotel's front door, a no parking zone, and as Jack watched, a porter in a striped vest came out and got in behind the wheel. He backed it away from the door and drove out of the square and down into the legal parking area beside the customs shed. The porter then began to lift the top up and lock it into place.

Jack pulled his own car in beside him, got out, and leaned in the porter's window. "Nice car," he said. "Whose is it?" He was speaking English, which he hoped the porter understood.

Most of these hotel people spoke some English, as this man proved to. "This is Monsieur Moro's car," he answered.

"I thought it might be Mr. Salazar's car." Jack had known a cop named Salazar. "South American guy." Jack handed the porter fifty francs, which disappeared instantly.

"No, Monsieur Moro."

"He's a Colombian, right?"

"No, American. From Puerto Rico."

"Is he alone?"

"Yes, alone."

"I thought it was Mr. Salazar's car," said Jack. "Stupid mistake on my part."

He drove back to Beaulieu, where he parked below Madeleine's windows and went up the stairs and knocked on her door.

When she opened to him her face looked suddenly pleased, as if she imagined that the brief interview with his ex-wife was over and he had come back to her.

Jack wasn't thinking about his wife at that moment, nor about Madeleine either. He went past her into the room. This was not a romantic visit, and as she realized it her smile vanished.

"What's the matter?"

He told her that he had had bad news and needed her help. She was not to get alarmed, but in fact Victoriano Zaragon had turned up. He was at the Welcome Hotel in Villefranche and—

She interrupted. "How do you know?"

"I tailed him there."

A detective herself, she began interrogating him. "You actually saw him?"

"Yes. He's registered under the name Moro. He's driving a rented Alfa. I have the plate numbers right here—"

"He see you?"

"He knows I'm here." Jack was determined not to overdramatize this.

"Spoke to him?"

"Yes." He had sat down on her bed. "We did have a few words."

Madeleine was pacing. "Did he threaten you?"

"Well . . ."

"He's put out a contract on you?"

Jack shrugged this off. "That's not important."

"Not important?"

Jack tried to calm her down. What was important, he told her, was that he knew where Zaragon was located and could lead the police there. Zaragon now could be arrested.

"On what charge?"

"There's an international warrant out on him."

"How do you know?"

"There must be."

"Maybe," said Madeleine.

Cops had to be found and persuaded to arrest him, Jack explained, and that's where he thought she could help.

He had given her no explanation about Flora or where he had been all afternoon, which was perhaps what she had expected to hear, been waiting for.

He wanted her to take him to the police, Jack said. Whichever police had jurisdiction. He was still sitting, apparently calmly, on the bed. He was trying not to alarm her. His own agitation did not show, he believed. Madeleine, pacing, was much more obviously agitated than he was. He wanted her to interpret for him, he said. He wanted arrest teams to surround the hotel at once, before Zaragon had time to disappear, before he had time to make any phone calls, if possible. Such speed wasn't possible, and Jack knew this, and he fell silent. He knew cops didn't move that fast, but a single phone call from Zaragon to some *milieu* thug, the "local talent" of which he had spoken, could be enough to seal Jack's death warrant.

Madeleine was looking at him thoughtfully. She said: "You want the police to arrest a foreigner on a warrant they have never seen and which perhaps doesn't exist."

"It has to exist."

"My experience with law enforcement is that somebody has to give the order to send it out, and somebody else has to remember to do it."

Jack studied her.

"A foreigner with a probably valid passport," said Madeleine.

"It's forged."

"Maybe. The arresting officers wouldn't be able to determine that."

Again Jack was silent.

"It's probably not a forgery," Madeleine said. "It's probably in the name of some dead man, and perfectly valid." She was thinking it out. "You want to know the number one rule of French cops?"

"The number one rule," said Jack. "What would that be?"

"Don't get involved in the quarrels of foreigners." Madeleine grabbed her handbag and started for the doors. She said: "I'm just getting you ready for what you're going to hear," and she led the way downstairs to his car.

≡ CHAPTER 15 ≡

In towns like Beaulieu, population under ten thousand, jurisdiction fell to the Gendarmerie, not the Police Nationale. The local Gendarmerie office was behind the tennis club, a kind of storefront set into the big building in which the gendarmes and their families were housed. The officer behind the desk was very young, very formal. He looked about eighteen but was certainly over twenty-one, and when Madeleine asked for someone of higher rank, the young man huffily refused her. But finally another gendarme, this one a sergeant, came out from inside. He was about forty, chewing on something and buttoning his tunic as he appeared.

"*Bonjour, monsieur, 'dame,*" he said politely. "What can I do for you?"

"This guy isn't high enough either," muttered Jack in English.

But he appeared to be in charge at the moment, so Madeleine described who Jack was, who Zaragon was, what was needed.

But the gendarme interrupted her. "Don't I know you?"

Madeleine said: "I don't think so, no."

"Yes, I do. You're that lady cop on television. Made a scandal. Broke the obligation of reserve." His manner was suddenly stiff and unfriendly, almost belligerent, and the expression on his face had changed.

"What's the matter?" said Jack, looking from one to the other.

"We have a bit of a problem," conceded Madeleine. This sergeant, she judged, was one of those who had obeyed the rules, written and unwritten, his whole career. He had no patience with public servants who considered themselves above the rules—her, for instance.

She had been afraid of running into a reaction like this. It was why she had not gone directly to the PJ in Nice.

The gendarme's attention switched to Jack: "Who's this *mec*?"

Madeleine resumed her explanation.

But again the gendarme interrupted, speaking directly to Jack. "You a *flic*?"

"Used to be."

"He said he used to be," said Madeleine. "He's retired."

"Papers," said the gendarme to Jack.

Jack, who carried a card that identified him as a retired New York City detective, passed it across the desk. To the gendarme it lacked official weight. He was looking for stamps, photos, raised seals. To him a card as flimsy as this had no heft and therefore proved nothing.

Which Madeleine realized. "His passport is on his boat," she interjected.

Eyeing Jack suspiciously, the gendarme glanced at the card front and back, held it between thumb and forefinger for a moment, then let it fall as if tainted to the counter. He said: "You say there's an arrest warrant? Let me see it."

"We don't have it," conceded Madeleine.

Jack retrieved his card.

"Come back when you have the warrant," said the gendarme.

"That's just the problem," said Madeleine. "We don't have time to wait for it to come through."

"No warrant," scoffed the gendarme. "What do you want from me?"

"This man Zaragon threatened to kill Mr. Dilger. You can pick him up on that and hold him overnight."

"Negative," said the gendarme.

"By tomorrow we should have the warrant."

"Lady, the story you told on TV sounded farfetched to me. This story you're telling now sounds farfetched too."

"He's not going to help us," said Madeleine to Jack.

"Try the Police Judiciaire in Nice," the gendarme said to Jack.

"What's he saying?" said Jack.

"Maybe you better go by yourself," said the gendarme to Jack. "Because I doubt they'll let this lady in the door."

"What did he say?" asked Jack.

"If the PJ buys your story, fine. I don't buy it, and there's nothing I could do if I did." The gendarme turned and walked out.

"He won't help," said Madeleine.

"I gathered that much. What else did he say?"

"He said to try the PJ in Nice."

"Then we'll go there," asserted Jack.

They walked along the sidewalk to Jack's car. "It will be the same story in Nice," said Madeleine.

Jack held the door for her. "Get in."

"I'm a pariah," said Madeleine in a small voice. She had hoped that other cops would approve of what she had done. But she saw it wasn't so. She had broken rules they continued to obey. This made her either better than they were or worse. Most, when they thought of her, were contemptuous. She was a traitor to their code.

And so she sat squeezed into the corner of the car and worried about how she would be received at the Rue de Roquebillière and who she would meet there. If she greeted her former colleagues, would they greet her back?

But the rush hour had started, and on the corniche the traffic was stopped up going through Villefranche, and again entering Nice. By the time they reached the Rue de Roquebillière it was late. Madeleine told Jack to park in the street, and they walked in past the barrier and up to the window, where she showed herself to the guard, whom she evidently knew. He waved them on, and she led the way up the outside stairs. By then she was so filled with dread she was almost trembling. The stairs were familiar stairs to her and so were the offices when she opened the door and stepped into them.

No one was there but her friend Inspector Bosco. To Madeleine this was a great relief. Bosco greeted her with an embrace, and kisses on both cheeks. How was she? he wanted to know. What was the status of her lawsuit? And they chatted in French while Jack waited.

Finally, switching from one language to the other, she identified the men to each other and they shook hands.

"Where is everybody?" asked Jack impatiently.

"Gone home," said Madeleine. "It's quite late."

"It's the hour when the crooks begin to come out," said Jack. "The stores haven't closed yet, the post offices are still open. How can all the detectives have gone home?"

Madeleine was breathing easier that they had. Three detectives, she explained to Jack, one each from Finance, Narcotics, and the Criminelle, would be on duty at the central commissariat on the Avenue Foch. They would respond to any crimes that happened during the night.

Jack's face showed amazement, but increasing impatience too. "So what do we do now?" he demanded, and he began recalculating his options. If no one would help him, he did what? He was certainly not going to sit around waiting to be killed.

"I have an idea," he said to Madeleine. "If your friend here will agree. Explain this to him . . ."

An hour later he sat with her in his darkened car under the trees in the parking lot at Villefranche, and together they watched the Welcome Hotel. Beyond it they could see part of the row of lighted restaurants along the waterfront. From time to time other cars came into the lot and pulled into slots nearby, and the passengers got out and strolled toward the restaurants.

Inspector Bosco had already been inside the hotel for some time. By now he would have flashed his credentials on whoever was in charge and begun asking questions as Jack had instructed him to do. He was to pretend to be interested in any foreigners who might be registered. Finance detectives had no authority in such matters, but the man he was questioning wouldn't know that and by now would be giving increasingly nervous answers. In America people, innocent or not, always got nervous when questioned by cops, and it wouldn't be any different here.

But Jack was getting nervous too, for Bosco was taking too long.

"Come on, come on," he muttered to himself.

The longer Bosco took, the more risk that Zaragon, either now or later, would become aware that the police had been there asking questions. Jack had instructed Bosco to conduct his interview in an office with the door closed and to put no special focus on Zaragon/Moro. But at this hour in a hotel as small as this one there might be only one clerk on duty, who might be obliged to stay behind the front desk the entire time. Suppose Zaragon walked past and overheard something? Or someone else did, and told him?

"Hurry up, for chrissake," Jack muttered.

It was then that the red sports car pulled into the lot into a slot only four cars away. Jack saw Zaragon get out, and that's all he saw, for he threw himself on Madeleine and buried his face in her neck. He had hit her with such suddenness that she gave a grunt and tried to fight him off.

"It's him," Jack hissed into her neck.

He felt her body relax. She even laughed. "For a moment I thought it was my charms. I could turn you into an animal without even doing anything."

"What's he up to?" said Jack into her neck.

"He's got a woman with him."

"What kind of woman?"

"A prostitute, from the look of her."

"What would you know about prostitutes?"

"Her heels are eight inches high, her dress is two sizes too small, and he's hurrying her toward the hotel with his hand cupping her bottom. Does that sound like a prostitute to you?"

"Sorry," said Jack into her neck.

After a moment Madeleine said: "You can come up for air now, I think."

Jack sat up and saw that Zaragon and the prostitute had almost reached the hotel. "Christ," he said. "He'll bump into Bosco in there."

"Don't worry about Bosco," said Madeleine.

"If Zaragon makes him as a cop—"

"I know he's only a Frenchman," said Madeleine, "but he's a very experienced detective."

About a minute later they watched Bosco come out and approach their car. In one hand he carried papers rolled up like a relay baton, and he leaned in their window.

"I told the clerk I was looking for illegal Arabs," he said, Madeleine translating. "That's always a good cover. Nobody likes Arabs."

He unrolled the papers, and plucked one out. "Is that the *mec*?" he asked Jack.

It was a Xerox copy of the second and third pages of an American passport. One page showed Zaragon's photo. The other gave the particulars of a man named Moro: date of birth, sex, passport number.

"That's him," said Jack. "Did he see you?"

"Was that him who just went into the hotel?" inquired Bosco. "I thought it might be. I was finished by then. I wished him and the *pute* bon soir, and walked out past them."

They decided on a plan. Bosco would go back to the Rue de Roquebillière. The Finance Brigade dealt regularly with the FBI, and Bosco knew the name of their principal FBI contact in

Washington. He would send a fax of Zaragon's passport pages asking for an immediate check of the passport's validity.

"If it comes back invalid," Bosco said, "we arrest the *mec* on a forged passport. We should get an answer by tomorrow. But it looked genuine to me."

"If it's genuine—" said Madeleine.

"Then where are we?" said Bosco. "Moro may not be his real name, but you'd have to have proof." He started to move off to his car, but turned back. "You better see about that murder warrant if you want to be sure we can take him off the streets."

"I'll call New York," Jack told him.

He and Madeleine returned to Beaulieu, let themselves into her brother's office, and Jack put a call in to Assistant DA McCauley. This was the same young man who had questioned him in front of the grand jury.

In New York it was early afternoon. McCauley was in court, he was told. There should be a recess in an hour. If she could get a message to him, the secretary said, maybe he could return the call then.

Jack hung up. "Can we wait?" he said to Madeleine.

"Of course."

"It might be an hour."

"We'll wait."

"It might be longer."

Madeleine came over and pressed his head against her waist. There were no drapes or shutters. A shot through the plate glass into the lighted office was all it would take. "Turn the lights out," said Jack.

The office went dark. Jack sat in a swivel chair at Alain's desk, Madeleine in an armchair across the room, and they waited. Presently Jack got up and moved the chair to a darker corner. "I don't want to make it too easy for somebody," he muttered.

They waited an hour with the lights off before the phone rang. Jack lunged for it.

"How you doing?" said Assistant District Attorney McCauley.

"Fine," said Jack, "how're you?" He remembered the attempt at a mustache that the young man had shaved off. He remembered he had been about to get married. "Did your wedding come off on schedule?" Amazing, he thought. Small talk. Even in times of crisis the amenities are most often observed.

"Sure did," said McCauley. "How's the weather there? On vacation, are you?"

Jack cut him off. Was there or wasn't there an international arrest warrant on Zaragon? he demanded.

"I thought there was," the young prosecutor said, sounding puzzled.

"You thought?"

"It's not my department."

"Jesus," said Jack.

"My job was to get the indictment, and I got it. The rest is up to somebody else."

Jack was silent.

"You sound troubled," said McCauley. "What's the trouble?"

"The guy is here," said Jack.

"Who's here?"

"Zaragon."

"You're kidding me."

"I saw him."

Now the young man fell silent. "Did he see you?" he asked finally.

"Yes."

"That's a problem."

"Yes," said Jack. "It's a problem. And the French police can't act without a warrant. So where's the warrant?"

"I don't know. Maybe I can find out."

"Find out," said Jack urgently. "And if it's not already here, get it here."

"I'm in court the rest of the day. I'll get started on it first thing tomorrow."

"Today," said Jack. "Today. Immediately."

He could not get a commitment out of the young man, who promised only to do the best he could.

"Take care of yourself," McCauley said brightly, and rang off.

Jack went to the window and peered out at the quays. The warrant might come quickly, but probably it would not. Meanwhile, how did he protect himself? Tonight, for instance? He could not spend the night in this office, or even in this port, but the only implements for leaving were: number one, his car; or number two, his boat. Someone could be waiting either place.

Some choice, he thought.

He stood far enough back from the window so that no light fell on him. Of the two he preferred his boat. If he could get it unmoored and out of the port it was doubtful that anyone would find him before morning. He might actually be able to get some sleep.

From the window he could see the main quay, which was dimly lit for its entire length and, at this hour, deserted. The finger quays that extended off it would be similarly dimly lit, but he could not see them through the maze of boats and masts in between. Especially he could not see his own boat, nor anyone who might be hiding on it or near it.

Madeleine said: "What are you going to do?"

"I'm certainly not going to wait around here for someone to shoot me," Jack said, and he gave her a smile which was meant to reassure her—himself too—but didn't.

Madeleine stood beside him at the window. On the quays that they could see under the dim lights nothing moved.

"You could stay with me," said Madeleine.

"A bit dangerous for you, don't you think?"

She shrugged.

He told her he meant to sail the boat out of the harbor and anchor it somewhere. He was thinking about himself by then, not her. Anything he did was dangerous, and he reached for the door handle. "Good night."

He stepped outside and felt bathed in the warm night air. It seemed to him he could feel his entire body. Being alive felt delicious. He had no desire not to be alive.

To his right the warehouses and stores were dark. To his left were the bright lights of the restaurants. People moved about down there, not many. He could hear voices, cars starting up. It gave him a sense of security that he knew was entirely false. As he moved down the quay toward his boat he listened for sounds that should not be there, watched for movement where there should be none. He was aware that there was nothing between him and bullets but his shirt.

To his surprise Madeleine came up and took his hand and walked along beside him. "You look like a man who needs company," she said.

He stopped. "I don't want to have to worry about you."

"I can worry about myself, thank you."

If there was to be shooting he did not want her caught in the crossfire. On the other hand he was touched that she was willing to share his risk.

"I'll get the boat," he said. "Wait here."

He went on alone. He was out on the finger quay now with the sterns of boats to both sides. No one lived on any of the boats along here, meaning that all should be empty, and he stopped again and peered ahead and listened hard, but saw nothing, heard nothing. Above him was the moon, which was a little past half, plus the usual billion stars. He took a deep breath and walked on past the boats and came to his own boat, then bent to disconnect the umbilical wires and tubes, and then the lines. When this was done he jumped aboard. No one had shot him so far.

He picked Madeleine up on the way by and they sailed out of the harbor and around the cape and along the coast. When they were a good distance out they passed the great scourge of light that was Nice, and all this time Jack was weighing his options. He could sail into some other marina, but you had to check into them. It was like checking into a hotel. The harbormaster would know he was there, and Zaragon's men might find him with a few phone calls. Nor could he just turn off the engines and drift. There was too much traffic in these waters, everything from fishing smacks to the liners to and from Corsica; in the night something might run him down. So he would have to anchor somewhere—but where? He would have to pick his spot, for the water most places was enormously deep.

"Where are we going?" Madeleine shouted.

He had the engines up close to full throttle.

He had decided to anchor between the two islands off Cannes, he told her, and she nodded.

He was at ease with this decision, and although they were far out he watched the shore, watched the towns pass, in his head identifying each cluster of lights, and for the first time in many hours felt safe. He had nothing to worry about out here.

In time they came to the islands, great bulky shadows dead ahead, and he steered between them. Madeleine, who had gone forward, tossed the anchor overboard, and he cut the engines. He listened to the sudden silence, felt the sudden peace. This seemed the last place anyone would look for him, and parked like this between islands the boat would not rock much in the night. He had no idea what the weather forecast might be, but if it turned bad the islands would offer some protection. Most likely the sea would remain as calm as it was right now.

"And tomorrow?" said Madeleine, who had jumped down into the cockpit and stood beside him.

"Tomorrow I'm going to buy a gun."

"That's interesting." She was immediately on her guard and he sensed this.

"How can I get one?"

"You can't."

"Come on."

"The laws are very strict here, sorry to say. Virtually no one gets a permit to carry."

"I'm an ex-cop."

"You're a foreigner."

"An illegal gun, then."

Madeleine said nothing.

"Can you get me one?"

"No."

It sounded like a no that permitted no argument. "In New York the laws are strict too," Jack said carefully. "But if somebody had to have an illegal gun, as a cop I would know where to get one."

Madeleine still said nothing.

"Every cop would know where to get one," Jack said, and he watched her.

"Good for them."

"Were you a cop or not?"

She chose to remain silent.

"Well?" he said.

"If you think I'm going to help you break the law, you're crazy."

A hard silence had fallen between them. Finally she said: "Look, I have an excellent chance to be reinstated. They find out I helped you get an illegal gun, and that's the end of that."

"How would it be traced back to you?"

"Because no one would imagine you capable of finding a gun on your own." He thought that her voice contained a certain measure of contempt, and he didn't like it. "You don't even speak the language," she said. "They'd blame me, and they'd be right."

"You won't help me?"

"No."

He was used to carrying a gun, wanted one, believed he had to have one, and for all these reasons was unwilling to let the subject lie. "If I get killed, how will you feel?"

She hesitated, and when she spoke refused to look at him. "I'm not sure I believe the threat is as real as you do."

"The only way to check it out is to let it happen. Which I choose not to do."

"Someone kills you, the investigation would be enormous.

They must realize that. We'd catch them. Maybe destroy the whole cocaine business on the Côte d'Azur."

"But I'd be dead. I've been dead once already. I didn't like it."

"Can I fix you a cup of tea?"

"Never mind, I'll fix one myself."

Choosing not to respond, Madeleine went into the galley to make the tea. It was her way of ending the argument. Perhaps also it was a way of getting as far away from him as the confines of the boat permitted.

They sat sipping tea in the balmy night, while the water lapped against the hull. But the closeness between them that used to be there, the comfort in each other's company that had begun on Corsica, was gone. Perhaps it had never really existed. In any case it was not there now.

"Tell me about your wife," said Madeleine. She was stirring up the embers, he conjectured, lighting a new argument off the old one. Or perhaps the first argument had not been about guns at all. Perhaps the argument had been about Flora all along.

He said: "What do you want to know?"

"I thought you were divorced."

"So did I."

"So why is she here?"

"I don't know," said Jack, though he believed he did.

"Are you divorced or aren't you?"

Above the bulk of the bigger island he could see the glow of light flung upward by Cannes. It hung in the night like golden smoke. He said: "She stopped the proceedings."

"How do you feel about that?"

"I don't know."

"I see."

"No, you don't see."

"At least you didn't lie to me. I appreciate that. Most men would just lie."

"Madeleine—"

She carried her empty tea mug forward toward the galley,

grabbing Jack's out of his hand on the way past. When she came back he reached for her but she avoided him and returned to her place on the rear banquette.

"Feel like a swim?" Jack inquired.

"No thank you."

"I think I'll take one."

She did not reply.

He stood up, took his clothes off, piled them neatly, and hesitated a moment. "Sure?" he said to her.

Again she did not reply.

He plunged over the side and came up blowing out a mouthful of spray. "It's nice," he called to her. "You should come in."

When she still said nothing he paddled about for a while, then climbed back up the ladder and into the cockpit. Water ran off him onto the deck, and he dried himself off.

"It really was nice," he said.

"Get some sleep," she told him. "I'll keep watch for a few hours."

He didn't think this was necessary and told her so. Criminals were stupid, he said. Hit men were especially stupid, and not capable of finding him here. "You give those jerks too much credit."

This was Madeleine's feeling too, though she didn't say so. "All right, we'll both sleep. You want the cabin or the banquette?"

He wanted her close, wanted to feel the old closeness, but was too proud to say so. "You can have the cabin," he said. He was annoyed at her, and at himself, but disappointed too.

In the morning he drove the boat back to Beaulieu. Last night's mood had hardened into anger: anger at Madeleine, anger at himself, and most of all anger at Zaragon and his thugs. Lying awake in the night he had made a number of decisions, and the first of them was that he was not going to let Zaragon intimidate him. His entrance into the yacht harbor was therefore as brazen as possible. He stood tall at the helm, saluted boat owners who glided past him en route to the open sea, and waved to the harbormaster and the men at the gas pumps.

"Bonjour," he called out. And again: "Bonjour."

But as the harbor narrowed, his eyes narrowed with it, and he scrutinized all the quays as they slid by. There were people he did not know on some of the boats, and sightseers or prospective buyers on some of the quays. As he penetrated deeper and deeper into the harbor he was forced to reduce speed still further, making himself the easiest of targets.

But nothing happened.

However, there were precautions he could take. Instead of tying up at the slot assigned him, he continued past it to a slot farther along that he knew to be empty, and backed in and tied up there. And once this was done he took a screwdriver and leaned over the transom and removed the plaque with the boat's name on it.

With a bemused expression on her face, Madeleine watched him.

"No sense making it easy for them," Jack said. "If they want to find me, let them work."

As they started back along the quay, Jack said to her: "Don't walk beside me. Walk behind or in front."

She gave an annoyed laugh, put her head down, and marched straight down the quay and into her brother's office. By then Jack could see his car. There was no one near it.

He unlocked it and was about to get in when Madeleine came out of the office. There had been a message from Inspector Bosco, she told him. The FBI had verified the passport Zaragon was using. The name Moro checked out. The passport number and date of birth checked out. The passport was genuine.

This was only what Jack had expected. Nonetheless, it was a disappointment.

He got into his car, put the key in the ignition, but hesitated before turning it. Madeleine was still standing nearby. The easiest way to kill him was to rig a bomb to his car, and he knew this. So did she, apparently, for she grinned at him and ran over and crouched beside the wall with her hands over her ears.

Jack, who was becoming more and more fatalistic, turned the key. They would have to hire a bomb expert first, and maybe they hadn't found one yet. When the engine came on smoothly he looked over at Madeleine, who gave him a wave.

He drove out of the marina. His first stop was the rental agency in Nice, where he turned in the car. Then he walked down the street to a second agency and hired another.

He drove it back to the Cap Ferrat to the Hotel Voile d'Or, where he found Flora beside the pool sunning herself in a modest one-piece swimsuit such as he imagined women still favored in Kansas City. Most of the other women around the pool were topless.

He waited at the bar while she got dressed, then took her up onto the high corniche to a restaurant he knew. His theory was that as long as he kept moving he was safe, and whoever was with him was safe. Zaragon's thugs could not find him except by accident, and there was no way to guard against accidents, so forget it.

They sat down on an outdoor patio under a trellis of vine leaves and ordered lunch. The view up here was different from lower down. The restaurant was on the reverse side of the mountains and faced north toward the high Alps. There were few trees so high up, nothing to obstruct the splendid view, and no other buildings within sight. The mountain ranges proceeded north in waves. Each succeeding range rose higher than the one before it, and the most distant summits were snowcapped even now in summer.

Flora was wearing a sleeveless blouse over a linen skirt. Though the sun came spattering down upon their table, the air was ten degrees cooler up here than down by the sea, and Jack went back to the car for a sweater that he draped over her shoulders.

They shared the patio with other couples, certain of whom, Jack joked, seemed to be hurrying through lunch.

"That couple over there, for instance," he said. "They're hurrying, wouldn't you say?"

Flora studied them, not yet getting the joke. "Could be."

"There are rooms upstairs, you know."

"Oh," said Flora. "Well."

"How old would you say the man is?"

"Sixty, maybe."

"And the woman?"

"In her twenties."

"An insurance executive," said Jack decisively. "The woman is his secretary. This is a very popular place with executives. Also with secretaries who enjoy a nice lunch."

Flora laughed.

"A place not normally frequented by wives. Close to the coastal cities, but isolated. Not even too expensive."

"It's got everything," said Flora.

"All French businesses are closed from twelve to two," Jack said.

"I didn't know that."

"If you eat fast, you have time."

It made Flora giggle.

As the couple finished their desserts, the man glanced at his watch.

"Now they'll go in and hire a room," said Jack.

The couple went into the inn and did not come out again.

"See?" said Jack.

Flora was laughing. "How did you know?"

"I'm a detective," said Jack.

They had nearly finished lunch themselves. As he poured out the last of their wine, Jack said with false casualness: "There's something I haven't brought you up to date on."

Flora had enjoyed lunch, he believed. She had been vivacious, had laughed frequently, her confidence growing. But now she looked down at the table.

"Is it that woman I saw you with?" she asked, and her eyes did not come up.

He had forgotten completely that she might be worried about Madeleine. "No," he said, "it's something else." And then: "Someone's after me."

"Here?"

"Here."

He told her about Zaragon, about the lack of interest of the French police, about the warrant from America that had not come.

"My poor baby," she said, not exactly the phrase he might have expected. It was a Kansas City–type phrase, he judged, sufficient in just about any situation. He could imagine girls being taught it throughout the Kansas City school system. A girl's reliable standby.

"So if I should drop out of sight for a day or two," he said, his big grin showing, "or not call you, that's the reason."

Her brows knitted together, and her hand came down over his on the table.

He realized that he had been trying to enlist her sympathy—he was not sure why. That he appeared to have done so was gratifying, though.

She played with his fingers. "Jack, what are you going to *do?*"

"As I see it," he said, "I have three choices."

Over her shoulder he could see clear-edged mountains that were thirty, maybe fifty miles away, and more mountains rolling farther back than that, with the highest summits golden white and glistening hazily in the sun.

"Choice number one," he said, "I can disappear into some other country; or two, stay where I am and wait to be killed; or three, I can get a gun and kill him before he kills me."

"Take number one," voted Flora urgently. "Disappear. Hide in Italy, South America, or—what about New York?"

"Number one is out. If the guy could find me here, he can find me anywhere. I don't see number one as a solution. I'd just be postponing it." After a pause he said stubbornly: "I live here. I'll be goddamned if I'll let some total piece of shit drive me from my home."

"It's not your home, Jack. It's a boat."

"It's home to me," he said stubbornly, and realized this was true. Home was where you tried to make or remake your life. You could only have one home at a time, sometimes none, but if you had one it was as important as life itself. Your entire psyche depended on it. Men had been defending their homes to the death since the beginning of time.

"You absolutely can't stay here," said Flora. "Number two is out."

"Number three, then," said Jack with a half smile. "Get a gun and kill him. Is that your advice?"

"No, absolutely not. Jack, you're not a killer."

Well, actually he was. He had shot a stickup man to death, and also Zaragon's brother. It seemed to him he could kill Zaragon himself and never feel a qualm.

But with what? He was still unarmed. His next job was to get a handgun, and he was not sure how to do it. Apparently it would not be easy. But until he was armed he could do nothing.

"When are you going back to the States?" he asked Flora.

"I'm staying as long as you need me."

He fell silent.

"I'm so afraid for you," said Flora, and she shivered.

They got into the car, turned their backs on the high mountains, went over the top of the mountain they were on and down the other side, down the steep switchbacks that descended first to the middle corniche and then to the lower one. The various cliffs, capes, and coastal towns came into view one after the other, some of them then disappearing, some reappearing for a second or even a third time. Always the sea was there below them.

Finally he drove out onto the Cap Ferrat and up to her hotel and parked.

"Do you want to come in?" Flora asked.

He was preoccupied by then, and declined.

"Stay with me, Jack."

"There's something I have to do."

"It will wait."

"I appreciate the offer, but no thank you."

"You'd be safe here."

"I'll protect myself, don't worry."

There were tears in Flora's eyes as she leaned over the steering wheel and kissed him. "I'm not going back to New York," she said. "I'm staying until this is over."

"Thank you."

"I'll wait for you," she promised. "If you need me, if you need anything at all . . ."

She got out and went into the hotel.

He watched her go, but did not immediately restart the engine. Instead he sat drumming his fingers on the wheel. In New York he knew where everything was, legal and illegal both. In New York if he needed an illegal gun he would go looking for street people he had arrested in the past, or informants to whom he had given money. Gun running was a trade like any other and easy to tap into. If they themselves did not have the gun he needed, they would lead him to someone who did. There were millions of illegal guns in America—millions in New York alone. It would not take long.

But France was not America. Where to look? Who to approach? French criminals had guns, same as American ones. Where did they get them? There must be a trade in illegal weapons here. All he had to do was find it. But how?

He drove into Nice, where he cruised through various neighborhoods. In New York he would have gone directly to one of the ghettos, and he was looking for the equivalent. That was where to find guns, drugs, stolen goods, and the men who dealt in them. A cop knew the underside of his city better than he knew its bright lights. In his own city a cop, any cop, was the ultimate insider, and the ultimate outsider was the tourist, any tourist. Jack Dilger, who had been the cop, was now himself the tourist. He didn't speak the language of the country. He didn't know where to look for what he had to have.

He cruised up and down searching for a neighborhood that looked the same, sounded the same, smelled the same as one of the New York ghettos. His plan once he had found it was go into a bar and talk to people, preferably Arabs. He was aware that the underclass here was Arab, not black. Therefore it was Arabs who would be hooked into street crime, and street crime meant guns.

Also, it was unlikely an Arab could be an undercover cop. He had no intention of winding up in a French jail on a gun charge.

But, although he drove round and round, he could not find the type of neighborhood he was looking for.

He did spot two Arabs loitering outside the railroad station. By then it was getting dark, which was at least the right time of day for an errand of this kind. He parked nearby, got out, and stood beside his car and watched the two men.

An hour passed, two. He was barely conscious of the passage of time. Other men came up to the two Arabs, not many, three in two hours. One of the Arabs, usually the same one, would go off with them and be gone awhile and then come back.

Jack became convinced they were dealing drugs. Crossing the street, he went up to them and wiped his nose a few times and in broken French asked what they were selling. He didn't know the slang word for drugs here and so used the American ones. Also, he flashed some American dollars.

The two Arabs moved off to confer among themselves, then returned, and one gave a jerk of his head, meaning that Jack was to follow.

He was led across the street and down an alley and into a side door. Inside was a staircase and no light except a dim bulb up on the first landing. Jack became immediately tense. New York undercover cops went into places like this every day, but never without backup, never without transmitters taped to their breastbones, never without small flat guns, .25s maybe, hidden in their socks. But often enough they got ripped off anyway. They got beaten up, even killed. Every cop in New York knew the stories.

So he did not like this setup at all. The Arab had turned and was holding out merchandise; a number of glassine envelopes. He was reciting prices too, so much for one bag, so much for purchasing in bulk. Peering up the staircase, Jack was listening for other sounds, the movement of a confederate. He was waiting to be pounced on.

The Arab was waiting too, palm still outstretched, but when his free hand darted down into his pocket, Jack grabbed him. The Arab let out a squeal, and they struggled. The two men were about the same size but the Arab was younger and presumably had not recently been hospitalized. Jack had one arm around his neck, and with his other hand was squeezing the hand in the pocket so it could not come out.

There was no gun in the pocket, Jack could feel that much, and a rapid pat-down disclosed no bulges anywhere else. Jack let him go and began apologizing in French and English both.

The Arab was on his knees scooping up the dropped envelopes, for they were worth money, first things first. Presently he had them all. After stepping carefully around looking for any he had missed, he again offered them to Jack, at the same time rubbing his neck.

Jack shook his head. He didn't want them.

Warily, slowly, no sudden movements, the Arab's hand went back into the other pocket. He eyed Jack speculatively the entire time.

When the hand came out it was offering alternate merchandise. Vials of crack, Jack saw. Courtesy of Victoriano Zaragon, probably, though it was unlikely that the Arab had ever dealt with Zaragon or heard his name.

Jack waved this away too. He needed a gun, he said. Could the Arab get him a gun? He spoke these phrases clearly, having memorized them earlier, and for emphasis he again flashed money.

The Arab shook his head.

Half the money down, Jack insisted, half when the Arab reappeared with the gun.

The Arab held out the crack in one hand, the heroin in the other. "You want?" he said in English.

"A gun," said Jack in English. "Can you get me a gun?"

The Arab put the drugs back in his pockets, opened the door, and stepped out into the alley. Jack followed a moment later. The Arab did not look back and in a moment had turned the corner and was gone.

In a grim mood Jack started back to his car. He had only one other idea, and he cruised the streets again, this time looking for prostitutes. A city the size of Nice must have plenty. The trouble was he had no idea how they worked here or where to find them. When he had been here in the navy there had always been lots of them hanging around wherever the launches came in from the ships. But the navy was not in port now. He remembered there had been streetwalkers on the Rue Massena and also the Rue d'Angleterre back then, and he checked out both streets. Nothing. These were bad times in the prostitute business, he supposed. The sexual revolution had become even broader-based. From teenagers on up, people were getting all the sex they needed from each other and not even hiding it. At the same time, because of AIDS, commerce with prostitutes had become scary.

Still, there must be prostitutes somewhere, and finally he spotted a woman standing on a sidewalk alone. She was wearing a skirt so tight it molded her ass. Early twenties. Nice-looking. Blouse tight across the bust. Very high heels. He supposed she was a prostitute. What else could she be? He circled the block, coming back for a second look to be sure. This time as he passed she was putting a coin into the slot of a sidewalk toilet. The door slid open and she went in.

Jack parked, hurried back to the toilet kiosk, and waited outside. Prostitutes frequently had organized crime connections, which in France meant the Corsican *milieu*—men who would have access to guns. New York prostitutes frequently had police connections too, detectives who used them as informants; it was probably the same here, and that could be a problem. Suppose she informed on him and the seller she brought back was a cop. You can't afford to worry about that aspect of it, he told himself.

He waited a good long time. What's she doing in there? he asked himself impatiently. Finally the door slid back and she stumbled forth and he saw that she was not as young as he had thought, and that she was wearing a wig. Also, she had the livid face and empty eyes of every junkie he had ever seen, and he understood what had taken her so long in the toilet. If he opened her handbag he would find her works.

Shocked to see him standing so close to the door, she began babbling at once. He made out very little of it, but enough to realize that she took him to be a *flic* who might lock her up. Without even being asked, she was giving this supposed cop information. It was an exchange of currency: information in exchange for freedom. When he didn't seem to react, she brought money out of her handbag. If information wasn't enough, then she would pay.

In disgust, Jack turned away, went back to his car and resumed circulating. He went up one street and down another, still searching. In time he went back to the railroad station where there were many cheap hotels, and at last he was rewarded—he spotted a girl coming out of one of them. The usual tight skirt. This one wore a hat and a veil as well. No one wore hats and veils anymore. No one had worn them, Jack supposed, since the convent girls of long ago. To wear hats and veils these days you had to be a whore.

At this time of night there were vacant parking slots in front of the station. He locked the car and walked across the street and up to the girl, who stood now on a corner as if waiting for someone.

Good-looking girl. "*Bon soir*," he said. And then: "How much?"

After looking him up and down, she gave a figure. "In advance," she said.

He nodded. "Where?"

She jerked her chin in the direction of the hotel he had seen her come out of and started walking, letting him follow. Nice ankles. Nice legs. Nice ass, of course. Nice bust too, if it was real. Why did a girl with that kind of attributes become a prostitute?

He followed her into the hotel and up a flight of narrow stairs. The desk was one flight up. A middle-aged woman sat behind it.

"You pay her for the room," the girl said.

The woman handed the girl a key and then a clean towel off the stack behind her. "Two hundred francs," she said to Jack.

He passed the money across the desk, then followed the girl up another flight and along a corridor and into a room. As soon as she had closed and locked the door the girl turned to him.

"The money," she said.

As he got his billfold out again he looked over the room: a double bed with brass bedsteads, two straight-backed chairs, a sink and bidet behind a curtain in an alcove.

The girl thrust Jack's money into her handbag and put the bag down on one of the chairs. She stepped out of her high-heeled shoes. She took off her skirt, folded it, laid it down on top of the purse, and then stepped out of her panties and put them folded on top of the skirt. He noted that she had thin, fair pubic hair. She did not remove her blouse, nor the bra underneath it that may or may not have been padded.

With the towel over her shoulder she moved to the bidet and squatted, and as she washed herself she carefully avoided wetting her shirttails.

When she stood up again, seeing he had not removed his clothes, she said: *"Monsieur, s'il vous plaît."*

"I need a gun," Jack said. Her legs were very fine indeed. As he waved a five-hundred-franc note at her, he wondered if, underneath the blouse, her bust was as good as it seemed to be. "Can you get me a revolver?" It was the same word in French, but pronounced differently. Jack wondered if he had pronounced it right.

"Revolver?"

"Revolver," said Jack, and he pointed his forefinger at her, pantomiming a gun. "Bang, bang," he said. A Frenchman would have said "Pow, pow!" but he didn't know that.

"Not this?" the girl said, making a circle of her thumb and forefinger and punching the other forefinger through it several times.

The universal gesture. Jack had no difficulty understanding it. "No, a revolver."

Briskly the girl stepped into her underpants again. The sparse pubic hair disappeared, the rounded behind. She buttoned her skirt, and the long silky legs disappeared. Kicking up first one heel, then the other, reaching behind her one-legged, she pulled her shoes onto her heels, first one then the other, womankind's everyday dance step. Briskly she picked up her handbag, and then snatched the five-hundred-franc note from his hand. Briskly she strode to the door.

"You wait," she said in English. She had not offered to return the money he had already paid her for the sex which had not taken place. "I come back," she said. The door closed behind her.

Feeling hopeful, Jack sat down on the bed. After a few minutes he stretched out, his head on the bolster, his ankles crossed, his shoes on the counterpane. The last thing he meant to do was fall asleep.

≡ CHAPTER 16 ≡

He came to suddenly, not knowing how long he had slept, nor what sudden signal had awakened him. A car door slamming, he thought, and he lunged for the window. The shutters were closed, but down through the slats he could see the sidewalk and part of the street.

The lights were still on in the room. He glanced all around, still trying to orient himself, then peered once more through the slats. A car was double-parked below. The whore had gone out through the bumpers to meet it and was leaning in the passenger side window.

A second car was double-parked a short way up the street, and its driver had got out and was coming forward. Was that the slamming door that had awakened him?

Now both men and the whore stood between the bumpers. The whore was talking and the men were looking up at the windows of the hotel. Both men were about his age, and both were casually dressed, one in dark pants, one in khakis, both wearing shirts open at the neck.

Gun dealers or cops? Jack asked himself.

Cops, he believed. To him they had the look of cops—something arrogant, aggressive about the way they stood, the way they moved. If they were cops, then slamming that door was a bad mistake. A New York detective would never have made it.

Options were flashing through Jack's head—there weren't many—but he wanted a gun so badly that he waited a bit longer to be certain. Perhaps too long. Dealers or cops?

One of the men reached back into the car, pulled forth a mike on the end of an expandable cord, and spoke into it.

That settled it: cops. The whore had sold him out. He was not really surprised. She already had his money; now she would earn herself some police goodwill as well.

Jack ran to the door, opened it onto the hall, and saw he had only two choices, up or down. Down was the two detectives, and he could already hear them, for they had entered the building. Quickly stepping out of his loafers, carrying them, he ran in his socks to the staircase and up two more flights. His hope was to get out onto the roof, perhaps jump to the adjacent roof, maybe two or three more adjacent roofs. It was as if he thought himself in New York. He would come out of some building down the street as innocent as a lamb. When he was a rookie detective he had several times chased burglars across rooftops in Harlem. The rooftops he was used to were always flat. There was an additional flight of stairs leading up to the roof and then a door you came out of.

Not here. The staircase had suddenly ended. He was in a kind of attic, and the roof sloped downward to the eaves on both sides. Even in the middle he could not stand erect. Above his head were laths, and on top of them lay tiles. A weak glow of light drifted up from the corridor one flight down and surrounded where he stood. The rest of the attic was in darkness.

Whoever heard of tile rooftops in a city? He had thought this the first time he ever looked down on Nice from above. Tiles that were bright orange. Who ever heard of a bright orange city?

He could hear voices below. He gathered that the detectives

had entered the bedroom he had just left. Finding it empty, they were discussing what to do next.

What would they decide? What would he do in their place?

They might decide the whore was unreliable and leave.

Unlikely, he believed.

They had no doubt planned to sell him a gun, then arrest him for it. Would they give up this idea? Yes, certainly. Just as certainly, he believed, they would decide to check out the whole hotel. They would want to find out who he was and why he wanted a gun. They would arrest him on some charge or other: suspicion of whatever unsolved crimes they had on their hands. They would take him down to the commissariat and grill him, maybe knock him around if they didn't like his answers.

He judged they would start opening up all the other rooms floor by floor. If they disturbed anyone, too bad. There were about four rooms to a floor. In New York, even in a hotel as disreputable as this one, they would need a search warrant, but he doubted such niceties were observed here.

Unless he could get out of this attic onto the roof that his head was touching, they would find him, and bad things would start to happen.

His hand stroked the undersides of the tiles. A tile roof would have to be serviced. Tiles tended to crack, to break. Or they got loose in a storm and floated down into the rain gutter or over the side. There had to be a way for roofers to get out onto this roof. A trapdoor of some kind.

He began to feel for it.

Below him doors opened and closed, voices were heard, most of them indignant. Footsteps climbed to the next floor. One more floor and they would find him. He was moving from lath to lath, sliding his hand up the wood to the peak and then down the other side as far as he could reach, then crouching and reaching farther. He was exceedingly angry at himself. He understood nothing of this country, and among the things he did not understand was the way they constructed their roofs. He was looking for a gap in the laths. There had to be a trap somewhere. Several times he was stabbed by splinters that he hardly felt.

He had started near the chimney at one side of the attic. When he found the trap finally it was all the way on the opposite side. Simultaneously he heard what sounded like the last door slamming on the floor just below, and he heard a French voice say:

"He's up there. He has to be." These were the words, and for once he understood them clearly.

The trap was some sort of vitrified glass, thick, very heavy. He pushed up and it came free. Carefully he moved it aside and could see sky, stars. Though the moon was out of his range of vision, he knew it was there somewhere because the sky, after the darkness of the attic, seemed to glow.

He hoisted himself out onto the roof and as soundlessly as possible replaced the trap.

And there he sat just below the peak of the roof and five stories above the street. The tiles sloped downward and they felt slippery. He felt himself sliding toward the eaves, beyond which was the void. He wasn't sliding, he told himself. The sensation was false, he told himself. He was only suffering from vertigo or panic, normal under the circumstances, and he tried to force his breathing to come slower and his heart to slow down, tried to force his rump to stick where it was.

The French detectives were in the attic now. He could hear their blurred voices and he could see the light from their flashlights as it filtered dimly up through the vitrified glass, which, he saw, was coated with filth.

He heard them go away after a time, but he remained where he was. How long he would have to stay on the roof he did not know. In their place, he would sit out in his car and watch the building for a while. Surely they would too, but for how long? Of course he could always go down and attempt to walk past them. He had committed no crime. No one had tried to sell him a gun. He hadn't bought any gun. They had no probable cause to arrest him. In New York no detective would dare do it. But this was a different country. Here they could hold him two days without charges, he believed, and under the circumstances probably would.

Two days in a cage.

Given that he had every cop's horror of being locked up—never mind how many men he had locked up himself—he began to wonder why he had let himself fall asleep in the whore's room. Had he wanted to put himself into a position of danger? Did he like sitting on this rooftop? Had he been trying to raise the level of excitement in his life? He was extremely excited right now, almost pleasurably so. Had he put himself out here in the night on down-sloping tiles on purpose? Was he willing to go to such lengths just to feel, as he did at this moment, so extraordinarily alive?

These were questions he did not normally ask himself, and he chased them away unanswered. Life did not bear too much scrutiny. Let things happen. Cope with them afterward.

But he felt almost drunk with safety, and therefore with pleasure. The detectives were not going to find him. Once again he had faced great peril and got out of it on his own two feet, and all his senses were working with extreme sharpness. The tiles pressed into his rump, he could hear all the noises of the town, and the sky was brilliant.

Of course he wasn't safe at all. The tiles continued to grate each time he shifted his weight, seemed to move each time he breathed, and the edge of the roof—the dropoff—seemed to pull at him. The tiles felt extremely unstable, as if at any moment they might all let go and start sliding, with himself at the heart of the avalanche. This, he decided, was either scary or funny, depending on one's point of view. How the hell did I wind up on a rooftop in Nice in the middle of the night? he asked himself, and he began to laugh. It started as a quiet chuckle, and ended with tears streaming down his face. He wiped them off and got up and walked to the peak and stood there like a man on Everest, and he marveled at himself. He felt like a climber looking around at the wonders of the world. Hey, look at me. Wow. Look where I have got to.

Wanting to see if the detectives' cars were still there, he walked downhill toward the eave. The tiles felt unstable and made noises under his shoes, and the roof was steeper than he had thought. When he came to the edge, he stood peering over.

He saw that one car appeared to have departed, but the other was still there. He watched it for a time. The detective stood beside it. If the man looked up, Jack was visible there on the edge. If the tiles gave way, he would land on him.

Jack turned around carefully and climbed back to the peak. He decided he would simply sit down and wait the detective out. He would use the time to study the stars. In the navy on clear hot nights he used to lie out on deck sometimes and count them and now he did likewise, though it wasn't the same. In the middle of a town the stars were fewer and less clear than at sea, but he began to identify the ones he could remember.

He sat counting stars for perhaps an hour, perhaps less, while becoming more and more impatient, more and more bored.

Finally he lifted the vitrified glass away, lowered himself into the attic, and went down the various flights of stairs.

The woman behind the desk was surprised to see him. "Monsieur," she called out.

But he ignored her and continued down to street level, only to encounter the whore entering the building, a new client behind her. She was dressed as before: stiletto heels, ultra-tight skirt, cream-colored blouse tight across her big bust. She was astonished to see Jack, and in fact he was startled himself. To avoid bumping into her he had had to put out both hands, which landed by chance on her outthrust breasts. Was it really by chance? She owed him that much at least. They felt real to him, so that he thought: I certainly am glad to have that question cleared up. He found also that his hands liked it where they

were, and he was in no hurry to remove them, but he had to, finally. *"Excusez moi, Mademoiselle,"* he said, and let go.

The whore had taken a step backward, perhaps in fright. She
must have walked on her client's feet, for he gave a squeak. Her
hands had come up to protect her face too, though Jack never
intended to hurt her.

"I looking for you before," she said. "Where you go?"

The client was middle-aged, wearing a good-quality suit that
was, however, well worn. Jack made him for a salesman in perfume or ladies' underwear—poor fellow was on the road for
weeks at a time. "Good luck up there," Jack said to him and,
laughing, he went out into the night.

He drove through the dark empty city. Even with the six-hour
time difference, it was now too late to phone New York about
the warrant. It was too late also to go back to his boat. Are you
afraid, or what? he asked himself. Well, it made no sense to drive
back to Beaulieu and park his car in a place where someone
could be waiting for him in the shadows. It made no sense to
step aboard a possibly booby-trapped boat in the dark.

He drove to another of the marinas, the one at Saint Laurent
du Var, and pulled into one of the angled parking slots under
the umbrella pines alongside the first row of yachts. There he
turned off the engine, screwed the seat down as flat as it would
go, and lay back on the headrest. This represented less than first-
class accommodations, but it would do for what was left of the
night, and before long he fell asleep.

The sunlight blinded him and woke him at the same time,
and he sat up and looked out at another three or four hundred
yachts, most of them, as at Beaulieu, for sale. Behind him was a
row of cafés, one of which was already opening, for a waiter was
bringing the plastic tables and chairs out onto the terrace and
setting them up.

He got out stiffly and stretched, and walked over and sat
down.

"Is there coffee yet?" he asked the waiter, and was pleased

with himself that he could now speak such simple sentences and be understood.

"Another five or ten minutes," the waiter said.

"I'll wait. Do you have a *Nice Matin?*"

The waiter brought him the paper and he looked through it, deciphering some of the headlines, while around him the waiter continued to bring out tables and set them up. The only news story Jack was interested in was of course not in the paper: when and how did Zaragon plan to have him killed? And its corollary: what could he do about it?

These questions caused him to ponder rather than read, and as he looked over the top of the paper he saw something that surprised him, and he stood up for a better view. Approaching the coast, though still far offshore, were a dozen or more warships— when he counted them the number came to fourteen. Among them he identified an aircraft carrier, two cruisers, and a number of destroyers and support ships. They must be American, for no other nation had that many capital ships in the Mediterranean.

The waiter came with his café au lait and hot croissants in a basket.

"*La flotte Americaine?*" said Jack, pointing.

"*Oui, Monsieur.* For the next few days." The waiter peeled back Jack's paper to a middle page, showing him the article. "They'll be anchored all along the coast."

"For the fourteenth of July," Jack said, and the waiter nodded.

Jack himself had been here twice on Bastille Day, the first time assigned to shore patrol all night. The following year he was with Claudia lying on a blanket on the beach at Nice watching the fireworks and doing things to her under the blanket even though there were people all around. Afterward they went dancing in the public gardens to the mostly accordion music.

And after that, he remembered, they carried the blanket back to the beach.

It brought a smile to his lips. The romance hadn't ended well, but he was over that part of it, and what he mostly remembered now was what it was like to be here that year, to be so young, so innocent, and so in love.

Whereas what he was right now was somebody's prey, and that's what he had best be thinking about. Forget the fireworks, he told himself. Forget the accordion music and the warm hands under the blanket, and concentrate on staying alive.

When he had paid for his breakfast he drove toward Beaulieu, bucking the early morning traffic that clotted the streets of Nice and finally coming out the other side. At Beaulieu he entered the yacht harbor, slowed, peered carefully around, and drove slowly up and down again looking for any man or men who did not belong there. He could not have said what he was looking for, someone whose posture seemed wrong, or who was wrongly dressed for the time and place, or whose eyes were moving too much, trying to watch in too many directions at once. A good detective should be able to pick such a man out, he believed.

He noticed no one, however. He did notice Madeleine having breakfast at one of the cafés, and he parked and walked toward her. With a half smile on her face she watched him come.

"*Bonjour, Madame,*" he said. "*Comment allez vous?*"

"Your accent is getting better," she told him.

She was wearing a yellow blouse, a navy blue skirt, no stockings or socks, and espadrilles. She looked, to him, very nice. When he leaned over to kiss her she offered her cheek, so he kissed her on both cheeks. She looked freshly scrubbed and combed, and he sat down at the table.

"You're out early," she said.

"So are you," he said, and that was the end of the small talk. "Listen . . ."

He wanted her to phone Inspector Bosco, he said, ask him to find out if the warrant from America had come.

She put money down for her breakfast and they walked toward her brother's office to make the call.

"You look tired," said Madeleine. "You didn't sleep well?"

"I slept in the car."

"The car?"

He felt a sudden resentment. He still had no gun, and partly at least it was her fault. She had put him through last night's experience, which in the cool light of morning did not seem nearly as delicious as it had then.

But this resentment lasted only a moment, for his attention had been caught by a man they were approaching. The man had a rolled-up newspaper in one hand.

During the time he had sat beside Madeleine in the café, Jack's focus had been partly on her, this woman who had once been a cop like himself, who was part of his own world, and who exerted over him such a strong sexual pull—intellectual pull too—this woman with whom he felt so comfortable at times as to consider trying to make with her a new life. But mostly, self-preservation being an even stronger pull, his focus had been on the rest of the yacht harbor.

Now the hairs on his arms suddenly stood straight up. At first he did not know why, but then his gaze returned to the man with the rolled-up newspaper—perhaps that was why. Jack had spotted him while still seated in the café: a man in a white shirt some distance off who stood in the roadway reading a newspaper—it was not yet rolled up at the time—as if some particular story had caught his eye that he could not wait to read.

A man reading a newspaper in the road seemed all right. It happened.

But now the man waited on the curb three restaurants up the line, and they were approaching him fast. He was about fifty, fat, bald; and although assassins came in all colors, creeds, and uniforms, still this was not the type individual Jack or anyone could consider an immediate threat.

But all along he had entertained the nagging suspicion that the man didn't belong there. He hadn't actually been reading the newspaper, Jack realized now. He had been holding it. Peering over it. And from time to time he had glanced around, had peered in their direction. Now, watching him, Jack was suddenly as alert as ever before in his life.

There is in that place a row of six or seven cafés and restaurants, most with nautical names. It was a hot sunny morning and the café tables and chairs were pushed out almost to the curb, leaving only a minimal strip of sidewalk facing a narrow roadway, and then the first row of yachts.

The man agitated the rolled-up newspaper several times as they neared him, the way a businessman might do when hailing a cab on a New York street. But this was not New York, there were no cabs here, which meant a signal of some kind. What signal? To whom?

As Jack and Madeleine came abreast of him the man thrust the paper under his arm, moved past them, and continued walking in the opposite direction. He never nodded at them as he passed so close, nor even looked at them, though people in marinas usually greeted each other, were usually friendly.

It was as Jack puzzled over what this might mean that he heard the motor scooter.

He threw a glance over his shoulder and saw it coming. Scooters could make about forty miles an hour flat out, and it seemed to be coming that fast, passing one restaurant after another, gaining on something, presumably him. There were two men on it, the driver and a someone riding pillion. They wore helmets with visors down, and leather jackets. In France helmets were obligatory by law, but visors were not, nobody wore them on scooters, didn't need them, scooters didn't go fast enough, and these visors were tinted so that both faces were obscured.

Jack had been expecting this, though not today, not so soon. No guns showed yet, though in his head he saw them already. He imagined how it would be, shot down at point-blank range, after which the scooter would merely keep on going.

It still had thirty yards to come, still no guns showing, no reason to show them until the last second. For the driver and his passenger there was still plenty of time. And for however much time this added up to, Jack was still alive. He was about to experience the favorite method of execution in France, the drive-by shooting, French style.

His second glance had swept all around him. Where in relation to the restaurants was he, where in relation to the scooter, where in relation to someplace to jump, duck, hide? The answers were a jumble, and they added up to this: he was no place. The two on the scooter were both probably armed, and he was not. Wherever he might try to run, the scooter would track him. It was faster than he was, and bullets were faster still. And what about Madeleine? She would be caught in the crossfire, or if she wasn't she became instead an eyewitness, the only one, and would have to be dealt with, probably on the spot, why not, assassins were not squeamish people. But being the only witness to murder was certainly a burden, wasn't it? It was a role he didn't recommend to anyone.

He and Madeleine were passing at that moment in front of the last restaurant in the row. It had a big awning out front, through which the sun shone down onto the tables and chairs. There were no customers seated outside, for by this time of morning breakfast was mostly over. There was a waiter standing in the doorway with his tray hanging down to his knees. His expression was rather vacant—he had no idea that a violent event was about to occur. No one in the entire marina did except the two men on the scooter and Jack.

Walking along beside him, Madeleine was saying something, idle conversation that did not register on him, he did not even try to comprehend it, and just then she chose to take his hand, but he shook her off instantly, pushed her away from him, and screamed at her: "Get down."

He saw the amazement on her face just before he turned to deal with the scooter. It was much closer now, not ten yards away, and it had slowed somewhat, not very much. The passenger had a gun out, a machine pistol of some kind, an Uzi or a Mac 10 or something, what difference did it make, and in another few feet he would use it, and Jack grabbed the nearest café chair and slung it into the scooter's path, and a fraction of a second after that he sent the table tumbling in the same direction.

The passenger had both hands on his gun, the same combat stance Jack himself had been taught in the police academy, for the gun was going to buck when fired, and unless the shooter used both hands, he would find himself shooting holes in the sky or perhaps through his driver's leather jacket. So the gun was as steady as could be under the circumstances, but the passenger, since he was no longer holding on to the scooter or the driver, was less so. He was trying to grip the sides of the scooter with his knees, as one would a horse, and normally, given a straight run, this would have been sufficient. But when the chair came skittering toward the scooter, the driver jammed on the brakes and swerved to avoid it. Then he ran head-on into the table.

The scooter as it went down slung the passenger sideways against the curb, and only the helmet he wore saved him from a crushed skull. The helmet striking the curb made a kind of muffled explosion like the boom of a bass drum. Because his hands had been out to save himself, he had been unable to maintain possession of the machine pistol, which had bounded onto the pavement and then slid some distance off. The passenger himself lay in the road stunned.

The driver had been more agile. The scooter had scooted out from underneath him, and he had gone striding along after it, several yards to the stride. This forward momentum carried him up to Jack's level, before he too fell down. But he was up in a moment and groping for his own gun, which he managed to get half out of his pocket before Jack clubbed him back down again with a second chair. Jack kept clubbing him, like someone slapping both sides of a face, back and forth. For the most part only one leg of the chair landed in any one swing, but the swinging was so vicious that each one did terrible damage, and certain of them broke bones: two fingers, a rib, a wrist. The man's helmet flew off. The chair leg raked his face, and the blood flowed. At that point the fight was effectively over, but Jack didn't realize it and kept on. Jack was fighting for his life, or thought he was.

"Jack, stop," cried Madeleine. "Jack, you'll kill him."

Jack didn't stop until he had brought the edge of the seat down on top of the man's head, and he went down and stayed down. Rushing forward, Jack ripped the gun the rest of the way out of his pocket, then ran to the machine pistol lying so innocently on the pavement and kicked it out of reach of either of them.

Five seconds had passed, perhaps less.

Jack was breathing so hard he felt like his chest might burst. He stood there training the gun on first one man, then the other, though neither showed any sign of getting up, and when Madeleine, now carrying the machine pistol, came into his field of vision he did not at first know who she was.

A car started up on the other side of the island of shrubs and trees. They both heard it, they looked at each other, and then Madeleine burst through the bushes and was gone. She came back a moment later prodding the fat man in the back with the machine pistol. She made him sit down with his hands on his head on the pavement, and in a sense she now took charge.

The waiter had come forward halfway to the curb, where he stood frozen, gaping. The owner or chef or whatever he was had come out from inside. He too gaped. "Police officers," Madeleine told him, so that Jack thought: how good it must feel to her to say that. The gun in his own hand felt good too. He was calming down now. It was a short-barrel Colt .38, he saw. It was similar to the off-duty gun he used to carry. To be a cop again really did feel good.

"Call seventeen," Madeleine ordered the owner. This was the police emergency number. "Tell them we're holding three prisoners." To Jack she said: "Search them."

From the restaurants down the line other people were approaching, but she waved them back with her gun even as Jack went forward. He didn't just pat the three men down. The search was as rough as he could make it. His hands slammed into them. He made the two gunmen scream and the fat man wince, and he recovered one more gun.

"They're clean," said Jack. He showed her the second gun. "The passenger had it."

"What did I do?" the fat man said. "Tell me what I did."

"I have to make a phone call," said Madeleine. "Beaulieu is gendarme territory. I don't want those klutzes handling this thing. I want us to handle it."

"Us?"

"The PJ."

They grinned at each other, and for a moment there was a warmth between them, a complicity so intense that it dazzled them both. They were cops again and they were cops together. "You know what I mean," said Madeleine.

"Yes, I know what you mean."

They started to giggle, but soon stopped. Their only worry now that the action was over was every cop's worry: how to keep jurisdiction. How to keep control of the case.

Carrying the machine pistol beside her skirt, Madeleine went into the café, the owner scurrying ahead of her, anxious to be of service. Jack watched her go, and then his sense of self-preservation came to the fore once more, and he shoved the Colt .38 into the waistband of his pants and arranged his shirttail to hide it. He had found the gun he needed, and no one was going to take it away from him. Today's attempt to kill him had failed, but if Zaragon remained at large there would be another, though it would take time to set it up. Armed, he would at least have a chance to defend himself.

By the time Madeleine came out of the café a panel truck had pulled up and a number of gendarmes in uniform had spilled out. The prisoners were handcuffed and hustled into the truck and the doors closed on them, while Madeleine explained to a sergeant, the same one they had talked to earlier, what had happened.

The sergeant, as he considered the magnitude of the case that had just fallen into his lap, was practically rubbing his hands with pleasure. It was a case that would bring him to the notice of his superiors. It could be the making of his career, and he began striding importantly about, giving orders. One gendarme was assigned to take preliminary statements from Madeleine and Jack. The sergeant himself took statements from the café owner, the waiter, and several other witnesses who had come forward. Other gendarmes on their knees worked with tape measures and chalk, and still another had a clipboard out and was working up an inventory: one wrecked café table and two wrecked café chairs that the government would have to replace; one wrecked motor scooter confiscated; plus two guns, one a Mac 10, the other a Manhurin .357 magnum.

"That's all you recovered?" inquired the gendarme with the clipboard. "Two guns?"

"That's all," said Jack quickly.

Madeleine gave him a look. Then she peered at the sky, and after that off across the boats. It seemed to him she even started to speak, but in the end her eyes came back to his, she seemed to look deep inside him, and she said nothing.

Thirty minutes had passed, perhaps more. The truck with its load of prisoners still sat there waiting, when suddenly sirens were heard and two carloads of PJ detectives came skidding around the corner into the port.

Seated beside the chauffeur in the lead car was Commissaire Divisionaire Demalet himself, the chief of the Nice PJ, who walked up to the gendarme sergeant and slapped him on the back. "Nice work, Sergeant," he said. "We'll take over from here."

After turning away to give orders to his men, he again addressed the crestfallen sergeant. "We'll take those statements your men have collected," he said. "We'll take the guns your men recovered as well."

≡ Chapter 17 ≡

At the Rue de Roquebillière an hour later Jack was allowed what passes in the police world for a moment of glory—he was actually invited into Demalet's office, invited to take a chair, even offered a cigar. "So you're a New York police officer," the divisionaire said. He was a heavyset man. They lit up together.

"Retired," said Jack. So far, so good as far as the French language was concerned.

"These people were trying to kill you, it seems."

"Yes, and I have a favor to ask you about that."

Jack started to explain about Zaragon, the murder warrant on its way from America, but Demalet interrupted. "Don't worry," he said, "we have the case well in hand now."

Jack started to ask to have Zaragon picked up and held until the warrant arrived, but it took time to collect the necessary words and arrange them in his head. Before he could do this, Demalet said: "What was your rank?"

"Detective," said Jack, "*inspecteur.*"

"Yes, but with what rank?"

"Just . . . detective."

Demalet's eyes narrowed. He had sat down with a man he

imagined to be equivalent in rank to himself, or nearly so, who had just engaged in extremely physical and dangerous police work. Three would-be assassins, all apparently connected to the Marseille *milieu*, were in custody. Arrests of this kind were simply not made by men of rank except in their daydreams, and Demalet had been extremely impressed. Men of rank, Demalet included, liked to imagine themselves one day collaring felons at gunpoint and being feted and congratulated as heroes, but in real life they sat behind desks and it did not happen.

But he had made a mistake. Jack had held no rank at all. A New York street detective was the equivalent of an enlisted man in the army, not at all a commissioned officer like himself. Furthermore, the American did not even speak French. Demalet's interest ended there, and so did the interview.

Jack, who saw the snobbery, ignored it. In the New York Police Department he had many times encountered the same thing—why should it be any different here? What was important to Jack was that he had finally got the words out about Zaragon and the murder warrant. That is, he had got some words out, he hoped they were the right ones, but Demalet, no longer listening, was shuffling papers. Jack went to the door and called in Madeleine to interpret. She entered warily, standing in front of the divisionaire's desk with her hands crossed in front of her skirt like a little girl, and she waited to be acknowledged.

No acknowledgment came, however. Demalet glanced at her and then back at his papers, and his attitude showed that he wanted nothing to do with her—regretted even that it had been necessary to permit her to enter the building—as if he feared she might contaminate his career.

So he stood up and came around the desk. Wearing a brilliant false smile, ignoring Madeleine, he ushered Jack to the door, Madeleine of course following. "You say the warrant's on the way," he said. "Good. As soon as it gets here we'll pick the guy up. Don't worry about a thing. Now if you'll sign the *procès-verbal* my men are preparing . . ."

Demalet closed his door behind them.

Jack saw how much this treatment had upset Madeleine. "Don't let that jerk get under your skin," he said, and put his arm around her.

"He makes me feel like I have a sickness."

"He's rude and he's stupid."

She looked completely disheartened.

"You're ten times the detective he is."

This won him a rueful half smile. "You think so?"

"I know so," said Jack, giving her a squeeze.

She stroked his cheek. "You don't know anything about it."

Banished to the outer room, they were interrogated by PJ detectives, Jack at one desk, Madeleine at an adjacent one, and from time to time he called across to her to interpret something. The statements took a long time and were interrupted at midday as food was brought in: beer and pizza purchased from a truck outside in the street. The detectives sat around a table munching and talking. Shop talk mostly. This case and that case—what else would you expect? Jack, who understood little of the conversation, decided that French detectives were no different from American ones. They didn't even eat any better.

The interrogation resumed. Much later Jack's *procès-verbal* was typed out, Madeleine vetted it, and he signed. She signed hers at about the same time. Now they were free to go.

So that they could not communicate with each other, the prisoners had been thrown into separate cages, and Jack went and looked in on them. A doctor had been in to see them, he was told. The doctor had found that the fat man was unhurt. In the other two cages he had done some bandaging, some stitching, after which he had pronounced all three suspects in sound good health and fit to go into *garde à vue*. Jack knew what this meant, and he gave a grim laugh. In America, he told Madeleine, the injured men would demand to be hospitalized, they would stall for a week, perhaps more, and after that talk only through lawyers. By then they would have lawsuits pending against the city as well, charging police brutality. Whereas here they faced forty-eight hours, two days and nights, of immediate grilling by relays of detectives with no lawyers present.

The world was strange.

He wanted to go back to his boat.

Madeleine wanted to stay.

A number of detectives had stopped to talk to her, he had noted. She looked a bit relieved, her presence accepted by at least some of her former colleagues. Having regained admittance to the building, she seemed reluctant to leave. Perhaps she wasn't as much of a pariah as she had feared.

By then it was late afternoon. A detective was assigned to drive Jack back to Beaulieu, where he looked into the office of Madeleine's brother and asked permission to phone Assistant DA McCauley in New York. This was accorded, and he dialed the number.

"What did you find out about that warrant?" he demanded when McCauley came on the line.

"The warrant exists," the young man said. "You don't have to worry about that."

"Then where is it? Why isn't it here?"

"It's a sealed warrant," the young man said. "They didn't want word of it to get out, so they sent it only to Colombia, which is where the subject is supposed to be. But the subject has not yet been arrested there. As a matter of fact, the Colombian police are having trouble finding him."

"Because he's here," said Jack. "That's why they can't find him."

"That must be why."

"I already told you that, for chrissake."

"Right, so you did."

"Somebody just tried to kill me."

"Now you're being dramatic."

"Will you get that warrant here, please? Will you get it sent here right away? Call me back and tell me when it will get here."

"I'll do my best," said the young man. "I have to be back in court. You take care of yourself, now."

Jack went into the grocery store on the port and stocked up on provisions: bread, coffee, milk, eggs, several cheeses, ham, some potatoes he could bake in the microwave if he decided to eat on board, some salad greens. He joked with the grocer, and he joked with the news dealer when he stepped next door to buy the *Paris Herald Tribune*. It was too early for dinner, but some of the waiters were standing in front of certain of the restaurants, men he knew by sight, and he greeted them cheerfully. He was in an extremely cheerful mood.

Carrying his groceries he walked out along the quay to his boat, and there he did remember to be careful, looking for any sign that something had been disarranged or moved, looking for booby traps. But there was nothing. He stepped on board rather gingerly, trying not to make the boat rock. When there was no explosion, he began to relax.

He steered the boat around to the pumps and refueled.

"Nice day, isn't it?" he said to the attendant there.

When the tanks were topped off he drove back to his own slip, tied up, plugged in all the lines, and even leaned over the fantail to screw the nameplate back in place.

After that he carried clean clothes over to the public baths at the edge of the harbor, where he paid the fee, shaved, and then luxuriated in a long hot shower. He dressed, combed his hair, and walked back to his boat, where he poured himself a stiff drink, sat on the fantail drinking it, and watched the sun go down. It seemed certain to him that Zaragon would come after him again, but it would take a while. For tonight at least he was safe, and probably tomorrow as well. By then the warrant probably would have arrived. The French police, after all of today's excitement, could be expected to move quickly once they had it, so probably he didn't even need the gun stuffed in his belt. It was nice to be armed again, though.

He took the piece out and looked it over. Guns held no mystery for him. He had carried a similar one every day of his life for twelve years. He broke it open and counted bullets: the usual five, not very many. He had no extras, but he wasn't going to have to shoot anyone, and once Zaragon was in custody he would throw the gun in the sea and wouldn't miss it. He would be finished forever with the world of cops and robbers, wouldn't need it any longer, and he looked forward to that day.

Did he really?

He remembered this morning's excitement the way a man would remember a delightful sexual experience. The rapid heartbeat, the sweating, the hairs standing upright on his arms. The pure sensuality of it. One never felt more manly than after moments such as that.

And now on his boat in the sunset sipping his drink he basked in the reflected glow of this idealized version of himself. The declining sun reverberated off the water, and he held his glass up to the light and realized he had not felt as alive and happy as this in a long, long time. He had been about to be killed. He had got out of it without help from anyone. What a man! The sensation was delicious. The most delicious, possibly, that anyone ever got.

But the events he had just survived were in their way as addictive as heroin. They left behind a kind of ache, a pull so strong it was almost a need. Already he needed another fix. He began to feel edgy, uncomfortable. The applause he was according himself no longer sufficed. He became possessed by the unreasonable and very, very dangerous desire to have it all again, quick. Experience that same high a second time.

And as this mood took hold of him he began to work out a way to remove Zaragon as a threat once and for all. If you want something done properly, you do it yourself, right? Why wait for the law to do it? He would do it, him, Jack Dilger.

And as the details fell into place in his head his excitement level rose once again.

He had held off having dinner, waiting for Madeleine, but the hours passed and she did not return. Finally he walked across to a café called Le Clipper, where he sat down outside and ordered a sandwich and a beer. The night got darker, and he looked across at the yachts under the dim lights of the quays and thought about Zaragon, who that day had paid men to try to kill him, and gradually, in addition to being in need of fresh excitement, he became angry.

Leaving money on the table, he got up, found his car, and drove to Villefranche, and as he came down the steep winding hill he could see that the entire harbor was lit up. The restaurants on the village square looked full, and so were those on the waterfront that he could see as they curved around the rade almost out of sight. At the edge of the square the Welcome Hotel looked ablaze, and out in the rade six American warships were anchored, one of them a carrier, and all six were strung with lights from prow up over the superstructure and down to the stern, and the American flags they flew were oversized and illuminated by floodlights. Onshore the sailors in their white uniforms were everywhere.

He drove past all this and into the public parking lot, which was jammed. He drove up one alley and down another until he found the red sports car. It was illegally parked, its front bumper touching a tree, its rear protruding and almost blocking that particular alley.

It was a big square lot with lines of trees delineating the alleys. To one side rose the Citadel's vast medieval bulk; on the other stood the customs building. The third side was the entrance to the lot, and the fourth was open to the sea. As he came around looking for an empty slot he could see most of the garishly lit warships. Their launches were moving back and forth bringing in still more liberty parties.

There was no empty space anywhere, so he double-parked deep in the same alley as the red car.

Having turned his engine off, Jack broke open his gun and counted bullets again.

He waited an hour before Zaragon walked into the lot toward

his car. He had a woman with him. The usual stiletto heels and ass-molding skirt. One of the local whores perhaps. The second one Jack had seen him with. He remembered his DEA briefing. This was a man who had killed a girl at eighteen, and who, despite all the drug money that poured in, kept whorehouses in Medellín and Bogotá and was said to be his own best customer.

Jack turned the ignition key and started his engine.

He followed them up onto the lower corniche, and from there up onto the middle one, where all the lights of the coast became visible below, and the American warships in the rade looked like toys, and from there east to Monte Carlo, to the casino, which, as it came in sight, proved to be as garishly lit as the warships had been. Zaragon steered down into the parking garage under the casino gardens; Jack found a spot on a side street. By the time Zaragon and the whore came up from below, he stood on the steps of the Hotel de Paris opposite, and he watched them approach the casino.

Was the young druglord a gambler? In a sense all criminals were gamblers. They gambled years in jail against immediate gain. They gambled against being shot down by cops or rivals.

But in Jack's opinion casino gambling didn't fit this man, or any of his Colombian colleagues. They had too much money already. The least of them had tens of millions of dollars in various countries and banks. They were the richest criminals the world had ever known. To men that rich, winning a pile of chips at a roulette table could not be too exciting.

More likely Zaragon would give the whore money and then watch her excitement mount, possibly get a hand up under her skirt while she was moving chips around. Gambling was very sexy. Get her aroused. After that, back to the hotel for the rest of it.

In every surveillance a detective had to judge how close he could get without being spotted, had to move up close enough, but not too close.

Zaragon and the woman entered the casino. After hesitating briefly, Jack followed.

Inside was a vast, high-ceilinged hall. Very crowded. Ornately decorated. Marble floors; Grecian columns; statuary on pedestals; and on the walls to either end, enormous nineteenth century murals in which fantasy women wearing see-through nighties flitted about in pastoral settings.

Jack searched carefully for Zaragon, did not find him, and concluded he must have gone through into the private rooms. These would be relatively empty, he believed. Serious gamblers only. Entry fee: fifty francs. Most tourists were not going to pay it. Zaragon would spot him. To go in himself was a risk not worth taking.

It was after midnight when he tailed the red sports car back to the Welcome Hotel. He watched Zaragon lock up the car and lead the whore into the hotel. More than an hour passed before the woman came down alone. She was counting money as she came out into the night.

Jack drove back to Beaulieu, parked, and walked down the quay to his boat, where he put on pajamas, put the gun under his pillow, and fell asleep.

The next morning Madeleine was still not back, or else she had gone out early. Sticking close to the *garde à vue*, probably. At lunchtime, when she still had not appeared, he decided to drive back to Villefranche and resume his surveillance of Zaragon.

The red car was in the parking lot below the square under the trees, which put Zaragon inside the hotel.

It was possible to sit inside one of the cafés on the square and still have a good view of the Welcome. Jack ate lunch there, a pâté sandwich and a beer, and in the course of the afternoon he drank several coffees. He read the *Herald Tribune*, looked out through all the outdoor tables and chairs, and watched and waited.

About three P.M. he saw two men come out and take up position on both sides of the hotel entrance. They stood with arms folded, and he made them for bodyguards.

During the next hour other men came up to the entrance, spoke briefly to the bodyguards, and were passed inside. They stayed for a while, then came out again. Jack decided Zaragon was holding meetings. Meetings about what? A contract to murder Jack Dilger would not take that long to arrange, nor would it require that many men. It must have to do with a drug network. Either Zaragon was setting up a network or he was assuming control of the one his brother had set up before him. Jack, who knew nothing about Musso or the need to replace him, had guessed closer than he knew.

The French cops should be watching this guy too, Jack believed. They could arrest him on drug charges, hold him until the murder warrant came through. Why weren't they doing their job?

All this time the bodyguards stood by the door, arms folded, looking surly. So where had they been when Zaragon visited my boat? Jack asked himself. Where were they when he went to casinos at night with women? And who provided the women?

By late afternoon the men were all gone. The bodyguards were gone too. He wants them around when doing business, Jack conjectured; they tended to scare people, which was good—it might give him an edge in a deal. When not doing business he didn't want them around. Didn't think he needed them around. Felt as safe here as Jack himself had felt only a few days ago. The bodyguards didn't seem to live in the Welcome. Probably he kept them in a smaller, cheaper hotel nearby. It was a way of keeping them in their place, perhaps.

A little later Zaragon and two other men left Villefranche in two cars, and Jack tailed them into Nice, where they drove into a parking garage. When they came out, they walked through the narrow streets of the Old Town to the Cours Salaya. They sat down outside a café but when Zaragon pushed money across the table, one of them left.

Jack was trying to decide who the two men were.

After about thirty minutes the man returned. He had a woman with him. Zaragon stood up at his table like a gentleman, and he and the woman shook hands. This one did not look like a prostitute. The woman sat down, and when the waiter came she ordered tea. Jack, who sat at a café across the square, couldn't hear the order, but when the waiter came back, a teapot and cups were what he had on his tray.

Another thirty minutes passed, perhaps more. Finally, after shaking hands all around, the two men left. Zaragon and the woman stayed a short time longer. She looked about ten years older than Zaragon. He presented her with an oblong box. Looked like a jewelry box. She opened it and pulled out a necklace. She had a big smile on her face. Turning in her chair, she allowed Zaragon to fasten it behind her neck.

A necklace? What's that all about? Jack asked himself.

Zaragon and the woman had their heads together in the center of the table, and she was obviously making up to him.

Later he tailed them to a restaurant in the hills behind Nice. The evening had turned windy, so they ate indoors. Jack moved his car up close and watched them through the glass. They drank nothing but champagne.

From the restaurant they drove to Cannes, where there was another casino. On the Riviera the casinos were everywhere. Jack gave them time to get settled inside, then followed. They were sitting at a roulette table and Zaragon kept handing the woman chips. He was concentrated totally on her.

When they finally left Jack followed them back to the Welcome. This time he did not wait for the woman to come down again, but instead drove home to Beaulieu.

As he parked he saw that there was still no light in Madeleine's room above the warehouse.

He walked out onto the quay toward his boat. The night was very dark, no moon, no stars. The wind was still blowing and the moored boats were moving up and down. There were shallow pools of light under the widely spaced streetlamps along the quays. They illuminated very little. Jack was too tired to be alert. He was safe enough for tonight, he believed. His boat came into view ahead.

It did not look right to him. As he got nearer he vaguely realized this. The line was wrong. There was bulk where there shouldn't have been. But he was so tired he did not immediately react, hardly cared, but only kept advancing. Suddenly he saw that the bulk was a person. Someone on board. Waiting for him. In a chair in the cockpit.

The realization gave him a terrific fright. It made him yank his gun out fast and jump backward into as much darkness as he could find. Not much, as it happened—a pile of mooring ropes and a parked bicycle. Drowsiness was gone completely. If there was one assassin waiting for him, there was probably a second. But where? Though he glanced around, he saw no one. Crouching, hugging darkness, he inched closer.

Presently he was close enough to identify the figure in the chair in the cockpit, and he rammed the gun back into his belt. There was no assassin. Waiting for him was Madeleine, and he noted that she was asleep.

He had to shake her awake. "What are you doing here?"

"Waiting for you," she said irritably.

His big grin came on. "Well," he said, "well, well." His good humor came back with a rush. "Couldn't live without me, eh?"

"Where have you been?"

"Want to go to bed?"

"No I don't want to go to bed. I've been waiting hours. Where have you been?"

He put his arms around her but she did not respond to his kiss.

"What time is it?" she said irritably. "There's something you have to know."

"What do I have to know?"

"I didn't come here to fall asleep. I came to warn you."

In her turn she too was glancing around, trying to peer into darkness.

"Warn me? About what?"

"Those men we arrested," she said impatiently.

"They've begun to make admissions," Jack guessed. "That's good. Makes it an easy case."

"Yes, they're making admissions, but no, it's not so good. Not for you."

"What are you trying to say?"

"That you were not their intended target."

"Not their intended target? Of course I was."

"They never heard of you. The target was someone else."

Jack was having difficulty understanding her. "Who?"

"Me, it seems."

"Jesus," said Jack, and he let go of her.

When she did not elaborate, he said: "You can't be sure. How can you be sure?"

"The prisoners haven't been to bed in about forty hours. It's pretty hard to make up lies when you're as tired as that. It turns out it was me they were ordered to kill."

Jack was speechless.

"It's a terrible blow to your ego, I know."

"Well, I mean, who hired them?"

"It's a *milieu* contract. They were just told to do it. They weren't told who ordered it."

"But—but—" If this was true then Zaragon's men were still out there, and ex-detective Jack Dilger was in immediate danger, had been all along.

"I had to warn you," said Madeleine.

Jack began to remember his visit to the grocery store, the refueling, his restaurant dinner, the hours working on his boat. He hadn't taken any precautions at all, and now he half expected to look up and see the assassins who had come for him—who could have blasted him at any time during the last day and a half.

"It's not safe for you here," said Madeleine.

Jack was suddenly angry—principally at the situation in which he found himself but at her too, the bearer of such bad tidings.

"I thought you didn't believe me. There was no threat, you said. Didn't you?"

"Yes. I'm sorry."

"They come after you, you change your mind. Oh, that's nice. That's really nice."

Though she put her arms around him, he kept peering over her shoulder at all the quays and boats he could see, trying to peer into every corner where a gunman might hide.

He had been living in a state of semi-euphoria for most of two days; that the euphoria was suddenly gone wasn't her fault.

"What about you?" Just as suddenly he had calmed down. "You're not safe either."

But she contradicted him. "We think probably I am."

He gripped her shoulders. "You need to be guarded around the clock. What are you doing out here in the middle of the night? What's the matter with your friends the cops?"

"The general feeling is that no one will bother me now. The person or persons behind the attempt to kill me will crawl into their holes. They have to. They have no choice."

"Did somebody guarantee that?"

"No, but I have nothing to worry about. It's understood."

Jack wanted to shout at her.

She said: "A major investigation is under way. The mayor, his party, the Sestris—no one would dare try anything now."

"Who told you that? Demalet? One of those idiots around him?"

"I agree with them," she said stubbornly.

"You believe in fairy tales too?"

"Fairy tales?"

"It's a crazy theory, crazy." He was once again glancing nervously around.

"Well, it's what we think."

"Somebody put out a contract on you. That contract has just

become even more urgent than it was. There will be guys on the next train from Marseilles."

"We don't think so."

"It's the craziest theory I ever heard."

"Look," said Madeleine calmly, "the attack on me was political. The people who want me dead are politicians, not criminals."

Jack gave a grim laugh. "Not criminals, right."

"You know what I mean. The political thing to do now is lie low, not bring on even more heat."

Jack was shaking his head.

"We had conferences all afternoon," said Madeleine. "The procurer general was there, and the *juge d'instruction* who has the case. Demalet was there, even Vossart. They talked to Paris, the minister of justice, the minister of the interior, five or six calls. Paris decided the news should be given to the press. Which proves Paris is behind us. The story was all over the TV news broadcasts earlier tonight. It'll be all over the papers tomorrow."

"You need guards on you," said Jack bluntly. "So do I, but at least I have this." And he pulled the gun out and waved it.

"They offered to put an armed guard outside my door. I refused. And I wish you didn't have that thing."

"You refused?"

"I don't need a babysitter."

"Jesus, Madeleine."

"Inspector Bosco drove me home. I'm going to sleep on the sofa at my brother's until this thing sorts itself out—for the next couple of nights anyway. If I want protection they'll give it to me, but nobody thinks it's necessary."

"And who's going to protect you as you stroll over to your brother's place now?"

She grinned at him. "You are, I guess."

Any thought of making slow, languorous love had entirely fled Jack's head. Where would he himself sleep? Not here, obviously. Exhausted, angry, frustrated, unnerved, he fell silent, and in his head he went back to the plan he had been piecing together all day.

"What are you thinking?" said Madeleine.

He said: "The warrant may never come, or come too late. I'm not going to wait. I'm going after Zaragon myself."

"I don't like the sound of that."

"I don't care what you like."

The suddenness of the rebuff made her begin to breathe a bit hard, like at the beginning of sex. She said icily: "What exactly do you plan to do, shoot him?"

"Not unless it's necessary."

"I see."

"I'm going to take him into custody."

"And do what with him?"

"Hold him until the warrant comes."

"Sounds like kidnapping to me. How and where do you hold him?"

He had some ideas that he did not wish to tell her. "Will you help me?"

She looked at him. "You're serious, aren't you?"

"Very. Will you?"

"Help you kidnap the guy? No, I won't."

In his head she was an almost wife, and wives were there to help. "Why not?"

"Because it's against the law."

"You're not a cop anymore."

"No. But it's still against the law."

His mouth hardened.

"Let the law handle it."

"The law is doing nothing. I'm liable to get killed before the law handles it."

For all he knew, the warrant was here already but the French police hadn't got to it yet. Every police department had limited manpower, and this one had just launched an investigation into the near murder of Madeleine. Because of the political over-

tones, it would be very deep, very careful. There might be nobody left over to work on a warrant from America concerning
two foreigners, namely Jack and Zaragon.

"The guy is a drug dealer," said Jack. "He's setting up drug
deals here. He's planning to poison your country. If you don't
care about me, do it for your country."

"It's kidnapping. You intend to break the law."

Jack shrugged.

"I can't help you do that."

He could feel his whole face go hard. He was worried about
himself, not her. He had no patience with her scruples.

"I can get reinstated," Madeleine said. "The climate just
changed. There's now a good chance they'll take me back. Better
than good. I can't risk it."

"You care more about that than you do about me."

"That's not fair."

"It's fair. Goddam right it's fair."

They eyed each other, both now angry.

"Go ahead then, but leave me out of it. Be careful you don't
get killed."

"Is that what you're worried about, getting killed?"

"No, I want my job back, and I'm not going to risk it over
some harebrained scheme by you."

"All right," said Jack coldly, "then there's nothing more to be
said, is there?"

Because the boat's cockpit was so small they stood very close
together, both breathing hard.

"Where will you sleep tonight?" asked Madeleine in a milder
voice.

"Right here," said Jack.

"You can't. It's too dangerous."

"I'm not afraid of those fuckers. They're not running me off
my boat."

Madeleine shook her head. "That's foolish."

Jack said nothing. They stared at each other.

"Suit yourself," said Madeleine. "I'm going to bed."

But Jack made no response to this statement either, which made her hesitate, as if giving him time to repeat his offer to walk her home or make some other conciliatory statement or gesture—something.

When this did not happen she stepped up onto the gangway. "I'll see you tomorrow," she said. "Or whenever."

He watched her walk down the quay in the lamplight, watched her bottom move under her skirt, a woman full of life, moving. She did not look back. When she had made the turn he leaped up onto the quay and hurried after her. Once she was in sight again he slowed, following twenty yards behind, making sure that no one waited to ambush her, that nothing happened to her. He saw her go into the building that held her brother's apartment on the top floor. The entire building was dark. Only when he saw a light come on up there did he turn away, and he strode across to the last café open on the harbor, where he asked to use the telephone.

It was by then almost two A.M., which was no time to be telephoning a man asleep in his bed five hundred miles away with a story that might sound insane—a man he didn't even know. But there was a certain self-indulgence to Jack. When he wanted something, he wanted it now, and if he wanted it enough he did not mind inconveniencing others, or care what anyone thought. Besides which, purely on a practical level, a call at this hour and from this distance was not a bad idea. It acquired a weight and an urgency that, during normal business hours, would not have been there. In any case, if his plan was to go forward, he couldn't wait. It had to start right now, and that was that.

Inside the café no one was left but the owner, who knew Jack, but was about to lock up. He had to show Jack how to find the number in Paris he needed, and after that how to call it. He did these things with bad grace, and then stood drumming his fingers on the bar while waiting for the call to be concluded.

Because of the hour it took some time before the man Jack

wanted, whose name was Foster, came to the phone. He sounded groggy with sleep.

Jack decided to unbalance him further. "How you doing?" he said. "How's the weather up there?"

"Who is this? What do you want?"

"Does the name Victoriano Zaragon mean anything to you?"

Foster suddenly was much more awake. "The magic name," he said. But he was cautious as well. "How do you know a name like that, if I may ask? Who are you?"

"You may recognize my name too," said Jack, and gave it.

"Two magic names," Foster said, fully alert now. "What's the connection?"

"I can give you Zaragon."

Foster was the Drug Enforcement Agency's country attaché in France. Jack's call had had to go through the American Embassy to Foster's apartment, where he had been asleep beside his wife. Foster was part of a clandestine business in which calls from informants frequently came in under cover of darkness. The embassy operators were under orders to route them through. This was not the first such call he had received in the middle of the night. "Where are you?" he asked cautiously. "And where is he?"

Jack answered both questions. "Do you want the guy or not?" he said.

"I have no police powers in France," the drug agent said cautiously, "and neither do you."

"Doesn't matter. I can still give him to you."

The café owner stood nearby, fingers still drumming on the bar. Jack begged him with his eyes to be patient a moment longer. "You come down here," he said to Foster, "and I'll show you a way."

From the Paris end of the line came silence. Foster presumably was deliberating. His job was to provide liaison between the DEA and the French narcotics brigades, and to pass on information, not to make arrests, and Jack knew this.

"There are planes every hour from six A.M. on," said Jack.

"The flight takes an hour and twenty minutes. You take a room in the Meridien. I'll meet you there at eleven A.M."

"I can't make it tomorrow," said Foster, and Jack understood this ploy too. He would not come until he had checked out Jack's current standing, Zaragon's as well. Besides which, a good agent was one who controlled informants, controlled a case. A good agent never let anyone else control it, and usually this meant making people wait. It was almost the first technique agents were taught.

Jack had been taught the same technique. He had no intention now of being controlled. "Be there," he said, and hung up. For a moment he stared at the phone. There was no question in his mind that Foster would come. The stakes—and Foster did not even know exactly what they were—were too high. He could not afford not to come.

Jack turned from the phone. "I really appreciate this," he told the owner. "Can I buy you a drink before you lock up?"

"Just let me go to bed," the man said.

At eleven the next morning Jack knocked on Foster's hotel room door.

Foster turned out to be a big man, taller than Jack and weighing well over two hundred. He had pudgy cheeks, gray hair, and looked to be about fifty years old. As he let Jack in he was not smiling and he did not offer to shake hands.

"Let me see some ID," he said.

Jack handed him his passport, which Foster tilted toward the light that spilled in through open French windows. He looked at it carefully, turning all the pages.

"You woke me out of sound sleep last night. You made me come a long way this morning. This better be good." He returned the passport.

Jack walked past him over to the windows and out onto the balcony. Below was the Promenade des Anglais and then the sea. "Nice view you have here," he said, turning back into the room.

"What have you got?" said Foster impatiently.

"Just what I told you on the phone. Zaragon is here, and I can deliver him to you. You then take him back to America and arraign him."

"As easy as that."

"As easy as that," said Jack.

"Who's going to arrest him? You?"

Jack shrugged.

"Last I heard, tourists didn't have powers of arrest."

"What do you care how it's done, long as you have him?"

"All right, you turn him over to me. He screams. He's being held illegally on French soil by a foreign police agency. What do the French have to say about all this? They find out, they'll put us both in jail and send Zaragon out on the street again."

"That's good, get all the objections out in the open," said Jack. "So we can dispose of them."

"Ever been in a French jail?" said Foster. "They're not too nice, I hear."

"The French won't even know about it until Zaragon's out of the country."

Foster had begun pacing so that Jack was talking to his back. But now he spun around. "What you're talking about, if I understand you, is called kidnapping."

Again Jack shrugged. "Forget the legal niceties."

"You kidnap him, and I just fly him out?"

"Your part shouldn't be too hard, the resources the DEA has."

"Negative," said Foster. "Kidnapping's a felony. The DEA can't be part of it, and I won't be part of it."

"The DEA has kidnapped plenty of people, and you know it."

"Even if we got him back to the States, it's an illegal arrest. The judge would throw the case out. We'd have to let him go."

"Horseshit," said Jack. "That Medellín cartel guy, Lehder, the DEA flew him out of Colombia within hours of capturing him. He was tried in Florida, and he's in jail today. One of the guys involved in killing the DEA agent in Mexico got shoved through a hole in the fence at the border where DEA agents just happened to be waiting for him, and he's in jail today."

But Foster walked to the door and opened it. "This interview is over."

"Sit down," said Jack. "You blow an opportunity like this, and what's over is your career."

They glared at each other, but Foster closed the door. He was running it through his head step by possible step, and Jack could see this.

"The kidnapping is my job. You don't have to know anything about it."

"Let's assume you kidnap him," said Foster. "How do I get him out of the country? Two tickets on Air France?"

Jack again walked out onto the balcony. "Come on out here," he said over his shoulder. "Look at the view a moment."

"Oh for chrissake," said Foster. But he followed as requested.

"What do you see?" said Jack when Foster stood beside him.

"I see the fucken sea, what do you think I see?"

"Note that cape off to the west. That's called Cap d'Antibes. There are some gray ships anchored offshore. You see them?"

"Yes."

"They're part of the U.S. Sixth Fleet."

Foster was silent.

"They represent American soil. You get on board one of those things and you're not in France anymore. Legally you're in the United States."

Foster still said nothing.

"There are more of them in the rade de Villefranche, anchored about half a mile off Zaragon's hotel. One of them is an aircraft carrier."

Foster was silent.

"Suppose Zaragon was to turn up on the carrier's deck. You could arrest him, couldn't you?"

Foster said nothing.

"Picture it," said Jack. "The dark of night. A little boat bumps against the side of the ship. Someone carries him up the ladder and drops him at your feet. You fly him to New York and you charge him."

This caused a moment of intense silence. "I doubt there's anything aboard that carrier could make New York nonstop," mused Foster.

"Then fly him to some U.S. air base somewhere. Frankfurt, Madrid. You pick it out. You transfer him to a bigger plane. Next stop the U.S. courthouse on Foley Square."

"When France finds out, they'll arrest you."

"On what evidence? France won't know anything about it until he gets a lawyer in New York who starts screaming. It'll take days, maybe longer."

"Deport you, anyway."

"I'll take that chance."

"How long is the fleet in port? How much time do we have?"

"It leaves tomorrow night."

"Is that enough time?"

"If it's not, you get one of the ships to stay."

"That will be harder," said Foster.

"But not impossible."

"Victoriano Zaragon," mused Foster. "His brother's dead, Escobar is dead, Rodriquez-Gacha is dead, Lehder's in jail, the Ochoas are in jail. Zaragon's the magic name right now. Mind you," he added hastily, "I haven't said I'll do it."

"You'll do it."

"I can't promise a thing until I clear it with Washington."

"There's the phone. Call them."

"Are you crazy? In Washington it's six o'clock in the morning." But he added in a conciliatory tone: "We'll have to wait a few hours."

Foster did pick up the phone, however. It was between the twin beds. "Let's have lunch," he said. "Let's go over this, make sure we have everything straight. What do you want to eat?"

Jack took the receiver from his hand and replaced it. "There are two other conditions." And then after a pause: "Small things."

"Small but vital," said Foster.

"Yes, vital. Deal-breakers, you might say."

"You want money—how much?" said Foster, and he waited. In Paris he controlled a fund, and buying information was what it was for.

"I want a press conference the minute you get him to Frankfurt or wherever you take him. I want the United States government to say he's in custody. If he's hired thugs to kill me, I want them to know he's gone."

Foster was amused. "No one's going to go through with a hit he might not get paid for. Smart. What's the second condition?"

"When this is over—he's tried, convicted, and in jail—I get picked up by the DEA."

Foster gave a rough laugh. "You, a federal agent?"

To Jack, DEA agents belonged to a lesser category than New York City detectives, but the NYPD didn't want him anymore, and as a federal agent at least he would be back in law enforcement. He would take second best because it was better than nothing.

"I thought all you NYPD guys held us in contempt."

Jack gave a slight inclination of his head. "Nonetheless," he said, "it's a condition."

The two man gazed at each other. Finally Foster said: "All right, I'll tell Washington." He reached for the phone again. "What do you want for lunch?"

"There's only one catch," said Foster, when they met later that day. "They'll hold the fleet until tomorrow night at one A.M. After that, they won't hold it. The fleet sails."

"I'll have him there," said Jack.

"Then all systems are go."

"I posed certain conditions," said Jack.

"Conditions?"

"The press conference. Being picked up by the DEA."

"I mentioned those things to them."

"And?"

"They don't see any problem," said Foster.

"And I'm to be picked up by the DEA?"

"I don't see why not," said Foster.

"Then everything is go?"

"Right," said Foster, not meeting his eyes. "The admiral has received his instructions from Washington. He'll be waiting on board the carrier. Our helicopter is already on its way down here from Frankfurt. The New York–Frankfurt plane is set up."

Jack believed what he wanted to believe. "All right, I'll deliver Zaragon to the carrier as promised."

"You don't have much time. Can you set up your end that quickly?"

"Yes. Probably grab him tonight."

"You're sure?"

"If not tonight, then tomorrow night." There followed a pause during which, as he considered the details of his plan, Jack saw all that could go wrong.

"When the carrier sails, your drug trafficker will be aboard," he said. Nothing could go wrong. He would bet his life on it, and in fact he just had.

≡ CHAPTER 18 ≡

From Foster's hotel he phoned Madeleine's brother, who promised to get a message to her: she was to meet him at the Beaulieu Tennis Club, and it was urgent.

He waited on the terrace. The tennis club was safe, it seemed to him, a place no one would think to look for either of them. When the waitress came he ordered a beer. He sat under an umbrella and sipped it and listened to the thunk of tennis balls.

And waited. The day was waning. There remained to him less and less time.

He needed Madeleine's help. There were other ways his plan could work, but using her was the surest and safest. She had refused him once, but heavy elements were involved now, the heaviest. When she saw the support he had brought up, the huge pieces he had fitted together, she would change her mind. She would want to take part.

More than an hour passed before he saw her come through the gate. He stood and kissed her on both cheeks like an acquaintance. She did not kiss him back.

Both sat down at the table.

She wore a sleeveless white dress and looked sulky. She said: "What's so urgent?"

Ideally he would have worked up to this slowly, carefully. But there wasn't time. "I'm going to ask you to do something. You can decline, if you wish." The words were awkward. He was more ill at ease than he had expected. "If you say no you have to promise not to burn me."

She gave a shrug.

"Is that supposed to mean you promise?"

She said sulkily: "I'm not in the habit of burning my friends."

Not meeting her eyes, he looked down at her shins, her ankles. "I have a plan you may not approve of."

"If it's what I think it is, we've already talked it out. You know I don't approve."

"There have been some changes. With your help it will work. Without it—"

Her face looked closed up against him. "What you are going to propose is against the law."

"You haven't heard all of it yet."

She looked at him.

"The Drug Enforcement Agency is involved now. The United States Navy is involved."

Her expression did not change.

As he continued it was as if he were adding weights to one side of a scale. "The carrier *John F. Kennedy* is standing by. A number of aircraft are standing by. Once on board the carrier Zaragon can be legally arrested." He began to explain the theory of United States soil. The quick flight to New York was already set up, he said, the arraignment in U.S. District Court was set up, and—

"It's kidnapping," she interrupted. "And it's against the law."

"You were a cop. Didn't you ever break the law before?"

"No, I never did."

"Then you weren't much of a cop." But immediately Jack fell silent. I'm not here to fight with her, he told himself.

"All I have to do is get Zaragon onto the deck and the case is closed."

"It won't work."

"Why?"

"It's too complicated, for one thing."

"I can make it work."

"In my experience," said Madeleine, "suspects don't often co-operate in their arrest. Arrests don't often go according to plan."

A tennis ball came over the fence and rolled to Jack's feet. He picked it up and threw it back.

"When you grab him," said Madeleine coolly, "be careful not to shoot someone with that illegal gun you have."

"I don't intend to grab him where there are people."

When she spoke she was almost begging. "Please think about this before you do something stupid. Suppose he puts up a fight. Suppose he pulls a gun. Suppose he has bodyguards around. Suppose people see you and intervene. There can be so much that is unforeseen."

"That's where you come in. I want you to lure him someplace where the unforeseen can't happen."

This statement left her momentarily speechless.

"I want you," he said, "to take a room in the Welcome. I want you to hang around downstairs until he notices you, and then I want you to lure him up to your room, where I'll be waiting. We hold him there until midnight or thereabouts. As soon as every-one's asleep we sneak him downstairs and out of the hotel. There will be no one around. We carry him across to my boat. I sail out to the carrier and it's all over."

She was shaking her head as if she found herself unable to speak.

"The only problem is time," Jack said. "We have only tonight and, if that fails, tomorrow night. Tonight would be better, ob-viously. We have to get started right away."

"Lure him up to . . . And how do you propose I do that?"

407

"You blink your eyes at him a few times. How do women usually do it?"

"I've never been good at blinking my eyes at men, as a matter of fact."

The waitress had come out of the clubhouse. "Do you want anything?" said Jack to Madeleine. "Coffee, tea, a beer?"

"No, nothing. I don't think I'm staying here that much longer."

"The check, please," said Jack. The check was under the saucer, and the waitress handed it to him. Jack put money down. After making change, she tore the check to signify that it had been paid.

"Your plan," Madeleine said when the waitress had moved away, "entails risks you haven't even thought about. Risks to you. Risks to me. That are totally unacceptable."

She paused. She was again breathing, it seemed to him, a bit hard.

He said: "I could use Flora, I suppose."

This gave her pause. "Was that a threat?"

"No, of course not."

"I think it was."

They eyed each other.

"Let's suppose you get Zaragon back to America," Madeleine said. "His lawyer asks the PJ to investigate the kidnapping of his client out of a certain room in the Welcome Hotel. He gives the room number. The detectives would find that the room was rented by me, wouldn't they?"

"Would they?"

"You have to show an identity card or passport to rent a hotel room in France, and unfortunately I don't have any false papers in my handbag this week."

Jack said nothing.

"They'd charge me as an accessory in a kidnapping. I'm a French citizen with no excuses the court would accept, and I'd go to jail."

The sun was very low. The tennis players made elongated shadows on the courts.

"I want my job back and I have a good chance of getting it back, provided I'm not in jail at the time. I think your plan is crazy, and I wish you'd drop it and wait for the warrant to come through and then let the police handle it."

Jack studied his hands.

"You don't even hear what I'm saying, do you? All right."

She sprang to her feet, but when she was two steps from the table she turned back. "You're right, your wife is the one to ask." She had waited most of three days for Jack to explain Flora's presence on the coast, to reassure her that the divorce was going forward and that their own relationship was intact.

But she had heard no such reassurance. Her mood had changed in that time: fear, depression, heartache, and now biting anger.

"Tell your wife to blink her eyes at him and lure him to her room. She looks like she's good at that type of thing. Probably done it before. And then I suggest you go back to her and back to America and get out of my life."

Then she was gone.

This tirade, her abrupt departure, left Jack half stunned. What got into her? he asked himself. That she could be jealous of Flora was a possibility, but it seemed so illogical that he discarded it.

He was annoyed to think that he understood women and what motivated them no better now than he had as a boy.

Flora looked perplexed. "Why not just stick your gun in his back and walk him onto your boat?"

"Where should I do this?" said Jack. "In front of one of the restaurants? In the parking lot?" He answered his own question: People might intervene, or bodyguards. If there were shooting, a bystander might get hurt. "A cop never makes arrests on the street if he can help it." He shook his head decisively. "You take the suspect off the street first. Into a car, into an alley. It's one of the first things they teach you in the academy."

They sat on the terrace of the Voile d'Or out on Cap Ferrat. Time was getting shorter. "That's why I need you," Jack said. "To take him off the street for me, so to speak."

Much had gone wrong with Jack's plan already. It was by now very late. There was moonlight on the water. Strings of lights traced the corniche roads along the mountains. And still nothing was in motion.

This afternoon he had hurried to Flora's hotel only to find she wasn't there. According to the concierge she had gone to Monte Carlo with other guests from the hotel.

On the terrace Jack had ordered a coffee and had sat down to wait. He had stirred the coffee around. Below him was the cape's tiny yacht harbor. Out here the view was back toward the coast and the mountains behind it. Off to the east in the late afternoon haze was Italy.

He had waited and waited but she did not return. The lamps came on outside the hotel. Hidden spotlights shone down on the flowers and plantations, and upward on the olive trees in the lawn. Lights began to show along the corniche roads up on the great cliffs opposite. As the night darkened the glow of Beaulieu appeared across the water.

He had felt the heavy pressure come down on him. Two chances to grab Zaragon had been few enough, but as time passed he saw them reduced to one. It had become too late to accomplish anything tonight. He would have one chance only. Tomorrow night or never.

Flora had not returned until past ten P.M., and when he started to speak she cut him off, said she absolutely had to have a bath before discussing anything important. And she invited him to her room: they could talk while she was in the tub. Knowing where this would lead, and the further delay it would cause, he had declined. He would wait for her downstairs, he had said.

She had smirked at him. "You are the most suspicious guy."

When she appeared she wore a black dress and high-heel shoes. They ordered a late supper on the terrace, and in between the attentions of the maître d'hotel and the sommelier, and the many waiters in dinner jackets, he explained to her what he wanted her to do.

Flora looked perplexed. "You could just knock on his door in the hotel," she said, "couldn't you?"

"He might not open to me. If he did, there would probably be a struggle. I can't afford a struggle." Flora nodded, but her brows remained knitted together.

"My way is the easiest and the safest," Jack added, "but I can't do it without your help. You can see that, can't you?" He gave her his most earnest look. "So will you help me?"

He looked out at the night view of the coast and waited for her answer. It seemed amazing to him that around here every conversation, including life-and-death conversations, took place in the context of this fabulous scenery.

"Are you sure there's no danger?"

Legally there was none, he believed. She was not French and she would be out of the country before queries about the hotel room, if any, ever reached the PJ.

As for physical danger, he was not going to let anything happen to her.

"I don't see where it could be dangerous."

"Because I don't want you getting hurt again."

This reply shamed him. She wasn't even thinking of the danger to herself. Was he so sure there was none?

If all went according to plan, he told himself doggedly, there was only minimal danger, probably none.

"How would I recognize him?" said Flora.

Jack had a photo of Zaragon. Foster had requested it from Washington and it had been transmitted by fax. Jack spread it out on the tablecloth. "A very distinctive face, wouldn't you say?"

"He's very good-looking, isn't he?" she said. "That scar makes him look rakish."

"You shouldn't have any trouble recognizing him."

She was silent a long time, too long, so that Jack began to suppose she would say no. But finally a big grin came on. "Okay, why not?" said Flora. The photo had made it all real to her. "Let's do it."

She remained registered at the Voile d'Or, but packed a small bag, and the next morning Jack drove her over to Villefranche, down onto the harbor front and into the lot under the trees. The red sports car was there, which put Zaragon inside the hotel. Jack steered into a slot about ten cars away, but when Flora started to get out his hand went to her knee to stop her.

She gave him a look, and they sat waiting. After a time she cleared her throat and said: "What are we waiting for?"

For a moment Jack missed Madeleine. If she had agreed to help, she would have understood everything without being told. More importantly, she would have been prepared to protect herself if need be. She would have been a colleague, in fact a partner. Whereas Flora had no idea what she might be getting herself into, she was not capable of protecting herself, and there was no way to justify what he was asking her to do. Flora was not a cop or ex-cop, but only a home decorator from Kansas City. Flora was in way over her head without realizing it.

Jack said: "We're waiting for him to come out to his car." Because of the presence of the red car in the lot he had re-adjusted his plan. "It shouldn't be long," he said. He had no idea how long it would be. Detectives were used to waiting. They sat on surveillances not moving for hours at a time, sustained by the interior excitement all hunters feel, whether hunters of game or hunters of men. At any moment the subject might appear in one's sights.

Madeleine would have known this. Flora did not, and it was not something that could be explained to her. She was studying her fingernails. With no sustaining excitement, she was bored.

How much boredom would she submit to? How long would she wait in a parked car in a parking lot? It was hot in the car. The boredom would increase, so would the heat, and if he kept her here too long she might back out altogether.

To keep up her interest he began giving detailed instructions. "When we see him coming toward his car, you get out. You leave your suitcase with me. As you pass him, you give him a smile. You say hello, as if you're both in the same hotel, as if he's someone you've seen around the lobby. Bat your eyes at him a few times, if you want."

"When it comes to attracting a man," said Flora, "I don't think I need any hints from you."

"Sorry."

"I've been doing it quite successfully, thank you, since I was about sixteen."

"With luck, he'll follow you back into the hotel, strike up a conversation."

"How do you know?"

"He likes women," said Jack bluntly.

"Maybe I'm not his type."

"Every woman is his type."

They sat another thirty minutes.

"If you get a chance to make a date with him, it has to be for tonight and it shouldn't be too early," Jack said. "We can't move him out of the hotel until the crowds are gone—midnight or so."

I should tell her how dangerous this could turn out to be, he told himself. Let her make her own decision.

But Zaragon suddenly appeared.

"There he is," Jack hissed.

The drug trafficker was alone, keys in hand, strolling toward his car.

Flora opened her door. "Go get him," Jack said, giving her knee a squeeze. He almost pushed her out the door. Simultaneously he slunk down in his seat.

Gradually he raised up enough to see out.

He saw Flora walk up to Zaragon, and then past him. She appeared to give him a smile and a nod. Jack could not hear if they spoke to each other. He saw Zaragon turn and stare after her, and he noted that Flora as she walked seemed to be wiggling her bottom more than usual.

Zaragon, who kept looking after her until she went into the hotel, seemed to hesitate. Then he put his keys back in his pocket, crossed the street, and went in after her.

Good, thought Jack. He felt himself grinning. A good start.

Zaragon came out again a few minutes later, got into the red car, and started it up.

Jack waited until it had wound its way up the hill and was gone, then carried Flora's suitcase into the hotel. He found her checking in, and the clerk asked if they were together. Jack said they were not, he was just carrying the lady's bag. The clerk nodded, and all three of them, tightly packed, rode up in the three-passenger elevator.

After throwing open the room and then the exterior shutters, the clerk handed Flora her key, took his tip, and left.

"Well?" said Jack.

"Well what?" said Flora, smirking, obviously pleased with herself.

"Did you talk to him?"

"He was quite charming, your dope dealer. Are all dope dealers as charming as that?"

"Come on, come on," said Jack.

"He inquired as to how long I was staying."

"Then what?"

"I inquired as to how long he was staying. Seems we're both staying till the end of the week."

"Wonderful," said Jack.

"What else would you like to know?"

"Flora, you can be such a pain in the ass sometimes."

She laughed. "Oh, I almost forgot. He asked me if I would be around tonight."

"And?"

"I asked what he had in mind."

"And?"

"He suggested dinner. I told him I had specific instructions from my husband to say no to dinner."

"You didn't."

She grinned at him. "I said I could meet him for a late drink, however. So we have a date. Ten, ten-thirty in the bar."

Jack stepped forward and gave her a resounding kiss on the lips. He was certain now his plan was going to work. "You are the most terrific woman," he said.

"And very underappreciated," said Flora.

Jack went out onto the balcony. The room was on the fourth floor and he could look down on the parking lot, and also out into the rade. All the warships were visible, and so were the liberty launches moving in and out. His eyes followed one of them to the pier, and he watched sailors piling out and making for the bars, for the waiting whores.

Back inside the room he noted that there was no closet, only a rather big armoire; well, the armoire would have to do. On the floor lay a rug of the size he would need; he would not have to bring one. Out in the corridor, he had already noted, was a door leading to fire stairs, and it was in the back of the building, leading therefore to a back exit. That was good too.

His entire plan was falling into place. He was no longer even thinking about danger to Flora, much less to himself.

Since he had much still to do, he kissed his wife, then went out into the hall and down in the elevator.

Once in the street he looked behind the hotel until he found what must be the fire exit. It seemed to come out through the kitchen. This meant it could not be used until the restaurant closed and the chefs and dishwashers were gone. What time would that be?

Across from the hotel was the customs shed, and at present there appeared to be two customs officers on duty. They watched the liberty launches come and go. Their presence was a formality only, but they were there, and for Jack that could be a problem. What time did the launches stop running? What time would the guards go off duty? The probable answer to both questions was midnight at the latest, Jack judged, remembering his own time in the navy.

He walked over onto the pier and allowed the memories to rush back. He knew just how to bring launches in to that spot. Long ago he had done it dozens of times. Then as now the launches were tied up in a kind of alcove tucked inside the seawall. Today a number of fishermen's boats were tied up there too, skiffs with inboard motors and nets piled in lumps in the bottoms. Villefranche had been a major fishing village once. Now only these few boats were left, and when it got dark the fishermen would go out in them, and far offshore they would spread their nets. Would these fishermen constitute a problem? What time would they go out?

This was the closest moorage to the Welcome, but it could be seen from the hotel's balconies, from the terraces of some of the restaurants, and it was totally exposed to people strolling from the restaurants to the parking lot. The Welcome and the restaurants would throw off a lot of light, which would be reflected off the water. It would be quite bright here, even at midnight. Of course by midnight most restaurants would have closed.

Where else could he moor? He walked back to his car and then past it to the edge of the lot, which was open to the sea. There was a low wall, and below it great boulders sloped toward the water, for the lot had no doubt been built on landfill. If he was careful he could drift his boat in sideways against the rocks and tie up to them. He might lose some paint. He could tie the boat snug, then step out and climb up and over the wall.

He gazed out at all the warships. Gray hulks. Blocky and angular. Not a nice line anywhere. The biggest was the carrier, which was moored to permanent buoys about a mile out in the rade. Some of the smaller ships were in quite close.

He drove back to Beaulieu, where he stopped in a hardware store in the town and bought two rolls of mover's tape.

From there he drove to the port, parked as close to his boat as he could get, and once again approached it warily, studying it with great care before deciding it was safe to step on board. The first business was to move the boat. After starting the engines he jumped onto the quay to disconnect all the lines, then drove it two quays away, moored it in an empty slip, then leaned over the transom and once again removed the nameplate. If anyone came looking for him between now and nightfall, they would have to look hard.

This much done, he made himself a cheese sandwich, opened a bottle of beer, and watched night come on. Since it was July it came slowly, too slowly to suit him, and the waiting made him extremely nervous. Nervously he went over all the elements of his plan. It still seemed sound to him, provided Flora did her part.

Darkness was taking forever.

Quit worrying, he told himself.

Finally the night seemed dark enough. It was not yet nine P.M., not very dark at all, but he started his engines and threaded his way out through the alley of boats, and then out through the seawall onto the sea. Since he had plenty of time and not far to go, he throttled well back. It took him more than twenty minutes just to round the Cap Ferrat. On the far side of the cape, he glided toward the carrier, which was again lit from prow to stern, circling it twice, studying its lines, and the positions of its boarding ladders. Finally he continued into Villefranche.

The night was now very dark, moonless, almost starless. When he reached the rocks at the edge of the parking lot he stood off for a time figuring out how to approach without slicing open his hull. It took several tries before he managed to arrange the boat so that it was virtually drifting, its flank floating almost imperceptibly in toward the rocks. When it was close enough he leaped onto the flattest and biggest, managing this without breaking an ankle or leg, and gently pulled the boat in the rest of the way, snubbing first one line, then the other. There are no tides in the Mediterranean. There was no wind. The boat would lie there unseen, unbothered, unmoving for as long as it took him to come back with Zaragon.

He turned in toward the cars parked in rows under the trees, searching up and down the rows for the red sports car, but it was not there. Where was Zaragon? Would he remember to keep his date with Flora?

Hurrying out of the lot, Jack crossed to the Welcome. A different clerk was on duty behind the desk. Jack nodded to him and got on the elevator.

On the fourth floor he knocked gently on Flora's door, and she opened to him.

She wore a tight skirt he had not seen before, and a blouse that was tighter still. Her breasts were high and pointing straight out.

She turned to face him. "How do I look?"

"Appetizing," he said.

"Will I do?" She spoke conversationally.

"You'll do." He himself felt the increasing strain, whereas she seemed to feel none at all. "Oh yes, you'll do."

She wore pancake face powder, much eye shadow, heavy lipstick. Her makeup was as garish as the tight skirt and the too-tight blouse. "I wanted to look the part," she said. "I mean, the guy's a drug dealer, right?"

"Are you padded, or what?"

She laughed. "You didn't know I had such big boobs, did you?"

He put his hands on them.

"I tightened the bra straps. I hiked them up real high."

He embraced her and she grinned up at him. "Don't," she said. "You'll spoil my makeup."

Jack was feeling a sudden terrific affection for her. Also a confidence that he could count on her, and that his plan would work out exactly as he had promised Foster.

Assuming Zaragon arrived on time and kept his date.

"I'd make a good-looking whore, if I do say so myself."

Jack wanted to pull her to him and kiss her. He wanted to do more than that.

"Afterward," he said, "we'll—" He stopped.

She stuck her tongue out at him. "We'll do what?"

"I'll go get the car and drive you back to your hotel," he said, and they both laughed.

Back to business. Opening the doors, Jack got into the armoire, sat on the floor under the empty hangers, and pulled the doors shut.

Flora pulled them open again. "You look silly in there."

He got out and studied the armoire.

"It's a nice one, isn't it?" said Flora at his shoulder. "It's Louis XIII."

"What does that mean?"

"It dates from about 1610, the reign of Louis XIII. In New York it would go for fifteen, twenty thousand dollars."

The year 1610 was a long time ago. To Jack the armoire looked exceedingly fragile.

"There's a similar one in the lobby," Flora said. "Didn't you notice?"

"No."

"This hotel is full of nice old pieces."

He drew her out onto the balcony saying: "We can watch for Zaragon from here. As soon as we see the red car pull in, you go down and flaunt those boobs at him."

Elbows touching, they leaned on the balcony in the warm night. Below were people sitting in front of all the restaurants, people moving up and down the waterfront. Many were sailors in their white uniforms. Jack and Flora could hear guitars serenading the diners.

Suddenly there was a loud report, and an explosion of color that burst over the rade. The noise made Jack jump, not Flora.

"Fireworks," she said.

"I forgot," said Jack. "It's the fourteenth of July."

"We're in a perfect spot to watch them," said Flora.

All the other balconies were crowded. With each burst they could hear oohs and aahs from nearby, and from below as well. The musicians had stopped playing, the diners had stopped eating. The waiters stood openmouthed among the tables.

The red car pulled into the lot. Seeing it was an immense relief to Jack. Presently Zaragon reappeared on the square where he stood watching the fireworks.

They lasted thirty minutes, ending with the so-called "bouquet"—the entire sky seemed to catch fire. The hotel itself seemed to tremble from the noise.

The colors spilled and tumbled down the sky, and then it was over. When Jack looked back, Zaragon was gone—into the hotel, he supposed.

"It's time to go to work, Flora," said Jack, and he began to give her final instructions.

Flora interrupted: "You get so tiresome when you try to tell me how to do something that I know how to do so much better than you."

It seemed to him she was like an actress anxious to go onstage. He said: "Be careful not to let on you know who he is. You don't know he's a drug pusher. Whatever he tells you he is, that's what you think he is."

"Yes, darling."

"Make the drinks last awhile."

"Coffee, cognac, the works."

"I don't want this to happen too early. About eleven o'clock you offer to show him the view from your balcony." If she could get him up here promptly, then this would give Jack most of two hours to capture him and get him out to the carrier.

She batted her eyes at her husband. "Suppose he isn't interested in the view from my balcony."

"Get him up here any way you can. I'll be in there." He pointed toward the armoire.

Then what will happen? he asked himself, and was immediately worried about her. He didn't want her caught in any shootout. He didn't think it would come to that, but one could never be sure. He didn't want her hurt in any way.

"Once you get him up here, you're safe," said Jack, "because I'll be here to look after you." But this only sounded fatuous; it was not what he meant at all. "I don't think he's armed, but it's possible, so once you get him in the room, try to get his clothes off him. Once his clothes are in a pile he's unarmed for sure. A guy who's naked has no fight in him, believe me."

"And how am I supposed to get his clothes off him?" said Flora, and this time she sounded a bit testy.

"You undress him. How do women usually do it?"

"And while I'm undressing him, what's he doing? Undressing me, that's what."

"Don't worry, I won't let anything happen to you."

"He'll be undressing me, kissing me, mauling me. I'm supposed to let this just happen."

"Think of yourself as an actress in a movie. You're pretending. Actresses do it all the time."

"Actresses do it with actors. This guy is a drug dealer."

"He's better-looking than many of those actors."

"All right," said Flora, "I'll go through with it all the way to the end. Stay in the closet until I'm finished. He'll be exhausted, easier for you to arrest."

They grinned at each other.

"You're in the armoire," said Flora. "I'm working him over. How will you know when I have him undressed?"

"Say: Ooh la la, so big. Or some such thing."

"Suppose it isn't so big?"

"Haven't you ever lied to a man before?"

421

Flora put on her most sultry voice. "It's—it's—so, so biggg." She dragged out the word *big*.

Good, thought Jack. She still imagines this is a lark, which it is not. At the door, he kissed her, gave her a pat on the bottom, and pushed her out.

"And as soon as this is over," she said from the hall, "we go back to America, right?"

"Yes," he said, knowing it was what she wanted to hear, "we go back to America." He thought he was saying this only to please her, then wondered, to his surprise, if it was not what he wanted too.

"Go to it," he said, and closed the door behind her.

Through the walls of the room he heard the elevator go down, and he went and opened the armoire doors. It was going to be cramped and uncomfortable in there. On the high shelf were two pillows, which he brought down, arranging one on the floor, one against a wall. The pillows would make his long dark vigil a little more comfortable, not much.

Well, he didn't have to climb in and pull the doors closed yet, and he broke open his gun and counted bullets still again. Still five of them. He went to the balcony and looked down at the restaurant terraces, at the people moving along the waterfront; and then out at the warships at anchor in the rade. Foster would expect him about midnight. He had spoken to him this morning. The fleet would put to sea beginning at about eleven. The carrier would be the last to sail. It would wait for him until one A.M., no later, according to Foster.

The feds had a lot invested in this by now. Jack was confident they would wait for him all night, if necessary.

One thing did worry him: the screws of the departing fleet would send waves in toward shore. These might lift his boat up and drop it down again against the rocks, probably several times, probably scuffing it, perhaps even gouging a hole in its side. It would be nice to get down there with Zaragon early, before the waves started coming in, get rid of him early. But that would mean crossing the parking lot with him at a time when many people and cars were coming and going. No, it was better to wait until most of the restaurants were empty, most parked cars gone. The small window of time was plenty big enough.

Coming in off the balcony Jack got everything else ready: the two rolls of mover's tape, the scissors. He placed these things atop the dresser. Looking over the throw rug on the floor, he lifted it to feel its weight, measured it with his eyes to be sure of its size. Again he decided it was adequate and would fulfill the role he planned for it.

What more was there to do to be fully prepared? What hadn't he thought of?

He studied the armoire. It was huge, heavy, and nearly four centuries old, if Flora was to be believed. Its outside was waxed to a shine, of course, but it was not nearly as solid as it had first appeared. It was worm-eaten in places, and all four legs were not the same length, apparently. He had felt its instability when he was in it, and now he was able to make it wobble just by pushing with his hand.

Its insides had never been meant to hold the weight of a man. Suppose, when he went to jump out, the flooring collapsed, dropping him below the level of the doors? He would still be able to get out, but there would be a delay. What would happen during this delay? Would Zaragon grab his gun, if he had a gun, at the same time grabbing Flora around the neck as a shield?

Suppose the whole thing fell over onto its face, with him still in it? He would not be able to get out at all, Zaragon would have his way with Flora, after which he might strangle her. The French cops would find a dead female body on the bed and a man inside a toppled armoire. Flora would be dead, and the French cops, if he knew cops, would pin it on him.

He decided he'd better practice getting out of the armoire. Fast but gentle.

Carefully climbing in, he sat down on the four-hundred-year-old floor, his back against the four-hundred-year-old side wall.

Sitting on one of the pillows, the other cushioning the knobs of his spine, he pulled the doors closed, took his gun out, and a moment later threw open the doors and jumped out, gun waving.

The first time, the armoire nearly came down on top of him.

The second time was better, and the third better still.

Hearing a commotion in the corridor, he scurried back inside and pulled the doors shut just in time. The outer door opened and someone came into the room. He heard footsteps moving about.

Flora? Flora and Zaragon? Someone else? Who? And why? In the dark one only had questions, far more than one would like.

After a moment he realized the intruder was a woman, for he could hear her humming. The maid turning down the bed, he judged. Came in to leave a chocolate on the pillow.

Suppose she decided to lay out the extra pillows as well, the ones he was sitting on? At the moment her footsteps were near the bed. Stay there, he thought. But he heard her approaching and he began trying to decide what to do if the doors opened. The woman would have a heart attack, or very nearly, and he would flash her a sheepish grin. Suppose she screamed? Then what?

She would certainly report him.

The footsteps had almost reached the armoire when they veered off. Jack heard her go to the French doors, open them, and step out onto the balcony. He had no idea whether she was young or old, white or black. Most menials in France were immigrants from Algeria, from Turkey, from Central Europe. She stood on the balcony for some time, enjoying the only perk that came with her job: for a few minutes she was able to contemplate a rich woman's view, breathe a rich woman's air.

Finally the windows closed and she stepped back into the room. She still might come for the pillows. But no, he heard her cross to the door and go out.

He decided to stay in the armoire rather than subject it to the strain of repeated entrances and exits.

By now he was satisfied that Flora and Zaragon had made contact—otherwise she would have come back upstairs to tell him the plan had fallen through—and he amused himself picturing the two of them together.

He himself had arranged assignations with women in bars. He knew about the tentative opening lines, most of them totally without imagination. Like: "Where you from?" You followed up with something equally scintillating, like: "What brings you to this part of the world?"

It would be interesting to hear Zaragon's answer to that one.

Next, one slid one's stool closer, and if this met with no resistance, one moved up closer still.

The technique for a woman was slightly different. It had to be more subtle. Women did it more with the eyes. They might show a little thigh. Would Flora be subtle enough?

The trouble was, she was not a woman to pick up men in bars, had never done so, so far as he knew, not once. Flora did not go to bars. He wasn't sure she would know how to proposition Zaragon, however confident she thought she was tonight. If she underplayed her hand she might fail to excite his interest, and if she overplayed it, he might get suspicious and walk away. He was a man traveling on a false passport. He was a drug dealer and murderer, a wanted felon. He was a man who had every reason to be careful.

But men were rarely careful where women were concerned. In Jack's experience both as a man and as a cop, almost never. A man's instinct, once he got a sniff of what might be available, took control. Caution vanished. He no longer considered his own best interests or the risks involved, did not even see them.

Flora must be leaning toward the guy by now. How much would he give her to drink? She didn't like to drink. She could get tipsy on almost nothing. Being tipsy loosened her tongue, and she would blab out whatever came into her head. If Zaragon plied her with wine, she might give this whole plot away.

In the dark in that narrow enclosure for what seemed to him

hours, Jack's concentration lost focus and he was beset by claustrophobia. He had the sensation that the walls were closing in on him. The armoire, which had seemed big enough, was suddenly far too small. There was less and less room; he was having trouble catching his breath. Claustrophobia he knew to be an illusion, a product of the dark recesses of his mind. He tried to force it back, and although he partially succeeded, he still couldn't breath properly.

His breathing problem was not an illusion at all, for the antique armoire had been impregnated with chemicals to kill the worms and had been polished with heavy waxes for decades, probably centuries. The resulting odors, to a man closed up inside, were not pleasant, they were intermingled, and they had begun to make Jack's head swim. When his breathing got no easier, he began opening and closing one of the doors, even sticking his head all the way out and staying that way until the beating of his heart slowed down.

And then a little later, having convinced himself that claustrophobia was not going to kill him, that he could breathe well enough if he tried, and that he must keep the door closed on himself at all costs, he at last began to feel comfortable, even extremely comfortable, though drowsy. Soon the claustrophobia was entirely gone, he was unaware of any odors, and in fact he had never felt more relaxed, more comfortable in his life. There was no reason, he decided, why he should not fall asleep and have a little nap. He had forgotten Flora, who in a few minutes would enter this room with a drug trafficker intent on undressing her. He knew only how tired he was, how much he wanted to sleep. His last coherent thought concerned the quality of the air. Perhaps those chemical odors had combined into a kind of poison gas. Perhaps it was lack of air inside the armoire that made him so sleepy. He thought this only vaguely. Perhaps he was about to fall asleep in a chemical haze.

He had to jerk himself awake. He opened the door a crack, enough to get his nose out, and sat in the dark shaking.

Just then he heard noises in the corridor, and he pulled the door shut. Again he was just in time. Again, locked inside what now seemed a condemned man's cell, he was listening to voices.

They were inside the bedroom. They were in fact only a few feet from him. Flora's voice was high, as it often got when she was excited, the man's voice low-pitched, seductive. There was the sound of movement—shoes moving—and then Flora's voice was suddenly choked off, which to Jack signified a kiss. He imagined the two of them in a clinch, the drug dealer's tongue halfway down his wife's throat. That was the way such things started, and he no longer felt sleepy. What he did feel was a strange tingling in his groin that seemed to him half a sexual response to what he imagined was happening, and half a jealous one, as if he were spying on a beloved wife who was about to betray him with another man.

The kiss must have ended, for he heard Flora giggle. The giggle was cut off, another kiss perhaps. Then came Flora's voice on a clear artificial note:

"But I thought we were just going to look at the view from my balcony."

How coy she sounded.

Zaragon muttered some response, Jack could not tell what, and there followed another long silence, this one punctuated from time to time by heavy breathing.

"Do you have hair on your chest?" said Flora in the same artificially high voice. "I want to see. Let me see."

All right, she must be working on his shirt buttons. What was he doing to her, meanwhile?

In order to know the optimum moment when to erupt from the armoire, Jack had to be able to see what was happening. But he could only listen to the sounds, only imagine. Based on what he was able to hear, he was supposed to determine how far the supposed seduction had got. He told himself he was focused only on when to make his move. This was not entirely true, for his mind had filled up with pictures—dirty pictures, as the little boys of his youth would have called them, the dirtiest. It was as if he were sitting in a darkened theater watching these pictures flash on the screen. He saw his wife in the arms of the drug dealer. It was much too vivid. Now Zaragon had his mouth buried in his wife's neck, now he was fondling her breasts, fondling her elsewhere too no doubt. Graphic detail.

Flora's voice came again, still high-pitched, almost squeaky. "You do, you do." And then, on a much huskier, throatier note: "I love men with hair on their chests." Her voice had gone blurry, as if she had buried her face in his curls. Biting them. Hairs in her teeth. She sounded the way she always sounded when sexually aroused. She wasn't putting it on, he decided. She was definitely aroused—not by Zaragon, necessarily, but by the thought of her husband in the armoire listening while she had sex with another man. The unfaithful wife who didn't have to worry about being caught. There was a danger aspect to this charade that all three of them were engaged in, for Zaragon was a killer, after all, but if she was immune to the danger, and she seemed to be, this is exactly what she would be thinking, feeling. She was enjoying herself, he was convinced of it.

"What else do you have to show me?" she said throatily. "Do you have anything else to show me? What's this big bulge here?"

Some of these lines Jack recognized. She had said them to him once, in another country, and in what seemed at this moment another life.

"No," she said, "my turn first. Ladies first."

Jack thought he heard his wife working on the man's zipper, thought he heard it slide. Well, she was following his instructions to the letter, was she not?

"There!" she said throatily. If Zaragon was waving in the air, what logically would happen next? What would any man do? Force her head down on it, that's what. Was she resisting? Women liked to suck it, in Jack's experience, and there was Flora's chance and at no risk to herself, because what was happening was only part of a play written by her husband. She couldn't be blamed—it wasn't really real. Or if real, then blame her husband.

"I want to see you," said Flora throatily. And then as if begging: "All of you."

There came the sound of rustling clothes, more heavy breathing, perhaps part of a struggle.

"No," said Flora firmly, "you first."

There had been a change of tone here, but Jack did not perceive it. She was enjoying this too much, he believed. He saw her in a mood to go through with it all the way, and to his surprise he became furious, though if asked he would never have admitted it. He was not jealous, not outraged, not upset at all, not a bit. Let her do whatever she felt like doing. He was not going to jump into the room just yet, and perhaps not until it was over. Let it go further than she wants, he thought. Pay her back for enjoying Zaragon's attentions so far. Pay her back also for evoking in her husband these too-ardent emotions. He saw none of this clearly. Some of it he was not aware of at all. Let her begin to worry, he told himself. For all she knows I'm not in this armoire. Let her sweat. Her rescuer went out to lunch. He's not on the scene.

Let's see how sexy she thinks herself then.

"Oh, it's beautiful," said Flora in the same throaty, husky voice. "And it's so big."

Jack did not move.

Let the scene run until Zaragon had got between her legs and shoved it all the way in, why not? Then, when Jack did jump out and stick the gun in his back, the drug dealer would be in even a more helpless, more docile position. Flora might be mad at him, but no woman ever died from sexual intercourse. You want to know the safest way to make an arrest of this kind, he told himself. You got it.

"It's so bigggg!"

Jack still did not move.

What was happening was not a classic ménage à trois situation, but it was close. Without realizing it, husband and wife had agreed to engage in a sexual perversion, and one could never tell in advance where the emotions would go, how these things would play out. The only difference between this scene and certain other types of wife swapping was the extra element involved: that one of the parties did not know he was a part of it, and was a dangerous criminal besides.

"Jack?" cried Flora. "Jack!"

As Jack erupted from the armoire, Zaragon spun around. If the sky had fallen on him he could not have looked more surprised. He stood beside the bed wearing a rampant erection and nothing else. Beside him stood Jack's wife wearing transparent white panties. Her bra was on the floor. He could see her breasts move as she breathed. Like Zaragon she was barefoot.

There was more than enough light. One of the bedside lamps was lit. From the open French windows came reflected light from outside as well.

Zaragon looked frozen in time, frozen in space. His mouth hung open. Only a few seconds had passed; his erection had not yet had time to wilt.

"What kept you?" demanded Flora.

"Actually, I think I came in too soon. Look what you've missed." Jack pointed at it with his gun. "That's good-sized," he said to his wife, "wouldn't you say?"

"You're repulsive," said Flora.

"Might have been fun for you," said Jack, and he walked over and clubbed Zaragon on the side of the head. He hadn't known in advance he would do this. Zaragon gave a grunt and went down.

Flora turned angrily on her husband. "It took you long enough."

Zaragon lay on the floor bleeding and groaning.

Jack grabbed one of the rolls of mover's tape and leaped on him, knees to the kidneys, a kind of profane genuflection. He yanked the hands back and got the tape started, wrapping it round and round, kneeling but not in prayer, joining both wrists, taping the dealer's arms together all the way to the elbows.

To Flora Jack said conversationally as he worked: "They ought to issue this stuff to cops. It's better than handcuffs." He was calmer now. "See the scissors there? Cut the tape. Right here. Good."

Next he taped Zaragon's hairy legs together from ankles to knees. Still half naked herself, Flora watched fascinated.

"Get me a washcloth out of the bathroom, will you?"

He rolled Zaragon over. The mouth still hung open. The black eyes were still unfocused, blinking slowly at the ceiling. The man's erection was gone, though, Jack noted.

When Flora handed over the washcloth, Jack stuffed it halfway down the dealer's throat. "Got any blocked nasal passages?" he asked him conversationally. "Hope not, because for the next hour or two you're going to have to breathe through your nose." He wound the tape round and round Zaragon's mouth and neck, forcing the washcloth deep, and then around his head. He did it roughly. Zaragon's head, except for the eyes and nose, became the head of a mummy.

When finished Jack continued to kneel there. He needed to uproot his kneecaps but for the moment couldn't. He was breathing hard. The danger was past, his plan was working perfectly so far, but when he stood up he was, to his surprise, trembling.

He turned toward his wife. He was no longer angry at her, and though she was still half naked he was no longer upset at what had happened—almost happened. Instead for the first time in his life he looked at her as a partner. He felt an overwhelming rush of love for her, for their partnership, for the danger they had just shared, for what they had accomplished together. He had never had a female partner, much less one standing beside him with her breasts exposed, and he embraced her murmuring: "You did a terrific job. Thank you." And he kissed her.

But she broke the kiss off, pointing at Zaragon on the floor, saying: "Jack, we're not exactly alone, you know."

"Oh, him," said Jack. "He won't bother us. Not ever again."

The glaze was gone from Zaragon's eyes and he was glaring at them with absolute hatred.

Jack glanced at his watch and was horrified to see how late it had become. It was twenty minutes to one. In twenty minutes the carrier would unhook from its buoy and steam out of the rade. There was an excellent chance he would not be able to get Zaragon out there that fast.

Nonetheless, he took the time to kiss Flora again. Then patted her rump, saying: "Get dressed. We have work still to do."

She stooped to pick up her bra, then bent to hook it in place. Jack went through to the balcony. The rade was nearly empty of warships. Only the carrier and one smaller ship, a destroyer, he thought, were still there. The garish illuminations were out on both ships, the giant flags stowed. Below him most of the restaurant lights were out too. The parking lot, what he could see of it through the trees, was empty of cars.

When he came back inside Flora was dressed. In fact she was in the bathroom. She had wiped most of the makeup off and was combing her hair.

He said: "Give me a hand with him."

Together they rolled Zaragon onto the throw rug, then rolled him up in it and tied him in there with mover's tape.

"You can stay here and go to bed," Jack said to his wife. "Or you can come with me."

"I've come with you this far. I'm with you all the way."

They gave each other smiles of a closeness that had not been there between them in a long time.

Jack went to the door, opened it, and listened. He could hear nothing: the entire hotel seemed asleep.

"Ring for the elevator," he told Flora, and he went back and slung the rug over his shoulder.

They rode down in the elevator, the rug standing up in the corner. One flight above the lobby they got out, descending the rest of the way via the fire stairs, coming out through the empty kitchen into the alley that ran alongside. There were pedestrians moving in front of the hotel.

Jack sent his wife forward to signal when the way was clear.

"Okay," she called back.

They crossed the street and entered the parking lot, the rug over Jack's shoulder. Headlights came on in one of the parked cars, and a moment later it edged out and rolled past them, not stopping, a man and a woman inside talking to each other, the woman giving them only a glance, the man not looking at them at all.

When they came to the edge of the lot Jack saw that the surface of the rade had become agitated from the departing warships. His boat rose and fell, repeatedly scraping its flank against the rocks.

Despite the burden on his shoulder he was able to step up onto the low wall and then down onto the ledge on the other side, and he began to make his way the rest of the way down the ragged slope. The rug was heavy, and he had to take great care not to lose his balance. Finally he reached the gunwale, stepped over and dumped his burden to the deck. He then reached up and helped Flora on board.

"I hope he doesn't suffocate in there," said Flora with concern.

"Me too," said Jack, "but I can't worry about that now."

The engines came on. He waited, watching impatiently over his shoulder, but Flora had trouble undoing the lines; he had to go over and do it for her. As the boat banged anew against the rocks he ran back and steered it toward open water. As soon as he had gained a bit of distance, he opened the throttles wide, and they surged away from the rocks, away from the town, and out toward the carrier. Jack checked his watch. It was five minutes to one. They had about a mile to go, which at sea is a considerable distance.

Behind him the town was still brightly lit, and ahead he could make out the bulk of the carrier: it seemed to have turned away from him, to be showing only its stern lights. Perhaps it was already under way. Close inshore there were small boats anchored here and there, and he had to thread his way through them, slaloming, throwing up a big bow wave. It was dangerous to drive this fast on so dark a night. There were no brakes on boats. He could ram a boat he didn't see in time. Worse, he could smash into one of the permanent buoys. These were huge heavy things, very low, lower than turrets, substantial enough to hold cruise liners, or aircraft carriers. The rade was dotted with them, and out on the water there was no light at all. The sea was black and they would be invisible until the collision.

All these possibilities flitted through his head, and he ignored them, driving full throttle toward the carrier.

≡ CHAPTER 19 ≡

By then the boarding ladder had been hauled up and the admiral, standing beside Agent Foster on the flight deck, had just sent an order to the bridge to get under way. The carrier was moving out of the rade, and in a moment would be moving fast.

Even though Foster had never fully believed in the capture of Victoriano Zaragon, nonetheless, because of what it would mean to his career, he had hoped that it would work out. Apparently it had not worked out, but so much was at stake for him personally that he was trying to convince the admiral to rescind his order now. He was begging for more time, thirty minutes, fifteen minutes—whatever he could get.

Foster's own neck felt exposed. He had consulted Washington, and even though he had done no more than lay Jack's proposition out there, he had been given the green light. By then, Treasury, Justice, the Navy Department, the White House—perhaps even the president himself—were involved, and if Zaragon was not now brought aboard, if at the end of the rainbow there was no Zaragon standing trial in New York, then not one of those Washington people were going to accept responsibility for anything. They would lay it all on him. They would band together to crucify him. Failure to accomplish his mission. His career would be destroyed.

The admiral had walked away from Foster. The narcotics agent was obliged to pursue him across the deck. But the admiral, worried about his own career, only shook his head impatiently. He had been ordered to wait until one A.M. he said; it was past one A.M. now. He had five thousand men on board, and he had the rest of the Sixth Fleet to worry about as well. He could not in conscience disrupt his entire command for one kidnapped drug dealer.

The admiral was not supposed to know anything about any kidnapped drug dealer. The orders he had received had been both specific and vague. A DEA helicopter would be coming aboard. Agent Foster would be coming aboard. The admiral was to hold the carrier at its mooring until one A.M. so that Agent Foster could take delivery of a package. If Agent Foster needed assistance loading this package onto the DEA helicopter, this was to be provided.

Otherwise the admiral had been told nothing.

As soon as he was advised that the DEA helicopter had landed, the admiral had sent for Foster. What was this all about? he had asked. Unfortunately, no one had ordered Foster to say nothing, so he had answered the admiral's questions. Although it didn't show, the admiral had gone into an immediate state of shock.

He wanted now in the night what he had wanted since his first meeting with Foster. To get away before this "package" arrived—to get out from under this highly irregular case altogether. He saw that Zaragon—or, more properly, Zaragon's lawyers—would make a terrific stink in court, no question about it. Illegal arrest, and so forth. The arrest itself a crime. He saw himself in court testifying. He would be obliged to give testimony that would both sink the government's case and ruin the witness, himself.

This being a risk he had no desire to run, he was at present rushing out of the rade as fast as possible. The deadline was past. He could not be blamed. If he got out into the open sea before any small boat showed up, he was in the clear.

As for Foster, the admiral reasoned, he had a DEA helicopter tied down on the flight deck. He could leave whenever he wanted, go wherever he wished. The admiral couldn't care less what he did.

With both throttles pushed all the way forward, Jack was fast approaching the carrier. He was looking for the boarding ladders—the staircases four or five stories high that had hung all week from the side of the ship—but he could not see them, which meant they had been hauled up. Then he realized that the carrier was moving, and he cursed. He could discern the beginning of a phosphorescent wake, and in addition could feel the throb of engines through the water, or thought he could. The big ship's vibrations moved through his own hull and up to his hands on the wheel. Once clear of the rade it would increase speed and leave him behind. It could make more than thirty knots. He could make fifteen tops. Any moment now the carrier would simply run away from him. He told himself he would chase it all the way across the Mediterranean, if necessary, though this idea was so unreasonable it gave him no comfort.

He was still gaining, though less and less—hardly at all, in fact. He was getting closer and closer to the exit from the rade, and the horizon was opening up, so that he could see better. Could he hope that someone would notice him? But he was a flea on the water compared to the carrier. Could he get close enough to start hailing? But who would hear him? The deck looked empty, what he could see of it. And probably his voice would never be heard over all the engine noise, his own and the carrier's, anyway. Then he saw he would never get close enough to be spotted or to hail, for the carrier had increased speed. Its wake widened. It was pulling away from him.

What was he to do now? How far should he chase it? How far off the coast would it come about, either to launch planes or begin fleet maneuvers? How much fuel did he have? Could he track it that far?

About to make his way up to flag country, the admiral was stopped by Foster urgently calling him back.

"Admiral, Admiral, there's a boat."

Suddenly Jack sensed that the carrier's engines had stopped, or nearly so. He felt this before he saw it. The warship lost way quickly, and as he closed on it a floodlight came on high above him and he was bathed in sunshine.

He wallowed at the foot of the great gray cliff. A face hung over the precipice above—he could not see who it was—and a voice drifted down. "Do you have a package for me?"

"Is that you, Foster?"

"Hold on, we're rigging up a winch here."

Jack glided close to the ship's flank and found a cleat to which he tied a line. He was out from under the flight deck's overhang, for he could see sky above. His boat lay eight or ten feet off the ship's flank, still wallowing, but less and less as the sea settled down.

They were well outside the rade by this time. The carrier, he could feel, was still making way, dragging him farther and farther out to sea. Well, this was to be expected. With a rocky shore at its back, you could not allow a ship this big simply to drift.

"It sure is high, up there," said Flora at his elbow. "I had no idea these things were so enormous." She was still extremely excited, and for a moment he observed the scene from her point of view. Together they had arrested a major drug trafficker. Together they had stopped an aircraft carrier on what amounted to the open sea. It must seem to her that she had got rather far from her decorating shop. Her veneer of New York sophistication was nowhere in evidence, and she had become as excited as a girl.

He gave her a fond smile, and they waited.

Finally an arm swung out and a cable started down. Attached to it was a wire litter such as would be used in wartime to lift the wounded on and off the ship. As the litter came within reach, Jack dragged it inboard. Now it lay on the cockpit deck, the slack cable leaning against the gunwale.

"I need to talk to you first," Jack called up to Foster.

"Negative," said Foster.

"There are things we have to go over."

"We've covered everything. Just send up the package."

Jack had passed through many emotions already that night. All of them, like blood when one has been slapped, were still exquisitely close to the surface. Now came anger again. It was directed not only at Foster, who had not made the carrier wait for him and who now tried to dismiss him, but also at Washington, at the New York Police Department—at all administrations that used men and then cast them aside.

Jack had risked his life many times in the past, had risked it again tonight, was still risking it. Alone and unaided except by his wife he was bringing in one of the two or three most wanted criminals in the world. Now he had questions he wanted answered, promises he wanted kept. He deserved respect, not a brush-off. He would not be brushed off by Foster or anyone else.

He was furious and wanted to scream up at Foster, but to do so was to waste breath. The DEA agent was too far away, and with the floodlight shining down Jack couldn't even see him.

His solution was to roll Zaragon in his rug into the litter— he did it roughly, and if the rough handling hurt Zaragon, too bad—and then with the litter beginning to rise he leaped on top of it, feet on the rims, hands clutching the cable, so that as Zaragon was lifted to the flight deck, Jack rode up with him.

The winch turned inboard. The litter was lowered to the deck, and he stepped off it.

Aircraft carriers were not new to Jack, he was familiar with flight decks, but this one looked odd to him, and then he realized he had never seen one so deserted. Flight decks, except in storms, were busy places, but in front of him now was a single helicopter still tied down and only four men. No one else was in sight. The flight deck was a vast empty plain. Even the winch operator was not there—he had apparently been working from one deck down. Jesus, thought Jack, they certainly are treating this with the utmost secrecy.

He had eyes for only one of the four men, Foster, who wore some kind of jumpsuit with DEA stenciled on it. There were two other men in similar jumpsuits whom he would realize later were the helicopter pilots. The fourth man, from his insignia, was an admiral. Jack did not recognize him. The commander of the Sixth Fleet, probably. Who else could he be?

Though he had no quarrel with any of these men apart from Foster, Jack shook hands with none of them. "Hello, Foster, how are you?" he said icily, though for the moment managing to keep his temper. Then: "Do you normally take delivery without verifying the merchandise?"

"You're not supposed to be on board, Dilger."

"What are you going to do about it, arrest me?"

He spilled Zaragon out of the litter, pulled out a penknife, and, kneeling, sliced apart the tape so that the rug of its own accord unrolled slightly. Jack stood up then and, grasping one end of the rug, rolled Zaragon most of the way out of it. As soon as the head showed he bent down again and sliced off enough of the tape so that the face became recognizable. Zaragon remained gagged, and his eyes looking up were blazing.

"I want to hear you say in front of these witnesses that this man is Victoriano Zaragon and that he's alive."

"Do you want a receipt too?"

"Let me hear it."

"Looks like him," conceded Foster.

Jack pulled the photo out of his pocket, unfolded it, and thrust it in front of Foster's face.

"Is it him or not?"

"I think so," said Foster.

"And he's alive and well?"

"He's alive."

"And well."

"Appears to be," conceded Foster finally.

"If he's dead when you land in Frankfurt, you killed him, not me."

The DEA pilots were looking from one of them to the other, but the admiral, Jack noted, had wandered some paces off and was gazing toward the ship's island. Bastard didn't want to know anything about what was going on here, Jack judged. Like the brass everywhere. Let some detective handle it; if someone was going to get in trouble, let it be some detective. Everywhere he had gone in law enforcement, the one out there on the limb had been some detective, most often himself.

"You made me some promises," said Jack.

"I made no promises," said Foster. "I told you Washington was inclined to agree to your demands." He turned to the two pilots. "Load the package into the helicopter."

Jack said: "Number one, you promised to hold a press conference the minute you touch down in Frankfurt." He had other items to discuss, but this was the most pressing. As soon as news spread that Zaragon was in custody, the contract on Jack's life would become inoperative, at least in France. Later there might be other contracts, but the one here would have become null and void.

The timing of the eventual press conference was critical. "I want to hear you say the press conference will be held today," said Jack.

"Negative," said Foster. "Washington changed their mind. It's not my fault. Washington decided no press conference till we get him to New York."

"I could be dead by then."

"There was nothing I could do."

Jack's rage showed in his face, his clenched fists, his eyes. "When does the plane leave Frankfurt?"

"As soon as we get him there. The engines are probably already warming up. Then eight more hours to New York."

Frustrated, impotent, Jack kept opening and closing his fists.

"Relax," said Foster. "You've stayed alive this long. If you can manage twenty-four hours more you're in the clear."

The admiral, who had been standing at the rail peering down, said to Jack: "Who's that down there in the boat?"

"My wife," said Jack.

"Hadn't you better get back to her?"

"What about the other thing?" Jack asked Foster.

"What other thing?"

"About the future, goddammit. About being taken on by the DEA."

Foster said: "If you can pass the physical, they will consider you."

"They'll consider me?"

"It's the best I could get. You testify at the trial, and once the verdict is in, they'll consider you."

"That's all you could get?"

"Your wife seems to be getting antsy down there," said the admiral, still standing at the rail.

"I tried real hard for you," said Foster.

"You just tell them that if they want a cooperative witness they better—"

"And I've got to get this ship under way," said the admiral.

Jack, who was beyond the age of being intimidated by admirals, ignored him. "Just tell them what I said, Foster. Just tell them."

"So I'd appreciate it if you two would cut this conference short," said the admiral.

The winch man, a tall sailor in dungarees and a white hat, had come up onto the flight deck. He stood nearby and was awaiting orders. "Lower this man to his boat," the admiral told him.

His fists clenched, Jack glared furiously at Foster.

"Now if you'll just move over there," the admiral said, "the seaman will drop you down to your boat and—"

Jack swallowed his anger, his pride. The elation he had felt at capturing Zaragon was already swallowed. He had been betrayed. He could accept the fact that the press conference was delayed; he'd just have to be careful a bit longer. What he could not accept was that the DEA, after an exploit of this quality, and after the promise Foster had made, would brush him aside anyway, and he was almost overcome by the intensity of his longing. He wanted the job he had asked Foster to secure for him. He wanted the DEA to take him on. He wanted law enforcement back. "You promised you'd help me, Foster. You've gotta help me."

"How long will it take you to get that bird in the air?" said the admiral to Foster.

"Time it takes me to send a message to Washington and get a reply."

"Get to it, then," said the admiral.

With a nod in Jack's direction, Foster went striding across the flight deck toward the island.

The admiral wrung Jack's hand. "Nice to have met you," he said, for even admirals pretend to social graces at times. Then the admiral too was striding toward the island.

"This way, sir," said the winch operator.

And so Jack stood in the night on the rim of the basket, which was swung over the side. The open-air elevator began to descend. The high gray flank passed in front of his eyes, a wall without windows.

Then he was on his boat, backing away from the carrier, but he lay to about five hundred yards off, engines idling, watching it, standing at the wheel while Flora beside him rubbed his shoulders.

"What are we waiting for?"

He wanted to see the helicopter take off, he told her. Although the machine itself was hidden by the flight deck, he could discern one of its still motionless blades against the skyline, or so he thought.

"Your shoulders sure are stiff," said Flora, rubbing them. "It's over. You won. Relax. Your last and greatest case."

"I'll relax when I see that helicopter rise up."

"I understand now what you saw in being a cop all those years. It really makes the juices flow, doesn't it?"

He nodded.

"It was exciting, what we just did. It was even, well, fun. It was really fun."

It pleased him that she saw this. Was it possible to base the rest of their lives on what they had shared so far in their marriage, and especially on what they had shared tonight?

Flora said: "Shall I make some coffee?"

She went below, while he continued to watch the carrier. It was making way now, and he pushed the throttles forward to keep up with it. The sea was still calm, and for a time he moved easily ahead of the wake the carrier began to produce.

Flora came back with the coffee. The steam rose up into the binnacle light.

"So what are you going to do when you get back to America?" said Flora. "Go into the security business like all the other ex-cops? Or try for something that might be bigger and better?"

"I'm not sure." Should he tell her about his conversations with Foster? Maybe he had not been brushed off. Maybe they would invite him to become a federal agent after all. To be a cop—a kind of cop—once more. He started to tell her, but then couldn't do it.

"You could be anything you want to be," said his wife. "If you wanted to go back to college, I could support us while you did that."

"That's very kind of you."

"I wouldn't be doing it for you. I'd be doing it for us."

"I'd have my pension," said Jack. He could not bear the idea of going back to school. Sitting in classrooms with kids? Impossible. But Flora was excited and happy with that idea, and with others she was formulating about the future, and he did not wish to jolt her just now, so he said nothing.

"Even law school, if you like," said Flora. "Or politics."

"Politics," he said. "Now, there's an idea." Join the crooks, he thought. Steal money on the grand scale.

But he kept this reaction to himself, gave her his big grin, and sent her below again to fetch him a sweater, for by now the night was blowing across his bare arms at ten knots an hour, and he was cold. Driving the boat had become chilly work.

The carrier was running southwest on a heading of about 210 degrees. The helicopter still had not taken off. Gradually the warship increased speed. He was determined to stay with it as long as he could. At first he could see the lights of the towns behind him, but soon only the glow above them remained. Finally he could see no coastal light at all, and as the carrier sailed farther and farther out to sea he began to worry about the helicopter's range, even if it had extra tanks. Frankfurt was about six hundred miles from the coast. How far out would they be before it took off? Why the long delay? What had gone wrong?

When the helicopter did take off he never saw it happen. What he did see, with the carrier now a considerable distance ahead, was the blinking lights that rose straight up into the night the way a roman candle did, only this time there was no incandescent burst at the top of the arc. Instead, the lights leveled off, hovered a moment, and then came skittering back in Jack's direction.

He saw it pass almost directly overhead, and heard it too, and despite himself he began to suck in the night air and to smile, and Flora put her arms around him and murmured: "There goes one very bad man to jail for life," and she kissed him. "Congratulations. You really are a great detective. And I'm terrifically happy for you that your last case was your best. Not many detectives get to have an encore like yours." And then: "Thank you for letting me share it with you."

She kissed him again, and as he let the steering wheel go, she began to dance him around the cockpit. He had never known her this happy. As she whirled him around, the binnacle light bounced in different ways off the planes of her face, and off the tears of joy in her eyes, so that she was gorgeous to him, and his stomach lurched and he found himself as overwhelmingly in love with her as he had been at the beginning.

"You don't have any champagne aboard this tub, do you?"

"Unfortunately not." He could not take his eyes off her, nor stop grinning.

"That's what we need, champagne." She held up an imaginary glass. "A toast to ex-Detective John F. Dilger, the best detective in the world, and my husband. A toast to my husband, now a prosperous lawyer. No, that's wrong. Now a congressman. A toast to my husband, one day—why not?—the ex-cop who becomes president of the United States."

She made him laugh, and the way she was whirling him about made him dizzy. Realizing that no one was steering the boat, he reached to push the throttles into neutral, and the sudden decleration threw them into each other so that they almost went down. Instead they became locked in a passionate kiss.

"What's this digging into me?" said Flora, and she plucked the revolver out of Jack's belt. "So that's what it is," she joked. "I thought for a minute I had got you all excited."

He let her study it a moment. She had never liked to touch his guns. She had never liked it that he moved through the city armed, and had sometimes said so. This was the first time she had shown the slightest interest in the tools of his trade, and he reached to take the gun back.

But he did not move fast enough. "We don't need this anymore, do we?" said Flora. "The case is closed. Detective Dilger is at liberty." And as casually as could be she slung the revolver out over the sea.

This Jack had never expected. If she had shot him with it he could not have been more surprised. He made a lunge for the gun, a lunge so frantic, so futile, that he nearly went overboard. He strained for it as if he had arms fifteen feet long and could pluck it out of the air. But he didn't and couldn't.

Still within the aura of light from the boat, the revolver fell with a very slight splash, and disappeared in water hundreds of fathoms deep.

Flora saw the stricken look on his face, and all the laughter went out of her.

"Well, you didn't need it anymore. You don't, do you?"

He assured her he didn't, though he thought it possible he might. He was not a man to have a tantrum over something that could not be changed. And he was so in love with her at that moment that he would have indulged her almost anything.

"No, of course not," he said, and even managed to give a semblance of a grin. "As you say, the case is closed."

But the dance had ended, Flora's happy toasts had ended, the former mood was broken, and he reached around her and grasped the wheel and put the pilotless boat back on course.

The gun was irrecoverable. It was too late to protest.

Nonetheless, he missed it. Missed it badly, as if he had lost something precious.

Precious why? he asked himself, as he steered by compass heading toward a coast he could not see. Was it psychologically precious, or security precious? Or was it both? Was his idea of himself mixed up with owning and carrying guns? People often saw guns as phallic symbols. A gun as a second penis. The fact that it was most often worn so close to the male organs was used at times to reinforce this notion.

Which in his own case was nonsense, Jack believed. If at the moment he felt a tremendous sense of loss—loss akin to grief—this was because he didn't yet consider himself safe, no other reason. He wouldn't be safe until after Foster's press conference had taken place in New York and the news had duly appeared in the French papers—say, two days from now. For that much longer a gun would have been nice to have. On the third day he would have thrown it away himself. He had almost been looking forward to doing so—scaling a handful of lethal steel into the Mediterranean Sea. An act of bravado, yes. But also proof that his manhood in no way depended on walking about armed in a world where other people were not. Getting rid of it would have been a way of saying: I wasn't safe before, but am now. He would have conquered Zaragon and his gang at last.

Conquered himself too, together with previous needs of which he himself had never been strictly aware.

Well, Flora had just made the gun disappear. She had done the job for him. It was less satisfactory that way, but no less final. And he realized to his surprise he didn't even begrudge it to her. Tonight she had earned the right to do with him whatever she wished.

He was even warming to her suggestion that he go into a business of some kind. If the DEA turned him down he would have to. He had got over his earlier anger at Foster. Foster was just another cop doing what he was told. The DEA had been Jack's last recourse. If the answer was no, then his law enforcement career ended for good tonight. Well, he could live with the idea, he supposed. At least, as Flora had said, he had had his encore.

As he steered back toward the coast Jack had no clear idea of where he was. He knew the carrier had led him off to the west, but could only guess how far. It didn't matter. He could not miss the coast of France, and whatever town he came in on he would certainly recognize. After that he could find Beaulieu easily enough. He had set himself a course of ten degrees, and to save fuel had throttled way back. He did not want to approach land in the dark anyway. Flora had fallen asleep on the rear banquette, leaving him alone with his thoughts.

As it happened he struck the coast west of Cannes, recognizing the two islands with the lights of the city behind them, remembering his first trip there with Madeleine. As he turned east the sky began to brighten. The summits of the Maritime Alps caught rays of sunlight still not visible lower down, and for a few moments he admired a glinting chain saw of peaks that floated in the sky with nothing whatever under them. But soon he was able to pick out the tops of the high hills behind the towns, and after that the lights that marked individual villas.

Flora came forward rubbing her eyes. "I didn't mean to fall asleep," she said. "I abandoned you. I'm sorry." She smiled at him. "Won't happen again, I promise." Their eyes met and held, and then both smiles abruptly vanished, for each of them understood that much, much more was being promised.

Jack, who was not much good with emotions as strong as this, was afraid to try to speak.

The sun chose that moment to pop into view, a sudden glare, lights of all colors bouncing off the water all around.

"Wow," said Flora, "look at that."

"Haven't you ever seen a sunrise before?"

"Not like this one, I haven't."

Jack, who had seen a hundred sunrises at sea, gave her a squeeze and sent her below to make more coffee. In a few minutes she came back up and stood beside him, and they sipped it and watched the sea around them change color as the sun rose.

About an hour later Jack steered carefully, slowly into the yacht harbor at Beaulieu and tied up and attached the various lifelines. They got off and walked along the quay. Jack glanced this way and that, but more from habit than anything else. It seemed to him much too early for anyone to be lying in wait for him.

One of the cafés on the harbor was just opening, so they sat down and ordered café au lait and croissants. These were brought to them, and when they were alone again Flora took his hand and said: "So when are we going home?"

Jack said: "I need a day or two. I need to turn in the boat, the car." He added, thinking of Madeleine: "And do one or two other things."

It was not going to be easy facing Madeleine, but he saw his life more clearly now, or imagined he did. He was an American, and a New Yorker, and New York was where he belonged. He did not belong here, would never be at ease here, would always be a bit off balance, always a foreigner. Furthermore, it was Flora who was his wife, and it was Flora who had stood by him, who had helped him capture Zaragon. New York and Flora represented home to him. It would be a different marriage from now on. A different Flora. A different him, as well. He would go home with her, and if he could not be any kind of cop anymore,

449

which was not certain, still he belonged there anyway. If he had to start a new life, he would find something.

He did not really need to tell Madeleine about his feelings for Flora, would just tell her about Zaragon—he was proud of what he had done and thought she would be too; in any case he wanted her to know. He hoped she and her friends in the Police Judiciaire would be able to put together their case against the mayor and bring him down. He would tell her that, and also that he hoped she would get her job back. After which, he would just tell her he was going home. He was grateful for every moment they had spent together, he would tell her. He cared about her and always would, but he had to go home. If he ever came back he would look her up, he would tell her, and if she came to New York she should be sure to call.

These thoughts came to Jack fully articulated. He could hear himself speaking them in a few hours. They were difficult thoughts, and were among the last he would ever entertain, for he did not have a few hours. He had almost no time left at all.

He strolled with his wife toward his car. Husband and wife had their fingers entwined, a yard of air between them, which was the way they had always walked when holding hands, signifying perhaps that although they were together, each of them was free and they were together by choice.

It was going to be another balmy day. The port was beginning to stir, and he could hear an occasional car out on the road. There is a row of trees between the first row of boats and the restaurants, with room for parked cars between the parked sterns and the trees. This was where Jack's rental was parked, the one he had recently taken in exchange for the old one. He thought of it as his new car; he thought also that he had not been driving it long enough for anyone to recognize it as his, and he came to it and inserted the key in the passenger door, opening it for Flora, and then walked around to the other side and opened that door for himself, for he intended to drive her back to her hotel, and perhaps stay with her there out of sight and out of mind for the rest of that day, and perhaps even until the press conference took place in New York.

There was room under those trees for a dozen or more cars, but in addition to Jack's there were only two others, one of them at the end of the row, and the other, a Jaguar, close by. There was no reason for it to be this close. In this Jaguar, a rich man's car, sat a man who looked rich enough. All four windows were open. The man appeared to have been dozing.

Jack's guard was down. He gave him only a glance, enough to decide he didn't fit the profile of a contract shooter. He was middle-aged and wore a white button-down shirt with a red tie. He looked like someone who worked for IBM or the FBI. His suit coat lay across the passenger's backrest. When he got out of the car he was carrying a briefcase, and Jack felt the first faint twinge of alarm.

"Are you Mr. Jack Dilger?" the man said. His accent in English was as American as Jack's.

Alarm came on strong: how does this guy know my name? The perfect accent was alarming too. My God, he thought, they've brought an American over to do it. But it was too late for alarm, or anything else.

"Who are you?" said Jack, at the same time moving out from between the two cars, opting for at least the appearance of aggressiveness, the only weapon, or pretense of a weapon, he had at his disposal.

"Yes or no?"

If he was going to hell, Jack thought, he was going under his own name. "Yes," he said, his eyes fixed now on the briefcase, knowing all of a sudden what he was about to see, and what the ultimate outcome was to be.

He was not disappointed. The briefcase was half unzipped. The man's hand went into it and came out with a Mac 10. Jack recognized it as such, of course, having seen many, a gun whose only usefulness was to kill people, and he even had a thought he had entertained many times previously: How did those things proliferate the way they have, who permitted it?

There was a moment during which he thought he could still save himself. Here on the Côte d'Azur he himself had been carrying a gun for only three days, but in New York before that for twelve years. He was used to a gun being there, could feel the weight of it where it was supposed to be, but when he reached for it his fingers came in contact with nothing, found nothing, and his hand came up empty—he held it out in front of him palm outward as one might attempt to block, say, a ball that was coming too fast to catch, attempting this time to block bullets that were coming even faster and could not be blocked by anything less than armor plate.

One of the bullets actually went through his hand. He saw it come out the other side and could not believe his eyes. All by itself his hand made a fist, he hadn't willed a thing. After the bullet went through his hand he could not tell where it went next, though something did smack him hard in the chest somewhere, either that bullet or perhaps the next one. There were many bullets, they were well-aimed and were all landing. He felt some of them like blows, some like bee stings. One way or another he felt them all—one rarely dies instantly when shot. He heard Flora screaming and wanted to tell her to run, he didn't want her killed too, but when he tried to speak nothing came out. Then he realized he was going down, he couldn't even stand anymore.

He struck the ground hard but didn't realize it. He did realize that he couldn't get up again. He tried but his muscles were no longer connected to his head, he couldn't make them work. He looked up and was staring straight into the sun, and he blinked a few times, and when he looked again he couldn't see the sun anymore, the man in the red tie and button-down shirt was blocking his view, was in fact bending over him. He saw the gun barrel come around. It seemed to be only inches from his face, and though it made no noise he saw it flame once, and that was the last thing he ever saw.

Flora was still screaming. She was standing over Jack and her hands were at her mouth. The man in the red tie gave her a look, then raised his machine pistol again, aimed at her, and fired. The bullet went between her arm and her left breast. It gave her in fact quite a burn on the inside of her arm.

After that the gun was empty. The man in the red tie had a spare clip, but it was in the car. What he didn't have was time. He would have to go into the car, reload, and then finish off the witness, Flora, but already there were people coming, what do you expect, he had fired between ten and fourteen shots, he didn't know how many. Some men, waiters or something, were running up from where the restaurants were. A woman in a bathrobe had come out of one of the nearby buildings; she was running toward him too.

The man tossed his gun into the Jaguar, jumped in after it, and left.

The woman in the bathrobe was Madeleine. She saw the Jaguar and tried to memorize the plate number as she ran. Then she saw that the man on the pavement was Jack Dilger, and the plate numbers fled from her head. She knelt down beside him and touched his shoulder and started to cry.

Flora had stopped screaming. Tears were streaming down her face too. Two women who didn't know each other, who had met vaguely only once, stood weeping over the man who had been Jack Dilger.

≡ Chapter 20 ≡

There are few enough gun crimes in France, and even fewer gun murders. Most that occur are contracts carried out at the orders of organized crime. That was the category into which the killing of Jack Dilger fell. The French police would like to have solved it, but hit contracts were notoriously difficult, especially this one.

A foreigner had been killed, apparently by a foreigner and apparently at the behest of a foreigner. The investigation was able to develop this much, but not much more. Flora was questioned for most of three days. She was practically catatonic at first, and even later could give only a vague description of what had happened. Finally she was allowed to fly back to New York with Jack's body in the hold of the plane.

Madeleine in her turn could describe the Jaguar—it had been stolen the night before and was later found abandoned—but this was all she had seen personally.

Having determined who Jack was, and at whose orders he probably was killed, the PJ detectives sent to America for information, for leads of any kind. They expected pressure from the FBI and from the DEA, perhaps even from the State Department. They expected help too, but in the end none of either ever came. It was not the FBI's case, and in Washington, after many high-level conferences, the DEA chose not to get involved—to do so, it was judged, would have called attention to "irregularities" in the arrest of Victoriano Zaragon. The French Embassy had already lodged the obligatory formal protest—something about a kidnapping on French soil—but so far was not pressing it. Better to let the whole thing die away.

Few enough mourners attended Jack's funeral: Flora, who wept all the way through it, and a few of her friends, and some cops and detectives from the 19th Precinct, and one or two others. The police department did send a color guard, and at the end the flag was folded and handed to Flora, who buried her face in it. But there was no official police representation. Agent Foster, who had accompanied Zaragon all the way to New York and who had stayed on for meetings with the prosecutors, had asked permission to attend the funeral, but the DEA had refused it. So he wasn't there. Some reporters were at the church, and even accompanied the hearse to Gate of Heaven Cemetery in Westchester, where Jack was laid to rest beside his parents. But the reporters departed shaking their heads. Ex-Detective Dilger's funeral had turned out to be a nonstory, they said.

Four thousand miles away a far bigger case had caught public attention.

Most mayors in France, the mayor of Nice included, are at the same time deputies to the national assembly in Paris. As such they enjoy a rather far-reaching parliamentary immunity from prosecution. This makes for so many legal difficulties that any attempt to indict and convict them is likely to fail. Most detectives, and especially detective commanders, not to mention prosecutors, are usually unwilling to try. To affront a major politician is an act of great risk to one's career.

But to the Nice PJ the attempted assassination of one of their own, namely Madeleine, was personal, and never mind difficulties or threats to one's career. If politicians could assassinate cops, even ex-cops, with impunity, then democracy itself was threatened, not to mention the personal security of each and every one of them.

The investigation that followed was carried out by men working mostly on their own time, and at first in great secrecy. They threw themselves into it.

They went to such depths that it took some months, but the evidence uncovered was persuasive, and they closed in simultaneously on the Sestri brothers and on several mayoral cronies who, once caught, began to talk.

Sestri Brothers filed for bankruptcy. The mayor fled to Uruguay, one of the places where he seemed to have been salting away money, and which supposedly had no extradition treaty with France. There he claimed political asylum, but he was arrested anyway, jailed, and ultimately extradicted. Once back in France he was tried, convicted, and sentenced to a long prison term. So were many members of his administration.

In the spring there were new elections, a new administration in Paris, and shortly afterward Ex-Inspector Madeleine Leclerq was exonerated of all past charges. Her gun and police card were returned to her, and she was awarded even her lost back pay. However, she was transferred out of Nice. Commissaire Vossart was being investigated on disciplinary charges by then, so perhaps he arranged it. In any case, someone did. She was assigned to the Finance Brigade in Lyon, and went willingly, for the Côte d'Azur had become a place of such heavy memories that she was glad to put it behind her.

In New York, there were delays as lawyers working for Victoriano Zaragon challenged the legality of his arrest. He had been kidnapped in a foreign country, they charged, and they demanded to know the identity of the woman who had lured their client to a hotel room in Villefranche, as she was a possible defense witness.

Flora was peripheral to the case, the prosecution countered, insisting that her name was confidential. The judge agreed and ruled it need not be disclosed.

However, during discovery procedures, a document with her name on it was inadvertently handed over to defense lawyers, who then presented it to their client.

Victoriano Zaragon flew into a violent rage.

Flora was never informed, no guards were provided for her, and she took no more precautions with her life than did any other woman of her age and station walking the streets of New York.

Zaragon's lawyers cautioned him to concentrate on beating the case against him; he should worry about Flora later.

He went on trial in state court for the murders of the art dealer Bulfinch, and Jack Dilger's two partners, and for the attempted murder of Dilger himself, but there were no surviving witnesses, and after two months of testimony and five days of deliberations the jury acquitted him.

A big smile came onto his smooth young face, but it did not last long.

The many delays thus far had given the DEA ample time to put together a federal drug case against him, and he was re-arrested before he could leave the courtroom. He merely changed prisons, moving from state to federal custody.

As he awaited this second trial Zaragon had still not been convicted of anything. Ample visitation rights were therefore permitted, and it was via one of his visitors, it was theorized later, that he now set up the hit contract on Flora.

Who still moved blithely through the city.

Finally the drug trial got under way. It lasted another two months, but this time Zaragon was convicted. The judge sentenced him to the federal penitentiary in Marion, Illinois, the toughest of all tough prisons, for a period of ninety-nine years with no possibility of parole.

At Marion he was locked into a narrow windowless cell below ground. It contained a cot, toilet bowl, sink—the usual. He was kept isolated from all other prisoners. For exercise he was allowed one hour every other day alone in a small empty courtyard. He got two showers a week. Even at mealtimes he was not permitted to mix with others; trays were brought to his tomb of a cell, and he ate three meals a day alone.

He would not see the sun again either, or the moon, or a tree, or a woman.

But the contract on Flora was already in place. It had an existence of its own and would proceed.

She was nearly over her grief by then. She no longer wept at odd hours for no reason. For many months she had not been able to sleep the night through, but now was sleeping well again. She had been in the habit of visiting Jack's grave every Sunday, but now had not been there in some weeks.

She had even begun keeping company with a detective she had met at Jack's funeral. He was a shorter, slighter man than Jack, but reminded her of him in so many ways. The detective was in the habit of dropping in to see Flora during the day, if he was in the neighborhood.

He no more knew that her life was at risk than she did.

It is true that she kept her shop's door locked during business hours. Customers seeking entrance rang a bell. She could see them through the glass, and if they looked okay she buzzed them in. But this system was normal on Madison Avenue; many of the shops and nearly all of the galleries employed it.

A man rang the bell at Flora's shop.

It was July again; one of her partners was on vacation, and the other was out on a job. At the desk sat an eighteen-year-old college girl interning for the summer, and she buzzed the man in. Flora probably would have buzzed him in also, for he was well dressed, carried a briefcase, and looked all right. He wore a tie.

Having heard the buzzer, Flora came out from the stockroom. She was smoothing her dress, professional smile already in place. "Sir," she greeted the man, "can I help you?"

But this was no ordinary customer. He said: "You Flora Dilger?"

Most of her customers still called her Flora Simpson, but

since Jack's death she had taken to using her married name, and so she nodded.

The man's fingers moved, the briefcase came unzipped, and he started to withdraw from it another of those ubiquitous machine pistols. Since Flora had witnessed this exact scene before, she recognized it at once, and froze.

The college girl's reaction was different, and it was virtually instantaneous. She screamed. From the stockroom the detective came running. He wasn't there on stakeout. He had only stopped to spend ten minutes with Flora. He didn't even have his gun out.

The customer must have thought this changed the odds, for he turned and sprinted for the door. But he had had to stuff the machine pistol back into his briefcase first, which cost him valuable time, and he was still a step from the doorway when the detective tackled him. As he went down two things happened: the machine pistol went skittering across the floor, and he hit his head on the jamb and went out cold. A second and a half later, he was in handcuffs. It was one of the easiest arrests the detective had ever made.

The story dominated that night's telecasts and the front pages the next day. DRUGLORD'S REVENGE PLOT FOILED was one of the less lurid headlines. Flora, who could barely talk when questioned by the police and who refused to be interviewed by the press at all, began to be portrayed as a national heroine, a national treasure. Her story dominated the news media for days. The arraignment and pretrial motions of the man who had tried to kill her made additional headlines. The shootout in Bulfinch's apartment was repeatedly dredged up, and the murder of Jack Dilger, and the two trials of Zaragon. Flora's was a story with legs. When she continued to refuse to talk to reporters, they filmed her through the windows of her shop or when stepping into taxis. Everything she did or didn't do was news.

The NYPD put a uniformed cop at her door during business hours. Precinct cars watched her apartment building around the clock. The heroine herself, thoroughly traumatized, would go nowhere alone; she jumped two feet every time a door slammed. Though the failed hit man was in jail, her immense fear remained. Despite it, she forced herself to go into court at each of the many stages of the judicial process against him. Each time, though unable to meet his eyes, she mounted the witness stand and testified as required. She was determined to see the case through to the end, however much it cost her personally, and she did.

The attempt on her life had brought down heat on every aspect of the drug trade. Speeches had been made in Congress. Hearings were announced. Increased diplomatic pressure had been brought to bear on Colombia. Zaragon's competitors there were infuriated at him, and they were worried about themselves. They were businessmen and did not need this. Probably the entombed druglord lacked enough access to the outside world to set up another contract, and perhaps he even lacked the means, for his rivals had shredded his organization, each one biting off as many pieces as he could swallow. But they were men who took no chances, and word went out that Zaragon's orders were not to be obeyed, that anyone who touched Flora Simpson Dilger would be dealt with.

This news was conveyed via informants to the NYPD, and then via her detective to Flora. After a number of weeks she began to believe it, and some of her jauntiness returned.

The cop outside her door was still there, and would remain almost a year. His presence, she had feared, would cause business to fall off, but the opposite had happened. She had become, in a manner of speaking, famous. People streamed in and out of the shop all day, some only to look, but many to buy. Business was better than it had ever been.

Her detective was still there too, dropping by to see her when he could, taking her to dinner, standing near her at vernissages and openings. Flora had thanked him in the best way she knew. And she continued to thank him. He had saved her life. Jack himself could not have done it better.